CRYSTAL CAVERN

Book Two

of Eugene Roberts' Ringmasters Chronicles

Eugene Roberts

Ordering Information:

For orders and inquiries, please contact:
1-888-404-1388
www.goldtouchpress.com
book.orders@goldtouchpress.com

Printed in the United States of America

Contents

Acknowledgments

Crystal Cavern has been a labor of love. Through the writing and editing of the manuscript, I became engrossed with its characters and the trials they experienced, and the bond of their family.

While my name appears on the front cover, I can't take full credit.

Friend and author Alan Bradbury spent endless hours putting my handwritten scrawl into digital format and endured my constant stream of edits and fixes. When I was about to give up, Alan spurred me on to finish.

No words can truly describe my thanks—and, he even volunteered to do it again.

I would also be remiss if I were not to also acknowledge the support and encouragement of my children, friend John, friend and mentor Keith, and my brother.

I finally dedicate this to the memory of my mother.

Chapter One
The Theft

"Y-you're sure you weren't followed?" stammered a short, thin-faced man with wire-rim glasses, wearing an overcoat atop a neatly pressed business suit; nervously glancing about. He had been impatiently waiting by a big tree next to the Greywacke Arch, a bridge to allow pedestrians to cross under East Drive in New York's Central Park. It was midnight, yet the park had many visitors; the early summertime temperatures were perfect for jogging and romantic strolls (and secret meetings).

"Of course. Relax. No one is taking notice unless you draw attention to us with your trench coat, sweating and fidgeting," said a tall woman wearing a jogging suit and a ball cap covering most of her black hair. A backpack was centered comfortably between her shoulder blades by its straps. "Besides, you're the Curator. If the theft has been discovered, you're the one who would be followed."

"I wouldn't d-do th-this, except I n-need th-the m-money... My w-wife, y-you k-know..."

"Yes, yes, we all have our reasons; yours are none of my concern. I assume you brought the requested item." She pointed at a rigid leather brief case he was clutching against his chest.

"D-do y-you have th-the g-gold?" He eyed her expectantly but remained wary.

"I wouldn't be here if I didn't. My employer keeps his word." She deftly unslung the pack from her back, reached in and pulled out her own leather briefcase that was obviously quite heavy. "It's all there—you may count it if you like, but we'll be here all night." Her case was identical to his.

"Th-that w-won't be n-necessary..." He waved his hand above his head. "I j-just s-set a v-vision shield... J-just o-open the c-case and l-let m-me have a quick l-look." He continued to stutter; he'd never anything illegal like this before.

The woman laid her case flat on the ground between them, spun the combination dials and eased up the lid. "Satisfied?"

"Y-y-yes!" was all he could mutter as his eyes opened wide at the sight of so many gold talons; more than he could make working many years as Artifact Curator at the Sodality Redoubt.

"That's the stuff dreams are made of..." She closed the case, snapped the latches and spun the locking dials. "While your shield is in place, let me see what we're buying."

The small man nervously turned the locks' dials, clicked the latches and opened his case. Inside lay a ½-inch thick object with a flawless, polished surface; almost twelve inches across at the bottom but tapered to six inches at the top. It was a deep translucent red, becoming darker at the top (almost black) and encased in glass with a wood frame engraved with ancient Celtic runes. The enclosure perfectly fit in a custom-designed, black velvet padded interior of the case. "No, that's what d-dreams come from..." He closed and secured the latches. Just then the cloudless sky lit up as a huge bolt of lightning streaked through the air above them, accompanied by a loud clap of thunder. They both thought it strange but concluded their business.

Nervously, the man placed his package into the backpack the woman held open for him, reached down and grabbed the handle of the gold-filled briefcase. But as he stood up, his mind seemed to explode and his legs folded under his weight. Some time later he arose but could not remember who he was, why he was in Central

Park or even where he lived. (Of course, there was no woman, backpack or case full of gold talons.)

* * *

"Was that truly necessary?" said the bespectacled man with a high-pitched voice. "I was quite willing to give him the money."

"He could have identified me if the investigators used a memory probe. He would not have held out. And through me they would have gotten to you. Is that what you want?"

"You didn't need to erase all his memory; just altering it regarding this matter would have been sufficient. The poor man can't even remember his own name."

"There wasn't time to be selective. Once the energy hit him, the vision shield went down and I couldn't do both. There were people all over the park.

"If it'd make you feel any better, I gathered his memories in this globe." The woman pulled a four-inch crystal ball from her backpack and handed it to the man who hired her. "I can find the Curator and give him back everything—except my identity, of course, and our transaction. I'll even fix it so he'll have a plausible reason for having the money. I will have to charge you extra for that service." She smiled greedily.

"Oh yes, of course—for an additional fee," squeaked the man's high-pitched voice. "It was never my intent for anyone to get hurt. My research is to benefit all Sodality; never to do harm." He handed the sphere back, noticing a swirling cloudiness inside the glass that was the sum of all the man's memories. "I will pay your price when you bring him here and I'm satisfied he has been restored exactly as you described. Joseph and I have been friends; I'll know if you were successful."

"It will take some time, but he should be paying you a visit within a week. You know, your high moral attitude seems strange

3

as you have just acquired a one-of-a-kind artifact that was stolen for you."

"I'm sure it appears contradictory, but my purpose is not for my personal gain or power—only to keep it out of certain hands."

"We all have our reasons for doing what we do; yours are none of my concern. I simply observed that you seem at odds with yourself."

"As you say, it is not your business. We both have work to do; I suggest we get to it. I will be anxious to see my friend made right again."

Chapter Two
Deep Questions

"Congratulations!" Brian was looking at his (newly adopted) brother's APT results before opening his own Progress Report envelope. "You scored Master level in every subject but History." They were standing next to the UTS receptacle in the hallway of his family's home at 128 Main Street. "I bet that's the highest score of anyone during Fifth Form." He nervously slid his finger under the seal of his own envelope. He knew he'd done fairly well, but one was never sure—especially with teachers like Professor Antetima.

"C'mon, let's see what you got," said J.J., anxious to shift the focus away from himself. Sometimes it was embarrassing to score so well with such little effort. He watched Brian open the envelope flap and extract a hand-written, folded parchment.

Unlike Fifth, Sixth and Seventh Form APTs that classify proficiency levels as neophyte, prentice, inceptor, master, licentiate or illusionist (depending on the subject), First through Fourth Forms are graded on the BME scale (Below, Meets or Exceeds Expectations).

"Hey, you did okay—four E's and two M's. You passed everything; you don't have to take summer school or tutoring to bring up any B's."

"Whew! I was worried Antetima wouldn't pass me." Brian was relieved—yet a bit jealous of J.J.'s top scores. "I still can't get used to it; in Meyor public schools a B is an excellent grade—in Sodality seminary, it's the worst."

"Yeah, I think they do that on purpose." J.J. then grinned and chuckled. "Just to keep us confused." He carefully refolded his Progress Report, slid it back in its envelope and tucked it between the other mail in the UTS box.

"We've been so busy with school and stuff regarding Reficul and Wizard's Cavern, we haven't talked about that article in the *Expositor*."

"You're right," said J.J. "What do you think? Could it be true?"

"I don't know—maybe. Let's ask Mom and Dad tonight. Maybe Grandma might even know. I'm sure they'll use our Progress Reports as an excuse to celebrate and have a big family dinner. I wonder how Nicki did." He held her (sealed) envelope—itching to tear it open. "Seems weird for her to get a Sodality Progress Report."

"She has to be tested on her tutored home-schooling, doesn't she?" remarked J.J. "I'm just surprised they gave her APTs this soon. Her tutor must really be impressed."

"Sis amazed me with some of the stuff she did in Wizard's Cavern. She's learned fast." For a moment, his mind drifted back to the last year, becoming Ringmaster, Reficul and Wizard's Cavern.

"I still don't think it's fair." J.J. grinned mischievously. "All those years livin' next door, she got to torture me and I couldn't use energy 'cuz she was supposed to be Nomag. Now it turns out she's got huge psionic abilities!"

"In some ways I'm glad her abilities developed later," said Brian. "Can you imagine how bad it would have been growin' up with her being able to channel?"

"I hadn't thought of it that way—you're right."

"I'm hungry. Mom said for us to fix our own lunch; she's at the Community Center helping plan the Fourth of July picnic."

"You're always hungry."

*   *   *

The house at 128 Main Street sat high on a hill rising above the tiny town of Meyor, Arizona. It was quite normal-looking to passersby, a two-story ranch style, painted white, with a picket fence along the roadway. There were several fruit trees scattered across the 1½ acre lot and a steep, curving gravel driveway that led up to the side—where a garage was planned. But number 128 was far from normal. Inside were wondrous things like the UTS (Universal Translocation Service) receptacle where packages and mail were instantly sent and received in a flash of light. There was the FON (Fiber Optics Network, which usually looked like a regular dressing room mirror) that allowed people to travel, even great distances, within seconds—after being dissolved into a shiny metallic liquid. But what was most wondrous was the family that lived there.

By all appearances the residents of 128 Main Street were average, patriotic, hard-working small-town folks. They participated in community activities, shopped at local stores, and helped their neighbors when there was need. No one would guess they were anything but ordinary. But ordinary they were not! Certainly other Meyorites had no idea their neighbors were descendants of 10,000 intergalactic voyagers who (mistakenly) came to earth in 21AD, or that they could channel energy using their mage power rings and psionics. Some might call the Everetts *witches, wizards, conjurors* or *sorcerers*, and their abilities *magic, spells, conjurations, witchcraft* and *sorcery*. But the Everetts (and the other descendants) called themselves *Sodality* and their special talents *powers, abilities, gifts,* or *psionics*.

Being Sodality, the Everetts were certainly remarkable. But they were more—much more! The occupants of Number 128 were the last descendants of Merlin, the fabled sixth-century magician (whose forefather was Captain C'Andro—who sacrificed himself to save his wife and children and the 10,000 voyagers when their intergalactic starship crashed into Earth's atmosphere).

The Everetts were a close-knit family. George had recently been appointed to a Sodality Council post that was third in line from the Chairman. Myrna was still a stay-at-home mom, but was becoming increasingly involved in community and Sodality volunteer activities. Nichole ("Nicki"), strikingly beautiful at 17, with long blonde hair, was a senior at Meyor High School and being tutored in psionics and other Sodality subjects (because she just came into her powers last year). Jeremy ("J.J.," age 15) was a real challenge. Short for his age, with flaming red hair, he'd been adopted by the Everetts after his parents were killed about year ago. He was one of the brightest psionics prodigies ever born but seemed determined to create more havoc than a whole class full of students his age. Despite his pranks and brashness, J.J. was intensely loyal to and loved his new family. Brian, nearing his twelfth birthday, was tall, thin, with golden blond hair, a never-ending appetite, and like his father and sister, had steely blue eyes. He carried a tremendous burden: After almost fifteen centuries (since Merlin), Brian was the *Appointed One* to make a *master ring* that would give him power to control all other mages' power rings. But he was not yet ready; there was much he needed to do and learn before he could become the *Ringmaster*.

* * *

"Thanks, Mom," said Nicki as she finished a helping of cherry cobbler; pleased she made high school honor roll and Inceptor on her APTs. "Dinner was great."

"Your fried chicken beats that bucket stuff any day," complimented J.J.

"Yeah, Mom, thanks," Brian barely got out between his last bite of dessert and starting another chicken drumstick—he decided he still had room for.

"You're all welcome," responded Myrna, basking in the attention and still gushing with pride at her children's excellent Progress Reports (especially considering their distractions of time traveling and the events at Wizard's Cavern). "You all deserve to be congratulated. I couldn't be more pleased."

As the Everett family and Grandma James finished their dessert (Brian had a second helping after two more pieces of chicken), there seemed to be an uncomfortable silence that no one felt at ease to break. Finally it was Grandma who interrupted everyone's musings:

"Brian, tell your father what is on your mind."

"How'd you—?" After almost 12 years of being around J.J.'s grandmother he should have been used to her ability to know what was going on in his head, but it still took him by surprise. "Sorry."

"It is no matter, but what you are concerned about, is."

"Dad, the first time Merlin's ghost visited me (after I got my ring), he said that it would be a mistake to think only he could invent a master ring formula. Do you really think someone else might be able to do it?"

"I would think, since he came up with two versions of the process, that it could be done. But the process is quite complicated and the formula requires some very rare ingredients. That's why no one has succeeded in all the centuries since Merlin."

"You mean—people have tried?" Brian looked at the adults.

"Oh my, yes," answered Grandma. "Many people have dreamed of becoming Ringmaster. Some have driven themselves insane in the pursuit—"

"*Power Press* reported a case like that just a couple of years ago," interrupted Uncle Paul. "It was sad—he was a respected Ord Seminary professor who completely wigged out and had to be committed. There was talk of sending him to that hospital in London, Saint Something-or-another."

"Son, why do you ask?" inquired Myrna. "Has something happened?"

"In all the excitement after Wizard's Cavern, catching up on homework and the APTs and stuff, we forgot to mention an article in *Sodality Expositor*..." Brian pulled the well-worn tabloid from his back pocket and passed it to his father. "I know most of the stuff they print is trash, but something about this story really made me wonder."

Everyone in the room became silent and didn't move as they saw George's face take on a look of intense concern while he read the headline.

"This has always been a worry," said George with a sigh. Then he turned the exposed front page and held it for everyone to see the large banner print:

SECRET ALCHEMY LAB DEVELOPING MASTER RING FORMULA

There was a collective gasp as everyone seated around the dining table stared at the words—all wondering if it might be true or if the article was another of the *Expositor's* flights of fantasy, like the story about Brian when he inherited Merlin's personal power-channeling ring. Yet, even in that report, there were small fragments of truth mixed in with gross exaggerations and outright lies.

"If anyone could figure out the correct formula, someone from that family might, because of their connection to Merlin," announced Grandma.

* * *

"What are we going to do?" asked J.J. worriedly. "Do you really think Mr. M can figure out the formula?" He and Brian were walking down the path toward Circle C.

"I don't know..." said Brian after a few moments' thought—his mind was in deep contemplation of the same questions. "It's not like we can confront him. There's no law that says he can't make a master ring or become Ringmaster."

"Yeah, but Grandma said you're the Appointed One—"

"That's true; as far as the formula created by Merlin is concerned. But when his ghost visited me, he said there would always be another who can do it. The only way to prevent it is for me to go ahead and make the ring from our family's records. There can only be one master ring at a time."

"Didn't he say you're too young?"

"I don't know what that means. Am I too weak? Does it require techniques I don't know yet? Am I really not ready for the responsibility?"

"Pro'bly all that and more. If you had it right now, what would you do?"

That question stopped Brian in his tracks. Since he was told about being the Appointed One, he'd toyed with various thoughts of things he could do with the master ring—kids' type of daydreams. But J.J.'s question was serious—what *would* he do? He did not even know what empowerment it would give him. Suddenly he knew why he was not ready: *I need to learn what it can do, how to use it and when I should use it.* In that instant, he understood that, despite the dangers, he needed to be patient and wait until he could fully answer those questions before he would try to become Ringmaster. And besides, he didn't even know what ingredients he'd need.

"Let's go get our Icers. It's hot and a big cup of juice with slushy, shaved ice in it sounds really good. Then I want to go across the highway and see if Laileb is still in the trailer park. And Phusikos; I could never figure out who's side he's on."

"That was so weird. We knew he was watching us at school and in contact with Laileb—probably even Reficul—but you never got any alarms from Monēo; and his warnings may have saved us—twice!"

They walked on down the trail toward the convenience store without any more discussion. They weren't in a hurry, just plodding along, kicking small rocks with their sneakers, sniffing the aroma of lunch being prepared in the cafe down the street, and listening to the melodies of birds chirping in the trees and watching for prairie dogs to pop their heads out of burrows. The summer midday sun was warm as their thoughts drifted. Brian wiped a bit of perspiration from his forehead; it seemed the responsibility of being the *Appointed One* loomed bigger than he ever imagined. The next Friday would be his twelfth birthday and he should have been happy, but right then he felt uneasy—even a bit scared. Turning twelve meant he was a year closer to fulfilling Merlin's prophecy that he would become Ringmaster.

"He's gone!" exclaimed Brian as they stood in front of the round-top aluminum trailer in space number eight. It was a rental unit and it was obvious the tenant had been gone for some time. They looked in the windows and everything was cleaned out; the only furnishings being the built-in bed, kitchen table and sofa. Even the curtains were removed (probably to get cleaned).

"What'd you expect?" countered J.J. "After they caught him in Wizard's Cavern, he was taken to the constabulary; probably in prison by now."

"For some reason, I don't think we've seen the last of him," said Brian, taking a final look at the trailer as if not believing the top lieutenant of Reficul and his Order of the Black Knights was actually gone. "Let's check out Professor Phusikos."

"I'm still here!" Brian and J.J. jumped and went suddenly pale as they realized the illusive instructor was right behind them. "I'm so pleased you have stopped by for a visit." The boys turned and saw the smiling bearded face they'd seen daily at Crown King Seminary. "Come; let's sit in the shade of my garden." The old-appearing man rotated on his heels and moved toward his mobile home across the gravel drive from the shiny, gray coach in space number eight. Brian still felt something didn't fit; the teacher looked old, but his gait, strong shoulders and stance were not how a frail, old seminary professor would usually appear.

Brian and J.J. followed the (seemingly) old man into a well-manicured and lush garden area just alongside a double-wide mobile home. There were climbing plants on a trellis, small trees and shrubbery growing so dense it created a room of living walls and ceiling.

"This is amazing," exclaimed J.J., waving a hand at the flora surrounding them; they were awed.

"Thank you, Mr. James—no, excuse me—it's Mr. Everett now, isn't it." He pointed at two comfortable wicker chairs. "Professor Flora Blender has been kind enough to provide some excellent advice which has enabled me to enjoy this bit of paradise. Please sit. I'd offer you some cold lemonade but I see you already have Icers from Circle C. I just baked some brownies. Please, do try them." He gestured his right hand at a low wicker table in the middle of the area and a platter of neatly stacked squares of moist, dark chocolate brownies suddenly appeared.

Brian didn't hesitate—as fast as the plate materialized, one of the luscious morsels flew into his hand and he took a large bite.

"Thanks," he said between mouthfuls. "These are great."

"If Mom saw you do that," said J.J., laughing, "she'd have you practicing etiquette for hours." He politely reached and picked up a brownie. "Thank you, Professor. They look really good. It's too bad my brother is eating so fast he can't enjoy them properly."

"Sorry." Brian swallowed hard and remembered his manners.

"It's okay. Growing boys need to eat. I'm glad you like them; it's an old family recipe. Now I'm sure you did not come down here just to get an afternoon snack. You're looking for some answers."

"Yes, Professor, but after everything—"

"You thought I'd be long gone, like Mr. Laileb, because you think I'm in league with Reficul and the Black Knights; yes?"

Brian stopped eating—it seemed as if the whole world stopped to wait for the answer.

"Well, obviously I'm still here. I've just renewed my lease on this space and my contract to teach at CKS. I am not going anywhere."

He finally sat in the last garden chair and (to make Brian feel less embarrassed) he floated a brownie into his hand. "As for the other question: I'm not at liberty to confirm or deny if I have any connection with the Order. I'm sorry."

"But, Professor," objected Brian, "last year we saw you and—" He grabbed two more brownies.

"I know what you saw and heard. You really must learn to shield your thoughts from empathic reading. I knew you were hiding on the hill. That's why I told you that 'often things are not as they seem when viewed later from a different perspective.'"

"But—but," sputtered Brian.

"Gentlemen, search your hearts. Especially in our world, what we see and hear can deceive, but your heart and the energy within you will always speak the truth. You both have special gifts. Discover them. Refine them. Use them. Prepare yourselves for the dangers ahead. I will tell you this: I am a dedicated seminary professor, and as such, I will never lie *to you* and will try to protect you whenever I can. I think I have already demonstrated that."

"Yes, Professor..." acknowledged J.J. "Your hints and advice were right on time. Thank you!"

The bearded man did not reply, but simply stared into the eyes of his two young guests and nodded. They all understood each other.

"It looks like I'll need to bake more brownies if there are to be any for my dessert this evening." He chuckled, pointing at the empty platter with only a few crumbs left.

"*Brian!*" J.J. blurted out.

"I'm sorry..." he said sheepishly. "I was hungry."

"You're always hungry. Professor, before we go, can you tell us what happened to Laileb?"

"As you saw, he's moved out of the trailer park—or I should say, someone cleared out his things. Of course, Mr. Laileb has been detained, but he's very powerful and has resisted all mind-probe attempts." He reached out his hand; a folded newspaper materialized within his loose grip and he reached forward, offering it to J.J. "As you can see, his present whereabouts are unknown."

J.J. unfolded the periodical as Brian looked over, recognized the familiar *Power Press* banner and read the large-type headline:

PRISONERS ESCAPE FROM CONSTABULARY HOLDING CELLS

Chapter Three
Strange Phenomena

Happy birthday to you... resounded through the house at 128 Main Street. Brian blew out twelve candles as the last strains of the traditional song ended and many pairs of hands clapped—eagerly awaiting the huge cake to be cut and ice cream scooped out. Unlike his last birthday party, which was a close family affair—the day that J.J. came to live with the Everetts—this was a large celebration. Almost the entire CKS Flipolo team and several classmates were in attendance—including Carl Fredericks. It was Saturday (the day after his actual birthday), so several of the party-goers' parents were also enjoying the festivities and catching up on the latest gossip.

After extinguishing the candles, Brian stepped back as his parents flew into action. The cake was sliced, put on plates and generous dollops of home-made ice cream were served on top. Brian smiled as he watched his mom and dad; they loved informal entertaining and were having as much fun as he was. The cake and ice cream were just the dessert; earlier all the guests were treated to a barbecue lunch. George grilled hamburgers, hot dogs, chicken and brats while Myrna laid out potato salad, fresh-baked bread, Cole slaw, corn-on-the-cob, macaroni salad, chips, pickles, olives and an array of condiments.

Around four o'clock in the afternoon the gifts had been opened, second helpings of lunch or dessert consumed and most of the gossip exchanged. Brian was near the hallway FON mirror saying goodbye, just before his guests stepped into the viscous portal and were seemingly dissolved by the liquid-metal. When most had left, Carl stayed behind.

"Are you scared?" he asked Brian quietly.

"What do you mean?" Brian scrunched his face, puzzled.

"You know about Laileb escaping, don't you?"

"Yeah—"

"Well, we *were* kinda responsible for him spending the last few months in jail—not to mention that whirlwind thing in Wizard's Cavern."

"I guess I'd not thought of it that way. Do you really think he'll come after us?" Brian's mind was racing; remembering the several other painful and embarrassing moments he had caused the Black Knights' top lieutenant—some of which Carl didn't know about. *Maybe he is mad*, thought Brian.

"It's hard to tell, but my parents aren't taking any chances. They're setting wards, shields and alarms; like the ones your uncle put on your house."

"I'm sorry your family is mixed up in this mess. It's too bad you were named in that *Power Press* article about us and the Black Knights last year."

"Are you kidding? It made me a celebrity at school for something other than being the class bully. Even Mom and Dad are happy with my new attitude, so they're taking it in stride."

"I guess that's good then. I sure hope nothing bad happens."

"We'll be okay. I'll bet you're the one he'll be after."

"Maybe... but he's had some ugly experiences messin' with my family. We'll be ready, just in case."

*   *   *

For the umpteenth time the small man pushed his glasses up on his nose; they were constantly slipping down. Unlike his usual (morning) dress of trousers, vest, high-collar shirt, tie and cutaway coat, he was clad in utility pants and a white, knee-length, starched white lab smock. Back and forth he paced in front of a laboratory bench laden with scales, microscope, beakers, distillation tubes, Bunsen burner, hot plate and a metal-firing furnace. Everything looked like a well-equipped university chemistry or metallurgy lab except for the leather case sitting in the middle which he had just opened moments before. The encased object reflected the ceiling's light and made the room have an eerie red glow.

With his hands clasped behind his back, the bespectacled man continued his pacing vigil. The object in the case was the only one like it (at least known to exist) and its value was inestimable. Yet, he was about to grind a portion to complete the experiment he'd been working on for years. He was unaware of the single dark cloud that was gathering directly over his old mining shack, in the foothills of Arizona's Superstition Mountains, in an otherwise cloudless sky.

After almost an hour of indecision, wrestling with his conscience, he finally plucked up his courage and stood before the ancient artifact. For long moments he stared at the engraved runes, wishing the translation would come to mind, but through the centuries no one had been able to come up with anything that made sense.

Outside, the single cloud remained stationary, directly over the dilapidated-looking building (that gave no hint there was a modern laboratory inside). The windows were blacked out so the man with his white smock and glasses (again at the end of his nose) was totally oblivious of the strange weather phenomenon looming over his head.

Not sensing any warning of impending calamity, the short man reached out, his hands barely reaching beyond the sleeves of the lab jacket, until his fingers touched the case's black velvet lining. Something deep inside him suddenly urged him to exercise caution, but he dismissed it as being the excitement of achieving something others had died trying to create.

Taking a deep breath, he stepped closer to the bench, began running his fingers around the rune-engraved wooden frame as if reverently touching a sacred religious icon. There was energy present; he could feel it. The power was building, like a huge capacitor being charged.

Beginning to feel deep concern, the small man wondered if the ancient relic or its reliquary were protected by a ward or shield set by those who long ago found it, put it in its case, or carved the symbols on the enclosure's frame. He assumed the Redoubt curators had not put any protection on the item or the case. There was only one way to find out. He worked his fingers between the frame's right and left sides and the velvet liner. Suddenly a bright flash of light filled the room—then everything went black.

* * *

"Hey, look at this!" Brian called to J.J. He had been watching the news on the special Sodality satellite channel on TV in the den down the hall from his bedroom. "In a minute they're doing a story about a theft from the Redoubt Museum in New York... It's coming on now."

> We're coming to you live from New York in front of the Redoubt Museum where detectives have just called in an inquisitor squad after a break-in and theft was reported.
>
> According to sources close to the investigation, the burglary occurred over a week ago but was not discovered until Curator Joseph Johnson's memory was restored and he remembered he had been preparing a valuable and rare relic for shipping when he was hit by a mind-altering spell.

> The Council's official spokesman refuses to disclose exactly what was stolen; saying only it is a priceless relic and was part of a shipment of items scheduled to be put on loan for an exhibition in England...

"I wonder what was stolen," said J.J., picking up the remote and turning down the TV's sound. "It seems weird they won't say what it is. If it was going on exhibit in England, it's not a secret that it exists."

"There's something about that story..." Brian seemed lost in thought—like he had not even heard J.J.'s comments. "I don't know how to describe it, but I feel like that theft is somehow connected to us."

"What do you mean? Was the thief a distant relative? Was the relic something Dad loaned out of his library or collection?"

"I don't think we're related to the thief." Brian laughed. "But I do feel we're somehow connected to whatever was taken. I don't know if it was out of Dad's collections. He's put a lot of family stuff from Captain C'Andro, Merlin and other ancestors out for study and display."

"I wonder if he knows about the theft?"

"He probably does; Dad always seems to know what's going on in Sodality world. When he gets home tonight I'm gonna ask." Just at that moment another news broadcast came over the SBN (Sodality Broadcast Network) that caught Brian's attention. J.J. turned the volume back up.

> An unusual weather event has been reported in the foothills of Arizona's Superstition Mountains, east of Phoenix and Mesa.
>
> Around 2:00 this afternoon a single cloud gathered over an abandoned mineral assay office, becoming quite dense and highly charged with static electricity. Witnesses say the cloud remained stationary until it

emitted a single bolt of lightning that struck the shack but did not do any apparent damage. Then the cloud disappeared.

While the area east of the Phoenix valley is renowned for unexplained lights in the sky, often attributed to UFOs, this is the first report of the formation of a lone cloud in a completely clear summer sky that then vanished after sending out a single bolt of lightning.

Brangler weather reporters cannot explain the phenomenon. Sodality in the area say they sensed power manipulation at work.

Now from the constabulary watch: There has still been no success in finding the Black Knight follower known as Laileb, who escaped from the Arizona Constabulary...

"That's really weird—"

"Which?" asked J.J. "The cloud thing or not finding Laileb?"

"The cloud—like the museum theft—I somehow feel we're connected to it all. Like the theft and the cloud are related to each other and us—or me, anyway."

"Okay, you're gettin' creepy again. We're not going to have another battle in Wizard's Cavern, are we?"

"How can I tell?" Brian was as worried about his gut feelings as J.J., maybe more. The last time he followed his instincts, people close to him were almost killed, including himself. Sometimes being Merlin's *Appointed One* was an awesome responsibility, especially for a (barely) twelve-year-old boy. He wiggled and scrunched his body to get his bean bag chair to conform to his backside more comfortably as he stared into the television screen, hoping for something to divert his growing sense of trepidation.

Sodality investigators are trying to identify a mage prankster who caused havoc at a zoo in Phoenix. Numerous animals had their voices changed: lions were meowing, tigers chirped, sparrows had loud growls, orangutans mooed and parrots barked. The scene at the zoo was chaotic: visitors were shocked as they laughed and sometimes cried, witnessing the bizarre scene. Zoo officials and veterinarians were unable to discover how the unnatural sounds came about or how to make it right.

Sources inside the Office of Brangler Relations say the Intervention Squad had a hard time sorting everything out and altering memories because there were many zoo visitors and they were scattered throughout the park.

"Now that's funny!" exclaimed J.J. as he saw Brian holding his sides, with tears in his eyes.

"C-can you imagine: a mooing orangutan o-or-or a barking parrot?" It was just the release he needed. "I bet the rest of the birds in the aviary went nuts when the sparrows growled." Brian was doubled up, almost unable to breathe as he continued to picture the animals with altered voices. "It's a good thing you have a solid alibi for yesterday—that sounds like something you'd do." He knew for certain his brother will have worked out the technique of changing animal voices before the day was over, probably even human voices.

*   *   *

The short man stood up on wobbly legs, straightened his lab coat and pushed his glasses back on his nose as he tried to clear the fogginess in his brain. *What happened?* he wondered, carefully looking around to see if there was any damage. All he could remember was starting to pick up the relic's enclosure, a flash of light, and then everything going black. The next thing he knew was finding himself in a heap on the floor in front of the lab bench. *How long was I out?* As he examined his surroundings, everything was in perfect order. Even the fragile glass pipettes were unbroken and undisturbed. The fluorescent lights were all lit and shining normally. He shook his head and stared at the custom-made briefcase with its padded velvet lining and the wooden frame of the glass reliquary with its carved runes. He was confused. *I have seen this thing on display without the leather attaché case. How did they handle it? I wonder... can it sense my intentions?* He carefully closed the lid, snapped the latches and spun the dials on the two latch locks. Very gingerly he picked up the case by its handle and walked to the FON mirror (attached to a far wall), then gave the command for his well-known shop.

After shaking off the queasiness of FON travel, the mage placed the case in a well-hidden recess of his large vault, closed the safe's one-foot-thick door and engaged the massive locks. He went to his private office and changed into his usual morning dress of trousers, high-collared starched white shirt, tie and cutaway coat. He glanced at his watch; it was almost eight o'clock, time to open for business. But what day was it? He walked into his sales area and toward the front door. Everything was in order. He smiled as he saw the front display window with its assortment of antiques on thin pedestals. Outside, the *Sodality Press* paperboy passed, tossed the morning edition at the door, cheerfully waved at the familiar face behind the glass and called, "Good morning, Mr. Mendacci.". The man waved back, pushed up his glasses, glanced at the paper's front page and gasped. He had lost a whole day on the floor of his secret laboratory. He would have to conduct some extensive research before again attempting to tap the secrets and power of the deep-red relic.

Chapter Four
Another Summons

"What are you laughing at?" Brian and J.J. turned and saw Nicki standing with both hands on the sides of the doorway into the den. Her long blonde hair was splayed about her shoulders and she was dressed in faded blue jeans, sneakers and a loose-fitting T-shirt. Now 17, she was quite beautiful, nicely figured and carried herself with confidence and strength.

"SBN just reported about somebody causing the voices of a bunch of zoo animals to change," said Brian, still out of breath.

"The tigers were chirping," added J.J., "and lions meowed."

"I wish I could have been there," said Nicki with a chuckle. "I bet the Branglers were in a panic."

"Yeah, it took the Intervention Squad a long time to sort it all out," said Brian.

"What have you got in your bedroom?" She stared at Brian with a questioning look and raised eyebrows.

"Nothin'—why?" He was totally confused.

"Well, I just went by your door and heard a flapping noise. Then as I walked past, it quit. I went back and it started again as I got close—like whatever it is knew I was there. Then I heard you guys laughing in here. Like before, the sound stopped as I went farther from your room. Did you collect another stray or abandoned critter?"

"No! I haven't got anything!" He looked at his sister's disbelieving expression. "Honest! I'll show you!" He wriggled up from the beanbag chair and headed toward Nicki and the door. She moved aside as he barged through and down the hallway toward his bedroom. But as he reached for his doorknob, he too heard the strange sound. "What is that?" he asked worriedly. "Did you bring something home that got into my room through the bathroom?" He looked over his shoulder at J.J.—actually hoping he'd say yes because the alternative could be something really scary.

"No way!" said J.J. "Whatever's in there is all yours. It's your room."

"That's what I was afraid of. You think there's any way Uncle Paul's shields and wards are down? Maybe something snuck in—or flew in. I agree with Nicki; it sounds like flapping." He kept his right hand extended but didn't touch the knob.

"You're not going to find out anything standing here," urged Nicki. "Either let's go in or get Father and let him deal with it."

"Deal with what?" George Everett's familiar voice sounded from behind the three youths. Brian felt comforted; he was brave, but having his father close when strange noises were coming from his bedroom made him feel much better.

Nicki quickly recounted what she heard while walking past the door. Brian and J.J. reaffirmed they had not introduced something foreign into the house. After some thought, George moved toward the door—in front of Brian.

"All of you, channel your power and put up a shield. I'll open the door and be prepared to stun anything we find inside."

They nodded their understanding, concentrated and muttered the shield command as George turned the knob and flung open the door.

At once Brian started laughing as they peered into his room. On his desk—right where he had left it—was the ancient tome of

Merlin's handwritten notes. The noise was from a large bundle of pages flapping back and forth rather forcefully, obviously trying to attract attention.

"I guess I'm missing something," observed George. "What does it mean when the book fans pages like that?" They all walked into the room and crowded around the desk. The book settled down, opened to a mostly blank page almost halfway through. The familiar bold print was flashing:

HITHER THY RIGHT HAND LAYEST
TRAVEL IN TIME THOU MAYEST

"Merlin's calling again, Dad. That's what it means."

As if sensing the question in everyone's mind, additional writing appeared below:

SIR BRIAN
SIR JEREMY
LADY NICHOLE

"Well, it appears you are being summoned, and your mother and I must wait here and worry."

"Maybe you could go," suggested J.J. "We could all go."

"I'd love to, Son, but we don't know what would happen if too many went through; especially uninvited. I haven't had time to research time travel and portals. So far, Merlin has never put you in a situation you could not handle. I'll just have to trust he continues to protect your well-being. And for you—all of you—to use good judgment and look out for each other."

"I wonder what season it will be when we get there?" Brian looked down and noted he was only wearing a T-shirt, short pants, socks and sneakers.

"Even in summer, England can have inclement weather," observed George. "I suggest you all go change into warmer clothes, including a jacket. Then go take leave of your mother; she'll not want you to go without saying goodbye and she'll probably pack some food." He turned and left the room to speak with his wife while J.J. and Nicki hurried to their bedrooms, leaving Brian to don fresh socks, underwear and T-shirt, blue jeans, flannel shirt and his Flipolo team jacket. He kept glancing at the book; its pages were flipping again—seemingly impatient or sensing it was being ignored.

"Cool your jets!" he chided. "We're coming; just have to get ready." He was surprised to see the ancient parchments instantly lay still—open to the portal call page. "That's better."

Within a few minutes the whole family was gathered in Brian's bedroom. Nicki and J.J. were wearing warmer clothes; George was reminding them to use caution, and Myrna was stuffing sandwiches, cookies, bags of chips, fruit and thermoses of soup into Brian's backpack. Each hugged their parents. Then the three youngsters stood in front of the desk and the ancient book. Just as Brian reached out his right hand, he heard the reassuring voice of his father:

"Good luck, and be careful..." Brian laid his hand on the open book and felt himself be elongated, stretched and sucked into the page. This time he was able to keep his eyes open while the swirling colored lights surrounded him and whizzed by. On and on he went; occasionally catching a glimpse of some long past event he'd barely heard about in history lessons and books. He could hear Nicki and J.J. moving along behind. He'd have to clear the landing spot quickly before they materialized right in his lap. Suddenly he felt himself coming out of the time tunnel (as he called it) and reforming. Immediately he could smell and feel the dampness of Wales, England. It was not raining, but it had not been long since it had.

He quickly stepped away from Merlin's end of the portal, glanced around and saw a familiar sight: the wooded lush valley where Merlin's cottage was located. The stream trickled down the valley floor and hundreds of birds chirped and sang in the surrounding dense forest. J.J.'s body stretched out of the book and regained its natural form, followed by Nicki.

"It's kinda like FON travel, except there aren't the thousands of branches that lead to various mirrors," said Nicki, checking to make sure all her parts were in the right place. "Where are we?"

"This is Merlin's cottage," answered Brian "where we fought his son and he hid Excalibur."

"Long time has passed since that occurrence," added the old man with a beard. "I have been waiting for you."

Brian, J.J. and Nicki studied their long-past ancestor and were surprised to see him appearing so much older—and he was not young before. Even the valley, forest and cottage all seemed to have aged.

J.J. moved first—remembering the famed wizard preferred the French greeting custom of a hug and a kiss on each cheek—and embraced the man he was now related to. "Hello, Grandfather. I get to say that now. Brian's parents adopted me after my folks were killed." They exchanged kisses.

"Sorry I am for thy loss—though pleased you are now grandson. The story I would like to hear when you are comfortable." The old mage looked deep into the eyes of the red-headed boy and tears welled up in both of their eyes as they touched each other's spirits.

After a long moment the spell was broken; Nicki and Brian rushed to embrace the fabled magician, their (too many greats to count) grandfather. "Oh, Nichole and Brian, how I have missed thee..." He gestured toward the door of his cottage. "If it pleases, victuals await within. We may sup as we discuss the purpose of mine summons."

Brian didn't hesitate. He followed Merlin through the doorway into a large room filled with books, a long table with bench seats, various rustic chairs and a cheery fire in a wide hearth that had a pot hanging over some coals. There was an aroma of new thatch on the roof, dusty leather-bound books, and a wonderful stew that was bubbling heartily in an old black iron kettle. The walls were made from large, smooth rocks held in place by gray-brown mortar. Several windows were open and the curtains were tied back, so the interior was bright and airy. The stone walls emitted a cool dampness, but the fire created a cozy warmth. Brian had often daydreamed about living in the splendor of one of the great medieval European castles, but he felt so at home in the simple comfort of that sixth century cottage, he could live there forever.

With a wave of his hand the hanging pot floated to the center of the table; four bowls, mugs and large spoons, bread board and knife all arranged themselves—ready for the feast. Merlin glided over, ladled out generous portions, sliced the bread, and bade them all share in the repast.

As usual, Brian tucked into his food with uncouth gusto—but he was certainly related to Merlin, for he too wasted no time before his first helping was gone. He and Brian were both reaching for seconds at the same time. Nicki and J.J. could only shake their heads with amusement and mild embarrassment.

After consuming his third bowl of stew and fourth slice of buttered bread, the old wizard took a deep breath and explained that he summoned the youngsters for instruction; no, there weren't any dragons with toothaches or powerful swords to protect.

"We go to a special school that teaches us how to use our powers. Isn't that enough?" asked Brian, but he wished he hadn't, for he knew the Sodality seminaries could not instruct him on how to be Ringmaster. He stared at his lap, but knew his brother and sister were glaring at him in disbelief.

"You know already the answer to that question."

"You're right—sorry—I'm sure I can learn a lot from you. I really need Ringmaster training."

"To be sure, all learning will benefit your task of being Ringmaster. The instruction I will give is not for that purpose particularly." He gazed intently at Brian. "Say again what training your academy does impart."

"Uh—hmm—we have lots of classes: history, herb and plant use, natural physics, astrology, math, transmogrification, energy and power control. In our community they don't call it magic."

"Well it is, as far as it goes. But more you must acquire." Merlin explained how the ability to tap into elements and energy existing outside the body had been mostly lost by his time. Brian's comments, along with what he had seen them do on previous visits, indicated things had not changed in the twenty-first century. Everything has energy from Earth, Fire, Water, Air, or Spirit. With training, wizards (and witches) can gather and use these powers. But just as certain gifts are dominant with individual mages (empath, seer, etc.), often the ability to use elements becomes focused on one, two or three. It is extremely rare for a wizard to have equal command of all five.

"Aren't we already doing that?" interrupted J.J. "We can light fires, move water, make holes in the ground, create breezes and do some mind control."

"If you do these things for an extended period, what do you feel?"

"Tired. It takes a lot of energy to manipulate elements for a long time."

"Yes, as you said, you have learned to use your powers, not gather the energies from them. To sustain your efforts for the tasks ahead, you must be skilled in all three disciplines: using personal power, enlisting the power of the elements, and gathering surrounding energies into yourselves. The latter requires great skill, for it is easy to take in more than may be handled and thus be consumed. For this cause the craft has become feared and not shared with new generations."

"When I read your book of notes, you mentioned these things," said Nicki, "but you never explained how to do it."

"The living book will have these lessons after you have learned them from me. Such skills may not be acquired by reading only. We will labor hard together that I may impart the necessary knowledge and wisdom. Also you must swear to not pass on the craft until you have practiced many years, and even then let the spirit guide your choices." He looked intently into the wide-open eyes of his grandchildren, reached out his hands to Brian and Nicki. "Let us all join hands in a circle and commit to the Wizards' Inviolable Oath." J.J. extended his arms and took the offered hands of his adopted brother and sister as they stood to form a circle around the table. The old man bade them repeat the words:

"I solemnly swear—the abilities to command and gather the powers—of the elements of Water, Earth, Air, Fire and Spirit—I will not teach until I have become master of the same—and then only to my immediate family—direct descendants or those the power of Spirit so directs—this I freely affirm by the Wizards' Inviolable Oath—and invoke its full force upon myself."

As they all pronounced the last words, energy freely flowed between them and around the circle. The youngsters were used to channeling and focusing power, but this was different: there was intensity—almost rage—as it swirled between and around them.

"Wow!" exclaimed Brian. "I've never felt anything like that. I get the feeling it would not be pleasant if we ever tried to break it." He sat down and scooped more stew into his bowl.

"What would happen?" asked J.J. with a mischievous grin.

"The Wizards' Inviolable Oath works differently for different mages. Sometimes it will cause the mind to not be able to do the forbidden thing. It will oft times punish—even to death—if the infraction is of such import."

"Quit looking for a loophole," ordered Nicki. "We must keep the oath, not just the words but the spirit of it."

"Okay—okay!" conceded J.J. "I was just wondering."

"What you have sworn will be recorded in the book to remind all."

After finishing their meal they followed Merlin outside and sat on round log sections that were sitting upright on their sawed ends. They were seated in somewhat of a circle around a fifth log section that had a bowl of water sitting upon it.

"Sit silently," commanded Merlin. "Concentrate on the water—nothing else. Extend the palm of your left hands and feel the water—sense its energy—ask it to share its strength—do not channel any power."

The four of them sat for some time. J.J. would occasionally shake his head, trying to clear his mind. Nicki was leaning forward with her elbows on her knees—keeping her left hand facing the bowl. Brian also bent forward, resting his upper body on his right arm that was folded across his lap. Finally the old magician broke their meditative trance.

"Jeremy, what do you feel?"

"I don't know. It seemed like I heard gurgle sounds, like a drip falling in a large pool and the ripples of the expanding wave."

"Brian?" he asked without comment, which made J.J. feel he'd done it wrong.

"I had a daydream. I saw water trickling down from a mountain creek or stream. Then it joined other water and became a river flowing toward the sea."

"Nichole?" (Brian too wondered if he had messed up the lesson.)

"I felt change, like the water was releasing energy. I think it was warm and it's cooling off out here in the open. I also felt a rocking motion, like being in a ship rocking back and forth and up and down with the ocean swells."

Still without interpretation Merlin arose, removed the water bowl, then picked up a handful of dirt and placed it on the rugged stand.

"Repeat, please, thine task on this earth." He sat back down on his crude chair.

The lessons went on for the rest of the day with a small fire burning atop a dish of lamp oil and air inside a glass beaker. Each time he would ask what they sensed or felt and they in turn related their impressions. It was late in the afternoon when they went inside. Merlin moved swiftly to prepare a supper as Brian, Nicki and J.J. cleaned up, unpacked the lunches and extra clothes from their backpacks. They all wondered at their host's reticence. During the whole day he had not commented on their performance. Was he disappointed? Did they fail? They all went about their tasks in uncomfortable silence. Nicki, Brian and J.J. would glance at each other questioningly with raised eyebrows; then an *I don't know* shrug of their shoulders. Finally, the smell of meat roasting over the fire and vegetables cooking in the black-iron pot seemed to lighten the atmosphere. As the large haunch of meat turned on the spit and broth began to boil, the delicious aromas of onions, cabbage, carrots, celery and garlic wafted through the large living room-kitchen area. Merlin smiled, clapped then rubbed his hands together and finally spoke.

"Lady Nichole, you may use the front, girls' bedroom. M'lords Brian and Jeremy will use my sons' old room in the back. There be plenty of clean linens, blankets and night clothes that should fit. Outside is a privy for necessaries. Water and washbasins are in the rooms. We bathe in the creek—we'll make sure Nichole has privacy. It's a bit cold, but I find it invigorating. I do have a tub if you really need it." He looked at them with a smirky expression, conveying disappointment if any of them should not be tough enough to take a dunk in the mountain stream. They all went to their rooms to wash, stow their extra clothes and check out their sixth-century digs.

Brian re-emerged in the great room carrying a large bag of nacho-cheese corn tortilla chips and tuna salad sandwiches his mother had made. He was sure Merlin had never tasted nacho chips and doubted if tuna salad was available in AD 500 (or whatever date it was). He pulled open the seal on the chip bag.

"Grandfather, here, try something from the twenty-first century." He held out the bag and watched the white-bearded man reach in and remove one triangular chip.

"Pray tell, what be this? What does one do with it?" He held it gingerly and examined the golden-yellow item from all directions. "It smells like cheese, yet the texture is strange." Brian broke out laughing, as did Nicki and J.J. (they had just returned to the main room).

"You eat it." He laid the sandwiches on the table and grabbed three chips out of the bag and stuffed them in his mouth. As he bit down, a loud crunch could be heard throughout the cottage; several crunches later, he swallowed them down. "They're really good. Try 'em." He watched the wizard tentatively nibble a corner of the chip. His eyes widened and a huge smile spread across his face as he devoured the rest of the morsel and reached for more.

"Beyond description this is. This must be food prepared for your royalty," he barely said as he gobbled a handful of chips. In a few moments half the bag was consumed as the twenty-first century youngsters looked on with glee.

"No, Grandpa," commented J.J. "Those are nacho chips. Big companies make them and everybody can buy 'em. And besides, in our country, we do not have any royalty, just elected representatives of the people, a president, and our Sodality Chairman."

"In a wonderful time, you live. Never have I consumed such a delectable treat." He looked down at the sandwiches on the table. "And these you eat as well? That clear covering does not appear as well-tasting." He gently prodded the clear plastic bag with the tip of his first finger.

Plastic sandwich bags were so common in their time, they didn't even think it would be a technological oddity in the sixth century. Brian set down the (almost empty) chip bag on the table, picked up a sandwich and peeled back the plastic to uncover about half.

"The clear stuff is called plastic. It's made from refined crude oil and keeps the bread from drying out and the contents clean." Immediately the distinctive odor of tuna, dill pickles, celery and mayonnaise wafted above the cooking supper. "I think our mother makes the best tuna salad sandwiches. She would be pleased if you had one. Don't eat the plastic." He chuckled as he watched Merlin seize the sandwich, take a large bite out of the middle of the exposed edge. The rest was rapidly eaten with relished gusto.

"Truly thy mother is a master cook." He turned the plastic bag over in his fingers, examining it from every possible direction. "Amazing this is. Hard it be to imagine how it is made from oil from the earth." He looked hungrily at the other sandwiches on the table.

"Here, Grandfather..." Brian picked up the two remaining tuna delights and held them out. "You can have these—we can get more when we return to our time." As the sandwiches were seized and eaten, Brian happily thought of how the sixth-century man would respond to the peanut butter and jelly sandwiches, fruit pies and Twinkies that were still in his pack. "Is our dinner cooked yet?"

"Oh, yes," he said between bites; waved his arm and the bubbling pot, bread, butter and rotisseried meat flew onto the table.

Nicki moved around, took a large knife and began slicing slabs of meat as J.J. ladled generous bowls of vegetable soup. They ate, mostly in silence, as the youngsters waited for some report on how their exercise had rated earlier in the day, except Nicki inquired:

"Grandfather, your English seems to be much more modern. You aren't using thees and thous very often. And according to our history books, Old English (also called Anglo-Saxon), was used until about 1150AD. Our modern American English is much different from what was spoken in the sixth century— the beginning of modern English. But your native language is Welsh-Gaelic."

"Wow, Sis!" exclaimed J.J. "You've really studied that stuff!"

"You are quite correct. However, much of my time-traveling has been spent in the late 1500s and after King James commissioned the translation of the Bible. It was important to blend in and protect my true identity, so I became quite well-versed with that speech and writing. Of late, I have studied the language after the eighteenth century, but ofttimes I slip back into those phrasings and words."

"Can you give us an example of Welsh-Gaelic from this—your—time?"

"I will write for you my most sacred (Druid) code." Merlin rolled out a scrap of parchment, snapped his fingers, and an inked quill appeared in his hand. He wrote two lines:

'Y *qwir yn arbyn byd.*
The truth against the world.

He passed the writing to Brian and then to J.J. and Nicki.

"Wow!" exclaimed J.J. "That's neat and a great code to live by! But how did we understand your son last year, and the others we've encountered here in the sixth century?"

"I placed a translation spell on the gateway you came through. It was made around 1600's English, so you heard much of that speech."

"Grandfather?" J.J. liked being related to the famous magician and he could no longer restrain his curiosity. "Did we not do well on the tests earlier? You seemed disappointed."

"Of course thou doest well, there was no right or wrong. Testing you was to determine in which elements thy strengths lie. Interpreting your words was I."

"What were the results, then?"

"You know already. Recall your feelings, visions and impressions." He stared at the red-haired boy and awaited his answer.

"I kinda felt something from all four, but Air, Earth and Fire seemed to give me the strongest responses." Again, Merlin was silent; he simply turned his attention to Nicki and gazed at her expectantly.

"Like J.J., I felt energy from each element, but for me, Water, Earth and Air were definitely the strongest."

"All witches and wizards may feel power from all four physical elements, yet most are gifted only in one or two. Blessed are ye both to be strong in three." Brian wondered why he had not yet been asked for his report ... maybe because he didn't feel any greater response from any element.

"What's wrong with me?" he wondered aloud. "They all seemed the same to me." He squirmed uncomfortably on the table-bench he was sitting on. "Am I not gifted with any of them?"

"Is that what you feel?"

"No—not really—I felt lots of energy from all four, but none were stronger than the others."

"You're gifted in all the elements!" blurted J.J. "That's really rare—at least that's what I remember reading somewhere—huh, Grandfather?" They all searched the face of the old magician for confirmation.

"Spoken true. Rare indeed for thy brother communes with the elements equally as they share their strengths alike."

*   *   *

"Try again," said Merlin, exasperated. "Draw the energy before directing it," he said for the umpteenth time.

For the past three full days they had been practicing the same task: urging a large granite boulder to lift off the moist earth and stay suspended for five minutes. The giant rock began to shudder, lean back and forth and ease into the air. J.J. was breaking out in a sweat.

"STOP!" They all jumped at the old man's sharp tone as the boulder splatted back on the ground. "You must not channel through your rings!" He was losing patience as he again explained: They were not to lift the boulder with *their* power; they could do that fairly easily from earlier training. Their assignment was to utilize the energies of the boulder and the ground below to oppose each other.

"This is really hard," exclaimed Brian. "We're used to channeling through our rings. When I try this way, I feel the earth energy, but to send it back I end up channeling my own power." He watched Merlin retreat into his cottage and return moments later with a plain-looking grey metal box.

"Remove your rings and deposit within this lead casket." He opened the hinged lid. "Your power will not penetrate within or without."

"But—but—Grandfather—Merlin—we can't," stuttered Brian. "We're taught to never take off our rings. I'm not sure they will come off."

"You may remove them voluntarily. Cannot be forced. You must have trust. No other way do I see. Ye may have them back at lesson conclusion." He held out the box and with hesitation and reluctance the three red-gold rings were placed on the plush fine linen lining of the casket's interior.

"I feel like I'm standing here naked—even though I'm fully dressed," said J.J. "Like I'm totally unprotected—exposed."

"You rely too much on the rings. You will learn they are not needful when command of the elements is achieved." He closed the lid and returned the box to the cottage. Only then did Brian notice Merlin was not wearing a power ring.

"Grandfather, I was told my ring was your personal mage ring, but you are not wearing one."

Merlin answered and explained that many years previous he made, used and infused the ring Brian inherited. It was impossible for him and Brian to wear the same ring at the same time—even though it had traveled back in time. He further told him that to become truly effective as Ringmaster he must be able to command the elements without using any channeling aid—ring or wand.

"If someone makes the master ring before me, does he have to learn all this stuff?"

"One may become Ringmaster without being master of the elements, but limited he will be and probably will not understand the cause. Only one gifted in all the elements, and skilled therein, may truly be Ringmaster."

"I guess I'd better learn the skills," he said with determined resignation, then turned to the boulder that seemed to mock his previous feeble attempts. He extended his left hand with its palm facing the large granite rock, closed his eyes and sought the great energy he knew was there.

After a time he felt a rush of power, like warm liquid was being poured down into his stomach until he was full. But he couldn't stop it coming. More and more energy flowed into him. He felt like he might explode. His face turned red and his body trembled.

"Release the energy!" commanded Merlin. "'Tis danger! You cannot hold more. Visualize Earth lifting the stone. Offer to share what you were given, and ask it to carry out your desire."

Brian tried to do as instructed and found he was supercharged. The boulder flew into the air—straight up until it was almost out of sight. He lost his focus and they all ducked for cover as the several-ton object came crashing back to the ground, landing almost in the same spot it left.

"You did it!" exclaimed Nicki.

Chapter Five
The Chase

ehind a dense copse of trees a man paced back and forth, trying to make sense of what he had seen during the past few days. With dark, unkempt shoulder-length hair, tattered clothes that had not been washed for weeks, scraggy beard and smudges of soot and ash on his exposed, weathered skin, he appeared to be a ragged beggar who had not eaten a proper meal in a fortnight—maybe longer.

Whispers in a nearby village told of an old wizard who lived alone in a cottage full of magical treasures. It was said he could even turn lead into gold. But there were warnings. Intruders who trespassed were severely punished: turned into toads, burned by dragon fire or made insane by powerful spells. So far none of those things had happened, but he was staying some distance away, watching the goings on. And that was the most confusing—even frightening. The old magician was there, but he seemed to be giving lessons to two boys and a girl—who were very strangely dressed. They all wore long pants—even the girl—that somehow fastened in the front, white shoes made of a material he could not identify and shirts that buttoned in the front (instead of lacing together).

Who are those children, he wondered. At least one of them—the youngest—was a powerful magician. Only moments before he made a huge boulder fly in the air—higher than the treetops—then it crashed back down, settling in the same spot it left. He had never seen anything like that. But what got most of his attention was the grey box the three youths put their shiny gold rings into. That would be a prize. He could eat well and sleep in inns for a year if he could get his hands on that box. He would have to work his way around the stone cottage—staying out of sight—where he might find a rear entrance.

He backed away, deeper into the heavily forested valley floor. Then, moving from tree to tree, he circled the house with careful stealth, making sure he could not be seen or heard by the youngsters or the old wizard. He knew how to be stealthy; many times he had trailed and poached the king's deer for a good meal and sold the remaining meat and hide. The royal game wardens were excellent trackers, but they had never been able to catch him. Silently he crept, taking a painstakingly long time. He could afford to be patient. He had already spent three days just watching. Each day the old magician brought his young pupils outside and they stared at a great rock—the same one that flew into the air earlier that morning. There was a satchel slung over his shoulder that still had some hard biscuits and jerky, so he would not starve. Soon he would be eating well and have new clothes.

It was mid-afternoon when he was finally able to see the rear of the cottage. There was a back door and some open windows—letting in a cool breeze. He snuck close enough and could hear the excited voices of the wizard and the children. They were again out front, following their midday break to eat. The aroma of fresh-baked bread and shepherd's pie still lingered in the air along with the damp mustiness of the thick forest ground cover of fallen leaves and rich earth. It was the perfect time. He could get in and out while they were distracted with their lessons. He planned to be long gone before the theft was ever noticed. As he thought about it, he did not want to be anywhere in the vicinity when that wizard and those witch-kids discovered their rings were missing. Visions of being turned into a toad, or something worse, made him become VERY cautious indeed.

No longer standing, the skinny robber crawled on his belly, trying to slither like a snake and be just as quiet. The grass and leaves were soft, but the occasional rock, twig or limb scratched his chest, arms and stomach. Several times he wanted to call out a curse, but he bore the discomfort in absolute silence; he still had frightening mental images of living out his days having green, warty skin, eating bugs and hopping from place to place. He shook his head to clear the mental images and continued his stealthy progress.

At last, he arrived and no alarm was raised. The rock walls, thatched roof and crudely-hewn, split (Dutch) door loomed above him. Without making a sound he stood up and lifted the latch. It was not locked.

* * *

"That was amazing!" exclaimed Brian. "It was almost like when I disintegrated Mendacci's door. The power flowed but I hardly felt it. It's almost like it did it on its own."

"Do you feel okay?" asked Nicki. "To lift something that heavy, so high, you should be exhausted."

"I don't feel tired at all." Brian danced and skipped around the area, full of energy. "I could do that all day long."

"Now that you've done it," inquired J.J., "do you think you can control it?"

"I think so. It's like when we first got our rings and had control problems. With practice and psionic focus, we can make it work." Brian turned back to the boulder, extended his left hand and began drawing power again. As before, it came as a rush, but this time, before he began to overload, he thrust forth his right palm. Instantly, the huge rock shuddered then rose out of the small crater: it created by crashing on the ground moments before.

J.J., Nicki and Merlin watched intently as the massive orb floated easily about six feet off the ground. They also noted Brian was not straining. His concentration was focused but there was little physical effort. He could even speak.

"I feel like a wire or conduit. The energy is just flowing through me."

"Float it over toward me," said J.J. He was a bit frustrated—maybe even a little jealous—he was always the first to perfect new psionic techniques. "I'm going to try to transfer control to me." He held out his left hand with palm up and closed his eyes.

Brian glided the rock through the air toward J.J. but held it some distance away so he was not underneath—not knowing what was going to happen.

Suddenly a gentle breeze blew their hair—it seemed to be centering around the red-headed boy.

"I feel it!" exclaimed J.J. "I'm drawing the energy!"

"Careful," admonished Nicki. "Don't take in too much like Brian did."

"It's hard not to. There's so much!" His shoulder-length hair whipped about and almost seemed to glow. He extended his right hand, palm toward the stone, and let the energy flow, focusing on the suspended rock. "Whoa! Now that's power."

The boulder seemed to be vibrating as Brian's Earth draw and J.J.'s Wind energy were both exerting forces.

"Take away your power," said J.J. "Slowly!"

Brian gently began to close his left hand—first curling in his fingers one at a time, then brought it into a fist.

All the while J.J. focused on creating a cushion of air to hold the stone suspended. Occasionally, flecks of dirt, a small clod of mud, or wet clump of grass that had been on the bottom, flew off from the roiling turbulence.

"You've got it! I've grounded all my energy." Brian was surprised how easy the transfer took place. "It's your turn, Sis—take it from J.J."

"Which one should I use?" she asked. "I guess I could draw Earth again—I don't want to create a water jet." She looked to the others with eyes wide.

"Make a cloud," said Brian. "It's water."

"You're right!" She threw both hands forward, closed her eyes and visualized a cloud cushion—heavy with water—holding the boulder.

Brian swallowed hard as his throat went dry. All the air around him was suddenly parched and arid, like the Arizona deserts in summer. But under the rock rain droplets formed and were caught up in the air pillow J.J. had formed. A tiny, dense cumulus cloud gathered up and began exerting upward pressure.

"You're doing it!" announced J.J. "I can feel less need for my support."

"Don't turn yours off yet," she directed. "I think I need to draw a little more moisture." She reclosed her eyes and visualized the water from the stream evaporating and joining the wet cushion. A long tendril of water snaked out of the nearby stream and wriggled its way through the air toward the bottom of the stone.

Just as the giant water snake reached its zenith over their heads, Nicki looked up and gasped. The loss of concentration resulted in a sudden deluge coming down on Brian, Merlin and herself. (J.J. was off to the side, still maintaining his focus.)

"Water aplenty you now have," spluttered Merlin. "Gather it and redirect it as before."

Nicki did not hesitate. She drew the water, gently speaking to it as if it were animate. "C'mon," she coaxed. "Form together—that's it—come out of the clothes—off the ground—out of our hair..."

Brian felt his clothes and hair instantly dry as if sucked out by the wet/dry shop vacuum his father had at home. He was starting to miss his parents; he was a bit homesick.

"There you go—y'all join together—now push up on the rock," Nicki softly continued. "That's it—hold it up..."

They all watched a column of water, two feet thick, form like a liquid pedestal from the ground to the bottom of the boulder.

Then, as if it had become ice—yet it was not frozen—the pillar supported the weight.

"I've got it—release your wind."

"Okay," responded J.J. He eased away the wind. "It's all yours." He dropped his hands and walked over to Brian and Merlin. "That's amazing how she did that," he whispered.

"Hey, Sis," chortled Brian, "what are you going to do with all that water when you set it down?"

"Oh, I've got that covered—just watch..."

Brian, his brother and grandfather did watch. The boulder began to slowly descend, as if on an elevator. The water shaft appeared to be sinking into the ground, but the ground was not wet. The liquid was dissipating, going back into the air as if rapidly evaporating. Just as the stone touched the ground, Nicki smiled mischievously, looking just over her brothers' heads. They did not see the thick, dark miniature cloud that had formed above them until it was too late. When the little cloud could hold no more, a narrow deluge suddenly cut loose and soaked them both. Merlin and Nicki broke out laughing. She did not see what J.J. was conjuring.

"That's just so wrong!" exclaimed Brian as he stood there, soaked completely. "Payback's gonna be a—"

"Eeeek!" screamed Nicki as she heard a whistling sound over her head and quickly looked up. A dirt devil had formed, with its eye just above her head, and was descending to envelope her completely.

"Be careful!" said Brian. "Don't hurt her."

"I'm gettin' good at these things." J.J. laughed. "It's just gonna take her a while to get the grass and leaves out of her hair!"

With that, the mini-whirlwind touched down at Nicki's feet and picked up grass, leaves, dirt and some moisture still on the ground. The debris swirled around as she held her hands in front of her face. Then, as fast as it formed, the tiny cyclone was spent, leaving the teenager completely disheveled. Her hair was twisted and full of chaff and her clothes pulled sideways.

"Hey, I like this elemental control thing," said J.J. "It's much easier to be sneaky!"

"Very funny," sniffed Nicki, realizing psionic-prank wars with her brothers was probably a losing proposition.

"You started it," laughed Brian.

"Yeah, I know. Maybe I should gather up another rainstorm and use it for a shower. Hey, that's not a bad idea—"

Suddenly both Brian and Merlin grabbed the sides of their heads, paused, then took off for the cottage door...

*   *   *

Once inside the thief couldn't believe his eyes. The interior was lined with shelves, piled high with hundreds—maybe thousands—of books, all kinds of odd contraptions, measuring devices, weight scales, jars, crystal globes and gold—many things made of gold. It was a king's ransom.

Louis, you've just found your fortune. If you can just get this loot out, he thought to himself—afraid to even whisper.

Carefully he moved around, eyeing the bounty, almost forgetting the rings in the lead box (that Merlin placed on a shelf). But he did find them and the small, grey-metal chest.

Quietly the burglar slipped the box into the flour-sack he carried and snatched a couple of gold items close by. *Canst not be greedy or get caught I will.* He was already easing his way out of the back window when, somehow, the cottage occupants were alerted—despite his stealth. The hairs on the back of his neck prickled, but there was no point in looking back.

If they are close, I'll soon be a toad. There's no help for it now, except run!

Up to that point he had been using every trick he knew to stay quiet and unobserved, crouching low and moving so carefully there was no visible trail nor even a dry leaf crunched under his foot. Just ten yards more and he'd be deep in the woods and he could run;

the thick ground cover, rustling leaves and chirping birds would conceal his tracks and sounds.

He had made it and there were no more sounds of alert behind him. Maybe his fears were only his imagination run amok, but there was no point in pushing his luck. *Now* it was time to run. He broke into a hard run, darting from tree to tree, to keep from being seen and to confuse any pursuers.

* * *

"What's wrong?" Nicki cried out. "What's going on?" She turned to follow J.J., who was already right on Brian's heels.

"I've seen that look before," shouted J.J. over his shoulder. "He's received a warning from Monēo." Just inside the cottage door he slid to a stop behind Merlin and Brian, who were intently searching about for anything askew or missing.

"Somebody was in here," said Brian. "I feel it. I can see his energy trails. He crisscrossed all over."

"You can see that?" asked J.J. "Was he Sodality?"

"Yeah, I can—he must be our kind for me to—"

"Nay, young wizard," interrupted Merlin. "All life has energy that can be seen by gifted ones. What you see are the strong remnants of one with dark intent. I doubt the intruder can channel power, but we cannot be certain; there are many who are not aware of their heritage."

"Can you tell what he did—what he wanted?" asked Nicki.

"He wandered around so much I can't tell, except he came and went through the back door," answered Brian, pointing toward the rear opening and the Dutch door that was left ajar.

"Is anything missing?"

"Only a few things: a goblet, spoons and a direction-finder is all I notice." Merlin kept rummaging about, trying to see if anything else was missing. "Those are not worth pursuing."

"He was only in this room," commented Brian. "There are no trails into the bedrooms..." He began to get a questioning look on his face. "Grandfather, we don't have our rings on. Why can I see the energy trails? I thought I needed my ring to enhance that ability."

"You are still charged with energy from exercises which works like the rings. Also, with practice, you will not need a ring or wand—except the Master Ring, when 'tis thy time."

"Speaking of our rings," asked Nicki, "where—"

"Fool am I! Hurry! Stole the box with the rings did the thief." Merlin was already breaking for the back door in hot pursuit with the three youngsters right behind.

Once outside, with robes billowing behind him, Merlin stretched into a run that one would not expect of such an old man—surprising his twenty-first century descendants. He was sprinting deep into the valley's thick forest. After crossing about two hundred yards, sometimes zig-zagging from tree to tree, the ancient magician suddenly stopped.

"Canst not see it further; I have lost the spore." He was breathing deeply but not yet out of breath. "Grandson, can you see it?"

"Yeah, it's right over there!" Brian pointed to a large tree about fifteen yards away. "It's getting dim, though—I need my ring."

"Let this be lesson. I am angry with me; losing focus and cannot invoke magic. You must not allow emotions to interfere." He took a couple of deep breaths. "Gather energy and focus—then seek the tracks."

As if in a trance Brian stood in the bright sunlight. He swayed slightly as he gathered energy from the sun, the breeze in the trees, the moisture in the air, power of Earth, and let the Spirit of the living things in the forest embrace him. He wrapped his arms around his chest as if hugging himself, then felt J.J. gently put his hands on his shoulders to steady him.

"Wow! Our rings could never do that!" exclaimed Brian. "I feel like I am a part of the forest—not just in it."

"Great!" said J.J. impatiently. "Now can we follow that guy? He's getting farther ahead."

"Please hurry, Brian!" pleaded Nicki. "I don't want to lose my ring!"

Brian opened his eyes and, without a word, broke into a run. The other three were startled by the sudden move and had to rush to catch up.

"Look at him," whispered Nicki to J.J. "It's just like when we were in Wizard's Cavern. He'll run that guy into the ground. I just hope we catch him before he sells or trades our rings."

J.J. smiled as he observed his brother, who was becoming more confident with every step and lengthening his stride. "Do you feel it?" he whispered back. "The power in him is radiating. I can almost see it."

"I thought it was just me—it's awesome! I seem to be soaking up energy just being close to him."

"We must be catching up," announced Brian quietly as he looked back over his shoulder. "The trail is getting brighter..."

*   *   *

This is impossible, the thief thought to himself. *Nary a king's game warden has been able to track me.* Yet there were voices coming from the direction where he had just been. *Maybe 'tis some hunters or woodsmen I passed but saw not*, he tried to convince himself for he had never been followed before; he was too good and careful for that. Whoever it was, they were close enough for their voices to carry. It was time to speed up and put some distance between himself and his pursuers.

He began to run flat out. He doubled his earlier pace, which was dangerous. Haste could result in a snapped twig, a slip and fall, or worse, a twisted or broken ankle. But he could not let himself be caught by anyone. He would not be able to explain how a beggar-looking man had several items of gold—including three rings that were an odd reddish-gold.

After traveling a good distance Louis stopped to catch his breath and make some decisions. If he was being followed, he couldn't just wander into the nearby village. Someone would see him with his bag of loot and surely the famous magician had acquaintances who would tell him about any strangers. He could skirt around the village, but if he were seen, they would think he was up to no good: by-passing a friendly village. Or, he could seek some hiding spot, hole up and wait for dark to continue his getaway.

In the end he made a fourth choice. He heard the familiar rattle and bang of pots, pans, shovels, big cooking ladles and spoons as they clanked against a peddler's wagon being pulled by a solitary ox. He could hear the four wheels of the canvas-covered wain creak and clunk as they were tugged over rocks and through ruts in the road leading from the village. He also heard the peddler's voice, as he cajoled and cursed the beast to move.

* * *

"Approach a village and yon be the road."

"He didn't go into the village," said Brian, looking off in the distance at the cluster of thatched roofs slightly obscured by a layer of smoke rising out of many chimneys. "The trail is confusing here. He moved back and forth several times, then went that way." He pointed to his right, away from the village.

"Toward the road..."

Brian was already moving again—almost sprinting—sensing they were close to their quarry. The others were right behind until they came to the road—or at least what Merlin and the rural folks of the sixth century called a road: a strip of cleared earth with ruts.

"This is a road?" asked J.J., laughing. "I'd hate to see something *unimproved!*"

"It may not be much, but it gets used a lot," observed Brian. "There's so many energy trails, I'm having a hard time making out our thief. It seems like his trail just ends over there by the wagon rut."

"Obtained conveyance has he."

"How do we follow that?"

"Now quiet—listen."

Through the sounds of a gentle breeze rustling the leaves and shifting grass, birds chirping and squirrels chittering they could hear another noise: wooden, spoked wheels groaning under a load, an ox braying and peddler's wares clanging against a wagon.

"What's that?" asked Nicki.

"'Tis a peddler's wagon; we must follow," instructed Merlin. "Ox drawn, it moves slowly."

"Let's go!" Brian didn't hesitate. He was jogging at a steady pace, still ahead of the others. "I'm *not* losing *my* ring!" He was surprised when a figure easily moved up beside him, making no noise, as if gliding.

"Do you have a plan?" spoke Merlin without effort—not winded at all.

"Yeah," panted Brian, the long run finally catching up to him. "I'm going to—tear apart—that wagon—until I find—the robber and our rings."

"Are you sure the peddler is guilty also? Might not he be innocent and punish him without cause?" They crossed a small hill and could see the road for some distance as it gently descended into a low area before starting to rise toward another hill. The forest was becoming less dense as the ground sprouted lush grass mixed with rocky stands.

Brian slowed to a stop, breathing hard; the others gathered and stood beside him as they viewed the wagon just topping the next hill, less than one-half mile away.

"I hadn't thought of that." He still breathed hard, but Merlin had not even broken a sweat. "No, I only want our rings. The peddler probably has nothing to do with this."

"Grandpa?" said J.J. "You said you were too upset to channel, but you had to be using energy to glide along like that. Was that another lesson to force us to use the elements?" He smirked, figuring he uncovered the old man's scheme.

"'Twas true, I could not focus." Merlin smiled as if caught with his hand in the cookie jar. "Though in the telling, was I able to regain control. Pleased I have been to observe thy brother's progress. Now we must plan." They gathered around the ancient magician and they carefully drafted a plan, keeping in mind the youngsters were barely beginning to employ elemental energies.

It was getting late in the day—the sun was barely glowing over the western horizon. They resumed their pursuit but left the road and circled around ahead of the wain to find a good place for an ambush.

They selected an ideal location. The road dipped into a shallow dale where it crossed a creek. Large trees were growing on each side. The water was not deep—easily forded except during the rainy season—though the smooth rocks were hard on wagon wheels, so it was crossed with great care.

They did not have to wait long. The peddler's constant barrage of encouragement and curses kept the old ox plodding along at a steady pace. He occasionally smiled as he pulled the solid gold spoon from his purse and reinspected it: excellent payment for helping a weary traveler.

It's probably stolen, he mused to himself. *But that's no concern of mine.* He slowed the pace as he approached the stream. Having previously crossed several times, he knew to proceed with caution; once before he'd split an axle on a rock.

"What doth impede?" came a voice from inside the canvas shelter.

"Nothin' t'worry, Guv. Only a stream ford—" he called back, but when he turned again to the crossing there was a large boulder right in the middle. He could have sworn it was not there just a second before.

Brian had to stifle a laugh as he saw the look of surprise on the peddler's face. He had put the huge rock in place much earlier, but Nicki created a sheet of water that kept it hidden until the right moment.

"Whoa up there," the peddler said to the ox; pulling back on the lead rope. He waded out to inspect the impediment. "How did such a thing become lodged here?" he grumbled aloud. "Even two men couldn' move tha'. Needs hitchin' to me ox." He turned to wade back to his wagon. "Hey, Guv, we camp here this night. There be a boulder in the cri'k. 'Tis late to remove it today."

"There remains daylight. We must go farther."

"If you can move yon rock, we will make haste. If not, you are free to go on alone. I will not require my beast to pull the stone after the day's toil. He is old but has served me well."

Louis looked at the boulder obstructing the way and all around and saw no other likely ford. "Very well, we tarry until morn." He scanned the area. Something didn't feel right. He wondered how the stone got there; surely it didn't just roll there. Why now—blocking the way of the wagon he was in? It was truly a good spot for an ambush—but there was no one to be seen—and if so, why had they not attacked? But still...

The plan was working perfectly. Once the man appeared who was riding in the wagon, Brian confirmed he was the one they wanted. He had the same energy print that was seen in Merlin's cottage. So far, there was no sign of the box with their rings. Brian figured it was probably hidden in the wagon. The four withdrew into a thick copse of trees on the far side of the stream where they joined to await the full cover of darkness and to finalize their scheme.

"I'm hungry," complained Brian.

"You're always hungry," said J.J. and Nicki simultaneously, and laughed.

"Hey, we've been running hard with nothing to eat since lunch."

"Nary have I succeeded at transmuting edibles—dost not ever taste right. We shall retrieve the stolen items, then sup."

After darkness fell, they went back to their ambush positions. The peddler had drawn the wagon off in the grass, beside the road, to make camp. A fire was burning and some vegetables were boiling in a pot. The two seemed relaxed. The last thing they expected is what happened next.

The plan called for Merlin to act first—hoping the box with the rings was still in the wagon—the wizard set a repulsion ward around the entire wagon. Any attempt to approach the wain would knock the intruder back with tremendous force.

Once the shield was in place, it was J.J.'s turn. To their utter amazement the cheery, warm fire went out—not *out* exactly—it left the fire pit. The wood, coals, ashes and cook pot remained undisturbed, but the fire and heat gathered itself into a ball and floated up into the air. Even the soup stopped bubbling as all the heat seemed to be sucked into the fiery orb. There was a sudden chill in the air as the suspended conflagration absorbed more and more heat.

The amazed traveling companions could not believe their eyes. They jumped up, yelled obscenities, and reached for the short sword and archery bow on the ground beside them.

Nicki then implemented her task. Before they could grab their weapons, she gathered energy from the water and quickly translocated the bow and steel blade to the middle of a deep pool below the road crossing.

It was show time for Brian. He stepped out from behind a large tree and answered.

"Here I am, peddler." J.J. moved the fireball where its glow lit up the tall twelve-year-old brightly. "You keep bad company; that man is a thief."

"You canst not—" Louis started to say.

"I'm not talking to you!" Brian roared back, then spoke levelly to the seller man. "What do you say, Peddler? Is this chap your partner? Are you in business together? If so, you will enjoy his fate with him."

"Nay—I only provide conveyance. I knew him not before this day."

As expected, the robber bolted for the back of the wagon, hoping to retrieve his loot. But when he hit the shield he was thrown backward ten feet until he landed flat on his back with the wind knocked out of his lungs—unconscious.

"M'lord," the peddler said as he dropped to his knees, "pray thee, have mercy. I knew nothing of this man's misdeeds or how he hath wronged thee. Clearly thou art wrought. Please, young lord, take it not upon me."

For full effect Brian gathered Earth energy and floated himself across the creek and into the campground. J.J. moved the fireball in perfect unison.

"May I search your wagon for the things stolen from us?"

"Pray thee, anything I have art thine. Thou hast my leave."

With a wave of his hand Brian knew Merlin had released the repelling shield. It took him only a moment to find the flour sack containing the box with the rings and the other gold items. He immediately slipped his ring on and knew he'd never take it off again—regardless of Merlin's lessons.

When he exited the wain, carrying the bag, Brian saw the peddler still on his knees waiting for a signal to rise. "Please stand, or sit, whatever you please. You don't need to kneel to me."

"M'lord honors a poor peddler." He started to stand but wobbled, feeling weak. He resumed his seat on a log near the cold fire. He untied a leather purse from his waist, opened it and withdrew a gold spoon. "M'lord, an honest peddler am I. Yon thief paid me this spoon for conveyance on me cart. Suspects I it was not his to give. Belongs to M'lord. Honest am I; everyone calls me Honest John. Pleased I be if M'lord takes it back." He dropped to his knees again, bowed his head and extended the spoon with both hands.

"Thank you, John—I'm glad to know your name. You are an honest man." He took the spoon but at that moment felt some weight in the front pocket of his jeans. He reached in and found two large gold coins and understood Merlin's intent. "My name is Brian—your actions should be rewarded." He reached down and pressed the gold coins in the man's trembling hands. "Go in peace; I suggest you not pick up any more strangers. You may not fare so well next time."

"M'lord Brian—this be a king's ransom! Thou art generous and wise. I will heed thy advice." He sat on the log again.

Brian surreptitiously signaled J.J., then made an animated gesture with his right arm toward the cold fire logs. "Your supper was interrupted. Here's your fire back." With a whoosh, the fireball returned to the pit and instantly a warming blaze crackled with a bright orange glow.

"It's a poor supper of boiled carrots and turnips. If it pleases thee, I will gladly share."

As hungry as he was, Brian was not a fan of turnips; it was meager enough for one man. He felt another coin in his pocket and smiled as he retrieved it. "Maybe you can afford a better dinner tomorrow." He laid the third gold coin on the log beside John. "When I leave, I'll take that garbage with me" (pointing to Louis) "Your sword and bow will be returned and the rock will be gone from the stream so your old ox won't have to pull it."

"M'lord, my whole family shall eat well and will pray for thee." His voice broke and Brian could see a tear in his eyes.

Bind, whispered Brian, then commanded, *Levitate*. Louis the thief floated in the air and followed the twelve-year-old from the camp and back to their hidden spot in the copse of trees.

"What do we do with him?" asked Nicki, after they all congratulated each other on accomplishing their parts of the plan. "Surely we're not taking him back to the cottage."

"Nay. I will replace Brian's binding spell with one that will dissipate on the morrow's evening. He can then go about his way."

"Won't he be mad and come back to get even with us—you?"

"Hmmm, 'tis possible. I will also alter his memory so he will remember nothing about this day or us."

"That's some stuff I want to learn..." J.J. laughed mischievously and rubbed his hands together as they watched Merlin invoke the commands.

"Grandfather, how are we getting back?" asked Brian. "You don't have fireplaces or FON travel and we haven't learned translation yet.

"With me you may travel—which goest first?"

"I'll go," said Nicki. "I can start supper, and I have some girl's personal things to attend to." She smiled as her brothers blushed a little.

"Take mine hands then." He extended two hands from under his robes. "Focus on landing just outside the front door of the cottage. Keep that image in thy mind." Brian and J.J. watched the familiar flash of multi-colored lights and heard the faint metallic-ringing sound—then they were gone.

"I can't wait—only two more years 'til I get to do that."

"Don't remind me; I have six years before I can test. It's still not fair! We both could do it now." Brian was recalling the same argument he'd had with his father many times. They stood in impatient silence waiting for Merlin to return.

Another flash of lights and metallic ringing and the old magician returned. "Master Jeremy, thou be next." They joined hands, then they were gone. Brian was alone with the robber, whom Merlin bound to a tree. His head lolled to his chest, still unconscious.

I wonder how the peddler will recall the night's events and his meeting 'Lord Brian,' he mused. *Will Merlin record this in the living book?*

Another flash and Merlin returned.

"How do you feel?"

"Fine, I guess—hungry!" He smiled.

"You misunderstand. Are you comfortable with Elements?"

"I think so. I know I need a lot more practice, but it's like when I first got my ring; it just seems to come naturally. I could really feel it after I put my ring back on."

"Tis well. Return to your time on the morrow..." The old man paced about as if wanting to say more but struggling to find the words.

"What is it, Grandfather? Is something wrong?"

Finally, after a couple of false starts, Brian was touched deeply as Merlin explained how he had grown to love him, J.J. and Nicki and he worried about what lay ahead for them—especially Brian, when he became Ringmaster. He was concerned he was not preparing him enough. He saw tears in the old man's eyes.

"It's okay..." He reached out and they embraced and stood for some time; and there seemed to be much more that passed between them than an emotional hug. Brian suddenly had an understanding of many things he had never been taught or practiced. He shuddered as goose bumps raised all over his body.

"Be thou cautious with what you have just received." They separated but held hands for the translation. "You can do it—take us." He looked deeply into Brian's eyes and nodded.

The blond boy almost objected but then nodded back. If Louis-the-thief had been conscious he would have seen a flash of colored lights, heard a metallic ringing sound and been astonished as the boy and the old man disappeared.

Chapter Six
The Reports

"Welcome home!" Brian heard as he was almost tackled by his mother's embrace. He had followed Nicki and J.J. through the time portal and was back in his bedroom at his family home.

"Mom, you're squishin' me," he playfully complained even though being held by his mother always felt good. "How long have we been gone from here?"

"Only about an hour," answered Myrna. She released her son and looked him over to make sure he was okay. "But it was the longest hour I've ever endured. I had no idea what dangers you might be facing. You cannot imagine the frights I was envisioning."

"Hey, there were no dragons or Black Knights. Hardly any excitement."

"Yeah, just days of lessons!" complained J.J.

"We did get to chase a burglar," added Nicki, watching the eyebrows raise of both her parents.

"Why don't we go into the living room? Then you can start from the beginning and tell us the whole story," suggested George. "I'll call Uncle Paul and your grandparents."

"Are you hungry?" asked Myrna. "I can fix something."

"We just had breakfast there," answered Nicki.

"I'm hungry!" announced Brian.

"You're always hungry!" the whole family said in unison, then laughed.

"I can't help it. I'm just a growing boy." Brian batted his eyelashes and put on his most innocent face.

"I'll put some snacks together. You probably should take quick showers and put on fresh clothes; these smell like your grandfather's cooking fire."

"Let me have all your clothes," said Mom as she eased into her son's bedroom. "With all the smoke, I don't want them in the hamper." Brian was standing near his dresser drying his hair with a large terry cloth towel, wearing only a clean pair of underwear.

"Here, I'll get them." He picked up the clothes he had been wearing, went to his backpack and pulled out the additional shirt, socks, underwear and pants that were soiled and smoky.

Myrna watched her son. There was something different about him... He was still lanky and tall for his age and his boyish (almost feminine) face was the same, but he had changed somehow.

Brian caught his mother's stare and suddenly remembered he was wearing only his boxers. "Mom, I'm not dressed!" He held the bundle of clothes in front.

"You seem to forget, I changed your diapers and bathed you until not that long ago." She laughed and took the clothes he was hiding behind. "And I seem to remember you were the toddler who hated clothes and ran around nude as often as you could."

He blushed deeply.

"And I wasn't admiring your body. I was noticing how you've grown. But there's more. You've changed somehow. I can't describe it—just something."

"I haven't grown two heads or nothin'. I'm still the same."

"I know," she said wistfully. "I guess it's just hard to see my baby grow up. And you are growing—those shorts barely cover your bottom. We need to get some larger ones."

"Yeah, they're gettin' pretty tight..."

Uncle Paul *banged* into the kitchen just as Myrna was floating trays of tuna salad sandwiches, various chips, sliced veggies and ranch dip, into the living room.

"It's a good thing I was expecting you," she said. "Your arrival pop could have made a big mess. Everyone is in the living room. Do something useful—bring the tray of Vainibier." She smiled at the perennial prankster.

"And I love you too, dear sister-in-law." He floated the tray and bottles of soft drinks behind those Myrna was levitating.

Over the next hour, the time-traveling trio related the events of the four days they spent with Merlin—including their lessons, the burglary and the robber chase.

"So, Nicki, you're gifted in three elements?" clarified Paul.

"Water, Earth and Air," she restated.

"And J.J, also three—"

"Yeah, Air, Earth and Fire," he said.

"And Brian, it's all five for you?"

"Merlin said I kind of had to be—to become Ringmaster."

"And you took an oath—"

"The Wizards' Inviolable Oath!"

"You promised not to teach anyone how to gather the elements?"

"Yep—well, not exactly..." Brian was recalling the oath in his head. *I will not teach until I have become a master of the same, and then only to my immediate family, direct descendants or those the power of Spirit directs.* "When we have mastered the techniques, we can teach you—our family—or anyone else the power of Spirit directs."

"When will you master it? How will you know?" asked George.

"We asked Merlin the same thing. He said we'd know when the time is right." Brian devoured his third tuna sandwich and started on a plateful of veggies and dip.

"Once we become fully proficient," added Nicki, "we won't need our rings at all."

"If that's the gauge, I have a long way to go," said J.J. "I did some neat things using only the elements, but I felt really limited."

"I'm sure that will change after some practice and gaining confidence," suggested Paul. "It's still all new. As you describe it, the technique requires a whole different approach."

"Yeah, kinda," said Brian, between bites of cauliflower he was dipping in ranch dressing. "The projected commands and manipulation are mostly the same. The big difference is where the energy comes from."

"He's right," continued J.J. "All the channeling we regularly do, the energy comes from within. That's why we get tired. This new way, we either gather and store the power from the elements or we draw elemental energy and focus it through us."

"Wow!" exclaimed Brian. "You said that really well. I couldn't find a good way to explain it."

"You said earlier that you *ask* the elements for energy," interjected Myrna. "That seems odd."

"Not really, Mom," answered Nicki. "The elements may seem inanimate, but it's *their* power we want to use—the energy given them when they were created. It only makes sense to *ask* them to share their blessing. That's how we become united with the elements. It's really amazing when it happens...it's the fifth element, Spirit, at work. Without it, we couldn't commune with the others. I know I'm not explaining this very well—that's why we can't teach the techniques until we've mastered them. Right now it's just something we feel."

"You did really well," announced Grandma, standing in the living room-hallway passage. "I apologize for being late. It could not be helped. Nichole, it will take us some time to understand what you explained. It is a deep concept that I have never heard expressed among Sodality scholars." The old empath was almost bowled over as J.J. ran and wrapped his arms around her. She held him tight, sensing how much he missed his parents. "Not understanding that concept is probably why channeling of the elements has not been successfully done for so many centuries. Only the simple acceptance by innocents could receive it."

"You said it hasn't been done successfully," observed Brian. "Does that mean—?"

"That it has been tried?" She and J.J. released each other and headed for two adjacent seats on the sofa. "Oh my, yes! Writings from Merlin, Mimm and other ancients mention the technique—even vaguely refer to the concept Nichole has just described—but nothing has survived that gives enough information to make the process work. As it taps into almost limitless power, many have lusted for the secret—almost as much as for the master-ring formula."

"You know, that *is* the key," explained J.J. "The whole time I was trying and failing, I was attempting to command the elements. Only when I asked—even said 'please'—did it work."

"Of course, there's much more—the stuff we can't teach now," added Brian. "But without that, none of the rest will do anything."

"Will you please show us an example of using elemental energy?" asked Uncle Paul.

"Sure," said Brian. He stood and started for the kitchen. "Let's go outside." He knew just the thing.

"Dad, you remember that big boulder that's right where you want to put the slab for the garage?" Everyone was heading out the back door. The Arizona summer sun was hot and they began sweating right away.

"Sure..."

"Why haven't you moved it?"

"It's mostly buried—it'll take blasting." They stopped in front of a boulder, in the hard earth, with only a tiny portion sticking up above ground.

"Please try to pick it up. Try as hard as you can."

"Okay," said George. He focused on the rock, reached out his right hand and commanded, *Levitate*. His body shook and he broke out in a heavy sweat as he applied all the energy he could muster, but even though it quivered a bit, it refused to rise. After several minutes he surrendered. "Okay—I can't do it."

Brian smiled, turned to his brother and sister. "Shall we play catch?" They nodded enthusiastically. "I'll pull it—you be ready." He saw them both reach out their left hands and start gathering energy—Nicki was pulling moisture from the air and a breeze was starting to swirl around J.J.

Instinctively, the onlookers started to back away—not knowing what to expect. Brian first held his left hand toward the sun, then in the air, gathered from the cloud Nicki was forming, and then turned toward the boulder. After accepting Earth energy, he held his right hand and gently—ever so gently—coaxed it to rise up. At first it barely moved. Then, as if shovels were at work, mounds of soil rolled off to the sides, exposing the whole rock from the top. A couple of wiggles back and forth, then it came out of the hole.

"Oh, my," said Myrna.

"I've never seen the like," added Grandma.

"I didn't think it was so big." Brian was surprised. It was twice as big as the one they moved at Merlin's cottage. It left a huge hole in the ground.

"Kinda like an iceberg," suggested Paul. "Ninety-five percent hidden below the surface."

The huge thing seemed to hover six feet above the ground. Brian showed no sign of struggle or strain—not a drop of sweat on his brow. He looked to J.J., who was about fifteen yards away. "Are you ready?"

"Sure! Toss it over," he said casually, as if catching a several-ton boulder were an everyday event.

"Here it comes." Brian waved his hand and the massive rock glided over toward his brother, who focused the cushion of air he had gathered. Easily, Air took the mass and cradled it. Brian dropped his arms.

"Hey, this is fun. I'd switch to Fire but I'm afraid the heat might crack the rock."

"Oh, don't do that," warned Brian. "I sensed a large fault-crack right through the middle."

"Nicki, are you ready?" J.J. saw her nod, so he sent the stone toward her.

Instantly a roiling cumulus cloud formed under the boulder and displaced the weight.

"If I hadn't seen it with my own eyes..." Paul stood watching, afraid to blink—he might miss something.

"I'm seeing it and am still not sure I believe it," said George. "Brian—J.J.—neither of you are helping?"

"No, Dad," they said in unison.

"Where do you want me to put it?" asked Nicki. "There's gonna be a bunch of water unless I give it back to Brian."

"Can you set it down on the hill behind the house? Some water there won't matter."

"Sure." She started moving the mass toward the hill. "Point out where you want it."

"That was quite a demonstration," said Grandma when they were back in the house. "Remember the saying: 'With great power comes even greater responsibility.'"

"That's very true," agreed George. "I'm sure we all understand, but I must say it. For now all this must remain strictly within the family!"

*   *   *

"You're sure he's okay?" inquired the short man, pushing his glasses up on his nose. "Joseph is a good man. He just let himself get overextended." He nervously paced about the back storage area of his shop. It was long after closing and his apprentices had gone home.

"Of course," sniffed the tall woman, sounding insulted. "I always fulfill my contracts. The curator has all his memories back except for his encounters with me and his removal of the artifact."

"Will a mind probe reveal anything untoward?"

"A very skilled practitioner might discover a gap in his memory, but will be unable to discover why or how. I suppose that could raise some questions, but they have no proof. They will look elsewhere."

"Then you have earned your fee." He held out an attaché case, using both hands as it was obviously heavy.

"Always!" she retorted, taking the handle with one hand and easily hefting her bounty.

"Aren't you going to count it?"

"You would not dare to cheat *me*!" She turned toward the back door of the shop that led out into a service area, and left without a single glance backward.

Chapter Seven
Back To School

"Mom, you're squishin' me," complained J.J., playfully repeating the line he'd heard Brian say many times, as he stood in front of the FON mirror at 128 Main Street.

"This is your first year since your adoption became final," sniffed Myrna as she fought back tears. "I just want you to know how much we love you and want you."

"I know, Mom; I love you, too." Now he had a tear welling up in his eyes. He pulled away, slung his book bag over his left shoulder and stepped up to the full-length mirror.

"Remember, all your registration has been changed—even the FON."

"Yeah, yeah, you told me a hundred times." He laughed. "Actually, I'm looking forward to it, but it's still a little weird." He put his hand on the rosette and commanded: *Jeremy James Everett to Crown King Seminary.* He stepped into the liquid and disappeared.

Myrna turned her attention to her younger son, scooping him into her arms.

"C'mon, Mom! You act like we're going away to one of those boarding schools in Europe." He jokingly resisted but was truly comforted. "We're gonna be back at four-thirty this afternoon."

"Any more, I'm not so sure. Between Merlin calling you to the sixth century and the turmoil surrounding the Ringmaster issue, I never know what's going to happen next or what danger you might be facing. I always want you to be comforted and strengthened by our love as a family."

"I know, Mom ... *Love is the greatest power in the universe* ... You've told us that hundreds of times."

"And I'll keep saying it; it's that important."

"I love you, too, Mom. I've got to go; I barely have time to get my first-day badge and get to Opening Assembly." Brian turned toward the mirror, called his name and destination and dissolved into the thick shimmering fluid.

"Well, if it isn't the Everett Brothers," called a tall, skinny, black-haired boy whose voice was barely recognizable for it had deepened considerably over the summer. "Can you guys sing?" asked Roger Johnson. "Oh, sorry, that's the Everly Brothers," he teased.

"Hey, Roger," answered J.J., looking up at a smartly-dressed, gangly teenager. "You must have bought some of that growth elixir at the fair. You're four inches taller!"

"I guess it seems like it. My mom's really frustrated. We had to get all new clothes and shoes twice during the summer holiday. She's been threatening to take me to Clinic and have 'em check for elixir." He laughed. "But I didn't; honest! It's all nat-u-raal!"

"You're lucky. Like you, I'm sixteen, but I still get my clothes from the junior boys' department."

"No, you're lucky. A growth spurt like this hurts, especially at night. I'm so uncoordinated I can hardly tie my shoes. It's embarrassing—and besides, you save your folks a lot of money!"

"At least adults don't pat you on the head and say, 'Oh, he's so cute!'"

They all laughed.

"We'd better go get our badges," suggested Brian. "If we're late to Assembly, we'll get detention on first day."

"That'd be a record even for me," said J.J. "I usually wait until at least second day." His mischievous grin made his red hair almost glow. They went to the reception room with the suspended illuminated signs over the various form registration tables.

Brian quickly spotted the Second Form sign—hoping Professor Antetima would be at the First Form table, like last year. But alas, there she was, standing with Professor Phusikos behind the Second Form table, looking like she'd just sucked on a persimmon.

"You are late, Mr. Everett. You would be well advised to hurry. If you're not seated when Superintendent begins Assembly, I will personally supervise your detention, which might affect your flipolo team eligibility."

"Nice to see you, too, Professor Antetima," said Brian as he put his hand on the soft, black registration pad. He was trying hard to keep his temper in check; she'd love for him to say something disrespectful and give her an excuse to punish him.

"Welcome to Second Form, Mr. Everett," said Professor Phusikos, seeming to come to his rescue. "I trust you had a good holiday."

"Yes, thank you, Professor Phusikos. It was very educational. I spent some time with one of my relatives."

"Excellent! Do move along, though; Assembly will be starting soon."

"I am on my way." Brian slapped the metal disk name tag on the chest of his Bradshaw Mountaineers T-shirt, picked up his class schedule, turned and almost collided with Roger and J.J. as they were all hurrying toward the exit door at the same time. Just as he left the room, Brian glanced back and saw Antetima and Phusikos in an animated discussion. She seemed to be trying to hurry him away and he appeared to be purposely dawdling. It was a curious scene.

"Welcome, students and faculty, to Crown King Seminary," Brian heard from the bald man with his quiet but authoritative voice—for the second time. As Superintendent Laedere introduced himself and the other staff on the stage, Brian couldn't take his eyes off the squat professor; seemingly torn between who she was the most angry at: Professor Phusikos, who obviously delayed long enough to insure Brian, his brother and Roger were seated in the auditorium, or Brian, who she hated, for some (unknown) reason, and had (again) escaped her wrath by another's intervention.

"And this year Professor Terrence Heady joins Staff to teach Basic and Advanced Psionics. For some time, our board of governors has felt the seminaries should offer psionics instruction in areas not covered by the traditional transmogrification, natural physics, astrology, translocation, personal protection and herb/plant use—especially in light of recent events."

That brought Brian back from his musings. "I wonder what he meant by *recent events?*" he whispered to J.J., yet he knew the answer. As if anticipating his next questions, Laedere said:

"This class will delve into areas that fell out of favor after the sixth century and are still somewhat controversial. Therefore, the class is an elective for all Forms, and parental permission slips must be signed before any student may apply."

Whispers and mumbles could be heard throughout the auditorium. The superintendent patiently waited for the din to subside, then continued, "Professor Heady will review all applications and will select students for four Basic classes. And from these students, an Advanced class will be created after Winter Holiday..."

After the usual pep talk about rules, safety and the upcoming flipolo season, Assembly was dismissed. Brian, J.J., Roger and the rest of the student body were crowding toward the exits to begin first-day meetings with their professors, to obtain class syllabuses, and to become reacquainted with the campus layout (that seemed to change every year).

"Hey, Bry," said J.J. softly, "have you looked at your class schedule yet?"

"No; we were running so late, I just stuck it in my book bag. Why?" He eyed his brother suspiciously, shifted his backpack and retrieved the parchment with his class list. "Hey, what's this?" he said after a quick glance. "You, too?" He looked into J.J.'s eyes and saw him nod in agreement. "That doesn't make sense; we're supposed to get permission slips signed and fill out applications, unless..."

"I wonder how long Mom and Dad have known?"

"I don't know, but I'm gonna ask. Oh well, I was planning to sign up anyway."

"Yeah, me, too." They heard a voice behind them.

"Hey, Brian, J.J.," called Carl Fredericks. He too had grown, but his hair was still slicked back, he had freckles on his nose and cheeks and his green eyes seemed brighter than last year.

"Hi, Carl," answered Brian. "Good summer?"

"Yeah—and no sign of folks from the Order." He smiled and raised his eyebrows. "You?"

"It was quiet for us at home, but we made another trip to visit Great Grandfather." He gave a knowing smile (they had kept their promise and told him about their time travel adventures). They all migrated into the main hallways where the crowds were dissipating. They found a quiet space between banks of wall lockers.

"Can you tell me about it sometime?" he said hopefully, but being careful as Roger was still tagging along.

"Yeah, some anyway. Maybe you can come over to our house after school one day, or on a Saturday."

"Cool! Anyway, I just wanted to know if you've already been assigned to the Psionics class?" He unfolded his schedule and handed it to J.J.

"Yeah! You, too, huh?" Brian offered his schedule to be examined, but it was Roger who took and scanned it.

"What?" inquired the tall fifth-former. "How'd that happen?" He handed it back to Carl and took out his own for another look. Disappointed, he would have to apply to get in the class.

"I don't know," said J.J. "Maybe they made arrangements with our parents after the thing with us and the Black Knights."

"That makes sense," agreed Roger. "*Power Press* and *Expositor* ran articles about that, although I always had the feeling there was a lot more to the story."

"Yeah, there was…" Brian's mind flashed back to the griffin, snake, mountain lion and dragon, none of which was reported to the news media or even to authorities. "But, I'm sorry, Roger, we still cannot talk about it. No offense."

"None taken; we all have family secrets. I'll catch you guys later. I'm going to start meeting with my professors." He turned and strode off down the hall—his long legs shortening the distance quickly.

"I guess we'd better get going," suggested Carl. "I'll see you in Psionics—we all have the two o'clock class." He set off for a different passage.

"Where is it?" said Brian—he spoke softly. Their surroundings were a damp, rock-walled hallway in a subterranean level, several flights of stairs under the main CKS campus. Electric light fixtures were placed near the rock-and-mortar ceiling but they were turned off or did not work. Torches were burning with their handles embedded in holes drilled in the walls. There was an eerie pervasiveness that seemed to demand hushed tones.

"I don't know," answered J.J. just above a whisper. "I'm pretty sure we followed the directions correctly; let me look again and see if we missed anything." Brain watched him unfold his schedule and held it under one of the blazing fires. "Ooo, wait a minute, it says go to the *Mirrose* door…"

"Yeah, I've been looking for that, but there's no sign of a door saying Mirrose—there's not even a door!"

"I remember somewhere…" said J.J., taking a long time to think. "Before there was the FON, mirrors were used for secret passages and other kinds of portals, but they had the same rosette for entry. Those portals were called a *mirrose* and the mirrors could be configured to look like anything—even a rock wall."

"Then all we have to do is find a rosette!"

"I think so. Let's look." They split up in opposite directions to examine every inch of the rock-walled passage.

"Here it is—at least, I think so," announced Brian. "It's real faint, but it looks just like the rosette on the FON-mirror frames." J.J. hurried over to join him at the far end of the passage.

"Yeah, it does look right—try it!"

"I'm not going to try it—you try it."

"Try what?" came a familiar voice from behind them.

"Carl!" they said in unison, smiling mischievously.

*   *   *

"Joseph!" The short, bespectacled man stood from behind a table at the back of Louigi's Italian Restaurant in New York City. As always he was impeccably dressed in a morning suit of dark colors—today it was a deep grey. He cheerfully extended his hand, as his dinner companion hurried to greet his friend. "I'm so glad you could come. It's been much too long since we've gotten together."

"You're absolutely right!" answered the gaunt man in a blue, pin-striped business suit. "We used to come together and enjoy Louigi's lasagna or spaghetti, at least once a month, but now—"

"I think it's almost been a year, though I still have lunch at his PV Mall cafe about once a week." He paused and took a deep breath. "How are you, my friend?" He spoke softly as they sat in the back corner booth on opposite sides of the table. "I heard and read about your troubles."

A waiter appeared before Joseph could answer. "May I get you some appetizers, something to drink, or are you ready to order?"

They both ordered fried mushrooms and herb tea to start, then salads and lasagna dinners with hot garlic bread and bread sticks.

"I am okay now," he said after the waiter retreated, leaving them ice water in tall crystal glasses. "It was touch and go for a while. As Curator, I was questioned, of course. I had nothing to hide; I agreed to a mind probe." His friend from Arizona nervously shifted his weight and pushed his glasses up on his nose. "I was cleared completely. Though it was strange, they discovered a blank area in my memory, but they could not connect it with the theft in any way. They tried to make something out of my recent inheritance, but that is all legitimate, so they're looking elsewhere."

"I'm sorry I didn't come sooner, but I was afraid the arrival of an out-of-state visitor would just complicate things." Their herb tea and fried mushrooms arrived, which they attacked with gusto.

"You are right; things were a little crazy for a while. And I feel terrible! As Curator, security is part of my job. I cannot figure out how the thief penetrated all my wards, shields and even Brangler motion detectors and lasers. I feel like it had to be some kind of inside job, but everyone who could possibly have access, cleared the mind probe as well as I did."

"That is a puzzle, but I'm glad you're okay. How is your wife? Is she doing better?"

"She's stable for now; it's expensive. The inheritance came at just the right time. Even our Psionics can't cure everything." Their salads arrived.

"That's so true. Is there anything I can do? You have but to ask."

"I appreciate that, my friend, but no, there is nothing—for now." They ate in silence until their lasagna dinners arrived.

* * *

"What?" exclaimed Carl, backing up three steps and eyeing the Everett brothers suspiciously. "Where's the door to class? This place is weird. I never knew anything was down here."

"We think the door is here." Brian pointed at the wall. "You wanna try it?"

"Sure!" He stepped forward. "CKS would never allow anything to purposely hurt us." He looked at Brian and J.J. "What do I do?"

"Well, duh." J.J. looked at Brian and shook his head. "We should have thought of that. We think it's a portal like FON. Just put your hand on the rosette carved there in the stone."

"Okay," Carl said cheerfully. "Yeah, it's pretty faint, but I see it." He put his hand on the spot.

Immediately a rectangle (the size of a door) became outlined and the rocky surface, inside it, liquefied to what appeared to be molten lava, but there was no heat.

"Ooo, that's neat," said Carl. He released his hand to walk through, but the passage instantly re-solidified. "Yeow! How do we get through?"

"Maybe it's like the FON—you need to identify yourself and your destination."

"You do it," said Carl, stepping back.

J.J. stepped forward and put his hand on the spot. When it liquefied, he called out: *Jeremy James to Psionics class.* He picked up his hand and again the wall went solid.

"Remember what Mom told you," said Brian.

"Oh yeah." He put his hand on the carving again. *Jeremy James Everett to Psionics Class.* He lifted his hand and the viscous cold lava remained. He walked into the roiling mass and disappeared.

Carl and Brian followed.

*   *   *

"Joseph, is your job secure? I understand you've been cleared of any criminal misdeeds, but do you still have the Council's confidence?" They were finishing their desserts of lime sherbet and vanilla wafers.

"Oh, I'm fine. The Council has been some of my greatest supporters, and besides, no one knows the collections better than

I do. But they are hiring a security consultant to beef up that end. And that is good. I will not have to worry about that as much."

"Is there any chance Reficul and his lot are somehow involved?"

"That question has been raised. It's hard to get a line on them, since the mess at Wizard's Cavern. They have really gone underground. But since I have been cleared, I'm no longer involved in the investigation."

"What's the word around the Redoubt? Why did he invade Wizard's Cavern?"

"For some reason, he seems to believe there's a Ringmaster formula hidden in a red-gold mine; one that was a natural formation and dates back to Merlin. That is why the Black Knights were rousting the mines around the country, but not taking any gold. They were only looking for the formula or ancient records that might lead them to it. Wizard's Cavern is an old played-out mine—both red and jeweler's gold. He just had the misfortune of running into the Everett, James and Fredericks kids who were up there exploring."

"How did three kids defeat Reficul and twenty or thirty Black Knights?"

"That's where the story gets murky. First of all, it was four kids. It turns out Nichole Everett is not nomag—just a late bloomer."

"Oh, yes, I heard that."

"And somehow, word got to Paul Everett—their uncle—and he was in the mix. But the captured Black Knights had the real tale. They were swearing (and confirmed by mind probe) the kids somehow coordinated their attack using rattlesnakes, mountain lions, a griffin and one is absolutely convinced she was pelted by a flock of ravens—but the investigators are sure it was a mind-altering spell."

"That cannot be true. They must have been hallucinating."

"Then they all had the same hallucination, and that's just as improbable as the story they told. The investigators were almost afraid to write up their reports for fear they'd be accused of fabricating a ridiculous story or having a mental breakdown."

"You're serious, aren't you?" Emilio chuckled then sipped the last of his tea, nibbled the final vanilla wafer and put several gold talons on top of the check.

"Oh, yeah," confirmed Joseph, leaning back in the booth, wishing he could loosen his belt. "Only the Everetts and Fredricks (Jeremy James is now Jeremy James Everett—he was adopted) really know what happened, and they are not talking. Personally, I think Brian Everett is the fabled Appointed One, but I have no idea if his family actually has the original halves of the formula. At any rate, the psionic abilities in that family are awesome. I know you won't confirm it, but I believe Brian inherited Merlin's ring."

"Well, if he's the Appointed One, and we're not sure the original formula has survived the centuries, someone better make sure he gets a formula from somewhere."

"Then it is true; that *Expositor* article. You have an alchemy lab and you're trying to develop a formula?"

"Shh! Not so loud!" he whispered. "But yes, I am—not for me, but for the Appointed One. It must be created before Reficul can do it; there can be only one."

"Have you succeeded yet?"

"No, but I'm close."

"You don't want to become Ringmaster?"

"No! My family has been serving Merlin's purposes for fifteen centuries. If Brian Everett *is* the Appointed One, it is he whom I serve and none other!"

"How did the *Expositor* get a line on you?"

"A disgruntled apprentice I let go told the story. But most people consider that tabloid trash and have already forgotten about it. Hopefully it stays that way. I don't need any more publicity."

*   *   *

"*Oh, you're not going to get any more publicity, but you're going to serve another master—real soon!*" thought the tall man dressed in

77

black clothes as he pulled the earpiece from his left ear, collected the small recorder and left the secluded alcove, in the alley, behind Louigi's. He had been shadowing the famed ring craftsman since the *Expositor* article came out. He had hoped to locate the alchemy lab, but the old man must be FONing or translating. Tracking him to Louigi's was easy. He had planted several bugs in his shop and phone, where he heard the call for reservations. It was a simple task to slip in and plant a bug under the table. The reservation had requested a specific table, which was good because Louigi's waiters were fiercely loyal and unbribable.

I may not know yet where the lab is. I learned so much more. He went out on the street and hailed a cab because he was not sure how translation or even FON energy might affect his recording. He would use Brangler transportation.

"Grand Central Station," he told the driver as he sat back and unfolded the train schedule to find the next departure for Boston. There, he would rent a car and drive to Adams, Massachusetts, Mount Greylock and his Master.

Chapter Eight
Weezer Hill

"Welcome, gentlemen," said a man's voice with a distinctive English accent, dressed in wizard's robes and a tall, pointed hat. He was standing on an elevated dais behind a massive antique double-pedestal desk. "Congratulations on solving the entrance puzzle. I am Professor Heady."

"We can't all take credit, Professor," said Brian. "It was my brother—we just followed his instructions." Carl nodded in agreement.

"Is that the way you saw it, Master Jeremy—or should I say *Sir* Jeremy?"

The three boys stared at the elderly man with the white hair coming out from under his hat.

"It is not polite to stand there with your mouths gaping open."

The distinct sound of three sets of teeth clamping together could be heard.

"Sorry, Professor. No, that's not the way I saw it. We all helped."

"And how was that, young Sir?"

"Yes, I solved the *mirrose* clue, but Brian found the etching. We were afraid to open the portal; Carl reminded us a CKS professor would never intentionally harm a student. Then I figured out the need for identification and destination."

"I believe Sir Brian had to remind you of your true identity."

"Yes, Professor," they all said in unison.

"Excellent! Then we've just had our first lesson. Master Carl, can you summarize?" He waved his hand and three antique wooden student desks appeared, side by side, in front of the dais; then he motioned for them to sit.

"We work better as a team—with all contributing—rather than individually."

"Spot on—if I could award you points, you would get them. I understand it is customary to distribute a syllabus and assignment lists at this meeting; however, I only arrived in country three days ago and have been quite busy getting organized. I will try and have them when the other students are transferred in." Brian held up his hand but the teacher continued, "You want to inquire how I know about your titles advanced by Merlin. It suffices to say your father does not have the only living book linked to Merlin—there is at least one other. By the way, King Arthur confirmed your investiture, though the official record has been lost. Beyond that, I know a great deal. Your parents have been most helpful, after Headmaster—sorry—Superintendent and I convinced them of our trustworthiness and absolute loyalty."

"We were really confirmed?" Brian stood up and paced about the large empty classroom (except for the dais and three desks). "I thought that was just a title Merlin used in the book."

"You apparently have not been studying your living book since your last training visit. It is all in there."

"What about my sister, Nicki?"

"In the sixth century women were not knighted but Nichole was formally recognized as being related and thus became titled nobility as a Lady. Which, if I am not mistaken, Lady Nichole should be trying to find this room as we speak." He gestured toward the door-frame. "Master Fredricks, would you please show the Lady in?"

Carl did not hesitate until he got to the etched frame, then looked back. "What destination, Professor?"

"Exit."

Carl put his hands on the crudely-carved rosette and called, *Carl Fredricks to exit.* He stepped through the cold molten rock. Moments later Nicki walked into the room—followed by Carl.

"Hey, Sis," greeted Brian, "what's up? Shouldn't you be at Meyor High or with your tutor?"

"Mom told me about Professor Heady—just after you guys left. She (and Dad) feel this new class is really important. Since I'm only attending Meyor High for half a day, here I am."

"Welcome, Lady Nichole. I am Professor Heady. I will be instructing you in various, sometimes unconventional, psionic applications and techniques."

"Professor, when Mother talked to me this morning, she said it would be a small class; lots of individual instruction."

"Right you are, M'lady. You have had lessons from Merlin. This is Advanced Class. I doubt any others from Basic will progress to this level during this form."

"Why am I here, then?" asked Carl. "I didn't time-travel and learn from Merlin."

"You earned and kept the trust of your companions. Through this course you will learn more. Your instructors have all given you high marks—since you gave up your brutish ways. You are expected to work diligently. I will not hesitate to transfer you into a basic class. Agreed?"

"Oh, yes, Professor. I'll work hard!"

"M'Lady, you also realize, even though you had elemental control instruction from Merlin, as a *late bloomer* you still have much catching up to do."

"Yes, Professor—I'll do what it takes. . . uh, uh, are you going to always use our titles?"

"Except when other students or faculty are about, yes. I am British, as you can hear in my accent. You and your brothers were properly and deservedly titled by a king. I will not dishonor the crown or you by familiarity. I realize titles are not used or recognized in the colonies, so in public I will not cause you unwanted notoriety. Those times will be few. You will rarely see me outside these confines—you probably noticed I was not at Assembly."

"Why now, Professor?" inquired J.J. "Why us?"

"During the last decade, the U. K.—even much of Europe—struggled with a particularly nasty megalomaniac and his followers, much like your Reficul and Order of the Black Knights. Those who would use their gifts to terrorize to accomplish their evil ends are becoming more powerful and brazen. It is time to train up those who oppose the dark forces. M'Lord Brian is the Appointed One and you, his companions. The Ringmaster's success depends on all of you!"

"That was weird!" said Brian, walking down the center concourse toward their lockers. "I didn't even know that lower level existed. And Professor Heady... I don't know what to make of him."

"Yeah," said J.J. "He's kinda creepy, but he seems to really know what he's talking about."

"I feel we can trust him. I guess it's the wizard's robes and hat that threw me off—" He heard a commotion down one of the hallways; there were several students grouped around an alcove, laughing, pointing and taunting. Something about the scene didn't feel right, and there were no other adults in the area. "Let's check it out." J.J., Carl and Nicki (who was still with them) followed as Brian strode over to the gathering. When close enough, he saw the object of their attention: a very small boy was cowering, sitting on his heels, crying, not understanding why he was garnering such treatment. Brian's heart sank as he saw the terror in the boy's eyes, shabby clothes, shoes with holes and mismatched socks. His face and hands were clean, but his hair was straggly and uncombed. His jeans had holes in the knees. He heard the crowd taunt:

"What's your name? Say it again!"

"Weezer Hill," he wailed in a broken, high-pitched voice.

"That's no name—what's your real name?"

"Weezer Hill!" The waif was sobbing.

"HEY!" Brian started gathering Earth and Air energy, then pushed his way between the tormentors and inserted himself between the rabble and the shivering child. "What's goin' on here? Can't you see you're scaring him?"

"We ain't hurtin' 'im," said a stocky fourth-former. "We're just askin' what his name is and he just says, 'Weezer Hill.' That ain't no name!"

"Yeah," said another boy. "We aren't askin' where he's from—and I haven't heard of any place like that. It's none of your business anyway."

"I'm making it my business!" announced Brian. "Real tough, aren't you—picking on a little kid." Everyone felt a slight breeze swirling around them, as he clenched his right fist and held out his left hand, palm up.

"Who are you?" asked the stocky ringleader, who was also clenching his fist—obviously channeling his energy.

"Just someone who hates to see defenseless kids being tormented." He opened his right hand, held it up in front of his face with palm up and fingers pointing toward the group. He grinned, then blew a breath across the flat of his hand. A sudden blast of wind hit the persecutors in their chests and drove them into the hallway wall behind them. Two of them (including the loud fourth-former) sank down to the floor, gasping for air.

"Hey, how'd you—"

"I suggest you get out of here," said J.J. as he, Carl and Nicki stepped into the area just vacated by the group. Brian turned, knelt down and gently wiped the tears from the boy's face, and slowly helped him to his feet as J.J. continued, "Bother young Mr. Hill again, and you'll deal with more than a little gust of wind—and believe me, that was little! You really don't want to get my brother angry." His red hair was blazing.

"Y-you're t-the Everetts," stammered one of the girls who was catching her breath. "I-I r-read ... y-you defeated R-Reficul's Black Knights." The rest of the group collectively gasped with recognition.

"Yup, and this is Carl Fredricks who helped us!" Another gasp. "Go on, get out of here!" Within moments only Nicki, Carl, Brian and J.J. were left. Brian was still soothing the boy's fears, dusting him off and picking up his tattered book bag. Nicki joined him and tenderly waved her ring over the holes in his clothes and shoes, which were instantly mended—even the socks became a matched pair.

"Mom taught me," she said, seeing the question in Brian's eyes. The boy smiled as he stood in silence for the gentle ministrations.

"Ah, I see you've met one of our first-formers," said Phusikos as they all turned to the interrupting voice.

"Well, I'm not sure we met exactly," said Carl. "He seemed to need a little help." He went on to explain what they saw and how they came to the tiny boy's help.

"It's unfortunate I did not arrive sooner. It sounds like you handled it admirably."

"I didn't want to hurt anyone," said Brian, "but I wasn't going to let 'em tease him any more. I'll report to the office and turn myself in for using energy against a student."

"That's not necessary. I'll report I reminded you about obeying rules and no further action needed. Frankly, they're lucky you dealt with them; I would have ordered four weeks of detention for the lot of them and recommend suspension for Mr. Farber. What they did was cruel!"

"He's okay now." Brian reassuringly put his hand on the boy's shoulder. "But we've gotta FON home now. What'll we do with him? He seems lost."

"No doubt he feels that way—being all alone on First Day is scary and then to have an episode like that. I'm sure he's grateful for your help. I will take him and make sure he gets to the home." He reached and took a small, timid (left) hand.

Brian bent down, smiled and looked him in the eyes. "I'll see you tomorrow. Don't be scared. Not everyone is like those jerks." Weezer Hill's eyes opened wide. He grinned, then reached out and touched Brian's cheek. To those watching, it was clear something passed between them.

*   *   *

"You have done well, my faithful servant," growled a deep, commanding voice. "Your fixation on Brangler toys has finally yielded results—excellent results." The tall man paced about in the library of his castle-appearing mansion deep in the forest of Mount Greylock. He rewound the tiny tape and replayed it again and again, listening to every voice inflection and nuance to find any hidden meaning.

"This presents two possible paths to success: the first is to take the formula from the old man—"

"And the second is to get the original formula halves from the Everetts," interrupted Laileb. "Just like we planned before. I knew I was right!"

"True, but both plans have possible major flaws: the old man admits he has not yet made a formula that works. Maybe he *is* close, but many have been close without ever succeeding. He may never get it right. And, just as he said, even if the boy is the Appointed One, that is no guarantee both halves of the formula have survived fifteen centuries. Further, some records say the formula is useless to anyone but the Appointed One—even though I too bear the family lineage."

"But, Master, surely you have the ability to remove the portion designating only the boy and leave the master-ring technique intact."

"I have always believed it so; we must pursue both possibilities. We must find the old man's lab, bring him and his equipment here and convince him I am his new master. And we must obtain Everett's formula. Even if I am unable to make it work for *me*, we will prevent *him* from using it." He waved his hand and a wooden table and two chairs on opposite sides appeared in the center of the main gallery. "Sit, my faithful servant. We have plans to make and carry out. There can be no failure!"

Chapter Nine
The Tiny Visitor

"Hey, Mom," called Brian from in front of the FON mirror. "We're home!"

"In the kitchen," answered Myrna. "I've got some fruit and juice—come tell me about your day."

They each waved a hand at their book bags, which floated to their individual rooms. Brian rushed to the kitchen table, grabbed a bowl of seedless green grapes and a tall glass of dark purple grape juice, plopped on a chair and threw a bunch of grapes in his mouth.

"We al-mos-ot-eten-sun." He swallowed hard. "We almost got detention today and lost our filpolo eligibility." He gulped down half of the juice, leaving a purple mustache across his upper lip.

"That would have been a record," said J.J., "even for me."

"Why?" She eyed her sons critically. "What did you do?"

"It was your fault," accused Brian. "We were almost late for First Assembly and Antetima was layin' for us." He wolfed down more grapes—hardly chewing. "One of these days, will you tell us why she hates us so much?"

"Yes, I think you should know, but it's for your father to explain—when the time is right. I suggest you ask him." She changed the subject. "How are your schedules this form?" She looked at J.J. "Sixth form is a tough year—at least it was for us. You're going into your advanced studies."

"I haven't looked very close at the syllabuses yet, but just scanning the books since we got 'em at the Mall was pretty scary."

Brian saw her shift her attention to hmself. "And how are things shaping up for second form—other than Antetima?"

"Dunno." He swallowed another handful of grapes—playing coy—he knew what his mother was trying to get them to talk about. "We barely made it around to all the classes—we got lost a couple of times; they moved everything around. Oh yeah, the PPO scored again. One of the pro teams had almost new 750s they weren't using ('cause they upgraded to the new Millennium 2000s) so they donated them to us! Wow! I can't wait to try 'em..."

"Yeah, Mom," J.J. joined in. "You should see them—not a scratch! They're just like new."

"Coach would have let us have a go, but by the time we were re-measured for helmets and pads there was no time," said Brian. "Some of the guys really grew over the summer."

"You should see Roger Johnson. He must be four inches taller and his voice changed. I hardly recognized him—and he's in my form."

"They gave me a new helmet and pads—last season's were too small, but I keep the same number."

"Lucky you—mine's been the same size for three years."

"Does that really bother you?"

"Nah! I like bein' different—I just enjoy gettin' a little sympathy."

"Enough already!" said Myrna, exasperated. "Tell me about your new Psionics class! What do you think about Professor Heady?"

Brian, J.J. and Nicki laughed.

"Mom, you weren't slick at all!" said J.J. "As soon as First Assembly was over and we looked at our schedules, we knew you were in on it."

"Why didn't you tell us?" asked Brian.

"If you arrived early and got your schedules, others may have seen them. Laedere wanted to make the announcement first," answered Myrna.

"Oh, so you made us late this morning on purpose..."

"Would I do that?" She blushed. "I was just having a hard time watching my babies go off to school."

"Oh, I'm sure that's true," said Brian. "But you also made sure we were late."

"Mother," added Nicki, "you're so transparent."

"Well, no harm done—though I did not figure on *that Antetima woman* causing a problem." She was breathing hard, with anger in her expression.

"Wow, Mom," observed J.J., "you really don't like her either. I gotta ask Dad!"

They spent almost half an hour talking about the underground classroom and the *very* British Professor Heady.

"Hey, Grandma!" called J.J. excitedly, the first to notice the sage empath step through the kitchen door. He jumped up and ran to her outstretched arms.

"I wanted to be here when you got home but was busy," said Grandma.

"Are you staying for supper?"

"I would not miss it!" She smiled. "Hopefully it will not be as momentous as last year's First Day get-together."

"We'll eat about six-thirty. It's a bit late; George is running behind."

"Excellent. May I help? We can have a visit."

Brian and J.J. took that as their cue to enjoy one last evening of video games; there would be homework starting the next day.

"Mom, you're squishin' me," complained Brian, lightheartedly. He was in Myrna's embrace after she came to the bedroom as he was putting on his pajamas. It was early, but he was tired.

"Why didn't you tell me? Grandma James just told us about the Hill boy."

"It's no big deal. He needed some help and we were there. And besides, I could have gotten detention for using energy on a student."

"That makes it even more special. Not only did you intervene, but you risked disciplinary punishment as well." She released him then sat in the shabby overstuffed chair Brian refused to get rid of, as he crawled into his bed.

"Who is he—did Grandma know?" He looked over and saw his father walk in with Nicki and J.J. in tow.

"That's not an easy question," said George. He sat on the end of Brian's bed as Nicki and J.J. settled on the floor's plush carpet. "He was found wandering alone, naked and dirty, in the foothills above Castle Hot Springs resort—north of Lake Pleasant. Fortunately it was Sodality who spotted him as he is very power-gifted. Without any formal training, he performed some amazing feats trying to avoid capture. It has taken almost two years for him to settle down enough to try CKS classes."

"He can talk," continued Myrna, "but speaks very little. Experts guess he's been on his own since age four or five. He learns fast; tutors have him reading and writing at grade level."

"He's really little," observed Nicki. "Is he really eleven?"

"Fairly sure. He's been thoroughly examined and physicians feel his small size is mostly due to existing on a diet of berries, roots, grasses and some occasional meat he would run across."

"Wow. Was it like the stories of feral children being raised by wolves?" asked Brian.

"There are no wolves in the Bradshaw Mountains, but some of his actions seemed to indicate he may have been assisted by coyotes or mountain lions. He may have your ability to mind-speak with animals."

"He can!" announced Brian. He saw the others stare at him. "When he touched my cheek, he said *thanks*—brain to brain—and a lot more, but I haven't had time to sort it out yet."

"Where is he living?" asked J.J. "Phusikos said something about taking him to *the home*."

"Despite exhausting efforts, there is no trace of his family or any report of a missing child fitting his description. He's currently living in a Sodality group home in Prescott."

"Don't they have clothes and stuff?" asked J.J. "His clothes were shambles."

"It's hard; the home doesn't receive public money so funds are tight."

"My folks never threw away anything. All my old clothes are still at the other house. I want to give him anything he can use—please!"

"Sure," said George. "I'll call the home and ask them to FON him here early in the morn—"

"Why not tonight, Dad? It's not that late," suggested Brian. "He can spend the night and go with us to Seminary tomorrow."

"I suppose they'd let him—but we'd better go get him. Brian, get dressed. He trusts you; you and I will go while J.J. and your mother go over to the other house. It still has the shields and wards Jason and Joan set."

"I bet he hasn't had a proper meal," observed Nicki. "There's plenty of leftovers. I'll warm up a good supper for him—yeah, you too, Brian!" She laughed.

"Wow! I didn't think anyone could out-eat Brian..." J.J. laughed. "This kid's acting like he hasn't eaten in months!"

"He sure doesn't get food like this," said Brian. "I saw what they had—they hadn't cleaned up yet. Their dinner was watery soup, bread and a piece of fruit."

"The folks who run the home are doing all they can and are genuinely apologetic. They simply have too many mouths to feed and no budget," said George. "We're going to do something about that—"

"Oh, yeah!" announced Myrna. "I never knew that place existed. It's now my mission to make every Sodality family in Arizona know and help!"

"What's his name?" asked Nicki—pleased her efforts were thoroughly enjoyed. "It's rude to keep calling him *boy* or *kid*."

"No one knows," said George. "The Home parents said he kept saying *Weezer Hill*, so they modified it a bit and named him Willard Hill. He seemed to like that, but he still pronounces it Weezer Hill."

"Hey, Willard," said Brian. "You want more meatloaf?" He pointed at the large meat platter.

"Is it okay?" the boy asked meekly, afraid there might not be enough for everyone.

"Sure! There's plenty—and we already had supper." He cut a thick slice and put it on Willard's plate, which was quickly emptied.

"I've freshened up quite an assortment of clothes J.J. outgrew and laid them out in Brian's room. He can try them on and decide what he likes."

"The group folks say he won't sleep in a bed. He pulls the bedding off and sleeps on the floor," said Brian. "We'll put a sleeping bag on the floor in my room."

"Mine?" Willard pointed to the array of pants, shirts, T-shirts, p.j.s, underwear, socks, shoes and jackets.

"If it fits and you like it," affirmed J.J., "it's yours."

Willard walked around the room, barely touching various items—like they might break or disappear, then kept looking down at himself. Brian got the message...

"Hey, Will!" Brian grabbed a pair of white cotton briefs he was sure would fit and headed for the interconnecting bathroom. "I bet you'd like to clean up before you try on these things. C'mon, I'll show you where." Willard's face brightened and he followed.

In the bathroom Brian turned on the shower and adjusted the temperature. "Just leave your old clothes on the floor. We'll take and wash them." He turned and saw him pulling off his well-worn T-shirt and dropping his pants—he'd guessed right—the home didn't even have underclothes for him. Timidly the boy approached the shower but hesitated before stepping in.

"Brian, I don't know how. At the home we only have a tub." He was almost crying.

"Hey, it's okay. Just stand under the water. You'll like it." The little orphan eased in cautiously at first but then smiled as the warm spray soaked him. "Take the soap and rub it all over—that's it—get lather everywhere—well, no, not in your hair—there's shampoo for that, but scrub your face good." He tossed him a washcloth.

"What's shampoo? We only have bar soap at home."

"It's special hair soap—it's in that bottle—here, hand it to me and lean your head over by the door." He poured a generous portion of the "no tears" thick golden liquid on the boy's head and worked it in thoroughly. He noticed the shower floor was streaked with the dirt being washed out. "Rinse out the soap and we'll do it once more." He repeated the hair washing with much less dirt going down the drain. "Okay, rinse off real good. Yeah, now you're clean." Brian reached and turned off the water, then handed him a towel. He picked up the dirty clothes as he passed the clean underwear to the boy.

In the bedroom Brian waited for Willard to come out of the bathroom. He heard:

"Brian," called the meek voice. "Can I use—?"

"Of course you can!" he called back. He remembered again this was the only time Willard had been away from the group home—except for living in the wild and his terrible first day at CKS. He didn't know that it was expected he'd need to use the toilet. A few moments later and a flush, he came out looking totally different. He was clean; his hair shone and he was wearing clean, white briefs. Brian went and grabbed his comb and hair brush, pulled out all the tangles and neatly combed the unevenly-cut hair, putting a part down the middle. "Now start trying on clothes—you don't have to ask—they're all yours. Whatever fits."

That broke the ice. Willard tried on several jeans, summer shorts, button, T- and polo shirts, socks, shoes; he even made sure which underwear fit. Brian and J.J. just chuckled. Finally he donned some flannel pajamas that had a bright checkered print, so he was dressed like J.J. and Brian, who had already changed for bed. There was a soft knock on the bedroom door, and Myrna stepped in.

"Boys, it really is bedtime—oh my!" she gasped. "What a difference! He sure cleans up beautifully."

"Yup!" said Brian proudly. "We did pretty well—and most of the clothes fit. He's gonna be one of the best-dressed kids at CKS. Most of the stuff is almost new."

"Brian?" The little voice floated from the floor through the dark. "Yeah?"

"Thank you!" Here there was a long pause. "Is it okay to say I love you?"

"Boys don't usually say that to boys, but, yeah, it's okay. We love you, too."

"Night."

"Good night, Will."

Chapter Ten
Another Day Of Infamy

"**M**OM!" Brian barely heard J.J. yell. Brian was still in his pajamas, sitting up on his bed with the room dark; only the old lava lamp and the orange-red glow of Arizona's sunrise backlighting the closed window drapes. He was holding the palms of his hands to the sides of his face and grimacing at the images in his mind. With his eyes closed squinting-tight, he did not see his brother standing in the doorway of their interconnecting bathroom with his wet red hair and bare shoulders, wearing only a large terry-towel wrapped around his waist. Nor did he see his mother enter his bedroom, wearing a bright pastel, mid-length dress and wiping her hands on her apron.

"He's been like that since I got up—all while I showered and stuff. I thought I heard him say something about a plane crash—American Airlines, Flight 11."

"What is it?" asked Myrna, sitting on the side of his bed and pulling him into her embrace. "What do you see?"

"What's going on?" inquired George as he eased into the room and sat on the overstuffed armchair. "Is he ill?"

"I don't know exactly," answered Myrna softly. "He's mumbling about people dying—burning. He's shivering yet his p.j.s and sheets are soaked from sweating. There's something horribly wrong somewhere."

"Oh, Mom," cried Brian, with tears streaming down his face. "It's so awful... People are burning in a huge fire in a tall building somewhere—and there's more to come; more crashes."

"Is it something that's already happened or are you seeing a future event?" asked George in almost a whisper. Nicki was now standing in the doorway—looking for the rest of the family.

"It's both! American Airlines Flight 11 has already crashed; United Flight 15 is heading for the same place; American Flight 77 is going toward another, odd-shaped, building and United Flight 93 has been taken over by bad guys." They all sat in stunned silence when their musings were interrupted by the front walk alarm, followed by a very insistent ringing of the front doorbell.

"I'll get it." Nicki turned and headed down the hall to the living room. After a few moments and hearing the distant sound of a very excited voice, she returned and announced, "It was Johnny Reeby from across the street; his mother sent him to make sure we're watching the news. A passenger jet crashed into the World Trade Center in New York." She turned on her heels and went back to the living room and switched on the large screen TV. The rest of the family quickly followed—except J.J., who needed to dress first. George watched only for a moment to verify it was the same scene Brian described, then frantically began making phone calls.

"I can't get through to anyone; all the phone lines are jammed!" he announced after many failed attempts. "I was hoping to warn someone, FAA. FBI, someone. I can't even reach anyone in *our* Redoubt. The UTS depends on fiber-optic lines and it's jammed, too." He paced about, frustrated. United Airlines Flight 15 crashed into Tower Two of the World Trade Center.

"It wouldn't do any good, Dad," said Brian sadly. "They're already in the air..." For a time they all stared at the incredible scenes unfolding on the TV. Then Brian got up, went to his bedroom and flopped on the bed—burying his face in the pillow. Some time later he felt his top sheet and light blanket being pulled over him and gently tucked around and heard:

"Mom translated to CKS to tell them you and J.J. would be staying home," said Nicki quietly. She pulled the desk chair close to the head of the bed. "Seminary has been cancelled. She found Willard wandering the empty halls, confused because the FON let him get there but, with the overload, he couldn't get back to the home. She wrapped him in her arms and brought him here. We tried to feed him but he is sitting in the hall outside your door and won't leave."

Brian rolled to face his sister. "Why did I get the visions and warnings if it was going to be too late to make a difference? It was awful to see all that and I'm still getting flashes if I let myself think about it."

"We've always been taught there's a reason for everything that comes into our lives, if we look hard enough to find it. Did you see Monēo?"

"Yeah, but not in connection with the crashes—it's like he was warning about other terrible things to come."

"Well, maybe that's it—you weren't given the opportunity to change what happened today, but to put you—us—on alert for the future."

"How do you do that?"

"Do what?"

"Come up with easy answers to hard questions? You did that all last year when we were sorting out the Wizard's Cavern clues."

"I just find it easier to reduce things to simple logic."

"Sometimes I think I do just the opposite; I make easy stuff more complicated."

"You can do lots of things I can't. It's all about making the best use of the gifts we've been given. Complex problem-solving is one of mine."

"Oh, Sis, it was so awful! All those people in the buildings were burned by fuel from the planes."

"Could you really see all that?"

"Not so much see—though I did see something like flash photo images—I mostly just sensed their emotions. I felt just a tiny bit of their fear and pain. But I also felt the plane passengers' anger at the hijackers and their frustration at not being able to do anything about it—except United 93. Even though they knew they'd probably die, they were relieved they kept the bad guys from flying to Washington. Sis, they were real heroes."

"Brian, none of that's been on the news—at least, not yet—are you sure?"

"Yeah. They were great. Americans owe them a lot."

"When did it happen?"

"It all started about ten or fifteen minutes before the crash, a little after ten o'clock."

"Brian, it's not yet ten o'clock."

"Eastern time—"

"What?"

"I felt it at their time; a little after ten in Washington."

"Freaky!"

"Yeah..." They were quiet for a couple minutes.

"I guess I'd better get up." Brian sat up on his bed, looked at the cowboy and horses print on his pajamas that were at least three sizes too small. He chuckled as he stretched out his arms, which were covered only halfway between his wrist and elbow. "And I think it's time to retire these PJs and start wearing the new ones Mom bought."

"Hey, Bro, you can stay in bed all day. No one would blame or bother you—especially since you seem to have your own personal security detail guarding your door. I had to promise to not wake you if you were asleep. When I mentioned you might be hungry, he said he'd bring it to your room."

"I am hungry—now, but I doubt he can carry that much—especially if he hasn't eaten, either. Thank you—it really helped." He put his feet over the side, stood up and stretched.

"Yeah, you'd better quit wearing those." She giggled. "They're not covering everything they're supposed to." She rose and strode out of the door as Brian looked down at his bare stomach and ankles, blushed deeply, then quickly changed into fresh boxers, sweat pants, Mountaineers T-shirt, sport socks and low-top tennis shoes.

"Hey, Will," he called. The undersized boy immediately stood in the doorway.

"Sir Brian?" his tiny voice answered.

"Why are you guarding—what did you call me?"

"Sir Brian," he said naturally, as if using the title since birth. "It's your name, isn't it?" Willard looked afraid he'd said something wrong.

"Well, yeah... But how'd you learn the title? Have you been talking to Professor Heady?"

"No, I'm not in his class yet. It's in your head—it's who you are."

"Can you read my mind?"

No, not that. When I touched you we traded things about ourselves: like who we are. If you think about it, you will know things about me, he projected without using his voice. It was so smooth Brian almost missed the change.

That was slick. You are good at this.

It's easier. I have been doing it with my animal friends for as far back as I can remember—much longer than lip-talking. When I talk I have to think about forming words as well as the idea.

"Wow!" said Brian aloud and projecting. "I've been talking since I was little, so I don't even have to think about it. I have to concentrate to project."

"I can't do that. Will you teach me, M'Lord?"

"Do what?"

"I can only mind-speak or lip-talk. I can't do both at the same time."

"Sure, I'll teach you, if you'll quit using my title—except in some formal thing where it's called for."

You honor me.

"Now, let's go eat. But first, why were you guarding my door?"

Through our connection I sensed you had lots of heart hurt and needed time to heal. You protected me. Somehow I think I am supposed to help you on your quest.

"What quest?"

You are the Appointed One, M'Lord. You must become the Ringmaster. Days like this must never happen again.

Chapter Eleven
Memories Revisited

Back and forth he paced through the close confines of the back room of his famous store. Emilio Mendacci had sent his apprentices and other craftsmen home an hour earlier, turned off the lights in the store's sales area and display windows, and turned the door sign to indicate "CLOSED"—even though several other PV Mall merchants stayed open until ten o'clock.

He walked up an aisle, between workbenches, where his artisans made the fabled power rings, then down another. He passed by his antique roll-top desk, where he paused and stared at a pile of extensive notes. He then retraced his steps—repeating the same circuit over and over, mumbling to himself: *What am I missing? What am I not seeing? If Merlin can figure it out, so can I!* Again he stared at his notes, made from his own experiments and years of studying Merlin's writings. *Why can't I pick up the artifact? It's been on display for ages—collectors and museum personnel handled it all the time. It makes no sense that I can't work with it. Maybe it can sense my intention to grind off a small amount.* He resumed his pacing and questioning vigil, until he heard the high-pitched ring-a-ling of the bell hanging on the store's front door. Grumpily he called out:

"We're closed! Come back tomorrow!"

He heard no response or another ring to indicate the late-evening caller had left. *I'm sure I locked that door,* he thought. But he knew locks were almost useless in Sodality world—only psionic energy wards, shields and alarms were effective deterrents. He'd failed to set any this evening.

"We're closed," he said again—more loudly—then turned toward the doorway that led to the display/sales area. There was still no response. *Maybe they didn't come in—saw the sign and left,* he considered as he stepped out onto the sales floor and looked around. He didn't see anyone, yet he felt something. The hairs on the back of his neck prickled and there was a faint aroma of a man's cologne. But there was no one—at least that he could see.

I'm getting paranoid, he convinced himself, then took one last look around and retreated back into the workshop to continue his musings. He went to the old desk, scanned the notes again—hoping for some nugget of inspiration. His back was turned toward the secured vault on the opposite side of the workshop.

Deep in thought, the short, bespectacled man habitually pushed his glasses back up on his nose, until he heard a slight rustle of clothes. He began to spin around, channeling energy, but a bright yellow flash of light erupted. His arms were solidly bound to his side and he glimpsed the glow of binding tendrils securing him firmly.

* * *

"Ouch!" complained Brian, rubbing his elbows and backside as he stood up. "I don't understand it! I've been defending against J.J.'s knockdown zaps for years. Now I can't seem to block anything."

"Sorry," said Carl. "I'm trying to hold back so it doesn't hit you so hard."

"It's not your fault. I'm just not concentrating." The dampness of the underground classroom seemed to be penetrating his bones.

"What are you thinking, M'Lord?"

"I don't know, Professor." Brian looked into the anxious faces of his brother, sister, Carl and the Advanced Psionics teacher. "I say *block* in my head, but it seems if I don't say it aloud, it doesn't work."

"As we have discussed, to properly defend yourself, you must be able to channel both offensive and defensive manipulations without verbal expression. To vocalize, it takes a fraction of a second to form the words. That can make the difference of whether you live or die. Your commands must become instinctive—almost without conscious thought. Please try again."

Brian watched Carl intently—looking for any eye movement or muscle twitch that would tell him when the energy-burst would be coming to knock him down again. But Carl was good; he gave no discernable warning. Suddenly a white streak was on its way and (again) Brian found himself on his back.

"Sorry," repeated Carl.

"Quit apologizing!" Brian took J.J.'s offered hand to help him up. He was really getting frustrated. "You're just doin' what you're told," he said angrily.

"Don't take it out on him," consoled Nicki, quickly stepping between her brother and Carl—knowing Brian's temper could sometimes get out of control, usually causing considerable havoc.

Brian flushed with embarrassment as he saw the worried looks on the others in the room. With command of all the elements (equally), there was genuine concern about some of his control issues when he was angry.

"Hey, I'm sorry! I didn't mean to take it out on you." He walked over to his student desk and plopped down in the seat. Everyone let out a sigh of relief. "I'm just having a hard time getting the September 11th images out of my head. I keep thinking if there had been Sodality on the planes or if I'd gotten the visions earlier, things would have turned out different."

"There is nothing you could have—"

"I know, Professor, but I wonder why I have these gifts if there's no way to prevent such horrible things. Ever since that day I've been having trouble concentrating. I wonder, if I can't do anything, then what's the use in practicing and learning all this stuff?"

"You finally reveal your problem."

"What do you mean?"

"You have been unable to focus when those terrible images haunt and you feel such futility. This we can cure."

"How?"

"Before I answer, do you completely trust these companions?"

"Yes," he answered without hesitation.

"Me?"

"Yes."

"Sir Jeremy's grandmother, Erin James?"

"Yes."

"I assume the answer is the same for your parents?"

"Of course."

"Excellent!" exclaimed the professor while rubbing his hands together. "Does your family have any plans for this evening that you know of?" He looked back and forth to each of the students.

"No, I don't think so," answered Nicki for herself and her brothers.

"Can you attend a special meeting tonight?" he asked Carl.

"If I call my mom, I'm sure it'll be okay..."

"Wait a minute—Willard Hill is staying with us for a few days while the Prescott Group Home is being painted and remodeled," explained Brian. "Mom has organized a fundraiser and has really been on a mission."

"I heard about that—even contributed. A most worthy cause. I understand you have a special bond with Master Hill. Can you trust him?"

"Sure."

"Then by all means; he may be of considerable benefit. I will contact your parents and we'll plan to meet here—"

"Professor?" interrupted Nicki. "I know our parents. They love any excuse for family dinners and to entertain. Does whatever we're going to do have to be here? I'll call to make sure, but they would be honored if you would come to dinner and we can conduct the meeting at our home."

"That is even better, for it will be more familiar surroundings for your brother; if it would not be too much bother."

"Believe me, Professor," added J.J. "Mom will be delighted! Er-er, Professor, what about our Uncle Paul, Dad's brother? He's usually part of anything we do as a family."

"Do you trust him?" He stared at Brian for an answer.

"Oh, yeah!" he confirmed without reservation.

"Then by all means, the more the better—if he's available."

As the ten people were finishing their hot, deep-dish apple pies a la mode, Brian was feeling a bit unsettled; unable to eat his usual four helpings of pot roast, oven-browned potatoes, carrots, onions and peas—he only had three. Professor Heady still had not fully explained what was going to happen. His appetite wasn't affected all that much; he was able to consume two full crocks of the deep-dish delight.

According to the professor's instruction, all the living room furniture was pushed against the walls, lights were somewhat dimmed and all ten participants formed a tight circle, sat on the floor and joined hands. Grandma James was on Brian's right, then Nicki, George, Myrna, Professor Heady, Paul, Carl, J.J., and Willard was holding his left hand.

"Professor," said George without preamble, "this is your show. We're here to help however we can."

"Thank you. We're going to try and help our young lord move on from the nightmare visions he saw on September 11th. Sir Brian trusts all of you implicitly, and has confidence in my intentions."

Brian stared at the robed wizard sitting directly across from him and wondered. The words were soothing, but he was glad to have his family close.

"I have some empathic ability, however, Ms. James is one of the most gifted we've had in centuries. I have asked her to make the mental connections while I narrate and make inquiries. During the session, if I ask a question and you know the answer, look at me and I will nod. Only then do you speak. Do not answer any questions put directly to Sir Brian. Much of what you see will be disturbing. Try not to react aloud; however, do not hold back your feelings or emotions. This is why we are here—to support and help each other.

"Often you have been taught love is the most powerful force in the universe, and never more so than what is found in a family. In love, reach out and help wherever you feel you can... Ms. James?"

"All of you, close your eyes." Brian did as Grandma directed and immediately felt energy flowing through him—oscillating from left to right then right to left.

"Everyone, except Brian, try to empty your mind—think only of a pure white room with no furniture, no windows and no door. You can only see white, with no blemish.

"Brian, think of a color—any color, do not name it, but see it in your mind's eye. Now give us that color. You love us and want to give us the gift of your color," instructed Grandma.

"Does anyone see, feel or maybe even hear, Brian's gift of color?" asked the professor, using very soft tones. Eight sets of eyes opened and made contact. He nodded at Nicki.

"I see sky blue."

He then nodded at George. "Yes, that's the color, but I also sense a sound of a gentle breeze."

"There's a faint tune—like humming," said Myrna, after she got the nod.

"I feel warm, like early summer sunshine," added Paul.

"I see light streaks of very high clouds," said Carl.

"I feel happiness and fear," announced Wil.

"What is the happiness, Master Willard?"

"He's glad the link up is working, and family is close."

"And the fear?"

"He's afraid you're going to make him relive the crash day."

"Will he take us there? It's his choice."

"He wasn't going to, but he feels our love and knows we'll help, so he'll do it." Wil's voice seemed to be changing and sounding more like Brian's.

"Brian?" he heard Grandma say softly; she reassuringly squeezed his hand a little tighter. "Brian, go back to very early the morning of September 11th. You were in bed and started seeing visions. Share those visions with us. You don't have to endure them alone. Give us your sight."

"Can anyone see it?" asked the professor. "No? Send your love to Brian. He knows his vision is ugly and painful, so it doesn't feel like a gift. Let him know it's okay. That's what families do—share each other's burdens." Nicki caught his eye and gasped.

"Lady Nichole? Do you see it?" She nodded her head, and tears began streaming down her face. "There's no need to describe it. We all know it's awful. But tell us: Is there anything you could have done to stop it? Even if you could have translated into the plane before it happened?"

"I don't see how..."

"Look hard! All of you! From Brian's vision, can any of you see a way to stop the first plane from crashing?"

"No," they all said in unison, just above a whisper—choking back emotions.

"Share your answer with Brian—through your connection. Send your views and analysis to him and relieve him of the guilt and frustration he feels."

"He's getting it," whispered Wil, "but can't talk right now."

"Brian, show us the second plane—from your vision," said Grandma.

After recounting the final images of each plane that crashed, each time they could see no effective means of intervention—even with their psionic powers.

"Now, Brain, honey," coaxed Grandma gently, "we know you were deeply hurt by those visions. Show us where it hurts. Yes, in your brain and in your chest—your heart. Just concentrate on the pain and those places where you feel wounded."

Myrna's and Nicki's eyes flew open and they gasped—almost breaking the circle as they wanted to grab their chests. One by one, they became aware of stabbing pains and pounding in their heads. All except Wil, who just squeezed his eyes tightly and scrunched up his face.

"Now, each of you reach out. Make extra blood flow into those areas," instructed the steady voice of the teacher. "Rub a healing balm on the sore spot to take away the inflammation. Send energy to speed up the healing. Drink warm herbal tea to calm your stomachs and nerves...

"With your own pain gone, become the physician. Reach out with your love and heal Brian. Use every ministration you know—even absorb it onto yourselves. Keep at it until there is no more, and he is well... Leave nothing behind..."

"It's working," announced Wil. "He can breathe deep again. His head doesn't hurt and his heart has room to beat freely."

Brian felt all the relief the little orphan boy described, and more, until everything went black...

*   *   *

"Are you sure you got everything?" asked Reficul in his deep bass—almost growly—voice.

"Yes, Master, I'm certain," announced Laileb. "He kept a complete file of notes in his Phoenix Valley Mall shop. In fact, when I went in, he was studying them, even speaking aloud about the missing element."

"Tell me exactly what you saw and heard."

"He kept pacing around the tables where they make the rings, mumbling about a dragon scale and not being able to put his hands on it. Then he'd go back to his old roll-top desk and stare at his notes again." Laileb went on with his detailed description, including when the bell rang on the store's front door, for no apparent reason, creating the perfect diversion. That's when he came out, bound the old man, probed his mind, copied the notes, and altered his memory.

As Laileb spoke, the fire crackled in the huge fireplace hearth, flames flickered from the candles, and the gray stone walls maintained their cool dampness that the Master always enjoyed. After he finished, there was a long, eerie silence as his master mulled over each word.

"What did your mind probe reveal?"

"Some of that was murky. I had to keep him semi-conscious with drugs because he was quite skilled at blocking the probe." Laileb shifted his weight uncomfortably as Refilcul's gaze made him feel like he were five years old and being questioned by an adult about some misdeed. "However, the images I could make out verified what I found in the notes."

"Then you're sure we don't need him?"

"As you pointed out, there would be a huge investigation if he turned up missing, and it appears the only thing he could not solve was where to obtain the missing ingredient." He shivered from the castle's dampness and Reficul's glare. "Surely, with your knowledge and resources, we can complete the formula long before he could, and we avoid the problem of his disappearance."

"Hmmm, you may be right." Laileb breathed a sigh of relief as his master continued, "I have examined the copy you made of his notes. Most of the ingredients are scarce, but not too hard to find. Like Mendacci, locating a blue dragon scale will not be easy. They are extremely rare. It's a good thing we don't need one from a red dragon."

*   *   *

Brian rolled over and saw the soft glow of a brilliant orange Arizona sunrise filtering through the closed curtains of his bedroom window. Groggily he rubbed his eyes, trying to focus and remember how he even got into bed. The last thing he remembered was sitting on the living room floor with his family, Grandma, Carl, Willard and Professor Heady. And even that memory was somewhat obscure. Now he was snug under the covers wearing only a T-shirt and underwear—which was strange because he usually wore only pajamas or a long nightshirt to bed.

Needing to visit the bathroom, he pushed off the covers and swung his legs over the side of the bed, but found the floor was obstructed by the legs of a body.

"How are you feeling?" he heard Willard's meek voice inquire. Brian looked down and saw the undersized boy sitting on the floor, leaning against the bedstand, with his legs inside a dark blue, down sleeping bag.

"Fine, I think," he said with some hesitation. "How did I get into bed—and why are you there?"

"You were so relieved when Professor's thing was done, you fell into a deep sleep. Your father carried you to bed. I have been staying close, in case you needed anything—"

"And growling at anybody who came close enough to disturb you," said J.J. from the doorway of their interconnecting bathroom.

"You needed to sleep," defended Willard. "Since that day, you have not slept all night through, until now." Everyone knew *that day* referred to September 11th and the tragic events that happened.

"Brian, will you tell your bodyguard he needs some sleep, too? He has not closed his eyes, or left your side, except to go to the bathroom. We even had to bring his meals to him or he wouldn't have eaten."

"Wait a minute," protested Brian. "You said *meals*. How long have I been asleep?" He looked around and saw the sun was becoming brighter behind his curtains.

"Please don't be angry, M'Lord," pleaded Wil. "This is Sunday morning—"

"I slept through two nights and a whole day?"

"You got up once to go to the bathroom," explained J.J. "But you seemed to be sleepwalking."

"I don't remember anything—and speaking of that, I got to go." He got out of bed, stepped between Willard's legs and headed for the bathroom.

"You should shower, too," teased J.J. as he retreated into his bedroom and closed the interconnecting door on his side.

* * *

"Ouch!" complained J.J. He pulled his feet under him and winced while shakily standing up. "You need to practice some control! That hurts!"

"Sorry," said Brian, grimacing as he watched his brother rub his backside and dust off his pants. "I have been so used to forcing my concentration, it's hard to pull it back. Maybe we should use wrestling mats or something."

"Nay, young Sir," answered Professor Heady. "Mats provide an excuse for lack of control. A few bruises will reinforce the object of the lessons."

"That's easy for you to say," grumbled J.J. in a whisper. "You're not the one with sore elbows and butt." He applied healing energy to his arms.

"I have excellent hearing, M'Lord."

"Sorry, Professor—"

"I know this is not easy, but you must remain vigilant for the times ahead."

"Professor, do you know something we don't?" asked Nicki. "We understand the need to learn self-protection, but you keep hinting around about something specific."

"No, nothing specific, but one needs only to examine events of recent history to have a sense of urgency to prepare—especially for the Appointed One, until he becomes Ringmaster. The world is facing terrorists' plots, slaughter of ethnic groups, environmental disasters, rogue countries with atomic weapons, corrupt governments, economic chaos, expanding illegal drug trade and a host of other potential calamities. And, of course, we must not forget Reficul and his lot. There is no telling when any of you may be faced with any of these threats."

"Whoa, you're talking about some big stuff," exclaimed Brian. "I know, when I become Ringmaster, I will be able to control others' use of their power rings, but most of that has nothing to do with Sodality or psionics. We're just kids—"

"In times past our kind lived apart from—you call them Branglers—and had little interaction with events beyond our personal concerns. That can no longer be the case. Each of us has the ability to influence what's going on around us. Evil must be confronted wherever it occurs, by whatever means at our command. Mug—Branglers will use their weapons, spy agencies, armies and mass media and we will perfect and use the gifts we have been given. And you, M'Lord, must become Ringmaster!"

"You mean we're coming out in the open?" inquired Carl, who was openly voicing the concerns of the four youngsters.

"No, that is not what we're saying." There was a sigh of relief heard through the rock-walled underground classroom. "The advanced psionics techniques you will be learning are to enable you to help in various ways, without being detected and to cause Brangler observers to think only natural forces were at play—even though they were a bit unexplainable."

"Then I guess it wouldn't be good to blast somebody across a room, when only some restraint or diversion would be enough," said J.J. as he glared at Brian and, again, rubbed his sore spots.

"Okay, okay! I need to focus more on control!" Brian looked around at the accusing stares and shivered a bit, thinking of the huge responsibility he would have as Ringmaster.

* * *

Arising from a small cot in the back corner of his store's workroom, Emilio Mendacci looked around in confusion. It wasn't as if he had never slept at the shop—that's why he kept the cot there. And, since his wife died (six months ago), his house was often lonely. But this was different. He could not remember going to bed—or anything—after his workers went home and he locked the doors at 8:00p.m.

"That's strange," he muttered to himself, shaking his head to clear the sleepy fog and think more clearly. "Such terrible nightmares!" He went in the restroom, splashed water on his face and donned fresh clothes he kept there for such occasions. All the while he strained to remember the night before, but the vivid nightmare kept replaying in his mind: There was a flash of light and someone dressed all in black, forcing him to explain his master ring formula and experiments. "It all seemed so real," he mumbled. Then, having a disquieting thought, he hurried over to his old roll-top desk, only to feel relieved. Everything was there—exactly as he left it.

"It seemed so real... I guess I'm getting paranoid." Then he chuckled, recalling: *Even if someone copied my notes, they'd get it all wrong. I recorded all the wrong key elements. In fact, if someone tries to make the formula, as it's written, they'll be lucky to survive the attempt.*

He laughed again and recalled the day, a few months before, when he knew he wanted to insert some misdirection in his notes—in case someone tried to steal or read them. He had been rearranging the artifacts in the store's front display window when the Everett family passed by, in the main concourse. The youngest boy, Brian, was wearing a bag on his back that had a beautifully-embroidered dragon across the front flap. That gave him the idea: He'd record the key ingredient as shavings of a blue dragon scale, instead of a red.

Chapter Twelve
Bandon, Oregon, Seminary

"What's wrong?" asked Brian. He looked down at an extremely excited, undersized Willard who could barely catch his breath. Brian closed and warded his locker, after putting his books away, to get ready for Personal Fitness class. "Calm down; take a couple of deep breaths." But all the boy could do was stammer:

"Notice—" he blurted out, then struggled to form another word: "T-t-team." Finally he pointed down the hallway where several students were gathered around the bulletin board where school and sports teams' announcements were usually posted. Brian did not hesitate. He headed for the gathered throng, but before he could get there, he heard Willard's projected voice in his head:

You and J.J. are both on the active team roster, as starters!

Brian skidded to a halt behind the assembled group, but too far back to see clearly. *Are you sure?* he mind-spoke back to Willard, as excited students pointed to the list and made various comments— including some grumbles from those who were disappointed from not being named. *You may have read the intramurals team list.*

I am certain it was the Interscholastic Roster.

The crowd ahead began to thin and Brian was able to get closer, as he felt others pressing from behind. After what seemed an eternity, the rosters came into view. "Woo Hoo!" he yelled. He was starting tosser, as Murphy had been made goal defender and team captain. He looked again and saw Jeremy James Everett was a starting pounder. Life just got much better for the Everett brothers.

Congratulations, Sir Brian.
Thank you—and to you, too.
Me? Why?
Didn't you notice? You are on Team 2 of the Intramurals.
I'll like that. Will you come to my games?
Every one I can.

"Welcome, flipolo fans." Brian heard the familiar, amplified voice of the announcer. He was getting used to it, somewhat, but there was something about walking up the tunnel from the locker rooms that made him feel like Roald the fire-breathing dragon was chasing a whole herd of red dragons right through his stomach.

"Last year's Interscholastic National Champions from Crown King Seminary welcomes the Northwest Regional Winner, the Bandon, Oregon, Seminary Condors... For those not quite familiar with the Pacific Northwest, Bandon is right on the coast, at the southern end of the Coquille River, and is considered the unofficial cranberry capitol of the Pacific Northwest. There's a lighthouse in the area that is one of the most photographed in the country.

"This year the CKS Spartans graduated out Giles and Roberts. Murphy is the goal defender and team captain, wearing Tunic number 4. Brian Everett is new starting tosser wearing number 33 and Jeremy Everett replaces Roberts as pounder, sporting number 5... And here they are: the CKS Spartans."

After the travelogue and introductions, Brian felt a little better. Maybe only Roald was in his stomach—without the herd of red dragons. As he ran out onto the field with his (almost new) 750 sledge under his arm, the team received a thunderous ovation—maybe the reds were back. He put down his sledge, slid his feet into the straps, picked up the control leash and he was off.

"And there they are, folks, the CKS Spartans doing their team warm-up laps. The Bandon Condors have some new faces: number 1, Richards, is captain and goal defender; number 4 Johnson is tosser with impressive stats; pounders are number 6 Marston, number 2 Anderson, number 7 Bates is new this year, along with number 12 Costello; number 3 Boyle, number 8 Payne and number 11 Manion are all from last year's squad. Give 'em a great welcome!"

Brian could hear the polite applause from the CKS side and loud cheering from the Bandon supporters, who watched them mount their sledges and begin their warm-up circuits. Then both teams faced off and the referee blew his whistle.

"And they're off! The first interscholastic game of the season, and Bandon takes early possession. Number 7 Bates is moving fast and he passes to number 2 Anderson, but he fumbled and CKS takes advantage. J. Everett makes a quick steal..."

Brian smiled when he heard J.J. make the play. The announcer's voice faded into the background as he searched the three-dimensional field for the elusive spherule (a 3-inch red ball that was empowered to avoid capture by flying in all directions). Last year he was lucky; as a second-string substitute for Murphy (who had broken his wrist) many teams underestimated him. They would not make that mistake again.

"Number 5 Everett passes to number 4 Randall, but here comes Condors number 8 Payne, who steals just before Randall can take his shot..."

"Drat!" exclaimed Brian aloud. Randall hardly ever missed. But he couldn't afford to get distracted, and went off searching for the elusive spherule. At least Johnson hadn't spotted it yet. Brian could not let the Bandon tosser get a head start.

"Flipolo fans, it does not get any better than this—even in the pro leagues. The score is still zero-zero. There have not been any fouls or errors—just good, old-fashioned glob handling and brilliant steals... And J. Everett has it again. He's got the glob and he's going for the goal..."

Brian couldn't help but turn and watch to see if J.J. made a goal.

"He's making a fast run, but Bandon Captain Richards is in position..."

Brian quickly scanned the area and spotted Johnson also watching the play below. He moved back to see what his brother would do.

"J. Everett is lining up..."

But Brian saw a better play: Reeves was totally unguarded at the far edge of the fifteen-foot barrier and could make an undefended shot...

Pass it to Reeves, thought Brian, wishing J.J. could hear.

"It's going to be close. Richards is set. But hold on, Everett angles a pass to Reeves, who is taking the shot—he scores! Reeves made the goal before Richards could change position..."

"Yeah!" yelled Brian, pumping his fist in the air, then climbing up higher to look for the elusive spherule. *At least Johnson hasn't seen it yet*, he thought as he saw J.J. gliding up toward him.

"Bandon's Castillo has the glob, but CKS defenders are blocking—he doesn't have a pass..."

"Hey, thanks for calling out about Reeves," yelled J.J. when he got close to Brian. "I hadn't noticed him. But it'd probably be best if you didn't amplify your voice—the other team can hear." He darted off to join the rest of the team, blocking Castillo.

"But I didn't amplify," called Brian to J.J.'s retreating back. *I didn't even say it aloud...* He wrinkled his forehead, trying to figure out what happened. *I can't project to J.J. He doesn't mind-speak—or can I?*

"Here comes number 11 Manion to assist Castillo. He's diving in low and takes the pass. CKS's Randall just missed making a steal, but the Spartans are is still lined up and keeping BOS from getting into scoring position."

Brian was almost in a fog; he was so distracted by the possibility J.J. had received his projected thought.

"There goes Johnson after the spherule," Brian heard, which snapped him out of his musings. He frantically searched the field to decide whether to try and outrun his opponent and grab the red ball first, or speed off to defend the goal.

"Johnson's captured it..."

There was no longer a choice. He began racing toward the goal, with all the speed he could muster. Fortunately he was already between the BOS tosser and the goal. Johnson was moving fast and calculating his run. It was going to be close.

"Johnson is going in low for his usual up-sweep. Everett will have his hands full; no one has blocked that toss and only once has it been caught..."

Brian was glad the announcer anticipated Johnson's run. He was so intent on getting to the goal, there wasn't time to look back and see where the bright green tunic, with number 4, was coming from. He had studied Coach's videos of Johnson and felt most missed the toss because they set up their defense low, and slightly right—anticipating the up-sweep—crossing right to left. But Johnson's toss was always late, waiting until he was high and left. Brian set his defense there.

"BOS's tosser is starting his run..."

Wow, thought Brian. *I'd never try it at that speed.* He was hoping slow-motion would kick in, but so far, he could not predict when it would activate (because he hadn't figured out exactly how he did it). He promised himself to talk to Professor Heady about setting up a practice program for the slow-motion—and some of the other, unexpected, gifts his ring gave him.

"B. Everett is in position, and Johnson is putting on even more speed..."

The excitement was building. The Crown King supporters were chanting: "Block that toss, block that toss—Everett, you're the boss—block that toss!" and the Bandon fans were yelling: "Make that goal! Make that goal—Johnson, you can do it—make that goal!" He knew he had to calm down and tune out the cheers and (armchair) coaching coming from the crowd and focus on the bright green tunic blazing toward him—and of course, the 3-inch red ball.

"Everett is on his own—Murphy is defending the glob goal as the Condor's number 7 Bates sets up. He takes a huge swing with his mallet..."

The announcer's drone faded out of Brian's consciousness as Johnson began his up-sweep. As expected he was starting from low-right (Brian's left, as he faced the oncoming Tosser) and was speeding up and across...

"Bates scores—but too late for Murphy to help Everett..."

Johnson cocked his arm back and Brian tensed, hoping he hadn't over-anticipated and set up too high (it was almost impossible to catch or block a spherule thrown under a defender).

"Block that toss..."

Again, Brian hoped the slow-motion perceptions would come. And, with the thought, Johnson's green blur resolved into sharp focus as he suddenly seemed to be almost stationary, floating suspended in the air, and just barely creeping forward, with his arm winding back to throw. At this speed, it seemed there was enough time to intercept anything. But, Brian reminded himself, it was only his perception of events that was altered. The game was actually moving at full speed and if he did not react fast enough, Johnson would make his ten-point goal. The only thing the slow motion provided as a bit of a jump on seeing exactly the moment of release and the ball's path.

Johnson began his toss, precisely like the videos had shown, and Brian knew his position should be perfect—hopefully not too high. But something was wrong. A cold feeling went through his gut. Monēo was not giving a warning—of that he was sure. Brian felt like a major event happened somewhere—almost like the way he felt when he woke up on the morning of September 11th, but there was no vision of calamity.

*   *   *

"I don't care what agency issued your press pass," huffed a harried New York police officer, standing behind police barricades, and yellow crime scene tape that was fluttering from a gentle breeze. He was standing post in front of the 77th Street entrance to the New York Museum of Natural History. "The mayor said only the CNA crew is to go inside to provide pool coverage. Ain't no one else getting in! Besides, Mr. Skeeter, what in blazes is the *Sodality Expositor?* Ain't never heard of it."

B. M. Skeeter knew he could translate inside, and the grouchy officer wouldn't know the difference, but he could not judge exactly where Branglers might be and his sudden appearance, amid a burst of twinkling, multi-colored lights and metallic ringing, could set off a panic. But he really wanted to get inside. His sources in the Redoubt had discovered that under-cover Sodality investigators where imbedded in the CSI, ATF and FBI units, sifting through the debris from an explosion down in one of the underground storage areas.

"Hey, Expositor guy," yelled the officer, pointing to an area roped off where several TV monitors were set up. "The pool monitors are over there. Maybe you can get your story off 'em." He was almost sounding helpful.

"Thanks! Maybe I can." The freelance reporter began walking toward the bank of TV screens sitting beside a big satellite news truck (with CNA painted on the side and a dish antenna sitting atop an extended mast rising from the roof). He was hoping to spot a vacant and secluded area where the monitor showed a clear location to focus on. Then he'd find a way to change the camera view angle. It wouldn't do to have a video recording of his "magical" arrival or for one of the other reporters to see it on screen—though he chuckled at the thought of disguising himself as some *man from Mars*... He could just see the headlines: *Aliens Invade Museum; Positive Proof of Extraterrestrials; E.T. is Back.* But such pranks were strictly forbidden and severely punished.

Skeeter stared at the screens. There were nine stationary views of corridors and the room where the blast occurred, and one that was moving—being held on the shoulder of a CNA cameraman. There was one larger screen that showed which picture was being broadcast live to CNA's viewing audience. Beside each of the stationary screens was a small lever—a joystick—that remotely controlled the direction the camera pointed. CNA always used the latest technology.

After a few moments he saw the perfect place—an empty hallway with several doors. He could easily focus on the spot in front of the door with Mammalian Fossil Department neatly painted on. The door was barely in the camera's view, on the left. Just a tiny adjustment to the right and no one would see him materialize in front of that door. Just then, the technician was distracted by one of the other reporters. Skeeter focused his energy on the little joystick which slightly tilted to the right. The picture from the camera panned a few feet away from the Mammalian Fossil Department door. No one noticed a thing. Skeeter eased his way out of the pack of newshounds and TV engineers. Quickly he found a hidden alcove away from the museum's excitement, and disappeared in a burst of twinkling lights.

Once inside the museum, the tabloid writer quickly consulted a museum guide map. He was in the Flick Building, on one of the lower floors. But the explosion site was at least two levels lower in the storage vaults amid the old catacombs—at least, that was what the CNA pool reporter said on the monitor. A stairwell was only two doors back from where he stood—away from the camera view. He hurried down.

It was not hard to confirm on which floor the explosion had occurred. The stairwell door had been propped open to help ventilate the dust and smoke. Skeeter doubted the blast was Sodality psionics. There was a strong smell of an explosive, probably a homegrown type with ammonium nitrate. The residual smoke carried the distinctive irritants that burned eyes and tasted bitter when inhaled, but that only added to the mystery. If it was not a psionic energy creation, why were Sodality agents involved in the investigation? Maybe it was more than a case of terrorist disruption—as CNA was reporting, from the FBI spokesman.

I wonder what was stored in that vault? He mused as he peeked around the doorway of the stairwell. He noted there was a haze in the air from smoke and dust, brightly lit up from portable lights on stands, provided by the CNA crew. There was a flurry of activity at the far end of the long corridor, as the various jurisdictions tripped over each other searching for clues. The scene was perfect. No one would notice one more body snooping around, especially if he stayed back and out of the way.

Slowly, Skeeter edged along the hallway, carefully examining every detail, hoping he might spot something the others might have missed. His movements looked exactly like the others moving around. He was several yards from the primary scene when his eyes were drawn left, to a door with an odd title: UNKNOWN/ OCCULT BIOLOGICS. And even more strange, it seemed slightly ajar. Upon first glance it appeared closed and locked, but close examination showed it was not quite secure. Seeing no one was paying him any attention, he eased the door open and slid inside—pulling it firmly shut (He could always translate out or use psionics to unlock it).

The room was dark and smelled of preservatives, old bones and mustiness. He held out his hand and lit a ball of white, cold fire, which provided plenty of illumination. There were several rows of industrial shelves holding a huge array of curious items. A whole section was allocated to shrunken heads, chicken bones, dolls and other voodoo paraphernalia. Other shelves held various carved statuettes of gods from assorted cultures and times throughout Earth's history. The area Skeeter seemed to be drawn to was dedicated to medieval magic. At first, he wondered why magic wands would be in this area, but then he remembered they were always made of wood—a biologic—and the cores were from some other biologic source (like a Phoenix feather).

After looking at several other items, and about to abandon his search as yielding nothing, his attention fell on a shelf labeled:

> Dragon scales: The existence of dragons remains highly debated among various scholars. The scales on this shelf cannot be absolutely proven to come from dragons, but there is no other logical explanation.

Even being a hard-nosed reporter for a tabloid, B. M. Skeeter's mouth dropped open and he caught his breath. Of course, being raised Sodality, he knew dragons have existed for thousands of years—though they were extremely rare in 2001. But their scales were even more rare, and he had never heard of any of them outside the possession of Sodality or wizarding communities. But here, in the depths of New York's Museum of Natural History, was a shelf with several various colors: blue, green, bronze, silver and gold. An amazing collection. He tried to remember the display at the Redoubt Museum. It was, maybe, a little more extensive, but not much. The most rare was from the red dragon, and the only one known to exist was stolen a while back. Skeeter still grumbled about that story—the Council had pressured everyone to not publish it.

Though tempted, Skeeter was not a thief. He was often quite unscrupulous about how he obtained his stories and took liberties with the truth (but only to add some flair), but stealing was not in his nature. With a sigh, he started to move on with his search when he noticed a discrepancy. The 3x5 index card by the blue dragon scale had 2pcs neatly typed at the bottom right corner. But, there was only one, lying above the card. He quickly scanned the whole area; maybe it had been mislaid. There was only one blue dragon scale to be found. He remembered seeing clipboards at the beginning of each row of shelves. No one had checked out a blue dragon scale for research or any other reason. One was missing, and he didn't believe in coincidence. The explosion wasn't a terrorist plot. It was a diversion to keep the theft of a blue dragon scale from being discovered.

Skeeter's discovery served only to create more questions. Blue dragon scales, while rare, were not the rarest or most valuable. Silver and gold scales were even less common, and were worth much more (monetarily). Those were still sitting on the shelf, above their 3x5 index cards. It just didn't make sense.

* * *

"Johnson scores! Everett seemed distracted and completely missed the toss. Crown King is going to have to make up that ten points..."

With the cheering of the Bandon fans and the groaning of the Crown King supporters, Brian snapped back to the game and everything was normal, full-speed again. Since last year, when he substituted for Murphy, he had never failed to catch or block a toss (if he could get into position—and he rarely missed getting to the goal on time). He sheepishly looked around at his astonished teammates, shrugged his shoulders, and flew off. He knew he would have some explaining to do after the game, especially if they lost by less than ten points.

"Hey, are you okay?" Brian heard J.J.'s familiar voice from behind. "Murph wants to know if you need to be subbed out."

"I'm okay. Just lost concentration for a minute. I'll tell you about it later." He sped up higher and resumed his search for the elusive red spherule—still unable to shake the weird feeling that something was amiss somewhere.

"J. Everett has possession again, and avoiding quite a rush of Condor defenders. He passes to Peterson, who tapped to Randall. But here comes BOS's Payne, for a steal, but fumbles and Everett has it back..."

Just then Brian saw a red streak, barely inches off the grass. A quick glance at Johnson—he was still looking high and had not yet seen it. Brian dove hard, aiming just ahead of the spherule's path. Johnson was still looking in the opposite direction. With any luck, Brian might be able to grab the spherule and make the toss before Bandon's number 4 even got turned around.

But, it wasn't going to be that easy. The crowd's yelling alerted Johnson, and he was speeding to deal with Brian's toss (it was too late to intercept).

Determined, Brian caught the red orb just as it tried to lift off and gain altitude. He looked at the goal ring. Johnson must have studied his videos because his position was perfect to catch or block Brian's favorite approach. It was time to come up with something unexpected. He sped to the extreme left side of the field, level with the goal, and started his run. As expected, Johnson shifted to put himself between Brian and the suspended ring. Brian raced hard, aiming for the fifteen-foot boundary with as much speed as he dared. He could see his opponent concentrating, trying to sort out the change in tactics. The fans were chanting again:

"Make that toss! Make that toss! Everett, you're the Boss... make that toss!"

"Johnson, Johnson, we all know ... You're the one to block that throw!"

"There's the two-minute warning. Number 33 Everett is starting his run while his brother, Number 5, is setting for a glob goal. If they both make it, CKS leads..."

Brian tried to block out everything. He had to make this toss or it wouldn't matter what J.J. did below. Both teams gathered around the goal area. At the speed he was flying, he hoped no one got in his way. He had a plan. At the last second he would fake diving down to toss when he came back up. But it was all a ruse. The feint would draw Johnson down but Brian would continue straight and level.

He bobbed low—Johnson followed. Then he went back on path and tossed when he was directly in front. The green defender didn't have a chance. Brian's aim was true and the spherule was through the goal ring before Johnson could get back in position.

"There's the whistle. The Everett Brothers both scored and Crown King Seminary wins its season opener."

The after-game celebrations at the Everett home had become a regular part of Friday evenings during flipolo season. Many parents attended. It was a good time to catch up on news and gossip. J.J. had been named Player of the Game and was enjoying the accolades. Brian was content to occupy the soft armchair pushed against the wall of the living room, close to the dining room where the big table was piled with pizza, Vainabier, sandwiches, cookies, ice cream and other items brought by various parents or team members.

"What got you so distracted?" asked J.J. as he slid a footstool in front of Brian, plopped down and took a long drink from his bottle of soft drink.

"I wish I knew. Just as I was setting to defend Johnson's toss I felt all cold inside—like something was wrong."

"Did you see Monēo?"

"No. It was more of a sick feeling like when I saw the stuff on 9-11, but there weren't any visions. I kinda wonder if someone else is in danger—not me—or us."

"Are you okay now? Do you still feel it?"

"Yeah, I'm fine. It only lasted a few seconds, then it went away—at least for now." He started wolfing down another slice of pizza, signaling J.J. there was nothing more to say on the subject, but of course J.J. wanted to have the last word.

"Well, if it happens again," said J.J., standing and pushing the stool against the wall, "try not to let a ten-point score get by you." He chuckled and padded off to the food table for a ham sandwich, being replaced by Team Captain Murphy.

"Look, I don't know what happened," said Murphy. "I'm sure you're sorting it out. Just let us know if we can help." Without waiting for a response, he walked toward a group of players who were retelling the game plays with increasing exaggeration.

"Thanks, I will," said Brian to Murphy's retreating back.

Chapter Thirteen
Willard's Pain

"Hey, Dad," mumbled Brian sleepily as he walked into the living room and spotted his father reading the morning edition of *Power Press* and listening to the TV turned on to CNA's early broadcast.

"Morning, Son," replied George cheerfully. "Did you sleep well? You look a bit out of sorts."

"Yeah, I'm good. Just had some weird dreams about—" His attention was diverted by a news report on the TV...

> I spent most of the evening inside New York's Museum of Natural History where federal agents are sifting through an underground storage area after an explosion. Government spokesmen confirm the blast was no accident. The exact explosive has not been confirmed, but the general consensus is a homemade device. No one was injured in the blast and damage in the area is relatively minor as the room was undergoing renovations and no artifacts were destroyed.
>
> No group has claimed responsibility but terrorism is certainly suspected. CNA cameras and crews have been on-scene throughout the night and will remain to provide the latest developments as they become available. This is Eric Newman for CNA News in New York.

"That's what I dreamed about!" Brian blurted out.

"What? Are you sure?"

"Well, I think so. It's kinda fuzzy and it's not a dream I remember clearly. It just feels like it."

"Maybe you should read this." George picked up a large (9x12) manila envelope, lifted the flap, chose a piece of paper and pulled it out. Brian approached, feeling surprised. Since his father had been promoted to the post of Ambassador for Brangler Relations (next in line to become vice chairman), each morning a top secret briefing arrived in a sealed envelope, just like the one the paper had been extracted from. No one was ever shown the contents and the topics were never discussed, but now one was being shown to him.

Noting Brian's hesitation, George extended his hand a bit further. He tentatively took the page and saw it was an office memo:

> To: Concerned Council Staff
> Subject: Explosion at Museum of Natural History
>
> Upon learning of the explosion in the underground storage areas of the museum, undercover Sodality agents made sure they were among the investigators assigned to the scene as many "magic" artifacts are known to be in the museum's collections. On the surface, it does not appear the incident has any connection to Sodality (or others with power abilities), however, a confidential source may have discovered a link. Unbeknown to FBI or museum authorities, it appears a blue dragon scale is missing from a storage area on the same floor as the blast.
>
> While all dragon scales are rare and valuable, there are many in the museum's collection worth considerably more than the blue that were undisturbed. This mystery causes concern and needs to be resolved. Council staff are encouraged to pass along any information or ideas they may have concerning this

matter. Ambassador Everett is hereby assigned to coordinate sharing of information with the Museum's director and/or other investigative agencies. As always, your cooperation and confidence are appreciated in this sensitive and classified matter.

Brian held the paper in both hands while he read and reread the text of the memo several times. At twelve years old, he knew it was important but he felt there was much he did not understand. He also felt somewhat connected but had no idea why.

"Dad, I'm not sure I know why you are showing me this."

"I was wondering—hoping it might help clear your thoughts about the dream."

"It doesn't, but—" Brian's mind was racing through the events of the last two days.

"What do you mean, 'but'?"

"What time did the explosion go off? Was it during my game?"

"Allowing for the time difference, yes, it would have been—"

"Just before the two-minute warning?"

"Well, yes—that's about right."

"Remember when I missed Johnson's toss? I was distracted by a cold feeling—like something was wrong. I think that's the exact same time of the explosion in New York, and the blue scale came up missing."

"Is there anything from your dream or when you had your cold feeling that might help discover who did it, why or what they're going to do with it?"

"I'm sorry, Dad, no. There was nothing but a sense of something being wrong and the dream only had shadows and like a flash of light. The only reason I think they're related is just an impression deep inside me. I can't explain it better than that."

"Don't apologize. We're always encouraging you to listen to your inner voice. That's what you're doing; keep it up. I only add: It appears you are in some way connected to this. Please stay alert to any other impressions you get and let me know—no matter how trivial they may seem to you. What you add may be just the key missing piece that goes together with other information that will allow us to solve this thing—whatever it may be."

"What are you going to tell the Branglers?"

"I don't know yet. It's only right to disclose the theft—so they don't keep trying to blame al Qaeda. Unfortunately, there is nothing more I can tell them. We don't know who did it or why. And I don't think they're ready for a briefing on the powerful properties of dragon scales. I'll try and convince them it was stolen because it's extremely valuable, which is about all we know for sure right now."

*   *   *

"Mr. Everett, I have been a confidential advisor to the president since long before he was governor. I was also a confidante of his father. I've quietly met with heads of state, corporation CEOs, union leaders, military generals, religious leaders and even some unsavory characters that will forever remain nameless—all to negotiate for the welfare of this country that I love and serve. Because of my service, I rather thought I'd seen it all and was beyond being surprised. So when POTUS asked me to meet with the Ambassador of the Sodality Council, I readily agreed, thinking I would fly off to some Third World country that had just undergone a coup, or was about to. As usual, I inquired what message I was to convey or position to negotiate for. I was simply told that Ambassador Everett would brief me. Now here I am, not in some distant land, but in the middle of Arizona in your comfortable home, having just been sucked through a liquefied mirror and deposited in your hallway. Somehow I get the feeling you are going to completely undermine my arrogance of thinking I've seen it all..." He shook his head in amazement.

"Mr. Jones—I assume that is not your real name—please drink the mint tea." He pointed to a tray with a tea service. "FON travel can make you a bit queasy and the tea settles that right down. I use the FON almost daily and it still leaves me a bit out of sorts. And like you did, I count my fingers and toes—just to make sure."

George and Mr. Jones both chuckled and relaxed a bit.

"Being you were sent to meet with me, we assume you can be trusted and can handle matters without revealing our identities. Further, like the FON, we have many abilities well beyond the typical human and one of them can detect deception. You have been tested from the moment you arrived and the president has good reason to put his faith in you. And besides, if you told anyone, they would not believe you.

"For this evening, there simply is not time to explain our whole history and everything we can do, so I'll just say we are people—humans—who have inherited the gift of psionics: the ability to control and manipulate elements and energy with our minds. Centuries ago we were called witches, wizards, sorcerers and the like. And even today, some of our kind—especially in Europe—still refer to themselves that way. Our abilities have been called magic, spells, conjurations and curses. We, here, prefer to avoid such terms as it tends to evoke such negative prejudices. Also, we call folks without psionic (magic) abilities, Branglers. The FON travel you experienced is but a simple example of our technical abilities. We do what we can to be good citizens and use our abilities to help our neighbors, however, we strictly forbid open display and jealously guard our privacy and existence of our powers, for obvious reasons. Everyone would want us to magically solve their problems, win wars, create weapons, manufacture wealth, or influence the outcome of events or sports. Believe me, anyone who attempts to manipulate us in any way is quickly dealt with and the same goes for any Sodality who try to use their powers in forbidden ways."

"You mean *you* have mag—these abilities? Can you—?"

"Give you a little demonstration?" George chuckled. "Sure. My wife is much better at this than I. Your teacup needs refilling." He waved his hand and the teapot smoothly lifted off the silver service tray, floated over to Mr. Jones and poured out a refill of warm mint tea, then also filled George's cup before alighting back on the tray. All the while Jones stared, wide-eyed with his mouth agape.

"If anyone told me I'd watch such a thing—I saw it—and I still don't believe it—'cept it happened right before my eyes. I suppose that's just a tiny fraction of what you can do." Then he watched his spoon retrieve two lumps of sugar, drop them in his cup, stir gently then turn itself into a fork. "Oh my... Oh my..." he just kept repeating.

"We understand your astonishment. It is certainly natural. Occasionally we even surprise ourselves. Recently my twelve-year-old son displayed some abilities far beyond any my generation has ever done. Of course we teach: with great power comes even greater responsibilities."

"I believe the president would vouch for that. Now, shall we proceed with the briefing POTUS told me you'd provide? I'm sure he didn't arrange this meeting so I could watch a magic show."

"Well said," confirmed George. "The Sodality Council is a group of elected officials who govern and protect our people in regard to our special abilities throughout North, Central and South America, Japan, China and Africa. There is also a Ministry of Magic in England that serves Europe, Australia, Russia, the rest of Asia and the Middle East. We diligently conform our laws to parallel those of the countries in which we live, while also addressing topics specific to us. As with any community, we have those who choose to function outside the law. We aggressively pursue those individuals and if intervention fails then they are prosecuted and punished. Rarely do any of our people end up in Brangler courts; as you can imagine, regular jails and prisons are incapable of holding us. However, since we do co-mingle in almost every local community, some of our law-breakers' victims are Branglers and sometimes Branglers prey upon Sodality. As Sodality Ambassador to the Branglers, it is my job to work with trusted government representatives (or advisors) to resolve issues of mutual concern."

"Forgive me, Mr. Ambassador, but you sure seem to be taking a long turn about the bush."

"Yes, I suppose I am. Since this is your first exposure to us, I felt it would be helpful to give you some background into why some of our ways are strange—even secretive."

"In my position, secrets are a way of life—though I must admit y'all put a whole new perspective on the subject." Jones chuckled. "Shall we get down to business of whatever initial concern caused the president to send me through that amazing mirror?"

George told Mr. Jones of the missing dragon scale and the Council's conviction that the museum bombing was only a diversion to disguise the theft and not a terrorist plot—at least for the simple act of terrorism. As planned, he did not attempt to explain the magical properties of dragon scales, but Jones was quick enough to ask:

"Admittedly, I don't know about such things, but you say there are gold, silver, brass, bronze and copper scales on that shelf in the museum... Wouldn't they be more valuable than the blue?"

"That's not always the case—the most rare are reds, but you are right, many are more valuable than the blue. We don't have an answer, except that the blue was the only specimen with more than one. Maybe the thief hoped that would forestall discovery of his deed. Please believe, this is something we are thoroughly investigating. Somehow, I don't think we've heard the last of this incident."

"How can I help?"

"First, please fully brief the president. There's no need for the FBI and CIA to be chasing foreign terrorists. With resources turned in other directions, we hope leads will help us find who did this—and more importantly, why. We have investigators who are also loyal FBI, ATF and CIA agents. If you can arrange to keep them assigned to this case, it will be mutually advantageous."

"You can consider it done. However, al Qaeda is already being blamed. I believe it serves both of us to leave that public perception in place."

"You are probably right."

* * *

"Hey, Brian," called J.J.'s cheerful voice. Brian turned to see his brother's beaming face and bright red hair approaching with a bounce in his step.

"What's got you so happy?" asked Brian, closing and warding his locker in the main concourse. "Didn't you just have history? After I finish an hour with Antetima, I feel like the joy of life has been sucked right out of me—like those demety-whatsits we read about that are in Europe."

"Well, that's just it." J.J. opened his locker and switched books for his next class: elemental physics. "Antetima's taken an extended leave and a Professor Elizabeth Preterit is filling in."

"Yahoo!" exclaimed Brian. "What's *extended* mean? Maybe the next ten years, I hope!"

"No such luck. Professor Preterit seems to think she'll be back after Christmas holiday or Spring Break at the latest."

"Well, we'll enjoy it while it lasts—hmmm, *Preterit*, that sounds familiar. I've heard that name before."

"You should! She wrote the history texts we've been studying."

"Oh, yeah. What's she like?"

"Hey, it's history—bo-oring! But she tries to make it interesting. Preterit has really traveled a lot and she tries to weave some of her experiences into the lessons—at least, she did for our form's class."

"After lunch, I have History and for once I'm actually looking forward to it. I wonder what's up with Antetima?"

"Yeah, me, too. None of my class can remember her missing a day for any reason."

The history classroom looked much the same when Brian sat in his usual desk at the back, however, he noticed some subtle differences. The teacher's desk was no longer on a raised dais in front but was on floor-level and moved to the side—near the windows. The drab, empty bulletin boards were adorned with colorful travel posters from various parts of the world. As the bell rang, a hush came over the students who were whispering: "I wonder what she's like?" "What happened to Antetima?" "Ooo, the room looks more cheery." "Who is Roger Johnson going out with now?" "How long's the sub gonna be with us?" "Did she really write the text?" Everyone became silent as a very frail-looking woman entered from the side, office door. She was tall, thin and smartly outfitted in a colorful dress that fit her perfectly. Her long brown hair was pulled back and tied with a bright ribbon. She wore no glasses but one could almost make out the glistening edge of contact lenses on her large, cheerful eyes. If she were younger, the professor could have easily been a fashion model.

"Good afternoon, ladies and gentlemen," announced a kind, firm voice that gave no hint of advanced age or weakness. "I am Professor Elizabeth Preterit. We will be enjoying each other's company for the next few weeks as we explore the wonders of our history and exciting heritage." There were a few grumbles of dissent. "Now, now," she continued. "I was not a history buff when I was young, and yes, it can be quite boring. But bear with me. I rather think you'll find we have a fascinating past filled with intrigue, wars and the triumph of good over evil.

"Many of you have wondrous family experiences that can add much to our discussions. I hope you'll share them to liven up our studies. I encourage questions and participation, however, I insist on respect and politeness. We never scoff at or belittle anyone's comments..."

Wow, thought Brian, *I might actually like this class*. While the syllabus was distributed, the instructor continued to review her plans and expectations for the coming weeks.

About halfway through the class a First-Form young boy opened the hallway door and excitedly announced, "Excuse me, Professor, Brian Everett is needed in Nurse Mederi's office!" He handed a folded note to Preterit, who quickly scanned it and held it out.

"Mr. Everett, please gather your things and follow this young man; take this note with you. I hope all is well."

Brian was up and moving before the professor ended her sentence, threw his books in his bag, almost tripped in his haste to take the note and catch up with the first-former who was already out of the door. Still moving, he slung his book bag over his shoulder and unfolded the note, which read: Brian Everett to report to CKS Clinic ASAP re: W. Hill, signed: *N. Mederi...* His mind was spinning. *Why would I be called if Willard is hurt or sick?* He tried to reach out to the young orphan with mind-speak, but he was blocked.

"Do you know what's going on?" he called to his young escort.

"We were in math class and Willard cried out in pain, grabbed the back of his neck, then broke out in a sweat. Professor Abacist asked me to escort him to the nurse and while she questioned him he kept asking for you. Then she sent me with the note. I don't know more. Sorry."

"Well, that makes two of us. I don't know why he'd want me, either," said Brian as they arrived at the open double doors of the school clinic.

"Thank you, Andersen; you may go back to class," Brian heard from inside a curtained-off examination area. "Come in, Everett," called the nurse's commanding voice.

Brian took a deep breath and followed the sound of Mederi's voice and stepped between an opening in the curtains that hung from a track on the ceiling. Inside, he saw a padded exam table, white cabinets with glass doors, a big swivel lamp hanging from the ceiling, and Nurse Mederi in her starched white uniform, sitting on a wheeled stool. Willard was stiffly sitting on the end of the table with his legs dangling motionless, looking pitifully distressed and pale, with his eyes closed.

"Andersen told you what occurred with Mr. Hill in math class," she stated—not as a question. Brian nodded. "I have examined him and cannot find anything wrong except a bit of tenderness on the back of his neck. He just keeps asking for you. Since he is orphaned," she began to speak more softly and compassionately, "maybe he will talk to you. He seems quite frightened." She stood and began to walk out. "I'll be at my desk if you want anything. I've been a seminary nurse here for a long time. He has nothing to fear or be embarrassed about. Please assure him we are here to help."

"Yes, Ma'am, I'll try," he said to her retreating uniform that crackled with stiffness. As soon as she was gone Brian felt the connection with Willard come alive.

Hey, Wil, what's up? Are you okay? projected Brian.

I—I don't know. Professor Abacist was talking about current events—

Yeah, he likes to do that, interrupted Brian.

He showed us pictures of the smoky mess at the ruins of the World Trade Center. All of a sudden the back of my neck hurt. It scared me— kinda like something was under my skin. Then I felt really angry— like I wanted to go hunt down the evil bad guys who did that stuff. Willard's color was slowly coming back.

I'm glad you didn't go after al Qaeda, teased Brian. *I think you're a bit young for that. Are you feeling better now?*

Yep. By the time I got to the clinic, it mostly went away.

Are you sure? Why don't you let the nurse check you one more time. Then we can get out of here.

Okay.

"Ms. Mederi?" called Brian. "I think he's okay now. You can check him again." A few seconds later the starched uniform rustled back into the curtained area.

"He just had a pain in his neck, but it scared him. He's still struggling to trust people. I'm sure you understand."

"Of course—after what he went through, being all alone in the wild..." She expertly felt along Willard's neck and back. "Yes, the muscles are still tense. I'll apply some healing balm and he'll be fine. Sometimes young people have aches and pains when they go through growth spurts." She went to the cabinet and retrieved a jar of some foul-smelling cream and rubbed it in. "There, that should do the trick."

"Thank you," said Willard meekly. "It does feel better."

"Uh, Ms. Mederi?" said Brian hesitantly. "Do you have something to help the smell? If he goes to class like that, they'll tease him terribly."

"Oh, sure!" She waved her hand and the odor vanished. "By the way, I was far away enough to give you privacy, but there weren't even any mumbles. How did you do the shield? I couldn't detect that, either."

"We didn't shield. Since Wil spends so much time with us, we learned a silent way to communicate; drives my parents crazy." Brian laughed. He didn't want to lie to the nurse, but for now their mind-speaking was a family secret.

"You may go to your classes. I will write a report and send a copy to the group home and your parents—"

"You only need to send it to our house. They're still remodeling the group home and Willard is staying with us."

"Oh yes, I saw something on that. I applaud your mother's efforts to organize such a project. I'm sure it will be much nicer when they are finished."

"Mom is going crazy—she's up there every day. The house is in the middle of all those Victorian homes on a busy street in Prescott so psionics can't be used, and she can't understand why the contractors are so slow."

"When it's all done, it will be worth it—I happily donated. Now off you go."

"The bell's about to ring." Brian looked up at a big clock on the wall of the school's main concourse. "It's too late for you to go back to math. What's your next class?"

"With Professor Heady," said Willard. Brian stopped dead in his tracks.

"I thought you went there in the mornings. Now is the Advanced class J.J. and I attend."

"My schedule changed today." Willard reached into the pocket of his jeans and retrieved a folded paper and handed it to Brian. He unfolded it and saw it was a CKS class schedule update. He had been reassigned and was now in the afternoon Advanced Psionics class. The hallway was filling with students heading to their next classes.

"Wow! You're right." He handed the paper back. "Professor H. must feel you're quite ready; he's real fussy about anyone transferring into our class. Let's go."

"Are you mad at me?"

"No! Why?"

"For getting you out of class and now the schedule change."

"I'd never be mad about getting out of history—even if we have a new teacher. I've always thought you'd do better in the Advanced Psionics class. It's okay with me." Brian kicked off a fast-walking pace that Willard almost had to run to keep up with. Soon they were descending the stairwell to the lower level (that students were now calling The Dungeon).

"Welcome, Mr. Hill, to Advanced Psionics class," announced Professor Heady with his distinctive British accent. "You have been moved up because other faculty and I have recognized some special abilities which may develop better in this environment. You are expected to work hard to catch up with your new classmates. I will not hesitate to send you back if you slack off. Agreed?"

"Yes, Professor," said Willard with his meek voice.

"Right then—"

"Professor?"

"You have a question, M'Lord—maybe you wish to add a word of welcome? Hmm?"

"You told us to bring up anything unusual. Last period Wil had to go to the nurse with strange pains in his neck and he became really angry when he saw the pictures of the Trade Center— Ground Zero they call it—"

"Wasn't it the other way around?" he asked the small boy. "You became angry then felt the pains? Hmm?"

"Yes, Professor."

"Yes, of course—that's to be expected. Nasty business that. People everywhere are having ill effects. One of the reasons you are in this class—all of you—is to learn to control your emotions in crisis or faced with powerful evil forces. In that way you can effectively choose how to respond best. Sometimes the wisest choice is to do nothing at the moment so proper response may be planned."

Certainly what the professor said was true, but Brian felt there was also something—a very big something—he knew but was not telling them...

Chapter Fourteen
Another Everett

"This is the most incredibly complicated formula I have ever attempted," said the deep bass voice of the tall man wearing the floor-length black robes. He was standing in a basement laboratory underneath his castle-appearing mansion located in the Mount Greylock area near Adams, Massachusetts. "We started after getting the dragon scale in late September, and now it's nearing Christmas."

"We've gone over every detail a thousand times," said the squat woman with her high-pitched voice.

"We've even made two duplicate batches to make sure we have a backup—and they're identical," said the tall man's faithful lieutenant. "I cannot think of any safeguards we've overlooked."

"Of course all our assumptions are based on Mendacci actually getting the formula correct," countered Reficul. "What makes us think he succeeded when, over the centuries, so many have failed?"

"Only his family's history of making power rings and he certainly seemed convinced when I probed his mind. His only problem was getting ahold of the dragon scale."

There was an uncomfortable silence as the tall Black Knights leader clasped his hands behind his back and slowly paced about the lab's confines—deep in thought. Back and forth he walked. The only sound was his shoes treading the large flat stones of the floor and the soft bubbling of the three identical formula concoctions. The laboratory was fairly modern with glass tubes, beakers, distillation units, digital scales and vented exhaust hoods, so the three matching cauldrons heated by blue wizard's fire seemed quite out of place. However, the ancient formula used cauldrons so Mendacci included them in his notes. Reficul meant to insure nothing of modern technology could alter the process. He even stirred the contents clockwise thirteen times and seven times counterclockwise. He would leave no detail to chance—no matter how small or seemingly trivial.

Several times the black-robed man stopped in front of the gurgling vessels while Laileb absently opened an ancient leather-bound book lying at the end of the lab bench. He gingerly turned the brittle vellum pages that were full of scripted writings, notes and formulas that had been passed down from Merlin through his eldest son (who became the first Black Knight). The discovery of the tome was almost accidental: At the suggestion of the seminary professor, they scoured Reficul's vast library collection for writings—especially for books—written by Merlin himself so they could compare Mendacci's formula against the famed wizard's unique style of assembly. The book was quite a find and happily it contained many notes that appeared to be Merlin's early attempts to infuse elements to create a master ring. Mendacci's formula was comfortingly similar and gave them even more confidence to proceed.

Their waiting and wondering was almost over. Laileb looked up and saw the countdown digital clock, on a shelf above the cauldrons, showed 1:30: one-and-a-half minutes until they would each pour in the precisely-measured last ingredient: ground shavings from the blue dragon scale. Laileb, Genoveve and Reficul each stood in front of a bubbling mixture, picked up a vial containing the blue powder and stared at the clock. 1:00 (one minute to go). Collectively they almost stopped breathing. 0:30 (30 seconds). It was almost time. In a few seconds they expected to finish the most sought-after infusion formula of all time. 0:10, 0:09, 0:08, 0:07, 0:06, 0:05. 0:04, 0:03, 0:02, 0:01, 0:00... They all tipped over their vials.

Simultaneously brilliant blue sparks arose from the three cauldrons along with big, glurpy, thick bubbles that popped loudly when they reached the surface. Genoveve and Laileb jumped back to avoid being splattered by the expanding glops or burned by the pyrotechnics, but Reficul stood mesmerized, still holding his hands over the brew as if being warmed. Then a big bubble arose and burst, sending a spray of thick, dark blue droplets onto his hands. He jumped back just as a large dollop hit his mage power ring.

Laileb and Genoveve shuddered and covered their ears as a bolt of blue lightning streaked through the room, accompanied by an ear-splitting explosion of thunder. The walls shook; beakers and glassware shattered. The three cauldrons rocked back and forth, spilling their contents on the lab bench, floor, and Reficul, who screamed as he was enveloped in a cloud of hazy blue smoke which still had bright, brilliant sky-blue sparks. Both Reficul's minions started to run to his rescue but suddenly a vortex of wind spiraled up from the open book of Merlin's writings. The whirling cone grew and snaked over to the blue cloud that seemed to have completely dissolved the Black Knight. The cloudy mist was sucked into the vortex like it was a vacuum cleaner, and then into the book.

With a flap, the book closed itself and there was utter silence, eerie nothingness. Reficul was gone. His faithful aides stood in shock with their hands over their gaping mouths.

*   *   *

"What's wrong, Mom?" asked Brian. He had been eating an after school snack of grapes, granola bars and apples. Sitting in the kitchen, he watched his mother fixing supper. But instead of her usual organized perfection, she was hurrying from place to place, banging things around, mumbling to herself, and hardly using any psionics.

"With the weather and winter temperatures in Prescott, the contractors now tell me the group home won't be finished until after the first of the year!" she said with considerable contempt in her voice. "If they had not been so slow, we would have been done before winter! They are so inept!"

"Wow, Mom, why don't you tell us how you really feel?" J.J. laughed and looked around the kitchen table at Brian and Willard. He hesitated, studying Willard for a moment, for he saw more than a smile at his sarcasm. The youngster seemed relieved to hear the re-opening of the group home would be delayed.

Myrna caught her (adopted) son's humored jab, chuckled with the others and slowed down some. "I guess I haven't been very patient. Sometimes it's hard for me to deal with things in the Brangler world. I don't know how your father does it—in his new assignment."

"How I do what?" George's voice came from the door to the hallway.

"Hey, Dad!" Brian jumped up and met his father with a hug as he entered the kitchen. He backed up as J.J. took his place, then Willard.

"I was just venting my frustration about dealing with things in Brangler world—not being able to use psionics." Brian watched his mother walk up and give her husband a kiss and embrace. "You're home a bit early—there are some snacks on the table if you're hungry. It'll be a while before supper."

"Would it be a bother to fix supper for a few more? We need to go over a few things with Grandma James, Paul, your parents and mine."

"It's a bit of short notice, but it's no problem." She broke away and went right to work—she was in her element and now a model of efficiency.

"C'mon, boys, let's get out of the way." He backed out with Brian, J.J. and Willard in tow. "I'll send Nichole in to help."

"Uh, Dad," said J.J., "can I talk to you—in your study?"

"Sure. Give me a few minutes to contact your grandmother and the others."

"Mom, can you take a break for a couple of minutes?" asked J.J. from the kitchen door. "I'd like to talk to you and Dad—he's waiting for me in the study."

"Everything's cooking—Nicki can watch it for a few minutes." She wiped her hands on her apron and followed the short, red-haired boy. Once in George's home office, J.J. closed the door and waved his hand to set a privacy ward, then sat on a chair next to the desk. He looked down as his hands fidgeting in his lap.

"I feel funny bringing this up—you've been so wonderful to take me in and adopt me..."

"Son, you're family and have been since long before the adoption," said Dad reassuringly. "Whatever you have on your mind, you feel it's important so it's important to us."

"We're about to break a little boy's heart!" he said without preamble, then went on to describe the look he saw in Willard's eyes when it became clear the reopening of the group home would be delayed. "Wil has now lived with a family who has loved and cared about him—a real family. He's feeling the same thing I did after my parents died. It was easy for me to stay here instead of with Grandma and even easier to be adopted and have Everett as my last name, but don't you see?" Tears were streaming down his cheeks. "No matter how good you make the group home, he'll never feel wanted and loved like he's experienced here. I know I'm asking a lot, especially since you—"

"Don't finish that sentence, Jeremy," said George with firmness. "I said you are family, regardless of how that came about. You are just as much entitled to bring something to our attention as Nichole or Brian."

"Oh, honey." J.J. was gathered in Myrna's arms. "I never realized... I've been so involved in the remodeling and raising money, it never occurred to me."

"Sometimes a kindness is not so kind if it has to be taken away," said George. "Hmm, that's a tall order, son. I guess I know how you'd vote if I called a family meeting." J.J. simply nodded his head, still wrapped in Myrna's embrace, who also nodded her agreement.

"Go ask Nichole to come visit with me—and then Brian. If everyone agrees, I'll call Social Services and see what they say. Then I'll talk to Willard. I don't want to get his hopes up if there's some legal problem." He reached in his pocket, pulled out a handkerchief and handed it to J.J. "You better dry your eyes or Nicki and Brian will think something is wrong."

Brian was finishing his third helping of hot cherry pie with ice cream as he watched his father stand to indicate the family meeting was to begin. The various muted conversations ended and eleven people expectantly waited for George to start.

"Sometimes unexpected things happen quite fast—as they did today—so instead of one announcement we have two. We'll start with the second as it tends to affect the arrangements for the first. Jeremy brought to our attention something we were being a bit oblivious to. So, with some fast negotiations we are now officially Willard's foster family—"

The whole room broke into pandemonium, cheers and applause along with several unabashed tears—especially from Willard.

"Dad, you said foster family," interjected Brian when calm resumed. "When you talked to us earlier you suggested adoption—like J.J."

"After checking with Social Services, we can immediately become his foster parents—which we have done. Adoption will be available once they are sure he has no other family. We're going to adopt—just as soon as he's cleared."

"Oh, that's okay, then. What about his name?"

"Willard Hill was just a name Social Services gave him because he kept saying Weezer Hill. He had no official name until now. Like Jeremy, Willard asked that all his paperwork be submitted as Willard Hill Everett—even the foster parent-child documents have been registered that way." There was more applause and congratulations offered.

"While we are gone, Sodality contractors are going to remodel the house and add a new room for Nichole. Jeremy will move into her old room and Willard will go into the room next to Brian—"

"Wait a minute, Dad," interrupted Nicki. "You went by that *while we are gone* part just a bit fast. Where are *we* going?"

"You caught that, did you?" George laughed. "Well, that's the other announcement. After seminary lets out tomorrow we are going to New York City for the holidays. There's the Vice Chairman Swearing-in ceremony, reception and other events we must attend, because of my new responsibilities. And, I hear New York is fantastic during the holidays."

Another round of excited applause erupted.

"Where are we staying?" asked Brian.

"Mr. Jones, our White House contact, has arranged a suite of rooms at the Plata Hotel. All first-class treatment."

"How are we getting there?"

"Technicians are installing a FON mirror as we speak. We considered flying commercial but the major airlines are still a mess from September 11th."

"Whoa," quipped J.J. "Won't the hotel folks get just a wee bit suspicious if a dozen people walk into their rooms through a liquefied mirror?"

"C'mon, Son, give us a little credit." George chuckled. "Mr. Jones has been quite helpful. He thought we might enjoy some Brangler travel that my Ambassador and SVC status warrants. He has arranged for a Gulfstream G-500 jet to fly us to La Guardia airport and then a limousine to take us to the hotel. The FON mirror is mostly for me to get back and forth to the Redoubt and for your grandparents and others to keep checking on the house and remodeling contractors. Also, we have arranged for all the domestics assigned to our rooms to be Sodality."

"All right, Pops," teased J.J. "You did pretty good for old folks."

"This is fantastic!" exclaimed Brian as he stepped out of the stretch limousine onto the tarmac at Prescott airport and spied the gleaming white jet. Classes had let out early for the holidays so it was only 2:00p.m. Most of their luggage had been sent ahead via UTS so they each carried only a small bag with a few personal items. Brian's backpack was slung over his left shoulder.

As the rest of the family exited the limos (it took two to transport all twelve) Brian watched a tall, thin, pilot-uniformed man approach his father.

"Ambassador Everett, I am Captain Gil Newton. We're scheduled for wheels-up at two-fifteen. I was told your luggage was sent ahead—that you only have light carry-ons. Your co-pilot is Ron King (we call him "Sky"), and cabin attendant is Marlene. Whenever you are ready, they will help you board and get settled. I will be making our final pre-flight inspections. If you need anything at all, please let us know."

Brian watched the pilot turn and ascend the steps of the air-stair door. Then he and his family followed, except Grandma James trailed behind, pausing to speak momentarily with Sky and Marlene.

Brian, Nicki, J.J. and Willard chose seats that faced each other directly across [the center aisle] from their parents, near the front. As Grandma James walked by, she bent down to speak to George and Myrna. He heard her say (softly): "The pilot and co-pilot are okay but there's something the attendant is very nervous about. She's not focusing on it right now, so I can't confirm if it involves us or the flight."

"I'll delay the departure. See if you can get her to focus. This plane doesn't move until we're sure." He unbuckled his seat belt and went forward to the cockpit. Brian could barely hear his father. "Captain, we need to hold for a few minutes while we check a possible security problem."

"I assure you, Ambassador, King and I are fully cleared—even to fly Air Force One."

"And Marlene?"

"She's not flying the plane, but I admit she's not on my usual roster. Everyone is usually screened pretty thoroughly."

"Everything may be fine. Just hold for a few minutes while we verify a couple of things, please."

"Per my orders, you're the boss. We'll wait until you give clearance."

"Please announce on your intercom: 'Our departure is delayed—we are awaiting additional clearance.' Thank you."

Brian watched his father return to his seat, speak quietly with Myrna as the cabin speakers made the announcement. Grandma James waved her arm and called: "Marlene, what's wrong?" She sounded agitated. "Is something wrong with the plane? Is there a bomb?"

"Oh, please," implored the attendant. "I'm sure everything is fine. Please, Mrs. James, we've carefully inspected this aircraft. There's no bomb aboard."

"Are you sure?" Grandma James sounded almost frantic. "Did the captain look everywhere and check everything?"

"It's my job to check the cabin. The captain inspected everything else."

"Oh, that's okay, then, as long as you can vouch for everything in the cabin." Grandma heaved a sigh of relief, stood and walked to George, then whispered in his ear.

He nodded, then called loudly, "Captain Newton, please come back into the cabin." The tall, sandy-haired pilot emerged from the cockpit area. George continued: "We understand you did not personally inspect the cabin area."

"That's correct. The attendant does that while we attend to the flight systems, mechanicals and flight plan."

"Would you please check the forward area—especially the bulkhead above the galley?" Brian knew his father could become stern when dealing with business and at work, but he'd never seen this side. His dad was being authoritative—even imposing, without any hint of the soft-spoken, somewhat geeky, family man.

Moments later the captain returned with a small black object that had a long wire attached. "I found this—it's a video camera lens that was attached to a recorder." He handed a video disk and the device to George. "You're in charge, Ambassador. I'll report this when we land in New York—or shall I order a new plane?"

"One moment." George stood. "Marlene, tell me why you are recording me and my family."

"Ambassador," she decried, "you have no proof—"

"Let's not play that game. I already know when and how you planted it. Now we *will* figure out the rest. Make it easy—why?"

"For the money," she said dejectedly. Her shoulders dropped and she began to sob into her hands.

"Who is paying you?" asked George firmly, but trying to sound kindly.

"I don't know his name, but it's somebody trying to find out about your connection to the White House; to discredit the president in the next election. I was told to remember anything you say about your job or the president."

"Are there any more recording devices on this plane—or is there any danger if we continue with this aircraft?"

"No, except this." She reached into her uniform pocket and produced a very small, light gray mini-recorder.

"That's it?" George took the small electronic device. "Nothing more?"

"Nothing more, Ambassador." She stared at the floor in shame. "I'm sorry! Please believe me. I just needed the money. My husband left and I'm trying to support my baby boy."

George looked at Grandma James, who nodded to indicate she was telling the truth. There was an uncomfortable silence while he considered the whole situation. Then he spoke, surprising everyone. "Brian, walk up and down the whole length of the plane.

Touch the right hands of Mr. King, Captain Newton and Marlene. Touch the body of the cabin in several places. Be very alert to any warnings Monēo might give you."

"Okay..." Brian released his lap belt, stood and did exactly as his father instructed, then reported, "Nothing at all!"

"I concur," added Grandma James.

"Marlene, do you want to get off here or go on to New York?"

"Please, sir, I live in New York. I'll continue as attendant, if you'll have me."

"Fine. Captain, let's get in the air. Do not report anything yet. I want to talk with my family and think about how I want this handled. Agreed?"

"As I said, you're the boss. I'll call in a revised flight plan with the delayed departure. Then we'll get underway."

"Thank you!" Marlene wept with shame and relief. After a long moment she recovered. "Please, everyone be seated and fasten your seatbelts."

Brian was fascinated as she described the safety features, emergency exits and oxygen system. He especially took note of the gourmet supper she would serve later in the flight. "And Master Brian, we were told you have a rather large appetite. We've included some extra servings just for you." His ears went pink and cheeks blushed.

"This plane can't hold that much," teased J.J. Then they all tensed up as the jet engines spooled up to a roar and the sleek Gulfstream took to the air.

"My apologies for the delay," said the Captain over the intercom. "We've got great weather and a smooth flight ahead."

Chapter Fifteen
The Little Bodyguard

Wisps of blue smoke still hung in the air as the smell of ozone from the lightning discharge penetrated the entire room. Laileb and Genoveve remained rooted in the same spot they were in when Reficul was dissolved by the cloudy mist and sucked into the book. They studied the carnage: broken glass was scattered on the bench and floor. Thick glops of the cauldrons' contents [that splashed out] oozed into puddles like Jell-o melting among the shards of glass.

"What happened?" whispered Laileb, seemingly afraid to speak aloud.

"I don't know," said the short woman—just as quietly. "Surely this was not the intended result."

"No, I don't think so. Any ideas where he went?"

"Maybe the more important question: Can he come back?" She cautiously stepped forward, picking her way between the broken glass and glops of syrupy formula until she reached the end of the granite-covered lab bench where the ancient book still lay closed. She saw a bit of debris between two pages and gently opened the tome to that spot. "I don't remember seeing this page before," she observed, and began to carefully examine the old wizard's writings. "Of course, we didn't study every page."

"What does it say?" Laileb started to exactly follow the woman's steps—gingerly avoiding the wreckage strewn across the stone floor until he stood behind and looked over her shoulder at the page she was viewing.

"There's a large drawing of a round seal named *Sigillum De Aemeth* and a discussion on travel to other dimensions or realms."

"Do you think that's where he went?" he asked with worry and awe in his voice.

"I don't know," she almost cried. "It says an inanimate object must be inscribed with the seal to form a gateway—" She took her hands away from the book and stepped back—bumping into Laileb. "Maybe this seal and book is a gate."

"That'd be my guess, but what opens it? It's obviously closed now. We must find a way to reopen it and bring Master back," insisted Laileb.

"We don't even know where or which one he went to—even if we opened the gate. There are hundreds of dimensions and realms—maybe thousands."

"Maybe there's a way to open the gate and discover the destination of the last one who passed through. We need to carefully go through every page of this book—we're *not* giving up! No matter how long it takes!"

"Ever faithful—that's you. But you're right. And we need to go back through his library again to see if we can find any other information."

"I'm going to find some paint. Before we move that book, let's mark its exact position—just in case location is critical to reopening the gate to wherever he went."

"You do that. In the meantime, I'm going to call up some of the other Black Knights to have them help clean up this mess, assist in the research, and make sure our other activities are being carried on."

"You—we—don't have authority to do that."

"The Master is gone; we don't know for how long. Someone must keep things going. When he comes back, it would be terrible if the Organization is all in shambles for lack of leadership." She turned and retraced her steps until she exited the lab and went upstairs—without giving Laileb a chance to object further—except he heard from the doorway: "As you said, we mustn't do anything that could possibly interfere with bringing him back. Do not use any psionics to clear up the lab!" she commanded.

"Who does she think she is?" he mumbled almost silently as he tip-toed around to find some paint. "Just 'cuz she's been a Knight longer than me. I've been his most faithful; doing some of the hardest assignments—"

"You would do well to remember Master had put in closed circuit cameras *and microphones* to monitor the lab—and an intercom." Genoveve's high-pitched voice crackled from the wall-mounted speaker. Laileb tensed and a cold chill went through his body. "Any time you wish to challenge my seniority, please let me know. In the meantime, there's something up here you should see."

Laileb did remember—it had been his idea. He had pushed long and hard to convince Reficul to have the equipment installed. Generally, he was against any mingling of Brangler technology and Sodality psionics.

* * *

"Welcome to the Plata Hotel, Ambassador Everett. I am Sebastian Abbott, General Manager," said an impeccably-dressed man with grey hair and wire-rimmed glasses. Brian watched him walk with a steady pace, leading the family through the hotel lobby toward the elevators—bypassing the check-in counter. "Your registration has been taken care of; your luggage arrived earlier and is in suite." As they entered the elevator he pulled a plastic card from his pocket, inserted it in a slot above the rows of floor buttons and said, "The presidential suite and accompanying rooms are on a secured floor and accessible only by a coded card." He passed out cards to each of the family. "The system is reprogrammed every day and new cards issued." Brian felt his feet press into the floor as the car began to ascend swiftly. "Only the domestics sent by your office will enter your rooms, and your team of technicians just finished making the custom installations." They exited the elevator and walked to an ornamental iron gate manned by a security officer wearing a gold blazer with the hotel's monogram embroidered on the breast pocket. "Your cards are also needed to pass this gate." There was an audible click and buzzing sound as the agent used his keycard to unlock the door.

"Is all this necessary?" Brian heard his grandfather ask as the gate closed solidly behind them with a firm clack.

"We don't always man the gate, Mr. Deering." (Abbott was obviously well-briefed.) "But we heard your security has already been challenged today. That won't happen in this hotel." He slid the same card into another slot to unlock the wide double doors of the Presidential Suite. As they walked in, Brian's mouth fell open. The suite was huge—with an elegant living room, dining area, study, kitchen and bedrooms on two floors. "As requested, the main suite will accommodate the Ambassador and Mrs. Everett in the master bedroom. Ms. James and Miss Nicole also have rooms on this level. Masters Jeremy, Brian and Willard share rooms upstairs, and Mr. Paul Everett is also on the second level. Mr. and Mrs. Deering have a separate, but adjoining suite on the left. Mr. and Mrs. Everett on the right." Just then four men and four women filed in and stood formally in a line. The women were all dressed in black maid uniforms with white aprons and the men wore black suits with long tails. "Two housekeepers and two valet/butlers will be on duty at all times—twenty-four hours a day. They are husband and wife teams and have rooms across the hall."

Another man joined the line of personnel. Brian saw he was dressed in a stiffly-starched chef's doublet. "A full-time chef is also on staff, and of course room service is on call if he is not available. I may be contacted at any time if there's anything—"

"You have been most helpful." Brian watched his father dismiss the talkative manager. "It's late and we have a busy day tomorrow."

"Of course, Ambassador. Good evening." He turned and silently exited through the double doors, closing them behind him.

After some quick introductions (and being instructed the valets were called by their last names and housekeepers by first) everyone was shown to their rooms where their luggage had been unpacked. Brian immediately noticed there were platters of fruit, finger sandwiches and pots of steaming hot cocoa. He and his brothers laughed when they noticed the pile of food on Brian's platter was almost twice the amount on the other two.

"Well, they did their research!" observed J.J. as Brian tucked into a ham sandwich half. "Couldn't you wait until you took off your jacket? Benson there is waiting to hang it up!" He pointed to the suited valet waiting patiently.

"I'm hungry!" protested Brian.

"You're always hungry!" said J.J. and Willard in unison, and they all laughed—even Benson. They removed their coats and the valet deftly waved his hand. The garments flew to the closet and settled perfectly on separate hangers.

"Hey, that's cool," said Brian, picking up a handful of grapes. "I could only do one at a time."

"Like most things, practice, practice," said Benson with a distinctly British accent.

"Hey, Benson," said J.J., "you're wearing a mage ring—I thought the English use wands."

"Aye, we do, though many of us are starting to use rings as well. I've trained with both."

"You're a skilled mage—wizard. Why are you our butler?"

"You would be surprised. When word came about these positions, many queued up; a trip to New York, good pay and excellent accommodations. And being part of your da's staff— the Ambassador—is an honor. A chance to do our bit for the cause."

"But Dad is just Sodality Ambassador to the Branglers. It's not that big a deal," said Brian.

"What's this? Don't you know?"

"Know what?"

"Your da—the ceremony tomorrow. Surely you know—I am to have you all dressed up to go."

"Oh, that, yeah. Dad's gettin' an award or something. He gets 'em all the time. But this is the first time we're all going."

"Oh no, this is much more than an award. The Ambassador—your da is being raised Vice Chairman."

"He did say something like that," commented J.J., "but I guess I wasn't listening very well."

"Me, either," added Brian. "Wil, did you know all that?"

"I think so, but I haven't learned that much about our government yet."

"But you did know it was another big promotion—to become Vice Chairman?"

"Yes," he said meekly.

"Wow!" exclaimed J.J. "No wonder there's so much security."

"Whaddaya mean?" asked Brian.

"Dad's gonna be next in line for Chairman!"

"Oh..."

"Great man, your da," said Benson reverently. "He'll be Chairman one day, mark my words. Soon, maybe. Me and the Missus are proud to serve your family. Now, young gentlemen, I've laid out your bed clothes and dressing gowns. Leave your soiled things at the foot of your beds and they'll be laundered tonight. I'll wake you early. Your mum wants you scrubbed before breakfast." He turned and left the room, closing the door softly behind him.

At breakfast the next morning the atmosphere was heavy. The usual light-hearted quips between Brian, J.J. and Willard were non-existent and the adults, especially George, seemed lost in thought—thinking about the new responsibilities and how everyone in the family would be affected. Even Brian, who by most standards ate a hearty breakfast, sat brooding; only twice visiting the excellent breakfast buffet.

"You're awfully quiet," observed Dad.

"Are we gonna have to move?" Brian glared at his father with frustration and resignation.

"Whatever gave you that idea?"

"You've always said how the chairman and vice chairman have much of the same responsibilities as the president and vice president. They live in the White House and Naval Observatory."

"No, the Chairman and I live at our homes. With FON and translocation we can be almost anywhere in the world within seconds. There is no need to have special residences for us."

"But I thought you said the house we went to for the Chairman's investiture is owned by the Council."

"It is. The Council keeps a house near the Redoubt for special functions—like today. Occasionally we may spend a day or two there if we have foreign visitors to host."

"That's okay, then!" Brian smiled, jumped up and filled a clean plate from the buffet with fried eggs, biscuits, sausage gravy, bacon strips and a cantaloupe wedge while Benson removed the plate he'd just finished. He noticed everyone watching as he sat down. "What? I'm hungry!"

"YOU'RE ALWAYS HUNGRY!" said eleven voices in unison, then laughed as he blushed and unabashedly tucked into the eggs.

The reception line had been long—at least it seemed that way to three impatient young men as they endured handshakes, shoulder and head patting, hair tousling, cheek kisses, and congratulations in dozens of languages. Brian spied the last of the well-wishers, a huge, middle-aged man who was wider than he was tall, no neck, wart-covered skin and wearing a suit that was barely able to button across the middle. Brian chuckled to himself, thinking of a comedy movie with a character "Pizza the Hut." The large man passed with a curt nod to the boys and the rest of the family, aiming only to greet Vice Chairman Everett, Sodality's second most politically powerful person throughout North, Central and South America, Africa, China and Japan. As he approached George, Brian felt a cold chill. Monēo was giving a warning! But there were so many people about—it could be anyone...

"Dad!" he called out sharply. "Monēo showed up!" That was their prearranged signal. Suddenly Brian was pushed aside; Willard was moving quickly to insert himself between their father and the large man.

It was an unbelievable sight—almost comical. An undersized eleven-year-old boy stood defiantly in front of a huge man who dwarfed most adults in the room. Brian could see Willard was in distress as he uncomfortably adjusted his head and neck and had the pool of a tear in his lower eyelids. But still he remained solidly rooted; staring at the wide man.

A silence started to spread around the room as onlookers began to notice the unusual showdown. Brian could not just watch. He immediately pushed over to the scene, with J.J. right alongside. They took up positions behind their little brother—also in front of their dad.

"You have an unusual security team, Mr. Vice Chairman," said the man; his voice almost a whisper, but never breaking eye contact with Willard.

"My sons tend to be very protective when they sense any possible threat."

"Is that so? Surely you don't suspect me?" He tried a disarming smile.

"I'm sorry," said George with his tone of authority. "I don't think we've met. Who are you?" From the corners of his eyes Brian saw security agents closing in around the family.

"Someone who does not appreciate being challenged by children!" The man huffed, turned and swept out of the room, rudely pushing people out of his way.

Willard started to follow the man but George quickly reached out to restrain him. "Whoa there, Son," he said softly. "We have a whole team of agents to handle things from here. Let's find a room and sort this out." The family (and two dark-suited agents) retreated into a study (and library) that adjoined the large living room. Once inside, the agents set a privacy ward and stood stiffly in front of the secured doors.

"Okay, boys, what was that all about?" asked George kindly.

"I got a warning from Monēo just as that guy walked toward you."

"I heard your signal. Are you sure it was him?"

"Not really. There were so many in the room it was hard to tell." Brian watched his father go and kneel in front of Willard and gently take his hands. "And you, my brave little bodyguard. What prompted you to do that?"

"He is bad," Willard blurted out angrily.

"Are you also receiving warnings from Monēo?"

"No! That man is bad!"

"How do you know?"

"Maybe I can help," interrupted Brian. "Remember when you got the note from the nurse?" George and Myrna nodded. "He gets a pain in the back of his neck—like something growing under his skin—and gets real mad when he senses something bad." He watched Grandma James walk over, lay her right hand gently on Wil's neck and say,

"You respond to the presence of evil. Yes?"

"Yes, Ma'am!" Willard seemed glad she put it into words.

"And you feel a power deep inside trying to break free and punish evil doers." She looked deeply into the small boy's eyes with love and understanding, then announced, "This boy has wondrous gifts of pure gold. He can be trusted to correctly identify evil."

George stood and walked to J.J. and put an arm on his shoulder. "You're uncommonly quiet. What motivated you to jump in that scene?"

"The Everett Brothers stand together!" he proclaimed. "I had no idea what they were up to but I wasn't going to let 'em face that monster alone!"

"Well, those are noble sentiments, but do you think they were alone? There was a whole squad of agents closing in, and the rest of the family was there. And, I'm not helpless, either!"

"Yeah, but—I—couldn't just stand there..."

"I know. 'The Everett Brothers stand together.' I wouldn't have it any other way. It's not just the brothers who stand up for each other. We stand together as a family—all of us, Everetts, Deerings and James. That's true power—our bond of love. Let's also remember: we have been assigned a whole detail of security agents. They'll be disappointed if we don't let them do their jobs."

Brian understood that he and his brothers were being gently admonished to be careful and avoid needless danger.

"We hear ya, Dad," said J.J.

"Good! Let's get back to the reception before all the food's gone. I assume neither of you sense any danger right now?"

"Nope!" answered Brian. He was anxious to attack the tables of catered delights.

*   *   *

"What is so interesting?" asked Laileb in a somewhat sarcastic tone as he approached the table with all the video monitoring equipment located in a corner of the large library and study of Reficul's mansion. Genoveve was pushing some buttons and turning some dials.

"The cameras' images were being recorded on a twelve-hour loop," she said. "We have the whole scene from the lab, preserved from four different angles—thanks to you, I might add."

"That's right! With everything else that happened, I forgot about the recording loop. What does it show?" He moved to where he had a good view of the video screen and watched her push a button and the large flat 27" monitor lit up, displaying four boxes with the cameras' views. Knowing the book was an important key, he focused his attention on the lower left, which most clearly showed the end of the lab bench. He watched himself somewhat absently walk up to the book, gently open the ancient leather cover and casually turn some of the pages—just leafing through them. Every few seconds he would look up at the digital clock.

When the clock showed 00:01:30 he suddenly moved, as if being brought out of a daydream. He quickly edged over to stand in front of one of the bubbling cauldrons.

"Wait a minute," said Laileb excitedly. "Go back and play that part again!"

"Why—what did you see?"

"I'm not sure. Just play it again." He watched her push a couple of buttons—the images on the screen went backwards very fast, then started forward again.

"THERE!" he yelled as he watched himself turn away from the book. In his haste, the edge of his robe billowed out and caught on the corner of several pages and turned them; ending up on the page where the round *Sigillum De Aemeth* seal gate was clearly visible. "I knew that was not the page I was looking at!"

"You're right," she answered. "Let's go on. It gets even more interesting." The scene continued to replay and Laileb watched carefully. The digital clock continued its steadfast countdown to the fateful moment when the unfathomable would happen. Laileb caught himself holding his breath as the last seconds clicked down. The moment came: Three vials with blue dragon scale powder were simultaneously poured into the cauldrons. Blue smoke and sparks erupted. He and Genoveve jumped back while Reficul remained transfixed by the event. A bit of formula splattered on his hand and mage ring, which then began to glow—emitting energy rays resembling laser beams. One of them hit the open page of the book somewhere within the circle of the seal.

Laileb again focused on the book; the *Sigillum De Aemeth* began to glow as if the lines were streaks of molten lava that became brighter and brighter until a vortex spiraled out just as the bolt of lightning blasted through the room. The mini-whirlwind grew and elongated, appearing like a long vacuum hose which wriggled and snaked over to the blue misty cloud that earlier seemed to have consumed Reficul. The smoky vapor was sucked in and disappeared—along with Reficul.

"We must carefully analyze this recording," announced Laileb. "If we can pinpoint exactly where that energy beam touched the seal, it may help us discover where he went and be able to reopen that gate."

"I assume that will be your first priority." She said as he watched her glance over her shoulder to see him nod. "Excellent! I will get you some help to clean up the lab and see if any of our associates have experience in video analysis or enhancement."

"What about Mendacci and Everett?" he asked. "We cannot allow them to continue to work on the formula and that kid become Ringmaster while we are laboring to bring Master back."

"You let me worry about them!" she spat. "It's time for the Everetts to get what they've got coming. And that old man should know better than to poke his nose in business not his own."

"You know Master ordered they not be touched—" he reminded.

"Well, things have changed, haven't they. He didn't plan on being zapped off to another realm—not knowing when or how he'd come back." She turned from the video console, gave him a dismissive wave and walked away.

Laileb stood for a few moments thinking: *Who does she think she is? I'll get Master back and then we'll see who he rewards as the most faithful.*

Chapter Sixteen
Mendacci's Trouble

"This is unbelievable!" exclaimed J.J. as he, Nicki, Willard and Brian walked along the visitors' path, escorted by a security agent and the ever-present Benson. "It's hard to believe the twin towers were standing here just a few months ago."

"I feel like we should be talking in whispers, as if this is sacred ground—like a church or temple or something." Brian felt his feet crunch on some gravel, heard the distant roar of diesel engines of huge cranes, loaders and dump trucks. He shivered—not so much from the cold, damp, New England December air—he was remembering the terrible events of September 11th.

"It's so sad," said Nicki in hushed tones. "All those people on the jets and in the buildings. I can't imagine how awful it had to be." She had tears in her eyes and also felt the cold as she pulled her coat tighter.

Brian turned to Willard. "Are you okay? Are you having those pains or stuff like when you watched that video?" He bent down close to their new (foster) brother and shook his head—he could have sworn he saw a flash of gold in Willard's eyes as they momentarily became narrow and slanted.

"Some of the bad men died here, too," said Wil in his timid voice. "But they're gone. There's no evil here anymore, but I still feel angry and want to punish them."

"Does it hurt?" asked J.J.

"No, I'm getting used to it." Brian turned as he heard the ring of a cell phone in Benson's pocket and saw the security agent speak into a microphone in his hand.

Benson flipped open the phone's cover, answered, listened then said, "Aye, sir, right away." He turned to the youngsters as the agent was drawing near. "Sorry. Need to go back. Yer mum and da need you to meet with someone."

"What's going on?" demanded J.J. "They told us we could tour the city all day."

"Didn't say, did he. C'mon, you lot. We have our orders." He opened his arms as if to gather them up and ushered them back to the waiting hotel limousine.

"But what'd he say?" persisted J.J. "Dad always explains things."

"Maybe to you, but all he said was there's folks from yer school and to get back as soon as possible."

"See? I told you!" said J.J. in triumph. "Someone from CKS has come. Hmmm, I wonder what that's about." Brian watched him bounce on his toes.

"Why would someone from school come all the way to see us in New York, while we're on holiday?" inquired Nicki.

"I don't know," said Brian as he stepped into the limo with the hotel's crest on the side. "It must be something serious..." He searched his mind to try to remember if he'd done anything wrong, skipped a test or forgotten an assignment. There was nothing. "Did you do something to get in trouble for?" he asked his brother.

"Me?" J.J. put on his most innocent face as he settled into the plush leather seat and buckled the seatbelt harness. "I haven't done anything—that Mom and Dad don't already know about." They all chuckled, knowing that despite his almost perfect grades, J.J. was frequently disciplined for minor infractions. "And besides, the professors aren't going to come all this way during holiday break just because someone made the silverware at the staff dinner table skitter away when they tried to pick 'em up."

"*You* did that? That was hilarious!" Brian vividly recalled Coach Fleogan almost jumping across the table trying to catch his soup spoon until Professor Phusikos calmly waved his hand and countered the repelling energy. "How'd you do it?"

"See? Even you think I did it. I get blamed for everything."

"But you did it, right?"

"Well, yeah, but that's not the point..." They all sat in silence, thinking about what tidings awaited them back at the hotel. The limousine driver deftly navigated the usual snarls of New York traffic until smoothly gliding to a halt at the hotel's covered, ornate front entrance. Doormen quickly opened the doors and Brian, Nicki, J.J. and Willard were protectively ushered inside, through the plush lobby toward an elevator held open by security agents and Benson.

"What's goin' on?" asked Brian as the elevator door closed. "You guys are hovering awfully close. Are our parents okay?"

"Aye," answered Benson. "Yer mum an' da are fine. We were just told to stay close. Didn't say why, did he."

Walking into the immense suite, Brian immediately glanced around to sense if anything were amiss, but all seemed normal except that Superintendent Laedere and Professor Heady were sitting in the living room with his parents, all the grandparents and Uncle Paul. He had a cold feeling in his stomach; this was not going to be good news.

* * *

"Nothing! Weeks of planning and we get NOTHING!" shrieked Genoveve's high-pitched voice. She was pacing large circles around the open area in front of the huge stone fireplace of Reficul's library. Her hands were shaking and her pudgy face was purple with rage. "I knew the school was a long shot, but the house—the plan was perfect—they're gone for the holidays." She stopped in front of one of the black-cloaked men in the circle she was pacing inside of. "We pay much for information... Why didn't we know everything had been moved out?"

"Our source did not see anything being removed," said the man.

"Why not?" She pushed so close he could smell her breath and see angry veins in her neck.

"Ask him!" he shot back. "I wasn't watchin' 'em!"

"No, Ralph! I'm asking YOU! You hired him."

"I guess he had to sleep sometime."

"Well, find out!" she yelled, and resumed pacing inside the circle. "Can anyone tell me... Are they gone for good? Have they moved to the Redoubt executive house?"

The silence in the room meant no one knew. The only sound was the crackle of the logs burning in the fireplace, the ticking of the grandfather clock, and the squat woman's angry, wheezing breaths.

"I want answers—and soon. Make contact with our sources in the Redoubt. And find out about our new *vice chairman's* security force. Can we get someone on the team?" She saw heads nodding in acknowledgement but bristled that they didn't answer like they would have for Reficul. She continued, "And make sure you all understand—tonight no mistakes! We make a move on that old man only if we can do it without being seen. No one touches him if there's any possibility a witness can identify us—or even that he was taken. He must simply disappear. As far as anyone knows, he was overcome with grief after his wife's death."

Again they silently nodded.

"Let's get going, then." She led the way to the mansion's FON mirror. They each stepped through after calling out *333 PV Mall*.

*   *   *

Without waiting for an invitation, Brian walked over to the gathered adults and sat down on the couch next to his father while J.J., Nicki and Willard squeezed in among the grandparents.

Brian smiled with satisfaction as he saw Willard being given extra attention by Grandma and Grandpa Deering, who seemed to have taken a special liking to the young boy.

"I'm sorry to call you back so soon. I know you had more sights to see today. Hopefully you will understand."

Brian watched Agent Bowyer approach the group but remain standing. Bowyer was head of the security team assigned to the family. George nodded to him.

"The Vice Chairman has asked me to brief all of you on events that have occurred over the last few days: Superintendent Laedere reports Crown King Seminary was broken into and student records were pulled and reviewed—"

"But I thought security protections at CKS are impenetrable," interrupted J.J.

"That's the problem," he continued. "Either someone has found a weakness we still haven't identified or a CKS employee is involved. Either way, it's a serious threat we cannot ignore.

"The next issue is the 128 Main Street house was broken into. It appears someone knew the family is away for the holidays and sought to take advantage of the situation. From some of the vandalism done, it looks like they did not expect everything to be out of the house for the remodeling, and were pretty upset. Almost all the repainting will have to be redone, and several other items replaced—which is no problem. Here again, we are concerned someone was able to breach several layers of security meant to protect all of you."

"Is all this because our father became vice chairman," asked Nicki, "or is it because some people believe Brian is the Appointed One?" Brian was glad she voiced the question almost everyone had on their minds—and she did not confirm his status to Bowyer.

"It's impossible to know for sure—"

"But we think it's most likely Brian," announced Grandma James. "However, the situation becomes even more sensitive because of your father's position."

"Did the same people do both break-ins?" asked Grandpa Everett.

"They left no fingerprints or other forensic evidence," said Bowyer, "so we cannot know for sure, but we think so." Brian watched him quietly withdraw to allow the discussion to continue in private.

"Wow! That's scary," said Nicki. "Someone was able to break into two very secure places and both are connected with us."

"What does that mean for us?" asked Brian, but as he looked at the Superintendent and Professor, he knew he wasn't going to like the answer.

"We can't go back to CKS!" answered J.J.

"What?" Brian jumped up, bristling. "No way!"

"Take a breath, Ringboy!" J.J. soothed. "Think about it! If someone is coming after us, it's way too easy for other kids to get hurt if they're close, or we're in the middle of a crowded school."

"And it makes it harder for the agents," added Willard. He didn't say much, but he was always listening carefully, so his infrequent comments were quite profound.

Brian's shoulders drooped in resignation. He plopped back onto the sofa, folded his feet under him, and leaned his head on his father's broad shoulders. "But it'll be the same if we transfer to another school. Our family is too well-known. What's the diff—" He looked around and it dawned on him. "Oh, we're not going to any school—we're gonna be—" He searched for the word.

"Home-schooled," answered his mother. "Professor Heady will give you your lessons and CKS will certify your APTs." Brian could hear her trying to sound cheerful and pique their interest. "You will get to visit many places around the world as your father travels."

"Oh joy." Brian sounded dejected as his mind was spinning. Then it hit him like a sledgehammer. "But no flipolo!" he said through clenched teeth, then pulled his feet out, stood and silently walked toward the stairs leading to the upper-level bedrooms. In the distance he heard his father counsel:

"Give him some time. This is hard—he's always had flipolo as a diversion and outlet from the burden of being the *Appointed One*."

* * *

For seemingly the hundredth time, the short, bespectacled man peered out through the dark curtains separating the back workroom from the sales and display area. His employees went home hours earlier. He was alone—as he frequently was—writing in his accounting books, taking inventory or trying to find a way to get that artifact out of its wood and glass case. Since his wife passed on, more and more he spent his nights in the shop—taking his meals at one of the Mall restaurants (even occasionally going aboveground to Brangler establishments). He always felt safe, at least he did until that bizarre night a few weeks back when he had the strangest dreams and couldn't remember going to bed.

Again and again he stood absolutely still and listened for anything unusual or he peeked through the curtains. There was nothing, but he could not get over the nagging feeling he was being watched or there was a plot against him. Still, there was no unusual movement or sound. He could see a few late night Mall visitors stroll up and down the concourse in front of the store's display windows; there was nothing out of the ordinary about that.

Finally, he dismissed his suspicions and decided to go to Louigi's for a large salad bowl and a plate of pasta. Before leaving, he rechecked the vault and went to the front door—the replacement for the one Brian Everett disintegrated a year-and-a-half ago. Carefully locking and warding the door, Emilio then strolled along behind a young couple holding hands until he spotted Louigi's *outdoor* patio with its the familiar red and white checkered tablecloths. He looked up and saw technicians had switched the projected sky to a beautiful red-orange Arizona sunset (even though it was almost 9:00p.m.). He hoped they would do the full moon night scene—that was always his wife's favorite.

He barely came in sight of the restaurant when the maitre d' rushed out with his hand extended. "Ah, Senor Mendacci," he exclaimed with a heavy Italian accent. "Bene, bene ... your table is ready!" He started to escort the ring maker to a popular outside table with a good view of the projected scenes on the walls and ceilings.

"Not tonight, Mario." Emilio hesitated; he was still feeling uncomfortable. "Inside tonight. A quiet corner, please." He saw the host nod in understanding. Often patrons of Louigi's wanted anonymous solitude with no interruption or anyone being able to approach unawares.

"Of course, Louigi's personal table is available; he's in New York today." He led the way to a dimly-lit corner booth with a single candle, in an old wine bottle, providing cheery illumination.

"This is perfect!" He discreetly pressed a gold talon in Mario's hand and slid into the booth with his back against the wall. He could see all who might come and go while he enjoyed a meal. "No menu; just a salad, veal Parmigianino and iced mint tea." He was much hungrier than he thought. The glorious aromas coming from Louigi's kitchen always piqued his appetite.

In moments the waiter brought iced water and tea, bread sticks, hot rolls and the salad. No one spoke to him; guests at that table usually had more on their minds than Italian food or idle chatter. Emilio enjoyed the repast. As usual, Louigi's offerings were exceptional and he was beginning to relax—chastising himself for being paranoid—until he saw a short, squat woman with two male companions. They were seated at one of the patio tables trying to surreptitiously get a look at the diners seated inside. He was sure he had seen the woman before, but of course, most Sodality had visited his store and he enjoyed an excellent memory. But it was more than that. He'd seen her somewhere else—but where?

The trio at the patio table did not eat meals. They only ordered some soft drinks and a platter of appetizers—maybe fried zucchini or mushrooms. Mendacci tried to ignore them by paying attention to the dessert he ordered (lime sherbet and vanilla wafers), but he was startled when he looked up and they were gone—nowhere in sight, leaving the platter of appetizers and glasses of soft drinks almost full.

Get a grip, he mumbled to himself. *They were just late shoppers who stopped in for a quick snack and they were curious about what the restaurant's interior looked like... You're letting your imagination run amok.*

*   *   *

Brian's eyes flew open. He sat up with a start and kicked the covers off his bed. The only light in the room (he shared with J.J. and Willard) came from a night light in the adjoining bathroom. His brothers' sleep seemed undisturbed as he frantically tried to make some sense of the dream he'd been having. Or was it a dream?

Earlier, after leaving the family meeting, he spent the rest of the day lying on his bed or sometimes just wandering around the huge penthouse suite without speaking to anyone. His family followed Dad's advice and gave him plenty of space and made no attempt to engage him in conversation—which he appreciated. He tried to put a positive spin on the latest developments, but he struggled to find any consolation. Benson had quietly brought up trays with snacks and meals.

Having eaten supper, Brian watched TV for a while until J.J. and Wil came in to get ready for bed. He fell asleep early. Now, sometime after midnight, he replayed the images of his dream over and over. They were so clear, almost like watching a reality TV program. He closed his eyes; Monēo flashed a warning and he saw it again: the old man was about to be kidnapped. Monēo's warning was enough! He jumped out of bed, grabbed his dressing robe and dashed for the door.

Running down the stairs, trying to pull the robe over his pajamas, Brian yelled, "DAD!" He hit the bottom floor as lights started coming on. Benson, his wife Madge, and two agents materialized. Out of the corner of his eye he saw Nicki emerge from the bedroom she shared with Grandma James. The old sage was right on her heels. He crossed the living room and saw the double doors of the master suite open and his father quickly emerged, pushing his arms down the sleeves of his robe, anxiously looking for the cause of the commotion.

"Dad!" he called again, then skidded to a halt as his father inquired:

"What is it, Son?"

"Mendacci—" He paused to catch his breath. "Mr. Mendacci! He's in trouble!" He took a couple more deep breaths.

"Are you sure?"

"He's being followed by two men and a woman—and there's others hiding, too. They want to capture him."

"Where?"

"He's in the main concourse at PV Mall." He watched his father nod at the agents, who immediately turned and started talking into microphones in their hands.

"That's a big place. Can you see where in the concourse?"

Brian closed his eyes—no one spoke or hardly breathed.

"He just left Louigi's and he's heading toward his shop." The agents moved quickly—three were lining up before the FON mirror, then were gone through the thick shiny liquid (one could not translate directly in or out of the Mall—the reception/ departure lounge must be used).

Mendacci emerged from the interior of the restaurant, patted his full stomach with sated satisfaction and weaved his way between the patio tables and chairs. He joined the throng of shoppers and Mall visitors.

Almost immediately the feeling of being followed returned. He stopped and looked around. Off in the distance he thought he saw the woman and two men from earlier, but just as he spotted them they turned to examine a shop window display. He shrugged his shoulders and started for his store. His pace was slow; most late-evening Mall patrons were not in a hurry—especially during the holiday season. Many came only to stroll the main concourse and look at the colorful displays and brightly-lit decorations.

Genoveve and her two companions quickened their steps as they saw their quarry turn and move along with the crowd in the middle of the great walkway. He was moving cautiously—as if he suspected something. But they had been careful and patient, spending most of the evening watching his store and movements. Despite the crowds, they had decided to take him. People regularly translated from shop to shop—often in groups. They would move alongside him, use a quiet stunner then translate to the reception/departure lounge, supporting his weight in their arms. From there they could exit. The perfect time would be just as he approached his shop door. Most stores in that area were closed and there was less pedestrian traffic. Two other Knights were staked out in alcoves nearby.

All was going as planned. The crowds were thinning out, when ...

Emilio was just about to again chastise himself for being paranoid when he saw them. Three men dressed in dark business suits and wearing dark glasses—despite the somewhat dim underground lighting. They were walking with a purposeful gait in a line to intercept him. He started to panic, channeled his energy and readied to defend himself.

But wait a minute—these were three large *men*—not one short woman and two guys. They were not being furtive at all. They were boldly and openly approaching with their hands at their sides.

"Mr. Emilio Mendacci?" said the one in front, smiling but very serious. "I am Agent Bowyer, in charge of Vice Chairman Everett's personal security. Please forgive the late hour. The Vice Chairman has reason to believe there is an imminent threat to you and has asked us to escort you to his temporary quarters to discuss the matter."

"Do you have identification?" he asked after recovering from the surprise.

"Of course." He took a black wallet out of his inside coat pocket and opened it; revealing a photo identification and gold badge. "He also told me to tell you Erin James still thinks you are an old reprobate," he said softly, so only Mendacci could hear.

"Ha! You're genuine, all right. Sure! I'd be pleased to visit with Vice Chairman Everett and offer my congratulations. First, I'd like to get something from my shop—if that's okay."

"Yes, of course, but please allow us to accompany you. Our orders are to not leave your side until your meeting."

A short distance away, Genoveve seethed as she helplessly watched—totally dumbfounded. Everett's security agents! She could not hear every word, but heard enough. Somehow, Everett knew Mendacci was in danger and was able to send agents just in the nick of time. Something had gone wrong and she was going to get to the bottom of it. And what was so important to Mendacci that he would need to take it with him to meet with the Vice Chairman? Curious, she waited, mingling about among the shoppers until Mendacci came out with the security escort in tow. She watched him seal and ward his door then pick up an aluminum-clad briefcase which he carried very protectively. She chuckled to herself.

It's probably his precious formula notes. The poor schmuck has no idea we already have them... Or what will happen when he tries it.

There was nothing more for them to do so she signaled for her crew to go to the FON reception/departure lounge and go back to Reficul's castle-mansion on Mt. Greylock.

Chapter Seventeen
Energy Trails

Brian watched his father pace around the large living room—frequently passing in front of the ornate, full-length (FON) dressing mirror. Despite the lateness of the hour (actually early morning) the whole family waited up to see if the rescue mission was successful. Even Superintendent Laedere and Professor Heady were seated on one of the sofas. (They had been given rooms across the hall.) Benson and his wife moved about with trays of snacks, sandwiches and hot cocoa—even though their shift ended hours earlier. One of the other valet-maid husband and wife teams was bustling around in the kitchen or picking up soiled plates and cups. Everyone in the room occasionally looked expectantly at the mirror—hoping the agents had arrived in time.

"Welcome, Mr. Mendacci!" said the Vice Chairman warmly, clearly relieved. Brian was picking up a sandwich and cup of cocoa from Benson's tray so he missed seeing the ring maker and the agents come through the shiny liquid metal. "I am quite pleased you were able to accept our invitation." George strode over to the bespectacled man, extending his right hand in greeting.

"Mr. Vice Chairman, thank you for your timely intervention." He took the offered hand which was firm and welcome. "From what your agents told me, it was pretty close."

"Yes, I think so." He pointed to the sitting room. "Please join us. We would be pleased to have you as our guest for a couple of days until we can sort things out a bit." They walked into the spacious room where introductions were exchanged.

"Stay here? But if I may ask, where are we?"

"Sorry. I forgot you missed the main entrance. This is the Presidential Suite of the Plata Hotel. We are staying here for a few days. There's an extra room across the hall. I'd like you to sleep there tonight and then we'll move you to a Sodality safe house for a few days."

"If it's not too much trouble... I will need to contact one of my employees; they can manage the store for a few days."

"Excellent!"

"Mr. Everett—Vice Chairman—please tell me—how'd you know?" He took a cup of cocoa and a sweet roll from a tray Benson offered.

"I'm sure you understand; in my position we have sources which cannot be named."

"Yes, I understand. I'm sorry if I inquired into a sensitive area."

"If I were you, I'd ask the same question. Now, it's late and I'm sure we could all use some sleep. If you'll give your FON address to Agent Bowyer, he'll arrange to have whatever you need brought from your home. If there's anything else you need, please don't hesitate to tell one of the agents or my brother, who has accepted appointment as my chief of staff."

Brian watched Bowyer escort Mendacci to the wide double doors and to a vacant room on their (secured) floor. Then his father spoke:

"As I said, it is late—or should I say early? Let's get some sleep. Then we can try to make some sense out of last night's events."

Brian went to his dad for a hug. "I'm sorry I got everyone up—"

George took him tight to his chest. "Don't apologize. You saved that man from being kidnapped or worse. You stay tuned into whatever source that's giving you these visions. If you *ever* see things like that, don't wait. Act. You were given wondrous gifts—use them!

"Good night, Son. I love you."

"I love you, too!" He went to his mother, hugged and kissed her good night, and headed for the stairs. He heard his brothers and sister say their good-nights to their parents and grandparents. He felt guilty ignoring the grandparents; turned and rushed back to embrace each of them. He was glad things turned out well.

*   *   *

"What happened?" asked Laileb in a firm-but-gentle voice that belied the humor and satisfaction he was feeling from Genoveve's failure over the previous days.

"Well, it's obvious, isn't it!" she shrieked, turning more purple by the minute. (It was all he could do to keep from laughing.) "There's a traitor in our midst who warned Everett!" Her voice was almost hoarse from all her yelling.

"And who might that be?" he said with almost irritating calm.

"How 'bout Phusikos? He's always been friendly with the Everetts."

"Really! Phusikos didn't even know there was an operation. I'm sure Master will be pleased to hear how you immediately accused one of his closest aides without any evidence or even the slightest possibility he could be at fault."

"And I suppose you'll tell him—"

"Look, Genoveve, you can play at running the Black Knights until he returns. I don't care, as long as you don't interfere with my efforts to bring him back. But understand: I have only one loyalty, and that's to Prince Reficul. I will not hide anything from him— ever! If you have a problem with that, then we'll call a conclave of all the Black Knights and see what they have to say about it."

"Okay—okay!" She conceded unwillingly but knew she dared not confront him before a conclave. That could be disastrous—especially since he was right. "But we're still faced with the possibility we have a spy or a traitor. Somehow Everett knew the old man was in danger. I heard that with my own ears."

"Maybe not. I seem to remember you or Phusikos mentioning that Brian Everett may have inherited seer abilities. With the help of that old empath, Erin James, he could be a force to reckon with."

"Hmmm, you may be right. If that's the case, it's all the more reason to make sure he cannot become Ringmaster."

"That much, we agree on..."

And George and Myrna will finally pay for what they did...

* * *

Brian walked down the stairs and saw the rest of his family and Misters Mendacci, Laedere and Heady milling about in the dining area. Sometime during the night, table leaves had been added or a larger one brought in; it was large enough to accommodate fifteen. He had been last to shower (after J.J. and Wil) and was afraid he'd be late, but the chef and the morning domestics were still putting finishing touches on the buffet table.

"Ah, everyone's here," announced Myrna. "Please, let's get started."

"Am I late?" Brian queued up for the breakfast just behind his dad.

"No, no," answered his mother. "Your father had some things to deal with already, so he just arrived."

Brian listened to various conversations going around the table. Most involved some recounting of the events of the night before (earlier that morning) but others discussed places to visit in New York, and Professor Heady was making arrangements with Superintendent Laedere for their home schooling. Brian would nod his head or offer a one- or two-word comment but mostly he was content to reflect on the dream that caused so much commotion—until:

"Is there any chance the attacks are related?" he heard Grandpa Everett ask George. All discussion stopped and fourteen pairs of eyes turned toward the head of the table. For a long moment there was silence, with the click of the pendulum clock in the living room the only sound. It seemed as if everyone was holding their breath, awaiting the answer.

"Thus far, there is no evidence that they are, though I'm not comfortable with so many coincidences. An investigation squad, including the FBI, is going over the scenes this morning but I doubt they'll find much. If they didn't leave fingerprints or other forensic evidence, we have no way to say for sure."

J.J. started to blurt out "Brian can," but stopped, almost choking on the words when he saw Brian glare and shake his head. From the corner of his eye he saw Dad take notice of the exchange but was distracted when Bowyer came up and whispered something in Uncle Paul's ear, who instantly got up.

"I'll handle it," said Paul, following the agent into the study.

"I'd better see what's going on." George started to put down his linen napkin and rise.

"Sit down, Mr. Vice Chairman," said Grandma James firmly. "You will not last a week if you refuse to let your staff do their jobs. You chose your brother to be chief of staff because he is competent and you trust him. He will let you know if something requires your attention." Brian watched his father settle back into his chair.

"Thank you, Grandma," said Myrna. "I've been trying to get him to do that for days."

"I'm just not used to having a chief of staff who filters everything and has so much authority."

"You will learn—if you will heed to your wife's counsel. You have a wonderful family with tremendous talents and abilities. Listen to them—all of them! You did well last night. You delegated the mission and let them plan and carry it out." Brian noticed Gradma carefully avoided mention his involvement in front of Mendacci.

"You have no idea how hard that was. I really wanted to take Paul and go handle it myself."

"Oh, we know it was difficult—even those who are not empaths could read your struggles." She beamed with one of her all-knowing, compassionate smiles.

"Was I that obvious?"

"YES!" said a dozen voices in unison, then laughed.

Just then Paul returned. Brian watched him fill a new plate with warm eggs, sausages and hash-browned potatoes, resume his seat at the table and say, "Mr. Mendacci, there's an apartment here in Manhattan ready for you. It's small but nicely furnished. The fridge and pantry are being stocked as we speak. It's fully warded against any energy transport. There's a FON mirror in a cupboard in the basement, which is high security restricted. If you go out, I'm sure you know disguise techniques."

"Thank you!" gushed the old man. "You've all been so kind and have done so much more than I deserve."

"You're welcome!" answered George. "I wish all this were not necessary but until we sort it all out, we appreciate your cooperation. You will be advised immediately if there's any change or progress."

*   *   *

"You wanna go where?" asked J.J. "You've got to be kidding!" Brian slipped on his coat and made sure gloves were in the pockets. Then he saw J.J. move to stand defiantly to block his path.

"Look, we've got to find out if it was Laileb—you almost said it yourself. I can tell if it was the same people at the school, our house, or the Mall—though the Mall may be harder 'cuz so many people go there. This is our best chance; everybody's gone to the Redoubt or shopping."

"Why not wait for Dad or Uncle Paul? If you explain it, I'm sure they'd come with us."

"I don't want the agents to know I can do this; they'd drag me off to every investigation they've got. And Dad and Uncle Paul, even Mom, can't go anywhere without 'em."

"How is it you make something so stupid sound reasonable?" J.J. stepped aside, went to the closet and started pulling on his coat. "If you're going, so am I!" Just then another, smaller coat flew off its hanger and into a pair of outstretched hands...

"You're not going to leave me to face Mom or Dad if they get back first!" Brian heard Willard say with more force than usual. "And I can help if there's trouble."

"And where might you lot be going?" Brian stopped cold when he heard the heavy British accent of Madge (Benson's wife) just as he was about to put his hand on the FON mirror-frame rosette.

"Mom said we could go to Louigi's restaurant for lunch—it's a Sodality-run Italian restaurant in Greenwich Village." That was the truth. They were going to Louigi's but planning to piggy-back from there to CKS.

"Right, yer mum mentioned that. It's okay then." She turned and headed for the stairs and the upstairs rooms—probably to clean up after three messy boys.

Okay, first hurdle, thought Brian as he put his hand on the ornate, carved flower. The mirror shimmered and became like a thick liquid. He gave the command for Louigi's then said, "I'll hold it open; you guys go on through." Willard and J.J. stepped in and disappeared. Then he entered the thick, viscous mass.

"Wow, that was easier than I thought!" exclaimed J.J. after shaking off the FON queasiness.

"Hey," whispered Brian. "Keep your voice down. Somebody might be around; one of the custodians or some kids to play on the flipolo practice field."

"Yeah, you're right. We should have come at night," answered J.J.

"We'd never figure a way out of the hotel then," added Wil.

"But it's winter and in the middle of the holidays—probably no one's here." Brian strode off toward the main doors of the campus interior.

J.J. followed, saying, "Have you figured out how you're going to get inside? I mean the FON room is easy—it's outside the main building. All the shields and wards start there." He pointed at the large, arched, Gothic relief-carved double doors protecting CKS. "One wrong move and alarms will bring all kinds of responses we don't want any part of."

"We don't have to go inside," announced Brian with a grin. "All I'm looking for are energy trails. They had to go through these doors, so if the trails are still visible, they're here."

"Can you see 'em yet?" asked Wil.

"No. Without a flash warning from Monēo, I need to draw elemental energy—like I did with Merlin. At least, that's the only way I know to do it right now." They all stood still as Brian held out his hands and began to gently talk to Air, Water (moisture in the air), Earth and Fire. They felt a slight breeze swirling around. The air became noticeably drier and colder. The ground under their feet seemed to vibrate through the concrete walkway.

Brian opened his eyes and looked around. He felt as if his whole body was charged like a giant capacitor, and said, "This is going to be harder than I thought. There have been a whole bunch of people in and out recently."

"You still remember what Laileb's looked like? Are any like that?" J.J. nervously looked around, shifted his weight from foot to foot and listened for any hint of trouble.

"Yeah, I remember, and he wasn't here."

"Anything look familiar or stand out?"

"Not familiar, but two are really bright, like they've been in and out many times—over a long period of time—but recently, too."

"One of 'em's got to be the Super."

"And the other is whoever broke in. Remember, he said it may have been someone on staff," added Willard.

"Phusikos?" asked J.J.

"No—I saw a bit of his in the trailer park. He hasn't been here recently."

"That should make it easy," said J.J. "I remember Super saying he didn't go to our house or hasn't been to the Mall in months."

"You're right!" Brian turned and went back down the hallway toward the FON room. "Let's get out of here."

"Lord Brian?" inquired Willard. "How long will the elemental charge last?"

"Several hours, unless I ground it." He walked toward one of the mirrors. "Wil, you're our brother now—family. You don't need to use those titles!" He put his hand on the rosette and called out their house destination.

"Sorry," said Wil and stepped into the shiny liquid. J.J. went through, and Brian followed.

*   *   *

"That's an incredibly elaborate scheme," said Laileb. "Brilliant. But elaborate and complicated. I like the fact that it is compartmentalized. No one, except you and I, know all the elements. So if there's a traitor, spy, or someone gets captured, he can only reveal or compromise a small segment—not the whole thing—or even the ultimate goal."

"Thank you," answered Genoveve. "Given our personal history, I take that as a high compliment. I hope you noticed your involvement is only advisory, so you, and the other team members you've selected, can devote full time to reopening the seal or gate or whatever you call it, and get Master back."

"I did see that—and that you'll keep me posted."

"Then you think we should implement the plan?"

"I told you before, my focus is the return of Prince Reficul. As long as nothing interferes with that, I have no problem with you managing the organization. It's your program—you don't need my approval. But since you asked, I think you should proceed without delay." *As complicated as it is,* he thought, *that plan will keep her busy and out of my hair for months... Though I hope she is successful—the boy must not become Ringmaster before I can effect Master's return.*

"Mr. Sutton," greeted Genoveve in her best silky, yet authoritative voice. "Thank you for coming so quickly."

"A Knight's call is not to be ignored," answered Leonard Sutton, a tall, muscular man dressed in the Black Knights' usual long black cloak. "How may I serve our Prince?"

Genoveve noted the man's specific reference to serving Reficul, not her—even though she held a greater rank (second-in-command). But of course, she could not say anything for he was correct: they all served Reficul. Still, it galled her that she was not afforded the respect she felt she deserved.

"Can you resume your position on the vice chairman's security detail?"

"It may take a while. When a chairman or vice chairman leaves office—as with the retirement of Vice Chairman Wright—the entire staff, including security, is replaced. I know some of Everett's people. He hasn't completely filled his roster. I may be able to get an interview."

"How will you get past Erin James? She is practically part of the family—since they adopted her grandson."

"As an empath, she's as good as they get. But even the best have weaknesses, if one has the ability. That's how I was able to remain so close to SVC Wright."

"So you can do it?"

"Deal with the old empath? No problem. And I'm fairly sure I can get an interview with the new SVC. I can't guarantee he'll offer me an appointment."

"I'll look forward to your progress reports." She watched Sutton turn and start to leave Reficul's study when she called, "By the way... Is there anyone currently on Everett's staff who might be approached?" She knew he understood her to mean people with debts, bad habits, secrets or other problems that could be exploited.

"Not that I know of." He hesitated but did not turn back around. "He has been very careful. I'll stay alert to any opportunities," he said over his shoulder. He walked to the door and let himself out—not waiting for her leave.

*　　*　　*

"This is going to take more than a little repainting," Brian heard J.J. exclaim, as they walked through the hallway, peering into various rooms of the house at 128 Main Street. "The FON mirror is about the only thing left intact." There were energy blast holes in almost every wall, closet and window. Cupboards were smashed or doors ripped off. The kitchen cabinets and appliances were in shambles.

"The only reason they left the FON was because that's how they got in and out," said Brian. "I can see their energy trails." He walked outside through what was left of the kitchen door and saw an energy dome over the entire property. "The bubble ward and shield are still in place—like Uncle Paul left 'em." The trio went back inside.

"Dad said something about lowering the FON security so the workmen could come and go," said J.J., as Brian watched him bend down and pick up a broken piece of glass from the kitchen floor and put it in a trash bin. The house smelled of smoke and the previously new paint. Dirt and debris crunched under their sneakers. "He wasn't worried about thieves—there was nothing in the house except construction materials."

"Are the energy patterns the same?" asked Willard, who was rubbing the back of his neck and looking very angry.

"Yes! One of the bright ones and at least three others, I think." Brian looked at Willard; it looked like his eyes had a yellow—no, it was gold—tint and slanted like a reptile. "Except the bright one, it's hard to tell. They're wearing off and there's been others in and out... Wil, are you okay?" He was distracted by his brother's change.

"People who did this were bad. I'm okay now..."

"We've done what we came here to do," encouraged J.J. "We better get back to Louigi's."

"We still need to visit the mall!"

"C'mon, Brian! Haven't you seen enough?" J.J. moved to put himself between Brian and the FON mirror.

"This only proves the house and the school are connected." Brian put his hands on his hips in defiance. "We don't know if it's the same people after Mr. Mendacci. We've come this far."

"Dad's gonna ground us for a year—if Mom doesn't kill us first."

Brain watched J.J. and Willard shake off the FON queasiness and announced, "C'mon, let's go back to Louigi's."

"What are you playing at?" gasped J.J. "We just got here 'cuz you insisted."

"We don't need to go any further. The same crew came right through that mirror over there." He pointed to a FON mirror across the room on the opposite wall.

"Are you sure?"

"As best I can. These trails are much fresher. I don't think it's any coincidence."

"Then let's go!" J.J. turned to the mirror he just came through. "I'll hold it open—you and Wil go through."

"Welcome to Louigi's," announced a heavily accented Italian voice to Brian as he stepped forward to clear the way for Willard and J.J. "Your papa just arrived and is already seated at your table." Brian recognized the man—Louigi.

The three boys froze in place with a deep feeling of dread in their stomachs, and minds racing in panic.

"Our dad is here?" asked Brian.

"Do you know who *he* is?" inquired J.J.

"Of course!" He turned to Brian. "You honor me again—heir of Merlin. And now your papa is our new Vice Chairman. Come, young gentlemen. Let us not keep the man waiting."

The strong smell of Italian food and garlic made Brian's stomach rumble—or maybe it was the thought of facing his father. Either way, he started taking tentative steps to follow the man in the silk suit. He swallowed hard as he stepped out from hallway and into the main dining room. In the very back corner booth he spied the familiar shape of his dad, and searched his face for some indication of how mad he was.

"He doesn't look too upset," whispered J.J. in his ear—from behind.

That's what worries me, he thought. *At least when he's yelling I know what to expect.*

Brian slid into the booth next to his father's left and J.J. to the right. Willard chose a chair right across.

"To save time, I ordered pizza, salad and spaghetti for all of us," said George cheerfully, taking a sip of his Vainabier. He seemed to be enjoying his three sons' squirming and guilty, downcast eyes. Their hands were in their laps, afraid to touch anything. "These soft breadsticks are wonderful!" He slid a whole basket of the golden delights in front of Brian, who looked at them wistfully. "Especially when you dip them in marinara sauce." He pushed a bowl of steaming red dip next to the basket. Brian's appetite won over his pangs of guilt. He picked up a breadstick, plunged it into the gleaming sauce and took a big bite.

"What?" Brian saw his brothers staring at him, aghast. "I'm hungry!"

Their response was immediate. "YOU'RE ALWAYS HUNGRY!" Then they laughed. The tension was relieved and the two other boys reached for the baked wonders and started dipping, just as their salads arrived.

"Well, did you find out?" asked dad, rather casually. "Was it the same lot at the house and the school?"

"You knew?" asked Brian.

"Of course we knew—except Mr. Mendacci. Don't you think it was a bit strange there was no one at CKS and not a single worker at the house? I must admit, your plan was bloody brilliant, except that you went FONing all over the country without permission."

"Why didn't you tell us?" asked J.J.

"And miss seeing you squirm like that? Not likely!"

"So we're not in trouble, then?" Brian's voice sounded hopeful.

"I didn't say that! You still must face your mother. I suspect you'll be doing extra chores and lessons for a while."

"That's not fair! You knew and you didn't stop us—that's like giving us permission."

"You've heard it said before, Jeremy: 'Life isn't fair.' I could say we were testing your integrity, but that's not entirely true. I think we wanted to find out the answers you were seeking as much as you did. So, just as I had to face your mother's wrath (for not stopping you), you too must learn to accept the consequences of your decisions."

"Is she really mad?" asked Willard.

"I think she's as upset with me as she is you—not because you were in danger but because none of us told her ahead of time."

"We couldn't tell you!" pleaded Brian. "If we had, you would have had to tell the security detail and I don't want them to know I can do this stuff. You didn't tell them, did you?"

"No. Paul and Mr. Laedere made all the arrangements so both places would be clear. The agents believe you guys were just curious and went exploring. That's also why you must deal with your mother—to keep up appearances."

"She's gotta be convincing, huh?" observed Brian, resigned he was probably going to be doing extra chores for the next fifty years.

"Oh, I'm sure she'll be that! Now, what did you find out?"

Over the next few minutes Brian, J.J. and Willard recounted what they saw and experienced. George listened without comment until:

"Wait a minute! You're saying the same people were trying to kidnap Mr. Mendacci?"

"I can't tell for sure; we only went to the FON lounge. But they were there. You've always taught us that true coincidence is very rare. I think there is some connection."

"I think you're right. That sure changes the nature of the investigations. I'm going to have to tell the detectives—without saying where the information came from." He watched the boys finish their lunches, then signaled for the check. "I think it's time to go."

Moments later Louigi arrived and again tore up the check. "You honor me with your patronage—and thank you for your trust with the earlier matter. You can always count on me."

As before, George left generous tips for the waiters. As they stood, security agents appeared from seemingly nowhere. They all went in the back to Louigi's FON mirror.

Chapter Eighteen
Everett Manor

━━━━━━━━━━━━ ✦═◦◯◦═✦ ━━━━━━━━━━━━

"This is not fair!" complained J.J., sweeping up a pile of glass into a dust pan and dumping it in a rubbish bin. "You'd think we made this mess."

"And we're not allowed to use psionics for anything—ugh!" Brian picked up the remnants of some cupboard doors and made another trip to the big collection hopper placed in the driveway at their house in Meyor. When he walked back in he saw Willard yanking on some ruined carpet that didn't want to come off the floor. "We would already be done if we could zap this stuff." He joined Wil and together they were able to pull up the stubborn material.

"It could have been worse," said Wil. "I was afraid they'd send me ba—"

"Don't say that!" yelled J.J. "Don't even think that! You heard Mom when you offered to go back to the home." Brian saw J.J.'s red hair was almost aflame and his freckled cheeks were glowing crimson. "You, me—we're part of this family. Nothin' changes that—no matter what we do."

"Yeah, that's true!" added Brian. "J.J. gets detention and letters from school almost every week and he's still with us." He laughed and tugged the carpet again toward the front door.

"Look, I know it's hard to completely accept being part of family like this—it took me a while, too—but believe me, we're in it now and this family is forever!"

Brian watched the exchange between his two brothers as their eyes glistened and tears started to streak down their cheeks—which created a muddy trail on Willard; he was covered in dust and dirt from the clean-up project.

"C'mon, let's get this done," said Brian. "Then we can FON back for supper. I'm hungry."

"You're always hungry," said J.J. and Wil, laughing and grabbing more trash.

"Done!" declared Brian after shaking off the FON queasiness and finding his mother at the desk in the study.

"Excellent!" she said, looking up from the pile of mail she was sorting through. "There's only two more days before Christmas. We need to do some shopping and get ready to move."

"Move? Where?" asked J.J. "There's a ton of stuff to be done before we can move back home."

"That's true, but we can't stay here. This was a nice vacation arranged by Mr. Jones. Since the house will not be finished for some time, we are moving into the Council Executive house on the 26th. Then, as soon as your father's security roster is filled, we'll be off traveling to visit some of the other countries under the Council's jurisdiction."

"Are Professor Heady and Super comin' with us?" asked Brian.

"No," she answered. "Mr. Laedere was here for only a few days. He has already gone home to his family. Professor Heady is spending the last of the Holiday with his relatives in England. He'll join up with us when we make a courtesy visit to the Ministry there.

"You've a bit of time before supper. After your showers, you might want to put some things down for shopping tomorrow."

Brian heard a rustling sound coming from behind, turned his head and saw Grandma James coming into the room.

"Willard, please tell us why you don't want Christmas presents."

"What?" Brian couldn't believe what he just heard.

"This is your first family Christmas!" exclaimed J.J.

"Honey, why?" asked Myrna.

"Mom, look around." He motioned to the opulent hotel room and the others. "I've been adopted by the greatest family a kid could want. We're spending the holidays in a luxury New York hotel. My new dad is now the Sodality Vice Chairman—and next in line to become Chairman. I have amazing brothers and sister and a wonderful mother who loves me—"

"And grandparents," interrupted the old sage.

"Yes, and grandparents. What more could I want or need? But there are other kids still at the group home who haven't been adopted. I can't give 'em a family, but maybe I can help them have a happy Christmas."

"What a great idea!" proclaimed Brian. He watched his mother almost leap out of the desk chair, run around and collect Willard in her arms as tears streamed down her face. "Let's all do it!"

*　　*　　*

Exiting the oversize, black SUV with its dark tinted windows, Brian looked around at the myriad of planes on the tarmac: There were small, single-engine Cessnas with their high wings; low-wing Beechcrafts; twin-engine King Airs; restored military fighters and various private and business jets. He could smell the asphalt tar and distinct odor of fresh jet-A fuel—that had just been topped off in the Gulfstream they were about to board.

There had been no time to settle into the Council Executive House. The instability of the world since the attacks on 9-11 required immediate meetings at the Ministry in London. The Council Chairman was too frail and old for such rigorous travel so the new Vice Chairman would go in his place.

Brian glanced toward the gleaming jet's open door. His father was already being greeted by Captain Gil Newton while ramp workers were quickly transferring their luggage from the cars to the plane—supervised by Co-Pilot King.

"Why aren't we FONing?" asked Brian, edging up next to his mother. "I know they've got fiber optics in London."

"Yes, they do, but some of the places we are going afterward do not. We need to have a plane for those visits, so it's best to start with one. Mr. Jones has been very helpful." Brian noticed Jones was traveling with them.

After the usual preliminaries, engine run ups and sudden acceleration, the powerful jet almost leaped into the air. As the power was reduced to cruising and the altitude leveled out, the Everett family relaxed into the luxurious leather seats. The flight attendant passed out blankets, pillows and steaming cups of herbal tea and hot cocoa. Of course, Brian's tray was piled high with sandwiches and pastries, which he immediately tucked into, as he heard his sister announce:

"That was the most wonderful Christmas I've ever had!" she exclaimed. "To see the look on those kids' faces was beyond exciting. When they said 'thanks' and gave us hugs, it was the best gift I've ever received."

"I wanna do something like that every year!" added J.J.

"M—tu—" Brian swallowed hard. "Me too!" He looked around and saw several looks of disgust and disapproval. "What? I'm hungry."

"You're always hungry!" came several voices from within the well-appointed cabin.

"Let's all finish up," said Myrna. "I've asked that the cabin lights be dimmed in a few minutes. It's been a busy few days and we need some sleep. It'll be late morning when we land and there's a full schedule for all of us."

Quickly Brian finished off three sandwiches, two pastries and the cocoa. He reclined the comfortable seat and curled up with the pillow and blanket. He was tired and was sound asleep within minutes; the drone of the engines was almost hypnotizing.

Brian woke with a start. Something had changed—and he'd been having the strangest dream about his great grandparents. They were on the gangway of a paddlewheel steamship just before something terrible happened to it. But that wasn't what roused him. There was something different about the sound of the engines.

He was trying to clear the sleep fog from his head when the cabin lights started getting brighter and the flight attendant began coming around and waking everyone.

"We are beginning a long, slow descent to London's Heathrow Airport." She passed out warm, moist towels and started collecting the pillows and blankets. "There's just time for everyone to freshen up, use the facilities and have a light breakfast—though I understand your hosts have a big reception and dinner planned."

A short while later, Captain Newton touched the plane down on the long runway with the slightest chirp of the wheels and the loud rush of the reverse thrusters. He then taxied to the general aviation area and into a hangar where four cars were waiting.

As the engines spooled down, the door was opened. Brian stepped down the stairs and saw a small group of dignitaries waiting to greet them. They were all dressed in formal wizards' robes and tall pointy hats. He watched the man in front approach his father.

"Ah, Chairman Everett!" said the man, extending his hand. "Welcome to London." He gestured toward the wide open hangar doors and the steady drizzle of rain outside. "Sorry about the weather. They say it's to clear this evening."

"Minister," greeted George. "It's good to meet you—though I'm only Vice Chairman," he corrected. "I've heard so much about London's rain and fog, I would have been disappointed to miss it."

Brian was fascinated to see his father in action. He knew just what to say to put folks at ease.

"We've arranged Ministry cars as you have underage wizards who cannot appar—uh, translate. Also, there is a lorry to take your luggage to the residence we have arranged."

At that moment, Brian protectively squeezed the padded straps of his backpack. He was glad he had carried it on the plane instead of putting it with the luggage.

"Thank you, Minister. You have been most kind. I hope our visit does not disrupt your routine too much."

"Not at all! With everything that has happened, we must be united in our efforts to resist dark forces that affect us all. Now, with your leave, we will place you in the capable hands of the drivers while we pop on back to the Ministry and make sure all is in readiness."

"Of course," said George, nodding his head with a slight bow.

Brian watched the ministry officials dissolve into the air with a sharp crack sound. As he walked toward the lead car, the driver rushed to greet him.

"Welcome to London, young sir," he gushed. "May I put your bag in the boot?"

"No, thanks." Again he felt his grip tighten on the straps. "I'll keep it with me."

"Very good, sir." He smiled and went to greet the others and hold the doors open while they piled in the back seats—which seemed much bigger from the inside. Even so, they split up between two cars, with their security escort in the third car.

The trip to the ministry was a unique experience. They never stopped at traffic lights, which were always green. Other cars and obstacles seemed to move out of the way for them, or the ministry cars would become long and thin—fitting between spaces much too narrow. Yet through it all, the interior of the car remained roomy and comfortable. Brian was amazed, yet wondered if this was a common way to travel; he understood the witches and wizards throughout Europe and other Ministry-controlled countries shunned Brangler technology. He made a mental note to inquire later.

As they sped along, the driver would call out various historical sites of interest. They passed by the Queen's residence, Westminster Abbey, the Tower of London and Big Ben. He also pointed out famous places where famous events for witches and wizards took place.

They were traveling along a busy street in downtown London when the driver announced: "Ah, here we are..." Brian could only see large business structures—nothing that looked like a government building. He wondered if they would have to climb into the call box he'd heard about that visitors used—described in some books.

Suddenly the driver turned the car and headed down a narrow alley he was sure was not there a second ago. He held his breath—there was a solid wall at the end of the alley and instead of slowing down they were speeding up! He couldn't help but close his eyes and brace for the worst.

But there was no crash. The car braked smoothly to a stop and as Brian opened his eyes, the driver was already climbing out and opening the back doors. Every sound echoed as they were in an underground garage—at least it seemed like a garage; there were other cars and marked parking spaces. But it looked more like a medieval castle's dungeon. It was damp and lit only by torches embedded in sconces on the walls.

It took Brian a minute for his eyes to adjust to the dim light and his heartbeat to slow back down. When he finally exited the car he saw the drivers were all smiling—clearly pleased with themselves for giving their passengers such a start. J.J. was laughing, and said:

"Now that was cool! I was sure we'd made a wrong turn and gonna crash. Well done," he complimented.

"That was better than a theme park ride!" proclaimed Myrna, surprising Brian, but he was shocked when Grandma James—who was always formal and reserved, said:

"Excellent, Gentlemen! Contrary to popular belief on our side of the pond, the English have a wonderful sense of humor. Yes, well done!" Everyone chuckled and began exchanging comments and observations about their ride from the airport.

The drivers led them to a pair of elevator (lift) doors embedded in the rock wall. When they stepped in, the doors closed. Brian wasn't sure if they were going up or down; there were no indicators. Moments later, the doors opened and they were greeted by a large crowd gathered in an expansive room—lobby—with a fountain in the middle. He was sure it was going to be boring, except, he could smell food—lots of it—on large tables against a far wall. He would go through the formalities, get his hand squeezed a hundred times, smile and say all the right things, then check out English cuisine—he was looking forward to some fish and chips.

* * *

"That was weird!" Brian looked around and saw his family all gathered around and still holding onto a large silver tray. "Almost like being sucked through time-travel, only much faster."

"Well, I imagine the principle is about the same," said Dad. "Even the names are similar: time portal, and didn't they call this a portal key?"

"Something like that," said J.J. "And you were right; it felt the same—just without the glimpses of history passing by." They set the tray on a nearby table and looked around.

"Wow! This looks like the inside of one of those English manor houses shown on movies and TV." Brian saw they were standing in front of a grand staircase that went up to second story rooms, curving both right and left. The wood paneled walls were covered with huge old paintings and tapestries.

"We're sure not in Kansas anymore, Toto." J.J. chuckled and Brian followed him as he began exploring and wandered through large sliding doors on the left that led to a huge library with a gigantic stone fireplace surrounded by ornate carved-wood designs. Suddenly he stopped short as he looked above the mantle and saw a deeply-carved family coat of arms, but not of some obscure, ancient family—it had the Everett family crest. After his adoption J.J. wanted to learn more about his new family and went through genealogy information in their home library. Many documents displayed the design in detail. He wondered, *Why would it be on that wall? Surely they didn't put it there for just our short visit.*

"Dad," called J.J., just barely loud enough to be heard—he was breathing hard.

Brian heard the distress in his brother's voice and immediately followed it into the extensive library, hearing his father's footsteps right behind echoing on the polished hardwood floor.

"Dad!" breathed J.J. again, pointing to the relief above the fireplace.

"Oh, my stars!" exclaimed George, stopping just behind his red-headed son.

Brian felt a shiver go through his body and the hairs on his neck and arms stood on end. There were more footsteps and gasps as the whole family viewed the surprising scene.

"Ah, I see you've found it."

Brian jumped, hearing the voice of the Minister from the library doorway.

"Didn't take long then," he said with solemn delight. "This property's ownership records have been lost for at least a couple of centuries. It fell into disrepair for a while. Then the caretakers restored it and allowed the Ministry to use it as a VIP guesthouse. No one knew about the coat of arms as there was a large portrait hanging just there. Then, last week while being cleaned for your visit, the painting fell down and that family crest was revealed. After some research, we were fairly sure it was yours."

"It sure looks like ours," said George. "There's been an old family legend about a house built on the lands given to Merlin by Arthur, but that wasn't anywhere near London."

"We're a long way from London, near Carmarthen—formerly known as Caer-Myrddin."

"Is this ours, then?" asked Brian.

"There's only one way to tell. This library—as amazing as it is—has not been studied in decades, maybe longer. Despite our best efforts, there are spells and enchantments preventing anyone from removing any of the books from the shelves."

"You mean like this?" asked Brian proudly as he held up one of the ancient volumes—he had walked over to the nearest shelf while the minister was talking.

"Yes—like that—how?—what?" sputtered the Minister.

"I just picked it up." Brian watched him rush over to another stack to retrieve a book but it was as if it was glued to the shelf. Other members of the family (including the adopted) went and lifted books from various shelves without any resistance.

"Clearly this house is yours," pronounced the Minister. "I'll have legal documents drawn up and recorded. We'll find a new guest house."

"Please, we will rarely be here," said George. "When we are not in residence, you may use this house with our compliments. Obviously the library is protected."

"As is almost everything else in the house. It seems anything from the early owners cannot be removed off the walls or from the rooms where they belong. Cleaning and restoration have been a challenge. Anyway, thank you for the offer. We will keep it in mind. You might consider some modern kitchen appliances. Like everything else, this house is holding fast to the antiques."

"Of course, but we're not going to have much time this trip."

"What about Grandpa Everett?" asked Brian. "He's not doing anything. I bet he'd love to update this place and go through the library."

"That's a good idea! We'll call him right away." said George.

"I'll leave you to it, then," announced the Minister. "Until we meet tomorrow." He bowed and with a crack was gone.

"This is unbelievable!" exclaimed Brian. "Look at this place!" He started meandering among the shelves with thousands of books—even some scrolls. Antique desks, chairs and other forms of furniture were neatly placed to take advantage of the natural light that would stream in through large windows overlooking a beautiful garden and perfectly manicured lawns. A movement by the huge sliding doors caught his attention—and the rest of the family's. There stood a man and woman who looked almost as old as the house. They were dressed in stiffly pressed, black and white servants' livery.

"Good evening," said the old man in a rich baritone, very English voice. "We are Mr. and Mrs. Hodgins. We and our ancestors have served the Everett house for generations. Our son Norman is in the village, collecting some fresh fruit for your breakfast—he has been keeping the grounds. Cook is also third generation in this house. We would be pleased to continue our service here, if you would have us."

Brian saw his mother start to answer but stop to first look at George for his approval, then Grandma James who was testing everything with her empath ability. George nodded his approval, as did Grandma. Brian was surprised though when she turned to him and Willard. He closed his eyes and searched for any sign of Monēo and Wil simply turned up his hands, meaning he sensed nothing. Like the others, he nodded.

"I am Mrs. Everett. Thank you for your offer to stay on, which we accept gratefully. The Vice Chairman—Mr. Everett—is very busy. All household matters come through me or the security team. We may not be here often, so when we are away, we have given the Ministry permission to continue using the house for VIP visitors."

"Very good, Mum. Rooms have been prepared for each of you and there are quarters for security personnel—"

"Wait a minute! Since your family has served here so long," challenged J.J., "why didn't you tell the Minister about the family crest and the history of the house?"

"The crest was covered by the last Everett to live here, and enchanted to stay in place until some future time. It was not our place to reveal what was hidden. When the painting fell, we knew the true owners were on their way. The spell was such that I do not think we could have spoken of it—even if we wanted to."

"I'm sure you did the right thing," said George. "Thank you for your loyalty."

"Cook is preparing guard-of-honor, cider-glazed gammon, jacket potatoes and Battenberg cake." The old woman spoke for the first time. "If it is quite convenient, we were planning to serve at seven-thirty."

"That's perfect," said Myrna. "Now, we'd like to see the house and our rooms, please."

*　　*　　*

"Are you sure you checked everything?" asked the short, squat woman. She was sitting on a park bench watching the famous changing of the guard outside London's Buckingham Palace.

"Each family member had a small carry-on I could not access. But I searched—even x-rayed—everything else," answered a thin, wiry, ruddy-complexioned man, speaking with a strong Irish brogue. "There was nothin' but clothes and a few personals; no old paper with handwriting." He took a bite of chips (fried potatoes) from a cone-shaped packet of fish and chips.

"I was sure they would have it with them." She shook out the newspaper she was pretending to read. "It doesn't make sense. They wouldn't put it into storage with the rest of their things. And they would have it preserved in some kind of container that would be too large for small carry-on bags."

"Need someone on Everett's detail, then." He munched a piece of fish from the paper cone.

"We're working on that—you want the job?"

"Gettin' on airport ramp luggage duty was easy—no way Everetts' screeners would pass me. Sorry."

"I figured that, but are you up to making a try for those carry-ons? We found out where they're staying."

"I thought you said it wouldn't fit."

"Maybe compression. What about the boy's backpack?"

"Wherever Everett is, won't be easy, will it?" He got a big grin on his face as he tossed a chip to some pigeons on the ground. "I likes me a challenge."

"Excellent! I'll try to find out more about their schedule. Meet me in front of Westminster Abbey this time tomorrow." She watched him toss another chip, causing quite a flock to gather. He stood and strolled off, whistling an Irish tune ("*Londonderry Air*") and didn't look back.

Chapter Nineteen
Gremlins In The Wardrobe

"Can you believe this place?" Brian was walking down a wide hallway lined with ancient statues, suits of armor, wood-paneled walls, paintings, candles in sconces and tall candlesticks. Polished wood floors creaked under his feet and the smell of burning candles and lemon-oil wood polish permeated the air. The antique eeriness seemed to prompt soft or whispered voices. "I bet we explored fifty rooms and haven't found 'em all yet."

"Yeah," added J.J. "If it had some towers and parapets, it'd make a neat castle. Sitting at that dining table, I felt lost. I'll bet you could seat almost a hundred around it."

"The food was a bit strange," said Willard.

"Not as strange as the names. I mean, they call sausages and mashed potatoes, 'bangers and mash'—and French fries are 'chips'."

"And potato chips are 'crisps'."

"I thought I'd lose it," said Brian, "when the reception waiter offered me *spotted dick*". They all laughed—which echoed down the long hallway. "Then I looked and saw it was a molded pudding of some kind. I was afraid to try it."

"You?" challenged J.J. "Afraid to eat a food?"

"Well, yeah. Somebody said it was made of suet, some kind of animal fat."

"Yuck!" said Willard. "I'm glad I didn't try it."

"I can't wait to explore the basement tomorrow," said Brian.

"I bet it's really a dungeon." J.J. rubbed his hands together expectantly. "Maybe even a torture chamber—o-o-ooh!"

"You really have a sadistic side, sometimes." Brian stopped in front of a wide, heavy, arch-top door with recessed panels that led to his rooms. "It seems strange... We're on the same grounds King Arthur gave Merlin almost 1,500 years ago. And if the story is true, then the Crystal Cave should be around here somewhere."

"I'd sure like to find it, but people have searched for centuries," said J.J. "Hodgins said Merlin's well is here on the property."

"But maybe the cave is only visible to Merlin's heirs—like the books in the library," said Brian.

"I don't know..."

"It could happen," encouraged Willard.

"There's so much to explore, and we're only gonna be here a few days." Brian turned and opened the massive door. "I'll see you in the morning." He watched J.J. and Willard head toward their rooms, then entered his.

His rooms were breath-taking. Dark wood paneled the walls, with polished brass candle holders and oil lamps providing illumination. From the wall opposite the door, a huge canopied four-poster bed extended into the room. Heavy matching drapes hung around the bed and on the windows on either side of the bed. A cheery fire crackled and blazed in a fireplace on the left wall and a door to his dressing and bath room was on the right. He had visited the facilities earlier and found modern plumbing—well, not exactly *modern*; for the sink was an antique porcelain bowl sitting on a pedestal. The tub was huge, sitting on clawed brass feet (no shower), and the toilet tank was mounted high on the wall with a pull-chain to flush. But, the plumbing fixtures seemed to be the house's only surrender to modern technology. Next to the bathroom door was a massive wooden armoire where his clothes were already hung. In a corner by one window a comfortable tall back arm chair beckoned to surround him in padded leather luxury and in front of the other window was an antique writing desk and chair.

Between Christmas, jet lag and a busy day, Brian was feeling extremely tired. Wasting no time, he slipped into the pajamas Benson had laid out on the foot of the bed, dropped his soiled things in a hamper and crawled onto the spacious bed. He blew out the lamps and slid under crisp sheets and a thick down comforter. He drew the bed curtains, and closed his eyes. Sleep came at once. He dreamed a familiar dream—about his grandparents, a boat and a tall man in a long, hooded black cloak, until—

"Good morning, young Master," he heard as the bed and window curtains were being drawn and bright light was trying to penetrate his eyelids. But the voice wasn't Benson—it was the ancient relic that still seemed to move with surprising agility: Hodgins.

"Where's Benson?" Brian was still groggy and rubbing the sleep out of his eyes. The sweet smell of hot cocoa sitting on a silver tray on the bedside table was inviting him to come to life—despite not nearly enough sleep.

"Rousing yer brothers, I expect. Come now, Sir, yer mum wants you bathed, dressed and breakfasted before the Chairman leaves for meetings."

"He's *Vice* Chairman," he corrected. "Okay! I'm up." He kicked off the heavy comforter and realized it was a good thing there was a fire in the fireplace—the old house was drafty and it was the end of December.

"Yes, yes—only a matter of time," mumbled the old man. "I've drawn your bath, laid out towels and small clothes. You're expected in thirty minutes." He turned and exited the room—softly closing the door behind him.

Since his bedroom door was securely latched, Brian did not worry about closing the bathroom door before stepping into the bath tub. The water was warm as he slid down. He wished there was more time, but he knew his family would be waiting to start breakfast. He quickly scrubbed all over, shampooed his hair and dunked deep to rinse off.

As he emerged from the water he heard a noise—a small rustling sound coming from just outside the bathroom door. Unsure of what he was hearing, he became very still so there would be no water dripping or splashing. He heard it again. It sounded like someone rummaging around in the big wardrobe. *Maybe it's Benson hanging clothes*, he thought, *but usually he announces himself.* He closed his eyes to see if Monēo was giving a warning: nothing.

Slowly Brian eased out of the water, trying to keep the noise to a minimum, and reached for a towel which he wrapped around his middle. If someone did come in, he didn't want to be completely exposed. He then called out:

"Who's out there?" He waited for a reply. "Hey, I'm taking a bath and not dressed!" Still nothing, except the same rustling and slight bumping sound. "Benson, if that's you, can you come back later—or, at least, close the bathroom door?" There was no response. This was too much. He channeled his power and gathered some energy from the tub-water, then waited. Still only the same noise. It was time to act.

Hoping his wet feet would not slip and the towel would stay in place, Brian jumped out of the tub. As his feet hit the tile, there was very little traction, but he scrambled through the door and into the bedroom. He slid to a stop halfway between the open (bathroom) door and the bed. But there was no one there. Everything was exactly as he left it, before his bath. It made no sense. He blushed, thinking how he looked: soaking wet, towel barely hanging onto his hips, slightly crouched in a defensive stance—ready for a power duel. But he heard it again. Inside the closet, something—someone—was moving around.

Again he searched for a warning from Monēo, but there was none. Then he thought: *This house is ancient. It's probably a bat, or some other creature rooting about for something to eat.* Whatever it was, he was not going to confront it wearing only a towel (that was threatening to fall off). He chuckled, thinking: *That'd probably scare it to death.* He padded back into the bathroom, dried and quickly dressed in the clothes laid out for him.

Standing in front of the deeply carved, ornate doors of the armoire, Brian debated whether he should call his father—or Hodgins, but dismissed it. He was a powerful mage, and besides, there was no danger warning—and his father always told him to trust that ability. He stood back about three feet from the closet, channeled his energy, extended his right hand and commanded the doors to open.

In his excitement, he slightly overpowered. The doors violently flew open, barely staying on their hinges, and crashed into the sides of the cabinet. The sudden movement and force caused a couple of hanging shirts to sail out and land on the floor. All this he ignored; focusing on trying to locate the source of the disturbance.

Suddenly someone was banging on the big arched bedroom door. "Brian, are you okay?" he heard J.J. yell. Then without waiting for an invitation, the heavy door swung open and J.J. came charging in with Willard on his heels. "What's going on? We were in the hall, heading to breakfast, when we heard a big slamming noise."

"Yeah, what's going on?" Nicki stepped through the open doorway. "You're not already tearing up the house, are you?"

Brian didn't answer his brother or sister. He only held up the first finger of his left hand to his lips and uttered, "Shhh!"

They all stopped and looked where he was staring: at the inside of the open armoire. When quiet resumed, they heard it: the rustling and bumping. Instinctively, each channeled their power and lifted their right hands.

"What is it?" whispered J.J., carefully easing around to possibly get a better view.

"I don't know. I was in the tub when I first heard it." He turned to Willard. "Sense anything bad?"

"No. I only feel energy—nothing alive."

"Look!" said J.J. "Behind your clothes—there's something in your backpack." They all bunched together to view what J.J. was seeing. "Was there food in there?"

"Did you rescue some critter while you were exploring yesterday?" asked Nicki.

"No and no! There was no food in there and I didn't rescue anything. I was just being careful because—" He dropped his hand and breathed a sigh of relief.

"Because what?" insisted J.J., still on alert.

"Relax, guys." He casually walked toward the open armoire. "Wil, go get Mom and Dad, please. Only them! No security, no staff or anybody else."

"What is it?" Nicki dropped her hand and stared at her little brother.

* * *

"Well, can you do it?" asked Genoveve. She was sitting under a covered bench at a double-decker bus stop across the street from the main entrance to Westminster Abbey.

"I popped over there last night just for a look-see." The wiry Irishman shifted uncomfortably on the bench. "That place is protected by some ancient spells. I've never seen the like. There are more layers than that school up north."

"You haven't answered my question." She saw a big red double-decker bus heading toward them, so she stood and began walking down the sidewalk. The Irishman followed. After the bus had passed (the driver seeing no one to pick up) they turned back and resumed their seats.

"Of course I can do it!" He reached into a bag, seized a small handful of shelled peanuts and popped a few into his mouth. "With enough time and talent, any defenses can be overcome. To get through that many layers, though, will take too much time. I've got to find a legitimate way to get onto the property, won't I."

"And you've found one?"

"Aye, I think so. Word in a local pub is they are looking for someone to help the gardener. That will get me past the outer layers and maybe further. I have an interview with the caretaker's son this afternoon."

"You have made good progress."

"It's what I do."

"Yes, well, here is a schedule of the Vice Chairman's meetings." She handed him a large manila envelope. "Unfortunately, they do not include any indication which ones the whole family will attend or any separate events the wife or children are going to attend."

"No problem! The old man's son will be most helpful." He smiled and his teeth showed a sadistic grin. "'E's a reg'lar at the pub I visited—ef yer catch me meanin'.'"

"You *are* thorough."

"That's what you pay me for, isn't it."

"You do remember—"

"Yeah, yeah!" he said with disappointment in his tone. "No one to get hurt."

"We cannot afford an open investigation."

* * *

"Merlin's book is calling us." Brian reached in the bottom of the armoire and pulled out his backpack with the embroidered blue dragon on the flap. "It's been in my backpack ever since we left for New York." He unzipped the flap, pulled out the book and set it on the desk. The cover and pages were insistently flipping back and forth.

"Are we going back to see Gran'pa Merlin?" asked J.J.

"I don't know—prob'ly."

"Not until you breakfast!" Brian heard his mother say as she was being led by Willard. The book kept flapping. "Enough already—they're coming," she snapped at the book. "They need to breakfast and get some things ready." The book suddenly opened to the page with the familiar:

HITHER THY RIGHT HAND LAYEST
RETURN IN TIME THOU MAYEST

"Who goes this time?" asked J.J.

"How did he know?" Brian stared at the bottom of the page and saw:

SIR BRIAN
SIR JEREMY
LADY NICOLE
MASTER WILLARD

"Hmmm, looks like the adults stay home again." Myrna sounded a bit disappointed. "Well, com—"

Brian stared at the open page—along with the rest.

Mother, Father, have a care
The time to travel comes when fair.

"As I was saying," she recovered to announce, "Well, c'mon! Let's breakfast and then get you packed."

Brian noticed his father was silent—content to allow his wife to fuss and keep busy. It helped her deal with the worry she naturally felt when her children traveled back to the sixth century and became involved in Merlin's dangerous adventures.

*   *   *

"Grandpa!" greeted four voices in unison as they ran to the white-haired and bearded old man. They hugged and kissed on each cheek.

"Grandpa—Merlin," said Brian, "this is our new (adopted) brother Willard."

"Well met!" He held the boy by his shoulders at arm's length and looked him over. "And welcome thou art. And very special, I see. In time thy true self revealeth."

Brian looked around—they were not at Merlin's cottage in North Britannia. They were standing on a hill beside an entrance to a cave. A prickle went up his spine as he saw some similarities to the land they just left.

"Where are we exactly?" said J.J.—thinking the same thing.

"You already know."

"That's it, then." Nicki pointed to the cave opening. "*The cave.*"

The old man simply nodded, and they all stood in silence for a few moments.

"Come—come. Warm within and cozy."

As they entered Brian saw this cave was much like the one overlooking the northern cottage. There were torches in wall holes, carved out shelves, a crude table, chairs and sleeping pallets. A cheery, smokeless (wizard's) fire burned in an alcove and the distinct odor of one of the old magician's herbal tea concoctions was steeping in a pot. Moments later they were all seated, sipping tea and honey and nibbling on bread and cheese.

"What's up this time?" J.J. smiled and his red hair glowed in the light from the torches and fireplace. "Some dragon dentistry? Sword rescue? Elemental power practice? Chasing thieves?" He greedily rubbed his hands together.

"As irreverent as always." Merlin's smile beamed through his beard and mustache. "Despite no blood ties, truly thou art my grandson." They all laughed and J.J. simply lit up with the compliment.

"This be short thy visit. A warning: thy foe entereth into the planes of alternate realms. He seeks to alter history and prevent the *Appointed One* from becoming Ringmaster. Stopped he must be. A catastrophic paradox will result. Even he will not survive."

"Can't you stop him?" asked J.J.

"He cometh from thine own time. I cannot interfere with the future—mine future. You must go back and prevent any change in history as it happened."

"How do we do that?"

They sat for some time as Merlin paced about with his hands clasped behind his back and explained about the *Sigillum De Aemeth*: a gateway or a seal to the alternate planes, realms and even time.

"If the seal is so rare, how'd Reficul get it?" asked J.J.

"Tis not the seal be rare. Knowing the means to open and use it."

"Then how did he learn to do that?"

"Methinks it was an accident. A seal was nearby and it was mistakenly opened, which prevents him from returning to his time; the portal was not held open."

"And so you're saying he's trapped in the alternate planes or realms until someone reopens the one he came through," observed Nicki.

"Aye. The seal was not opened properly, so it closed after he went through."

"He's gone, then!" said Brian. "He can't hurt us."

"Nay. He can do much. Thy foe has since learned to open and use the seal he has acquired and plans to change a past event—your past—mine future."

"Grandfather," said Willard meekly, "can I ask—how do you know all this? It's all in your future." Brian watched the old man wielding his wand. A rough-hewn three-legged stool appeared, and he sat down.

Merlin went on to explain that he often traveled the other realms, places, planes and times to learn about events in those existences. He would watch events unfold. But he frequently had to remind himself to not interfere in any way. Usually that meant not even being seen. It was quite by accident, while visiting a world of orcs, hobbits, elves and dwarves (which may have been the inspiration for some famous books—or the other way around), he heard about a man who exploded into their realm out of a column of blue smoke. He made friends with an old wizard who taught him about the seal—which he later regretted. Merlin overheard the man plotting to return to earth and interfere with a past event and steal a document.

"He's going after the formula!" Brian jumped up from the crude chair and began pacing around the cave's interior. "He's going to attack one of our great grandparents!"

"But the two halves didn't come together until Mom and Dad married. He will only get half, and that won't do him any good."

"That's enough!" proclaimed Nicki. "It may not make him Ringmaster, but it'll stop Brian—the *Appointed One*. He could also try to go after one of Mom's ancestors."

"But that'll affect all kinds of things. Not just Brian."

"That's what Grandfather Merlin told us earlier," said Willard.

"How do we stop him?" asked J.J.

"We have to travel to that time and find some way to interfere with his plans." Brian continued his pacing but his shoulders were dropped in resignation, and his voice sounded sad.

"And we'll have to do it without changing anything of the actual history," said Nicki, "or we'll create a paradox mess—maybe even bigger than he will."

"Understanding the problem it seems." Merlin sighed and Brian continued his pacing, his mind racing.

"And we don't know when he's going to do it or what he's going to do. Do you, Grandfather?" asked J.J. "I mean, if he's got over 1400 years of our family history to work on."

"It has to be some well-known event," said Nicki. "Otherwise, he has no idea about when or where a specific family member might be."

"I am afraid I am no help," said Merlin. "Save it be to instruct you in the use of the seal—*Sigillum De Aemeth*."

Brian felt sure he knew the event and who Reficul was going to attack or alter, but for now he chose to not complicate things with his suspicions. Now he needed to learn how to travel between realms, planes, dimensions and times.

Over the next several hours Merlin explained that the seal was like a maze. Each line and intersection was a gate to a specific portal leading to alternate realms, dimensions, planes or time travel. A very skilled practitioner could even combine time traveling with a realm (world), dimension or plane—otherwise it was necessary to travel in two steps: first, go to the desired location and then travel to the sought time period. He also reinforced the necessity that the portal must remain open to allow traveler(s) to return to their time and place of origin. Merlin liked to use books, as it was easy for them to have the seal icon drawn on a page, and can usually be placed where they will not be disturbed. But almost any inanimate item can be a portal—as long as the seal can be drawn, etched or engraved on a surface—even very small.

"Did you use the seal to bring us here—to your time?" asked Brian.

"Aye. An open gate at each end transports any who touch it. And I put a spell for it to open with the rings I created."

"But there's no *Sigillum De Aemeth* on the page of our book," protested J.J.

"What thou canst not see mayest be present still." The old man grinned mischievously. Brian saw J.J.'s face almost burst with recognition.

"Ha! Invisible ink—you were famous for it," proclaimed J.J., jumping up and down in his chair—excited he solved the old wizard's trick. "But how did you make the book stick to Brian and do all that flapping?"

"Some secrets are mine to keep. You may discover them in time." He smiled again—obviously pleased with himself.

"In other words—"

"In other words, little brother," interrupted Nicki, "since you're so smart; you figure it out!"

"That's okay. I love a challenge." He clapped his hands together and rubbed them with mischievous delight.

"Grandfather, you have no idea what you just set in motion," said Brian with a chuckle. "The alternate realms may never get over it!" They all laughed but Brian saw the gleam in J.J.'s eyes and his hair aflame.

"That's not as hard as I thought." Brian was pacing again, but this time it was around the library, back at Everett Manor. They had practiced using the seal to travel to various times, planes and realms, then went back through the books (always the same gate must be used to return to the same place and approximate time). "I thought it would be really complicated or take a huge amount of power." J.J., Nicki and Willard were sitting in various chairs.

"Remember," said J.J. "Merlin told us that's part of the secret. No one wants to believe it's that simple. They wanna make it hard and confusing."

"Kinda like the old saying: 'Hidden in plain view'," added Nicki

"Are we gonna tell Mom and Dad?" wondered J.J. aloud.

"Merlin didn't say not to, but he didn't let them come for instruction."

"Let's talk to Dad when he comes home and see what he thinks."

"Talk to me about what?" Brian heard his father's voice from the big doorway between the vestibule and the library.

"DAD!" they all shouted and ran up to give and receive hugs and greetings. Then Brian explained:

"Merlin told us about the *Sigillum De Aemeth* and how to use it as a gateway to travel to alternate planes, realms, dimensions and times." Brian talked about Reficul being trapped but planning to interfere with a past event that would keep him (Brian) from becoming Ringmaster.

"Of course, we've known there is a gate," said Dad, "but how to use it has been lost for centuries—especially how to select destinations. This knowledge is huge—and has even bigger implications."

"Unlike the oath we swore about the elemental power, Merlin didn't say we cannot tell you how this works," said Nicki.

"And you're wondering if you should tell me."

"Yeah—"

"Don't," he insisted. "If we were meant to know the secret he would have told you. Anyway, I'm not sure I want to know. I might be tempted to send some dingy ambassador off to some world of dragons."

"Wow, Dad, did you have a bad day?" asked J.J. with a smirk.

"No, not really, but some of the foreign representatives sure have their heads in the sand about current events and how they affect all of us."

"Tell me who they are—when we were practicing, we went to an ice planet. Someone from the desert would love that!"

"Believe me, it's tempting. That's why this knowledge cannot become wide-spread."

"Are you sure?" asked Brian.

"Completely. And besides, if I need such travel, I have four children who can arrange it." He started to turn to leave the library.

"Dad, before you go, can you tell me the story about your Grandparents and that ship that sunk in New York?"

"Wow—I haven't heard or thought about that in years." George walked over and sat in a comfortable, padded armchair. "As I remember it, Grandma and Grandpa volunteered to help a neighbor, German immigrant family with five children who were going on a church outing aboard a paddlewheel steamboat—the General Slocum. Just before they were to shove off, a woman had a premonition and convinced the neighbor something horrible was going to happen. The woman, the neighbor, his family and my grandparents rushed off before the gangway was removed. About twenty minutes after the boat headed up the East River, it caught fire. The Captain ran it aground on North Brother Island, but it burned to the waterline and over a thousand lives were lost."

"Wasn't there something about luggage or something?"

"Hmm, yeah. After Grandpa was sure they were okay on the dock, he tried to get back on board to get their light bags, which were still on the steamer. The captain wouldn't hear of it—he wanted to get underway. A few minutes later he couldn't figure out how Grandpa was suddenly standing there in the Third Street pier with all their things. It would have been funny except for the disaster that happened about a half-hour later."

"Was the—?"

"Yes, it was!" George cut him off from saying anything aloud about the formula.

"That story is not a family secret, is it?"

"Oh, no—except for what was in the bags. The local Sodality newspaper (I don't know if it was the *Power Press* back then) reported the story."

"I've had some dreams about that event."

"I'm sorry to hear that. It was a terrible tragedy, though it turned out okay for us. We'll always be grateful that lady, Mrs. Strabe or Strube or something, had that premonition." He stood and headed for the door. "I need to find your mother; she's got some things for me to do."

"Being Vice Chairman doesn't get you out of anything, does it?" said J.J.

"Nope."

Chapter Twenty
The Discovery

"I bet this stuff would be worth a fortune," Brian heard J.J. say as they were rummaging around in the basement deep below Everett Manor. There were rows and piles of old furniture, paintings, tapestries, toys, clothes, weapons, bedding and an array of garden tools. "The appraisers from that PBS show, *Antiques Roadshow*, would go crazy down here."

"I thought you'd be disappointed we didn't find a medieval dungeon or torture chamber." Brian opened a box of old wooden toys.

"Well, if we don't have a nice stretching rack..." He laughed with a sinister cackle. "We might as well have a great load of treasure!" They all laughed as they uncovered more items.

"The condition of this stuff is amazing." Brian wiped his fingers across the polished wood top of an old oak table, then rubbed them against his thumb. "There's not even any dust."

"Mrs. Hodgins said she uses a cleaning and preserving spell that keeps everything like new," said Nicki.

"Have you seen her use her wand?" added J.J. "She's brilliant."

"I wonder why they let the place fall into disrepair then," questioned Brian.

"They didn't," said Willard, who was examining some of the huge boulders that made up the foundation wall. "I heard Hodgins tell Dad that it was all done on purpose. During the wars and other problem times—when there were no Everetts in residence—they made it look all broken down so no one would bomb it. There were repelling spells to keep out thieves, vandals and local kids (and adults)."

"Oh wow!" Brian pulled a large, intricately-engraved sword from its scabbard and tried to swing it in the air. "What a great way to preserve the place—this thing is neat!" Unable to wield the sword with one hand, he grabbed the hilt with both hands and swung it over his head—but almost dropped it.

"You better put that down," teased J.J. "You're gonna chop off your foot."

"I don't know how they fought with these things. It's lighter than I expected, but it's still so long." He worked the blade back in its thick leather scabbard that was covered with embossed runes that looked Druidic.

"Wouldn't it be something if it's Excalibur?" said J.J. with a mischievous glint in his eyes and hair almost flaming red.

Brian felt a slight warming in his hands from the sword's grip and there was a faint metallic ringing sound in the basement.

"Yeah, it would, but I remember it was given to the Lady of the Lake."

"But what happened to it after that? Wasn't it the Lady of the Lake who entombed Merlin in the Cave? It could have ended up here."

"You really are a romantic," said Nicki.

"Hey, it could happen." J.J. blushed deeply.

"About as likely as you becoming an NBA center." Brian chuckled and rolled the sword (and scabbard) back in the velvet cloth it had been wrapped in. "And besides, if it were here, wouldn't it be upstairs on display or something?" He looked at J.J. and could see he wasn't convinced.

"Sir Brian," called Willard's tiny voice. "There's a room or something behind this wall."

"Are you sure?" Brian, J.J. and Nicki walked over to where Willard was standing: next to a large, flat rock embedded into a very solid-looking wall. "How can you tell?"

"I think so. It just feels open on the other side."

"Hmmm." J.J. began running his hands over the flat surface and tapping various points with his knuckles, like knocking on a door. "Sounds pretty solid. Maybe there's a torture chamber after all." He chuckled evilly.

The room suddenly felt drier, colder and a bit of a breeze swirled about—like a window was open. Brian was gathering energy. He closed his eyes for a moment then opened them, staring at the wall.

"Wow! There's a lot of energy around that stone."

"Can you pull it out?" asked Nicki.

"I'm afraid to; the foundation is really old." Brian walked over to the wall, at the far left of the rock. He seemed to trace some invisible lines with his finger, then reached up and grabbed a small stone jutting out from the mortar at the edge of the boulder. With a gentle pull the stone slid out about an inch with an audible click that sounded metallic.

"How'd you do that?" asked J.J., but before Brian could answer, a low hollow rumble and grating shook the wall and basement floor. Brian jumped out of the way as the huge stone started swinging toward him, seeming to have hidden hinges buried along the right side of the boulder.

"I don't know. I could see lines of energy swirling, but they all went to that spot—but that's not it either. It's like when we were in Wizard's Cavern: I just suddenly knew the lever was there, as if I've known all my life."

"That's really scary—brilliant—but scary!"

"Yeah, really scary." Brian barely mumbled, breathing hard.

The big flat rock was a door, flat on both sides, about eighteen inches thick. When fully swung open, it created a jagged opening about five feet wide and seven feet high. They peered inside and saw a large stone room filled with scrolls and ancient books.

"Well, here's your dungeon, but no torture devices or treasure," said Brian.

"Are you nuts?" J.J. was jumping up and down with excitement. "In ancient times, books were more valuable than gold." Brian watched him bound into the room which lit up as he entered. Ancient, glass-chimneyed oil lamps on the walls and on the tables all began to burn brightly. "Whoever sealed these in here must have thought they were even more valuable than the ones in the library upstairs." He grabbed a scroll and began to gently unroll it until he looked up and saw Nicki, Brian and Willard staring past him. "What?" He turned and his mouth dropped open. "Oh!"

Brian too had his mouth agape as he took in the sight. Beyond the stacks of books another doorway led to a long tunnel which was slowly being lit up by glass-chimneyed lanterns hung from brackets on both sides of the walls. As if being turned on by switches, the lamps came to life one at a time, side to side, about every twenty feet. On and on they went until the newest to light were beyond what they could see. A cool gentle breeze told them fresh air as blowing through, though smelling like damp earth.

"Well, Cavern Boy," said J.J. gravely in a hoarse whisper. "Does your sudden knowledge tell you where that leads?" His sarcasm suggested he really did not expect a positive answer.

"Yeah, I think so." Brian began taking tentative steps toward the long tunnel's entrance.

"Really?"

"It's the crystal viewing room—the Crystal Cavern."

*　　*　　*

Laileb looked deeply into the faces of the three women and two men seated at a large rectangular table, laden with books, scrolls, computers, pads of paper and several cups with pens and pencils. He had recruited them to form the team to research how to reopen the seal and allow Reficul to return to the present realm. They were thorough; having borrowed (or stolen) books and research materials from libraries and personal collections around the world. The piles on the table were only a small portion of what they had amassed. They had taken over the large, open area in Reficul's Mount Greylock library. A cheery fire burned in the fireplace, yet the pervasive gloominess of the castle-like rock walls, ceiling and floor always kept a damp chill in the air.

While each recruit was learned and dedicated to the task, CKS's Professor Phusikos was, in his opinion, Laileb's greatest asset. The bearded teacher's expertise as a researcher was almost legendary. If anyone could find the answers, it would be him. Even the Sodality Council consulted Phusikos on matters needing historical or technical perspective, which gave him access to materials not usually available to the (Sodality) public. Unfortunately, the professor would soon have to return to Arizona and resume his position at CKS. Antetima had already taken an indefinite leave of absence. They could not afford to attract more attention.

"What do we know so far?" asked Laileb.

"Not nearly enough," responded one of the women. "We know the seal is the gate for hundreds—maybe thousands—of destinations."

"Our Master cannot return unless we open a seal and gate—from this side," said another woman.

"A spell or incantation does not open it," said the man sitting beside Phusikos. "It requires some other means of energy."

"Does the location of the seal (or book—in our situation) matter?" asked Laileb.

"No," answered Phusikos. "Only the exact spot on the seal—that gate—is critical."

"You're sure?"

"Yes! Much of the seal's information is obscure—at least what we've found so far—but that's one element that's clear."

"If it doesn't require a spell or incantation, what triggers the gate to open?"

"After critical review of the video recording loop and a few obscure bits in the research, an argument can be made for introduction or application of energy," explained Phusikos. "The problem we haven't solved is what kind of energy and how to precisely control it."

"Why don't we just start experimenting?" asked one of the women.

"Because we might run out of experiment*ors* before we have the answer." Laileb stood and chuckled at his bit of sarcasm.

"Until we know how to control it," continued Phusikos, "any energy applied to the gate could open a portal and whoever is close might be sucked into some distant time or realm and be trapped."

"Or course, Mabel, if you're volunteering to be first—" said Laileb.

"Oh no—no, thank you!" she said, holding the palms of her hands out-stretched. "I hadn't thought of it that way."

"Then I suggest we dig deeper to find the answer, or we may just have to start experimenting."

The meeting broke up and each researcher returned to their individual projects, except Laileb pulled Phusikos aside for a private conversation.

"You know, she's right—we are going to have to open some gates—and see what we find—eventually."

"Hopefully, we'll know much more before we do that. Who knows what horrors we might stumble into?"

"And we must learn how to keep the gate open, so we can get back."

Chapter Twenty-One
The Crystal Cavern

J.J., Nicki and Willard faithfully followed Brian, who padded along almost as if in a trance or being pulled by an unseen force. The floor of the tunnel was clean except for a few very small pebbles and some bits of sand that had fallen from the ceiling, which crunched under their shoes. Brian's pace was steady. They could easily see, even though the lanterns' illumination was somewhat dim. Deep in the tunnel the air was slightly musty, but there was enough fresh air (from some source) to prevent staleness or foul odors from building up. Though centuries old, the tunnel seemed to have been dug out recently. The walls and ceiling were smooth—covered with an ancient form of whitewash or plaster. Neither roots nor animal debris encroached on the passageway.

After walking a long way, the quartet of youths reached what appeared to be a dead end. Out of the corner of his eye Brian saw his sister give J.J. a threatening signal to stop him from blurting out one of his usual quips. He smiled, thinking how hard it was for his brother to restrain himself. After only a moment's study and searching his mind, he cautiously walked up to the end wall (that looked exactly like the side walls), placed his right hand on a spot about the height of his chest, closed his eyes and channeled energy. A metallic click echoed through the tunnel and Brian easily pushed the wall away. With a low groan and a bit of grating, it pivoted on a hidden hinge, exposing a passageway similar to the one in the basement. The heavy door opened to a darkened chamber.

As before, lanterns lit up with cheery flames and the glass chimneys provided warm light that flooded the room. But unlike the chamber with the books, scrolls and a bit of furniture, this room was sparsely furnished with only a couple of crude chairs. When the last lantern flickered to life the chamber was suddenly filled with a rainbow of colors. Smooth flat walls showed brilliant bands of reds, blues, yellows, greens, violets, oranges and thousands of blended shades. It was breathtaking.

From the center of the ceiling hung a suspended, absolutely flawless clear crystal. It was over eight feet tall and so wide, Brian doubted his arms would reach all the way around. As he ventured forward he could hardly take his eyes off the huge stone. When he did, there were hundreds, maybe thousands, of other, smaller, crystals suspended from the ceiling and jutting from the floor at various heights around the room. At first the placement seemed random, but as he walked in and looked further, there was a familiarity and symmetry about it. He couldn't remember from where, but something he had seen before. From each small crystal there was an interplay of light between it and the large one in the center—and sometimes with another small one.

"Wow!"—"Unbelievable!"—"Oh, my!" Brian heard his two brothers and sister whisper as they followed him into the room and witnessed the spectacle. He could hardly breathe.

"This isn't quite what I expected after reading the books about Merlin and his crystal cave," said J.J. softly after several minutes of walking about and examining the ancient chamber from several vantage points.

"Very late in his life, after he defeated Viviane's entrapment, Merlin remade this place."

"Wait a minute," objected J.J. "There's no record of him breaking free from Viviane or anything except to appear to Sir Gawain—and his ghost coming to us."

"I know. He didn't appear to anyone, in this plane, as himself. He stayed here and built this—and the tunnel. Of course, in disguise, he went on his time-travel adventures he told us about."

"Your connection to him has given you a lot," said Nicki. She too was in awe, walking about the room.

"It seems to come only when a particular fact is needed, and it's not everything. There's some stuff he wants us to work out for ourselves—like how this room works."

"Oh, ho! I love a challenge." J.J.'s hair seemed to be ablaze as the prism bars of color touched him.

"Yeah, you would—and most of the answers are in that study room at the other end of the tunnel."

"There's no other way in or out," observed Willard. "That's why no one can find the surface entrance anymore. He must have closed it off when he finished the tunnel."

"Good guess," confirmed Brian. "There's no more hidden doorways—" He grabbed his head and swayed where he stood. Willard rushed to steady him.

"Owww!" he complained.

"What's wrong?" asked J.J. "A Monēo warning?"

"It kind of feels like that, but no vision appeared."

Suddenly one of the walls flickered and like a TV screen without a picture, a staticky and snowy scramble showed. Instinctively Brian closed his eyes and concentrated. A picture appeared. There were two men seated at a small table inside a pub. One was Melvin, Hodgins' son, and the other was a sandy-haired, thin man with a ruddy complexion. There was no sound but they were shaking hands and smiling: an agreement had been reached. Then the picture flickered again and was gone. Only the color bands remained.

"What was that?" demanded J.J.

"I don't know!" cried Brian—still hurting but starting to feel better.

"How'd you make that happen?"

"I don't know!" he repeated. "Like I said, it's one of those things our dear great-grandfather wants us to work out for ourselves."

"I think that scene is important somehow," suggested Willard.

"And it's probably not good, either," said Nicki. "It's getting late. We should get back before Mom and Dad send a search party after us."

"You're right there. With all the remodeling and some of the old buildings on the estate, I'd hate to think what extra chores Mom could dream up," said J.J.

"And I'm getting hungry," announced Brian.

"You're always hungry!" echoed throughout the room.

As they backed out of the doorway, the lamps snuffed themselves out and the thick rock door closed itself and locked with a metallic click and deep clunk, like a bank's heavy vault door locking. They jogged through the tunnel and each lantern went out as they passed.

Exiting the tunnel, they passed right through the study room and finally stopped when the basement's stored furniture came into view.

"Tha – ws – fa'er – than – I – tho't," gasped Brian, panting hard and holding his side. Then, like the other door, the big stone slab closed and sealed itself shut. It was amazing—he looked at the wall and there was no trace of the huge, rock (open) doorway that was there only moments before.

"Grandpa! Grandma!" called four voices together as they stepped into the main foyer of the manor house; then broke into a run to embrace their father's parents.

After warm hugs, kisses and greetings Brian watched J.J. take the elder Everett into the library and showed him the relief carving of the family coat of arms.

"That's really something," said the old man. "I could hardly believe it when your father called. We couldn't wait to come see." He then turned to Brian. "I understand you object to my quiet life of retirement and think I need something to do."

"That's not—I don't object—you do lots," stammered Brian, dropping his shoulders and staring at his grandfather—hoping he wasn't really offended.

"You're good, Grandpa!" quipped J.J. "Not much will make Ring Boy speechless."

Brian's cheeks were glowing almost as much as J.J.'s hair as he realized he'd been so easily had by the old man's teasing.

"I grew up hearing stories about this place, but we thought it had been destroyed in one of the invasions or other conflicts Britain has been through." He pulled Brian close with a strong arm. "You had me pegged right. I would love to do some remodeling, install some modern utilities and appliances. And your grandma is looking forward to babysitting you guys while your parents are away."

"What?"—"Babysitting?"—"Mom and Dad leaving?"—"When?"—"Where?"—How long?" blurted Brian, Nicki, J.J. and Willard faster then answers could come.

"Oops! I guess I let the cat out of the bag. I thought you knew."

"Nope. We've been exploring underground and the basement all day," said J.J.

"Your dad and mom need to meet with leaders in some other countries and the schedule is so tight there won't be time for sightseeing. They felt you'd rather stay here than sit in some boring waiting room."

"You got that right—and I guess they can travel faster (translating) if we don't have to go."

"And you need to get back to your school studies," said a familiar voice.

Brian turned toward the library entrance and saw Professor Heady gliding in, dressed in long, black wizard's robes and hat.

"Is it that time already?" complained Brian. "I thought we'd have another week."

"Nay, young lord," he answered. "Yer holiday be over."

"Er, Professor?" J.J. had a smile on his face, clearly indicating some deviousness was running amok. "Didn't you say we were going to have to do a Sodality history report?"

"Yes—" said the professor hesitantly, sensing his brilliant student was setting him up. "Since you cannot attend class lectures and discussions, several of your subjects will require research and written reports."

"What about combining subjects, say, history and advanced psionics?"

Brian watched J.J. put on his most innocent look: cheeks dimpled and blushed, downcast eyes, feet shuffled about, and hands pushed deep in his jeans' pockets. Truly a master at work.

"Seems a noble task, M'Lord." The teacher had seen the boy ply his charms before and was not about to agree before knowing more. "Present your proposal tomorrow then, and we'll give it due consideration."

Just then their brother's plan dawned on Brian, Nicki and Willard. "You'll like it!"—"It'll make a great project!"—"Wait 'til you see it!"—"You won't believe what we've found!"—"It's brilliant!"—"It'll take lots of study—and practice!" they all joined in, but careful not to reveal too much where so many could hear.

"I'm sure you have a great plan." Brian watched Grandma come to the besieged professor's rescue. "But for now let's let Professor get settled in his rooms and you lot need to clean up for supper. Your parents are leaving for meetings afterward." Right on cue, Hodgins appeared.

"Welcome to Everett Manor, Professor. Your rooms are prepared. Please follow me." He waved his wand and Heady's bags and trunk levitated and moved ahead like a luggage guide dog.

* * *

Brian selected a desk and sat down. He looked around. Overnight, an unused room on the second floor had been converted into a classroom. Four antique student desks were in a semicircle, facing a larger teacher's desk. Chalkboards were on a wall behind the teacher's raised dais. Maps, charts and books were arrayed on the other walls. Nicki, J.J. and Willard were milling about when Professor Heady came in, followed by Hodgins.

"Excellent!" said the teacher as he circled around inspecting the room, his robes flowing behind with each step. "Hodgins, you've outdone yourself."

"Not at all, Professor," he said, obviously basking in the praise. "This is not the first time young wizards (and witches) have studied here. It's good to have the house used again. Please let us know if you need anything at all." He retreated from the room with a slight bow, closing the door behind him.

Before anything else could be said, Brian stood, pulled a piece of paper from a pocket of his jeans and handed it to Heady.

"What's this?" he asked, but when Brian did not answer, just stood staring at the paper, he unfolded and quickly read it. "Right! Please be seated while I attend to a couple of details." Brian watched him pull out a wand from his robes and walk about the perimeter of the room, mumbling power commands—touching the doors, walls and windows.

"I think everything's secure now. We cannot be overheard by electronic or magical listening means. Would one of you tell me what this is all about, then?"

Brian watched J.J. stand and wave his right hand. The floor-length heavy window curtains closed, several of the lamps dimmed and the room became dark. Another wave and a three-dimensional hologram was being created in the air—each line lit up like a laser beam.

One of these days I'm going to have to learn how he does that, thought Brian to himself as he watched lines fill in. After a few moments they were staring at an illuminated scale model (hologram) of the thick rock basement door, study area, tunnel and crystal viewing room.

It took the professor a few minutes to understand what he was looking at. "Is that—?"

"Merlin's crystal viewing room?" answered Nicki. "Yes."

"Have you? Is it here? Is it still in working order?" he stammered.

"Yes, yes and yes!" Brian's eyes were so bright with excitement they almost seemed to glow in the subdued light of the classroom.

"Does anyone else know?"

"Only you—that we know of. Mom and Dad left before we could talk to them. But I wouldn't be surprised if Hodgins knows about it; they seem to know everything about this house and the grounds."

"That's something we should make sure of." The professor walked around the image J.J. was projecting. "What's this room?" he asked, pointing to the study room. Nicki told him about the scrolls, books and study table.

"You say it works—have you used it?"

Brian explained the details of what they had seen and the momentary image of Hodgins' son and the other man.

"And you have no idea how you activated the projection."

"Nope."

"Now I understand your research project and report. You want to study the materials in that room to learn about the crystals, perfect how they are used and write a report."

"Yup!" J.J. grinned, face and hair glowing red, clearly pleased with his idea.

"Excellent plan, M'Lord." He gave J.J. a formal bow. "We will need to bring those materials up to the library or this room. Spending too much time down there may attract unwanted attention."

"Let's put everything in the library," said Willard. "Anything on those shelves is protected by powerful spells; only Everett family members can remove items from them."

"Spot on! We will make sure no one is in the house after dinner, then pack off everything to the library."

"Er, Professor, it's okay if our grandparents know what's going on," said Brian.

"That's even better. They can organize a shopping trip and ask the Hodgins and Cook to go with."

"And their son?"

"Especially him—until we know what that vision meant."

Chapter Twenty-Two
The Break-In

"Well, that's the last of it." Brian placed an ancient, leather-bound book on a shelf they had cleared in the main library of Everett Manor. Professor Heady had quietly spoken to the grandparents and arranged for them to take the Hodgins (including their son) and Cook on a shopping trip to select paint colors, appliances and other supplies for the house's remodeling. They would also order groceries to feed the craftsmen and ever-growing number of household residents; they would be staying for a time while the 128 Main Street house was being rebuilt to accommodate a newly-adopted son and the security required for Sodality's Vice Chairman.

"Do the old spells work on this stuff," asked Nichole, "even though it wasn't there when the energy was placed?"

"Wow, I'm not sure. I just assumed it would," answered Willard.

"All of us are Everetts," said J.J. "We'll have to get Heady to try."

"Try what?" Brian and the others turned and saw their teacher entering the library through the large double doorway, then wave his hand; the heavy sliding doors rumbled, rolling to meet in the middle with a deep bump. "M'Lord Jeremy?"

"Er, sorry, Professor." J.J. understood he had just been gently chastised for his discourteous familiarity.

Brian jumped in quick to relieve the tension. "Professor, would you try to remove one of the tunnel-room books from the shelves? We want to know if the spell works on anything placed on the shelves."

"Certainly, M'Lord." Brian watched him reach in a leather briefcase he was carrying and extract a small book, then walk to the shelves they had just filled. Setting the book on the shelf, he reached over to one of the antique volumes (brought up from the basement) and found it impossible to move—as if it was glued or bolted in place. He then reached for the small book. It came up easily. "Ah, just as I thought..."

"How'd you—m?" stammered J.J. "You're not supposed to—"

"Be able to remove anything from the shelves, hmmm? Au contraire, M'Lord. The spell works only on items placed by an Everett."

"That's why you had us—"

"Put everything on the shelves. I wasn't just making you do all the work."

Brian suddenly swayed as if dizzy and almost lost his balance, then put his hands on the sides of his head. Willard rushed over to help keep him from falling. The quick movement stopped the banter between J.J. and the professor as Nicki joined Wil's efforts to prop up their brother.

"M'Lord," said Heady. "Are you not well?"

"Give him a second," suggested J.J. "We've seen this before." He eased toward Brian as he closed his eyes. "Something is going on."

Before Brian could open his eyes and speak, Willard started squirming, turning his head from side to side as if his neck was hurting. He wanted to rub the back of his neck, but he wouldn't release his steadying grip on Brian.

"Somebody is in the house," whispered Brian after a long, uncomfortable silence.

"A bad person," said Willard with unusual power in his voice.

"Where?" insisted J.J. "This place has lots of rooms."

"Mom and Dad's bedroom!" He broke free from his brother and sister, heading toward the doors, which J.J. already slid open. Following J.J, he started up the center grand staircase and heard the professor's voice in the distance.

"Gather elemental energy." It was clear his students were not waiting for him to take charge. "Stay shielded!" he called after them.

Trying to keep up with J.J. and still feeling the crush from the vision, it was not easy to concentrate on gathering energy, even though there was plenty of heat in the fireplaces (which were burning brightly) and air swirling all around. Reaching the second floor landing, the teacher was already there by translation. Brain slid to a halt, breathing hard.

"We don't want him to get away. I will hold a translation barrier (you haven't learned yet) over the whole house, but that'll take everything I've got. You should wai—"

"There might be important stuff in there," interrupted Brian. "Who knows what might get damaged." He was remembering the robbery disaster at the Meyor house. "We gotta stop him!" He led his brothers and sister as they started jogging down the long right side hallway toward their parents' rooms. He heard Heady invoke the barrier commands (which J.J. carefully listened to).

Nearing the door to their mother and father's large suite, the quartet slowed, walking softly and watching for any movement. The door was open and they could hear the sound of things being moved about and quiet cursing. The intruder was looking for something but could not find it. Brian eased his gathering energy from the fireplace. He didn't want to extinguish the fire in he bedroom and alert the intruder. Wind was swirling around him. He could sense Nicki and J.J. also taking in elemental power, (probably more than he was). He surrounded himself with a shield and moved boldly into the center of the (open) doorway.

Seeing the movement, the ruddy-complected intruder whirled and quickly fired off a powerful stunner, which was absorbed by

Brian's shield, but he swayed and almost tripped—still feeling the effects of the warning vision.

"Well, young wizard, and who mi'cha be, eh?" he said with a strong Irish accent. He was clearly stalling for time to formulate a plan.

"I live here." Brian put on a brave face (but grimaced, still in pain). "But more to the point, what are you doing in my parents' bedroom?"

"Aye, Laddie, 'tis a good question, but alas, no time for small talk."

Brian watched him wave his wand and there was a sharp crack. The man was enveloped in a puff of smoke, then another crack. Dumbfounded he stood in the very same spot. Brian would have laughed, but at the moment it would have taken too much effort.

"Looks like you have more time than you thought. Why don't you toss that wand over here? Then we'll wait for my father's security detail to sort things out." He watched the man ever-so-slowly ease to his right, hoping for some advantage.

"I think I be keepin' me shillelagh, if it be all the same to ya, and best forego meetin' yer da's lackeys. So if you'd be so kind t'step aside, I'll be on me way—seein' ya can't hold them shields forever."

Brian saw him begin to lift his wand and heard him start to say, "*Cruc*—" when he sensed slow motion changing his perception. Before the man could complete the infamous curse, he combined air and heat (fire). A blast of hot air hit the man in the face, knocking him down on his backside.

"Did you really think you could use a forbidden attack in this house?" roared Brian with anger he didn't know was in him, but his knees almost crumbled under him.

Quickly J.J., Nicki and Willard stepped into the doorway, taking positions between Brian and the Irishman.

"Oh, what be d'matter," he taunted. "Needin' reinforcements, I see. You be comin' t'rescue yer brot'er..."

"No, we're rescuing you!" said Nicki. "We don't want your demise on his conscience. Believe me, you have no idea what he's capable of—and really don't want to find out."

Brian had to smile, listening to his sister, as he saw J.J. quickly create a shield to cover all four of them—and just in time.

"Ah, noble sentiments, me lass, but now it be time to leave!" He jumped up, flicked his wand (shillelagh) and sent a fireball at the four youngsters.

Brian was glad J.J.'d chosen absorption shield instead of reflection. The powerful wave hit the dome and dissipated. He gathered the heat within himself. He could see the look of shock on the man's face.

"Hmmm, that feels good," he said. "You got some more?" A bright energy aura formed around him—making him look like he was glowing and his red hair seemed ablaze.

In all the commotion no one noticed Willard squirming with discomfort. His skin had taken on a gold tint and its texture changed—almost scaly. He squatted down on his heels, raised his arms just above his head. Brian noticed the curious movement, and saw him open his mouth. Willard then let out a low rumbling sound, creating a cone of air disturbance and a mist between the intruder and himself. When it hit the man, he collapsed to the floor—not unconscious but so weak he could hardly control any muscles.

Seeing the man go limp, Nicki quickly sent bright yellow energy binder ropes to hold him fast, but they weren't really necessary. The man was unable to even lift his head off the dark hardwood floor.

By the time Brian looked down again (having been distracted by the man's sudden weakness and Nicki's golden ropes) Willard was standing again, skin color and texture were back to normal; acting as if nothing had happened. Nicki was the first to move. She walked over and picked up the man's wand, still holding the binder.

"What do we do with him now?" she asked. "His weakness may wear off and—"

"We'll handle it from here." Brian heard the familiar voice of Agent Bowyer, head of his father's security detail. He waved his hand and another set of binders secured the Irishman's hands and feet (like handcuffs and leg irons). "You may release your energy, Miss Nichole." Another agent levitated the man's limp body and they started for the door. Nicki sidled over to J.J. and whispered:

"You'd better ground that elemental power before you hurt yourself—or someone else."

"Good idea," he agreed and headed for their parents' bathroom to find a plumbing fixture. That was one advantage of the antiquated utilities: most of the pipes were exposed and mounted on the walls. It was easy for him to discharge the excess energy he had gathered.

Brian was so weak and relieved, he collapsed where he stood and held his head (that was still hurting).

*   *   *

"Well, what happened?" spat the short, squat woman. She was again sitting on a park bench in a nondescript part of London. It was cold and threatening rain (or snow) so there were few passersby. At the other end of the bench sat another woman, who could have been her twin (in physical size and shape), wearing a ridiculous-looking cardigan.

"He was captured in the Vice Chairman's bedroom, rummaging through their things."

"The house was supposed to be empty."

"The children and tutor stayed home to do studies."

"A school professor couldn't hold him; he's much more powerful than that!"

"It wasn't the professor—he only held an apar—you call it 'translation' barrier. The Everett brats did the rest."

"That can't be—"

"I watched the interrogation myself. They gave him a truth potion."

"Did he say anything about me?" asked Genoveve with obvious worry in her voice.

"No—but only because they didn't ask. They were satisfied when he said he was working for Reficul's Black Knights as a contract operative."

She breathed a sigh of relief, then asked, "How did those kids defeat him?"

"The reports say the boy Brian started it. He held a shield that was impenetrable against stuns and then hit your man with a blast of hot air that knocked him down."

"That's impossible. One cannot hold a shield like that and do offensive attacks—especially one that manipulates two elements (air and heat). The others must have been helping."

"That boy apparently can. His brothers and sister weren't even in the room yet."

"What happened then?"

"The others did come into the room—protecting your man from the boy. Then the redhead created an absorption shield and seemed to gather energy from the fireball. Then the youngest growled. Your agent collapsed on the ground, so weak he could not move."

"He what? Lost his energy because a little boy growled?"

"There's no evidence to connect the boy's sound to the weakness, so most at the ministry believe the youngster did not cause it. But, nothing else explains the loss of energy."

"I don't understand it. Last year, four kids (and their uncle) defeated Reficul and over thirty Black Knights, and now, one of the most talented and powerful operatives is put out of commission by actions thought to be impossible and the growl of an eleven-year-old." She slid a bag of gold coins over to the other woman, then stood to leave. "Thank you for your valuable information. Please keep your ears open for anything else that might help us."

"It's been a pleasure doing business with you!" She placed the newspaper she was carrying over the bag and watched her employer turn and walk off without looking back.

Chapter Twenty-Three
Auntie Winifred

"Congratulations!" Brian heard his father say. The whole family was gathered in the large sitting room located on the opposite side of the manor's expansive front foyer from the library. A cheery fire burned in a huge fireplace, warming the thick walls which reflected the subdued lighting of oil lamps and several candles. The massive carved-panel sliding doors were closed and anti-eavesdropping wards were in place. Colorful Persian rugs were on the hardwood floors and large tapestries hung on the painted or wallpaper-covered walls, creating a cozy, yet somewhat formal atmosphere. "Your mother was worried that we didn't leave any agents here, but I felt you would be fine. All of you performed admirably." He took a long sip of his hot, mint tea.

"But don't you think this proves they need a detail assigned to them?" questioned Myrna, sounding worried and unconvinced. "The interrogation revealed Reficul's still after us."

"What more could agents have done?"

"Please, Mom," pleaded Brian. "It's bad enough that we can't go to Seminary, play flipolo and stuff. We don't want bodyguards hangin' around all the time." He took a big bite of a cream-filled pastry, which oozed white filling around his mouth.

"I don't know..."

"What was he looking for?" J.J. changed the subject—hoping to get his mother thinking about something else.

"The master-ring formula, of course," said George. "I can't imagine they think we're stupid enough to leave it lying about in our bedroom."

"How'd—e—ge—n—da—ows?" Brian swallowed the last of his pastry and saw everybody staring at him. "What? I'm hungry!"

"YOU'RE ALWAYS HUNGRY!" the whole family erupted, then laughed.

"I said: how'd he get in the house? There were no alarms."

"We gave Hodgins permission to hire another groundskeeper. Their son met and hired him."

"How'd he get past Grandma's screening?"

"My abilities are not without limits," answered the old sage. "The man was very skilled at keeping just the right thoughts and avoid revealing his intentions."

"I wish I could do that," mumbled J.J. quietly; grinning at his grandmother—knowing she empathically heard him.

"You might develop that skill, Jeremy, but with our connection it will never work on me."

"That's not fair!" he complained playfully. "I know; you don't have to tell me—life's not fair."

"It's good to see you're learning something," teased George.

"Is that guy okay?" asked Nicki. "He was sure weak and pale when they took him away."

"When I left the ministry he could sit up and answer questions, but was unable to stand up. I suspect he'll be much better in a day or two. Which reminds me," he turned to Brian, "how'd you do that? Local healers are baffled; they have no counter spell. It'll just have to wear off."

"Me? I didn't do anything!" He saw his dad look at him somewhat skeptically. "Honest! Wil just sorta growled at him and he collapsed. C'mon! I know it sounds weird, but we didn't channel anything. Maybe he was just sick or something."

"I hope it's not contagious," observed Nicki.

"Are any of you feeling ill or weak?" asked Myrna, but her expression suggested she knew more.

"No," the four youngsters said at the same time (but Brian added *not now* in his mind). J.J. was getting an idea, but needed to do some research before saying anything. And Brian wondered why it took so long to recover from the vision—keeping him from gathering energy.

"Well, it is late and we have all had a busy day." Grandma eased out of the plush armchair she was seated in, cutting off the discussion. "I am sure things will become clearer when we have had some rest and time to investigate today's events. And, Mr. Vice Chairman, I believe you are expected in Capetown, South Africa, early tomorrow morning." Without waiting for further comment she waved her right hand at the large paneled doors, which smoothly slid back into their wall pockets. Then she opened her arms, signaling she wanted good night hugs from her grandchildren. Brian rose instantly and as he approached, a small linen handkerchief appeared in her hand, which she used to dab a bit of white pastry filling from the corner of his mouth. She smiled; they exchanged kisses on each cheek; then she held him close. "You must learn from today," she whispered. "Be careful of your temper, take time to prepare properly and study hard. Much is yet to be revealed. Remember you are loved and—"

"I know, Grandma," he interrupted. "Love is the greatest power in the universe." He felt her squeeze him a bit harder.

* * *

Brian walked over to the tilted reading desk he was using and set down the armload of books he had just retrieved from the shelves—the ones from the basement tunnel collection. He looked around and saw his brothers and sister were also studying books or scrolls at similar desks (Hodgins found and brought up from the basement). Professor Heady was leafing through a textbook he was making lesson plans from. Merlin's notes about the crystals were amazing but there was no index or guide to the order of how to make them work. So far, they had not determined which one was first. So their initial task was to catalog them by subject and sequence.

Before starting on the pile he'd just retrieved, Brian went to a side table with pitchers of water, pots of cocoa and herb tea (no drinks were allowed at the desks or near the ancient tomes). After several sips of cocoa he headed back to his desk, glancing at J.J.'s work as he passed. The book he was examining wasn't one of Merlin's—it was a detailed practical guide to dragons. He was about to inquire about what dragons had to do with the crystals, but his brother looked up with an expression of pleading and eye contact, imploring him not to say anything. Accepting there was a good reason for his brother's actions—and that he'd find out later—Brian passed without a word and continued his cataloging chore until:

"Professor, Milords, Milady, I understand Cook gets cranky if dinner is allowed to get cold—"

"Benson!" yelled Willard, first to recognize the impeccably-dressed valet who had been with them in New York and during the move into Everett Manor. He jumped up and ran over to greet the man. "I thought you were going off to another ministry assignment."

"Yer da offered me and the missus permanent appointments on his staff and Mr. Jones arranged for work visas when we go back to the U.S."

"That's great!" added Brian. "We've missed you the last few days. Did you hear about that guy breaking in?"

"Aye, M'lord. Agent Bowyer briefed us. The Ministry is grateful t'yer lot. Been looking for that Patrick O'Connor bloke for years. With Professor's leave, let's get you to dinner while still hot. Then after your afternoon studies, yer mum wants you scrubbed and dressed in formal robes. The Sodality South African ambassador will be here for supper and reception. The Minister and a group of ministry officials will also attend."

Brian stepped out of the bathroom, which was still steamy from his hot bath. He had a towel wrapped around his middle and a bath robe hanging loose about his shoulders. The crackling fire made the air warm; smelling of pine and oak. Yet the old windows were drafty and the wet and cold of British winter crept in through the wood paneling on the thick stone walls, producing a slight chill. He hurried to the big four-poster bed to don underclothes and formal dress robes laid out by Benson. In Europe's wizarding community robes were common attire, but they felt strange on a Sodality youth from the United States. He chuckled when he saw a long, thin pocket sewn along the inside to hold a wand—where it could easily be drawn if needed.

Moments later, upon entering the long, second floor hallway, Brian met up with his brothers and sister. They were all heading downstairs to the large sitting room to meet the South African ambassador and the other guests. Nicki seemed to flourish at such functions, but Brian, J.J. and Willard felt awkward—never knowing what to say. But now that their father was vice chairman, formal dinners and receptions were part of the job. And it would only become worse when George became Chairman of the Sodality Council.

Entering the sitting room, Brian was shocked. It had been completely redone. A chandelier hung from the ceiling with dozens of candle flames reflecting brilliant light off hundreds of polished glass crystals. Oil lamps glowed from golden sconces attached to the walls. Comfortable chairs were set about in clusters to allow several group conversations.

Brian followed his sister toward the nearest gathering of dignitaries—he knew they were expected to make the rounds and Nicki was perfect at polite and unobtrusive introductions. Also, if he (or his brothers) blundered or couldn't think of anything to say, she would brilliantly smooth things over—which did not take long.

"Oh, aren't you a darling little thing!" said a short, fat woman with rings covering her pudgy fingers and wearing a lurid cardigan. She extended her hand to tweak J.J.'s cheek but he quickly backed out of her reach. "Your red hair is so cute, and your freckles, too."

"Yeah, and you look like a badly transfigured warthog!" J.J. blurted out before he could check himself.

There were gasps from those nearby.

"What did you say?" she demanded.

"That you remind him of his great aunt Winifred Terrogg," said Nicki smoothly, without hesitation. "And I can see it—yes—I think he's right. One of our favorite aunts, Auntie Winifred."

"Oh," said the woman, her eyes darting back and forth between Nicki and J.J. (who was furiously nodding in agreement). "That's okay, then... One of your favorite aunts, hmmm?" She seemed almost proud of herself, for she felt some connection to the very powerful Everett family.

"Oh, yes, I shall mention it to Mother," continued Nicki without missing a beat. "If you'll excuse us, we must say 'hello' to the other guests." She reached, grabbed J.J.'s hand and pulled him away before he could blunder into anything else.

"Good one!" complimented Brian, catching up with Nicki (still dragging J.J.). "I thought we were about to kick off an international incident."

Away from guests, Nicki stopped and whirled on J.J. (and Brian and Wil). "Look! Dad's barely holding an alliance together by a thread. Most of the wizarding communities want to just go deeper into hiding from Branglers and pretend nothing's going on in the world. You saw Ground Zero. And Brian, you felt a little bit of the horror of 9-11. Just one stupid comment like that can unravel months of work!"

"Okay, I'm sorry!" said J.J. "I just get so sick of looking like a ten-year-old. Brian's four years younger yet he's bigger than me. But you're right; Dad's depending on us."

"Just stay out of reach of the cheek tweakers," said Willard. "That's what I do—and I *am* smallest and youngest."

"But you don't have red hair, freckles and dimples. Those seem to be tweaker magnets."

"C'mon, let's make the rounds," said Nicki. "Oh yeah, Dad wants us to keep our ears and other abilities alert to any hints of problems."

Chapter Twenty-Four
The Gold Dragon

"**D**inner is served!" announced Benson with a formal tone, just loud enough to be heard over the din of conversations. Brian watched his father lead the crowd through another pair of double sliding doors and into the gigantic dining room with the long, rough-hewn wooden table that surely dated back to medieval times. His mother joined them to walk in behind the guests.

"One day you must introduce me to your favorite Aunt Winifred," whispered Myrna in a jovial way.

"I'm sorry, Mom," said J.J. quietly. "I lost it and Nicki bailed me out."

"Yes, I know. Madge was nearby with a tea tray and heard it all, and gave me a heads up. It's a good thing; that woman approached me a few minutes later. Next time, come to me directly," she gently chastised.

"There won't be a next time—I will—"

"Oh, I'm sure there will. It's all I can do sometimes to keep from telling off some of these snobs." She led them into the dining room after the last stragglers went in.

"Wow, Mom," whispered J.J. "Why don't you tell us how you really feel?" They all sniggered quietly.

"Ladies and gentlemen!" At the far end of the room George stood at the head of the table with a golden goblet in his right hand. "A toast to our new friend and South African Ambassador and to our unity to defeat evil and dark forces that confront us all!" He raised his cup high in the air and the entire assemblage stood, copied his salute with many saying, "Hear, hear!"

"Unity!" responded all those around the table.

Brian raised his drink with the others and sipped the contents. He tasted sweet, bitter sparkling (carbonated) grape juice (alcoholic beverages were never served by the George Everett household—despite the large wine cellar the previous owners of the manor had left behind). The imitation champagne was so convincing, he heard several comments around the table:

"Excellent vintage!"—"Wonderful bouquet."—"Fine wine!"

Smiling, he thought: *if they only knew.* Then he saw his parents simultaneously sit, signaling for everyone else to do the same. He was almost taken by surprise as empty soup and salad bowls were suddenly filled and hot bread was steaming in napkin-lined wicker baskets. Muted conversations resumed as everyone tucked into the perfectly-presented first course.

When the soup and salad was finished, Myrna waved her hand. The bowls disappeared and were replaced by plates with prime rib, baked potato, green beans and sweet yams. Platters, tureens, boats and bowls appeared in the middle of the table filled with turkey, gravy, stuffing, sausages, sauces, steak and kidney pies and assorted warm breads for those wanting seconds (or, in Brian's case, fourths or fifths). Brian was now in his element. He knew just what to do with a whole table laden with glorious food. With a bit of concentration, he could consume copious quantities and still be a perfect gentleman, not spilling anything or dropping a crumb.

No one seemed to be in a hurry (which was excellent for Brian); they were content to enjoy the marvelous meal, continue political discussions and work out ways to anonymously use their powers to deal with terrorists. As requested, Brian listened for any hint of dissidence or anyone working against his father's plans, but there were none. In fact, everything he heard was quite supportive—even enthusiastic. One discussion even praised the Vice Chairman for bringing together groups that were usually less than cooperative with each other. He marveled at this; to him George was just his geeky dad who, while fairly strict, loved his family passionately. The confident, soft-spoken, politically-masterful SVC George Everett was a whole new dynamic in the family. Even Uncle Paul had transformed from the immutable bachelor and prankster to a model of professional efficiency who tolerated no disloyalty; a perfect chief of staff.

With another wave from Myrna, the main course plates, platters and bowls disappeared and Brian almost went into sensory overload. The huge table was suddenly filled with éclairs, ice cream, sherbet, kettles of mint tea and hot cocoa, pies, cakes, tarts, puddings, custards, donuts, trifle and streusels. He heard many "oohs" and "aahs" from the other diners. A great thing about dining with a bunch of folks with psionic powers is never needing to reach, wait or ask for trays to be passed. With a wave of a wand or ringed hand, the desired items were simply translocated from the platter to one's plate. Advanced practitioners were able to be so discreet in their actions, it seemed the food just appeared out of thin air. Others loved a showy display and were quite animated— even flying the food through the air (instead of de/regeneration), which was considered very poor manners by the more high-brow types. Here again, Brian was a master. He could focus on a desired item and it would dissolve and then reappear on his plate or in his bowl—always plated in an artfully pleasing manner (appearance was important).

Brian took a bite of a chocolate covered éclair and noticed a dark-suited man enter and discretely walk toward Uncle Paul. This was a new addition to the security team he had not seen before. Suddenly Brian felt a headache like "brain freeze" but he was not eating or drinking anything cold (he was saving ice cream for last). He closed his eyes tight, holding the sides of his head. Behind his eyelids he saw a spectral vision of a very gaunt face—almost ghostly skeletal— with dark recessed eyes and a long, pointy nose. Something was wrong or danger present—he had a vision of Monēo.

Opening his eyes, he glanced at Willard. He was rubbing the back of his neck and his skin was taking on a gold-looking tint. Brian knew if he suddenly stood and walked to his father he would attract a lot of attention, but he couldn't ignore such a warning. He was in a quandary. Who was it? Everything was fine until the new agent walked in, but the security team was carefully screened and vetted. Maybe it was someone else in the room and they didn't plan to act until now. He watched the agent deliver his message to Uncle Paul and leave—and so did the Monēo warning. The prickly feeling on the back of his neck went away. That was just too much coincidence. But what to do, and when to do it? He looked at Willard, who nodded and projected:

"That is a bad man."

"The agent? Are you sure it's him?" replied Brian in mind-speak.

"Aye, M'Lord." (Wil was picking up a British accent.)

"Follow my lead, but first I'm going to try to project to J.J."

"Can you? Will it work?"

"It did once, I think, at a flipolo match."

"Try it—it could happen."

Brian closed his eyes and focused on J.J., willing him to hear.

"J.J., can you hear me?" he shouted in his mind.

The reaction was instantaneous. Brian watched his brother almost bite off the end of the spoon that held his ice cream (which was now either choking in the back of his throat or drooling from his mouth and chin). Coughing, he dropped the spoon in his lap. His cheeks began turning red and tears were leaking from his eyes. He quickly put his napkin over his mouth and uttered a muted cough so those near him would think he'd swallowed something wrong. He looked across the table with his eyes wide open, brows raised, and nodded.

"That new agent who just talked to Uncle Paul is a bad guy. Even Wil picked it up," projected Brian with less force.

J.J. turned up his hands as if to say 'what do we do?'

"Can you do a translation barrier like Professor did?"

J.J. grinned mischievously, then nodded.

"And ward the doors?"

This time J.J. hesitated, rolled his eyes toward the ceiling in thought. After a moment he nodded.

"Done?"

His grin was unmistakable: yes. Brian politely stood, sliding his chair back, and said quietly to those nearest and loud enough for his mother to hear, "Please excuse me; I need to freshen up." He looked at his mother, who mouthed:

"Of course."

"Me, too?" Willard quickly followed.

"Go ahead," said Mom quietly.

As Brian headed for the side door—the one the agent used— he smiled as he heard comments from some of the adults that were sitting near: "Such polite boys." "I wish my children were so well-mannered." "The Vice Chairman and his wife should be proud." Willard was right behind him as they stepped into the large vestibule which was lined with chairs. Aides and security personnel for several of the VIP guests were eating from plates of food (resting in their laps) or simply relaxing—waiting to respond to any need of their employers.

Seeing the children of their host, several men respectfully stood and one of the Ministry aides spoke: "May we be of service?"

"Which way did the agent go who just came out?" asked Brian.

"Toward the staircase to the upper floors, just there." He pointed to one of the back staircases usually used by Hodgins, security and other domestics.

"Thanks!" Brian (and Wil) broke into a fast jog and took the steps two at a time.

"Do you have a plan?" projected Willard. *"Shouldn't we wait for Dad or security?"*

"No! I'm making this up as we go. We're just gonna check this guy out."

On the second floor, in the wing their parents occupied, there was a room where the security detail kept an office. One had to pass it to get to the Everetts' bedroom. Brian guessed that's where the man was headed. He knew Willard was right but did not want to cause a scene if it was not necessary.

Down the hallway, lit by candles and lanterns, light was coming from the open door of the security office. Brian slowed, caught his breath, gathered and channeled his energy, then boldly stepped into the room. The (new) agent was sitting at a desk, looked up and was surprised to see the young Everett boys.

"Can I help you?" He made no move to stand but seemed tense. "I am John Sutton. We haven't met. I just joined your father's security detail." He was trying to be pleasant but was obviously nervous about the boys' sudden appearance and determined stance.

"Who hired you, Mr. Sutton?" demanded Brian.

"I was on the previous SVC's detail, so—"

"That's not what I asked! Who hired you?"

"I came—in case your father needed—"

"You still haven't answered! Who hired you?"

"Now see here! It's not your place—" He started to rise.

"Don't move!" Brian extended his right hand and ring and out of the corner of his eye, Willard seemed to be glowing—gold. "I don't know what you're about, Mr. Sutton—if that's your real name—but your loyalty is not to my father or this family."

"And what makes you think that?" he sneered. "I'm a trained agent. Do you think I can't handle two underage mages?" He realized his mistake: A loyal agent would never threaten his protectees—even their children—the way he just did. The only thing he could do was escape—leave the manor. But there was just one teensy problem—no, make that two: young or not, there were mages all channeled up for battle, standing in front of him. And, there were the wildest rumors about the abilities of the Everett kids. They, with little help, took on and defeated Reficul himself and a couple dozen Black Knights. The fact that they were standing their ground before a skilled agent said a lot.

"Look, I think we got off on the wrong foot. Let's start—" He dove sideways to the floor and rolled to his feet, sending the chair flying the opposite direction and crashing into a wall.

The move took Brian by surprise. He fired a powerful stunner but it missed and blew out a window in the back wall. Fortunately he had put up a shield. Sutton fired back and Brian staggered when it hit the dome of energy, but he remained standing. Just as he was about to return an energy bolt the man suddenly put his hands in the air; surrendering with a twisted look of surprise and shock.

Brian felt a nudge against his protective dome and assumed it was Willard, but there was a nagging thought: *Dad says to never assume anything*. Afraid to take his eyes off the traitorous agent, he quickly glanced sideways. "What the—?" It was all he could do to keep his composure. Instead of a tiny boy there was a dragon—not a very big one, but a magnificent, sleek, brilliant gold dragon who was staring at the agent with a menacing look that was terrifying. There was a pile of clothing on the floor that moments before was on Willard.

As if Brian was not even there, the dragon slowly advanced on the man, never taking his eyes off him. As soon as Brian was out of the way, the gold maw opened and a low growl and vapor came forth, enveloping the astonished Sutton, who folded in a heap as if he had no bones or muscles to hold himself up.

Grateful as he was for the man's incapacity, Brian had many other pressing concerns. The first:

"Hey, dragon," he confidently called, "Where's my little brother?" He really had a pretty good idea, but again that old advice: '*Never assume anything.*' "I've dealt with dragons before. If you ate my brother, I'll—"

"*You'll what?*" Brian heard Willard's projected voice say in his head. "*It's me, Milord. I'm Willard,*" the voice almost pleaded.

"*Well, can you change back or do we have to put in a cave and straw for your bedroom?*" He laughed.

Like the air going out of a balloon, the not-so-big gold dragon became a smallish eleven-year-old boy who stood there with a huge grin on his face.

Brian quickly bent down, picked up the pile of clothes and tossed them to Willard. "You better put these on before someone comes." He turned to face away while the boy dressed.

"What do we do now?" asked Willard, tying his robes and shoes.

"You should go down and find Agent Bowyer, or Dad if the dinner is over. I'll put a binder on this guy and hold him until you bring someone back."

"Do we tell anyone about me?"

"That's for you to decide, but I think you should tell Mom and Dad."

"But they might send me away. They didn't plan to adopt a dragon." Tears were welling up in his eyes.

"They didn't plan to raise the appointed Ringmaster, or to adopt a red-headed troll. They love you—all of us. Boy, what a weird family. Some day an author is going to write our story and chronicle the Ringmaster, Sodality Chairman, Merlin's heirs, gold dragon, the highest I.Q.'d mage in history, and a nomag who becomes a powerful negotiator mage before she's eighteen. See, Willard, love is greater than all that. You're not going anywhere! So I think you should tell 'em—"

"Oh, you got that right," said Myrna as she stepped into the room. "And tell us what?" She waited a few seconds, then said, "That Willard is a gold dragon?"

"You knew?" asked Brian with a surprised expression and voice.

"Of course we knew!" She went over and gathered the small boy in her arms. "We've known for some time. There were many hints, but he had to discover it for himself."

"Why didn't you tell me?"

"As close as you are, could you not tell him?"

"Prob'ly not. Is supper over? Why'd you come up here?"

"Yes. Everyone is back in the sitting room. It seems there are wards on the doors and a translation barrier over the whole house. Your father and uncle are creating some last-minute conversations so no one tries to leave. We figured you were up to something."

Just then three security squad members entered the room, led by Agent Bowyer, who instructed, "You can release your binder. We'll take it from here."

"Hold him until the guests leave," ordered Myrna. "We'll sort this out then. Let's go down and find your brother—I figure he's holding the wards and shields."

"How'd you figure that out?"

"I asked him where you went and he could only say, 'Chasing a bad guy.' He was obviously concentrating very hard."

Chapter Twenty-Five
The Chairman

I t was almost midnight and the last of the guests had finally left. The South African ambassador and his party were among the final departures. The evening had been a complete success: A formal accord was agreed upon, between the attending communities to share information and cooperate in exposing, resisting and punishing evil or terrorist activities. Numerous details were yet to be worked out and many other countries were needed to sign on, but it was a start. And none of the guests had any idea a traitor (spy) had been caught or that a (not so big) gold dragon had been using his breath weapon right over their heads.

"I'm sorry to keep everyone up so late," said George, looking about at the ten others in the room. They were in his study with everyone seated in deep plush leather arm chairs and he was behind a huge dark wood desk. "But we need a few facts so we'll know how to deal with earlier events. Brian, Willard, would either of you like to explain why a security team member is in the basement's temporary holding cell, unable to even lift his head?"

Brian stared at his father for a moment then shook his head.

"No? It was all a mistake then?"

Again he shook his head, but allowed his eyes to dart toward Agent Bowyer, suggesting he could not hear the answer.

"Oh, right; Agent Bowyer, are you still prepared to swear the inviolable loyalty oath as we discussed?"

Brian turned toward the chair where the dark-suited man sat, and watched him solemnly nod in agreement, and say, "Yes, sir!"

"For some time I have felt our chief of security needed to know some things and I believe he's earned our trust. Does everyone agree—if he swears the oath?"

All quickly agreed, except Brian who hesitated, searching his abilities for any sign of deception. Finally he said, "It's okay, as long as you and Grandma James seal the oath."

"Fine, Mr. Bowyer, Grandma..." They rose and joined George behind the desk. "Better idea! Everyone, join hands—we'll all seal it." The eight Everetts stood and crowded around the desk. They held hands to form a circle with Dad, Grandma and the agent.

"Does everyone feel the energy flow?" Brian heard his father ask and he watched all nod in the affirmative. "Bowyer, you know the words."

"Yes, sir," he said, then began: "By all the Powers, I swear loyalty to those in this circle and their families, to hold secret all their personal affairs unless specifically given permission and hereby invoke the Inviolable Loyalty Oath."

Brian felt a surge of power flow through him and knew the man was bound. They each shook the agent's hand, then went back to their seats.

"Right. *Now* will you tell us why—and how—Mr. Sutton was reduced to a babbling blob?"

"When he came in and spoke to Uncle Paul I got a clear Monēo warning. I saw Wil rubbing his neck, so I knew he sensed it too. He and I mind-spoke. I was afraid to say anything that would make a scene, so I projected to J.J. to put up the barrier and wards—"

"We knew you and Willard could mind-speak—Jeremy, too?" interrupted Uncle Paul.

"Maybe; he hasn't learned how yet, but I can send to him."

"Hmmm, interesting. Continue," said Dad.

257

"Wil and I excused ourselves and followed him to the second floor security office—just to check him out. I asked him who hired him but he wouldn't answer. Then he dove to the floor and tried to stun me.

"I tried to zap him but missed and blew out the window. Then, much to my surprise, Wil transmuted to a gold dragon and used his cone-of-weakness vapor breath weapon. He changed back, got dressed and then Mom came in." Brian looked at Bowyer and chuckled; his jaw was working and mind spinning but he was trying hard to be totally nonchalant and said:

"Well, it sounds like we need to use a memory probe or get some more truth potion from the Ministry folks and find out who this guy is working for. We also need to alter his memory about Willard."

"Understand something, Bob." George shifted in his chair behind the massive desk and took on his most authoritative demeanor. "You will come to know you've only learned a small fraction of the abilities of these four children. I suspect—I am certain—there are many things they have not yet told their mother and me. As tempting as it may be, they are not to be asked to use those abilities in any official capacity without our approval—and we won't authorize anything against their wishes."

"Tell him, Dad," said Brian with quiet resolve.

"You're sure?"

Brian simply nodded in affirmation.

"Agent Bowyer," George became formal again. "Even though I may become the Sodality Chairman, the time is coming—possibly soon—when Brian will be able to influence my psionic abilities—yours, too. He is Merlin's appointed heir to become Ringmaster."

"It's true then? The legend and rumors are true..." Bowyer sighed. "What an awesome responsibility for a young boy—"

"You have no idea," interrupted Brian.

"That explains a lot: We have been assuming Reficul's Black Knights' attacks are somehow tied to the Vice Chairman, but it's his obsession with the master ring. He's trying to prevent Brian from becoming Ringmaster."

There was a long, uncomfortable silence while the man let what he just learned sink in.

Finally Brian spoke. "Dad, there's something you should know." He took a breath and steeled himself for this one. "Merlin's crystal seer cave, the Crystal Cavern, is here."

"Intact?" George couldn't hide his astonished excitement.

"Perfectly. There's a long tunnel to it through a secret door in the basement."

"Can you use it?"

"Not yet—at least voluntarily. The day we found it, we saw a scene with O'Connor, but we have no idea what made that happen."

"We're studying Merlin's notes," said J.J. with his mischievous smile. "We'll figure it out. I love a challenge."

"Somehow I knew you'd say that," said Mom.

Just then Brian heard an urgent-sounding knock on the door. George waved his hand to release the privacy wards and answered, "Come."

The door quickly opened and four senior Sodality Councilors (two men and two women) entered, each followed by their aides and a discreet video photographer. Agent Bowyer jumped up and stood protectively on George's left side while Uncle Paul assumed his traditional position on his right. For the last time George Everett stood up as the Sodality Vice Chairman...

"Pursuant to Sodality law and custom," said one formally, "and by unanimous, and may I say, enthusiastic vote of the International Sodality Council, George Alan Everett, you have been confirmed as Chairman." Everyone in the room gasped and held their breaths. "Sir, do you accept?"

* * *

Activity at Everett Manor, near Carmarthen, England, was fast and furious. From the moment George uttered the words: *I accept*, not only did he officially become Chairman of the International Sodality Council, but some awesome "powers" were inherited by transference. It was difficult to do anything; security was everywhere. Since George became CSC (International was usually dropped to shorten things) the vice chairman position was vacant, making him the lone authority in the executive branch, who just happened to be in a foreign country—not under his jurisdiction.

Brian was frustrated. With well-wishers (literally) popping in and out and a myriad other issues requiring the Chairman's attention—not the least, planning a traditional formal investiture and gala—he had not been able to speak with his father about the seer cave. For some time he had been having dreams about his great-grandparents, a boat on fire, and a bad guy (he was sure was Reficul). He was convinced the cave would help him get more information so he wouldn't mess things up too badly when they met in 1904.

Brian was in awe. He watched his mother move from room to room deciding which items would remain and which would go back into the basement (which J.J. called 'the dungeon') for storage. And, which would be used in the 128 Main Street house. He intercepted her on his way to make another attempt to see his father. When he rounded a corner his hopes rose. The study door was open and no one waiting outside to see him—only the agent who stood by the door.

"Anybody with him?" Brian asked the dark-suited man.

"Only your Uncle—"

"Excellent!" He didn't wait for permission or to be announced; he hurried right past the stiff guard and burst into the room.

"Hey, Dad!" he called cheerfully. "Got a minute?"

"For you, I've got two!" George stood and opened his arms which were soon wrapped around his son.

"I know you're busy, but I really need to stay a few days to do something with the cave."

"You can't stay here. Everyone must be present for the investiture and reception." He felt Brian's shoulders slump.

"But Dad, it's important—really important!"

"If you say so, I'm sure it is, but—"

"How 'bout going back and forth by FON," interrupted Paul, who was sitting in a somewhat darkened corner at a small desk. "This place needs to have fiber optics, internet and utility lines installed. I'm sure we can use some influence to get it done in the next few days."

"Yes, that would work. They would be available for the mandatory functions—"

"And we'd be out of your hair the rest of the time." Brian picked up on the plan right away. "We can carefully package and ship a few books and be studying while the lines are being installed." He felt his dad push him back to arms' length, then look deep into his eyes.

"No argument! Professor, Benson and an agent will accompany you every time you return here. And you will not leave on any time-travel adventures without clearing it with your mother and me."

"I promise! However, when we go into the Crystal Cavern or tunnel, only Professor goes with. Okay?"

"I will give those orders, but you must let security know you're going down in the basement so they don't think you've gone missing."

"Deal," said Brian, pulling himself back into his father's embrace.

"You know, after the festivities are over, Grandpa and Grandma are coming back here to finish the upgrades. We still haven't unraveled those old spells that only allow an Everett to do anything to the place."

"I almost forgot about that," said Paul. "I'll get Dad to put up the FON mirror and utility service boxes before we leave tomorrow. That should satisfy the old place an Everett wants the stuff installed. He can translate back and forth if there's a problem. We'll make sure everyone has international satellite cell phones."

"I want that FON installation thoroughly tested before my kids use it." George's air of command authority had returned.

Chapter Twenty-Six
Back To The U. S. A.

ondon's famous fog and rain postponed their departure
only an hour—which was good because last minute delays
at the manor house ran just about that long. The Ministry
arranged another portal key to get them directly to the protective
hangar and the waiting G500 jet. A customs inspector quickly
stamped their passports and Brian was pleased to see Captain
Newton standing at the foot of the airstair door.

"Mr. Chairman." He extended his hand for a handshake.
"Congratulations. We are fueled, pre-flighted and there's a break
in the weather. We're wheels up whenever you're ready." Brian
watched as they shook hands. Brian followed his parents as they
boarded the sleek white jet. Inside the luxurious cabin smelled of
lemon oil polish, new furniture, jet fuel and the galley food.

Everyone quickly belted in, and a tug pulled the jet through
the giant hangar doors as the powerful Rolls-Royce engines started
up. Moments later (12:00 noon) they lifted off and Brian settled
into the plush, soft leather seat for an eight to nine hour flight
(depending on the winds aloft). *Flying is fun but it's such a waste of
time,* he thought. *We'd already be there if we translated—but nooo,
we have to wait till we're seventeen. If only they knew Merlin already
taught me...*

"Hey, Dad, why aren't we FONing? Grandma, Grandpa and the rest of the staff are translating. I know there's a FON mirror at the Ministry. It'd be a lot faster."

"We could've and it's sure faster, but the jet was already at Heathrow and we certainly don't want to deprive the staff, who went on ahead, of a chance to organize a surprise party." He chuckled.

"They're not very sneaky, are they?"

"I wouldn't have it any other way. We're fast building a core group who not only work well together but are loyal and truly care about each other. So be sure and act surprised."

"Hey, Pops," jibed J.J. "Since you've been promoted, do I get a raise in my allowance? Chairmen's kids gotta put on a proper example." He blushed, grinned and made his dimples and freckles show.

"Yes, Father," added Nicki. "I'm going to need a whole new wardrobe to wear at all the special events." She batted her eyelids and gave him her sweetest girlish smile. She knew exactly how to ply her daughterly charm to melt his heart.

"That reminds me, Dear." Myrna could not resist such an opening. "We're certainly going to need a bigger household budget."

"Okay, okay! I can see I'm fast getting outnumbered—at least I have my chief of staff."

"Oh, really?" Paul had a huge grin on his face. "I was just about to remind you the contractors at the Meyor house need their last quarterly payment."

"Hmm, let me see." George prided himself on his memory, so he was going to get this just right.

"First, as to allowances, if you do well on your ATPs, you'll get 'em. Yes, Nichole, you're going to need some new clothes. I've noticed some being too tight and not long enough. We must always be attentive to our modesty and standards. Yes, dear, some adjustments in the household budget are going to be needed. Of course, the Bensons and Hodgins are domestics, so you'll be taking care of their salaries, and the remodeling of the manor house. And finally, yes, Paul, we will take care of the contractor. We need him to finish that project so we can move back home!"

They all groaned—George Everett didn't miss a thing. Allowance raises were coming, but only if grades came up. Nicki would get a new wardrobe but not the latest "hip" styles. Mom would get a bigger household budget but was given huge new expenses to pay out of it. The only one who came out even was Paul; the contractor's payment was due anyway. They should have known better. Brian saw his dad grin quite contentedly. He knew they should have waited until he was extremely harried or sleepy.

"When *can* we go home?" inquired Nicki. "Now that you're Chairman, we have to make even more modifications to the house."

"Right after your brothers went in for clean-up chores, the contractors found some major structural problems—it was an old place and not built well. It was also about that time Chairman Anderson's health took a bad turn. It was easier and faster to build a new home than to try to fix the old. The new house is finished except for some trim work, painting and decorating—which each of you will choose your own. We should be home within a week of the investiture ceremony."

"We can decorate our rooms however we like?" J.J. had a huge mischievous grin and was almost jumping out of the thick, overstuffed seat.

"Within reason!" snapped Mom quickly. "There will be no immodest pictures from magazines."

"Yeah, right—like we could even buy that stuff. I just want to customize the wall colors and put up a bunch of flipolo posters and stuff."

"Well, it'd be a shame to cover all that new paint, but sure, you can do that."

J.J. reached down, pulled the seat's swivel release and spun around to face aft and Brian seated behind. They leaned together and began plotting their new digs.

"Hey, Dad," said Brian across the aisle. "Where are the Bensons and agents staying? Not in the house, I hope."

"We bought the properties on either side of ours. The Bensons will move into the little house on the left and security will be set up and housed in the North Ranchette. Also, before the (new) house went up, a two-story basement was dug in, which can be used for many purposes."

"Any secret passages?" asked J.J. teasingly, rubbing his hands together. The answer surprised them all.

"Actually, there are, but you're just going to have to find them, aren't you."

Brian saw J.J. rub his hands ever harder, his cheeks blush and his hair seemed to glow a brighter red (if that were possible).

"Oooh," he said. "I love a challenge—and a mysterious one." Just then the cabin attendant brought plates, silverware, and tables that snapped in between J.J. and Brian; George and Myrna; Nicki and Willard; Paul and Grandma James. Agent Bowyer had his own table up near the galley.

"I'll be serving your lunch. Please raise your seats to their full upright positions," she announced as Brian anxiously awaited his meal.

They didn't have to wait long. Expertly-presented dinners of fried chicken, mashed potatoes, corn, gravy, coleslaw and broccoli appeared on their plates. Tall glasses of iced mint tea and Vainabier finished out the offering.

"I didn't know she's Sodality," whispered Brian; he raised his eyebrows and smiled, noticing his portions were almost double the servings on the other plates. "She didn't use psionics on the flight to London."

"Mr. Jones was with us, wasn't he," said J.J. "She prob'ly didn't know it was okay to do that in front of him." They watched her walk up and down the aisle and point to a plate which would get a second (or third or fourth) helping of whatever was desired. She paused at Brian's plate and he kept nodding until there were four drumsticks and thighs and two breasts piled on his plate. He looked up to see scowling stares on the faces of those near.

"What? I'm hungry!"

"YOU'RE ALWAYS HUNGRY!" clamored the other nine fliers (including the attendant). They all laughed and continued the excellent nosh.

After dinner, Brian reclined in his seat and curled up to take a nap. Due to time changes, his day would have an extra five hours—meaning they would land at Washington, D.C.'s, Dulles Airport between 5:00-6:00PM, local time. He went to sleep grumbling about the crowds of people who would be pressed into the Council Executive House: old biddies pinching his cheeks, creepy old men tousling his hair and squeezing his hand like a vice. Still, he smiled; he was very proud of his dad. Tears came to his eyes when he thought about it: Sodality Chairman for North, Central and South America, China, Japan and Africa—about one-half of the world's population.

Sleep came quickly, but he woke just a half-hour later, struggling to breathe. He had dreamed a five-hundred-pound woman with four arms, four legs, dressed in witches' robes and pointy hat, was pinching his cheek with one hand, tousling his hair with another, patting him on the back with a third and burying his face in her chest with a tight hug with the fourth.

"Wha—whazzup?" J.J. stirred at Brian's sudden movement.

"Nothin'. Just a nightmare—a horrible nightmare." He pulled the blanket back to cover up and drifted back to sleep—hoping that was not a "seer" premonition, and for no more dreams.

But he did dream; not about the gargantuan woman, but about his great-grandparents, a paddle-wheel steamboat and Reficul. Also in this dream was a woman who gets scared, then convinces a couple (man and wife) to leave the boat with their five children, before it sailed. Brian's great-grandparents also left. They had volunteered to help corral the five kids during an excursion and

266

picnic. Everything in the dream was just like the story that had become a family legend, except, Reficul was there. *How could that be?* he wondered, even in his dream. Reficul wasn't even born in 1904, when the General Slocum burned (without the Everetts on board—thanks to Mrs. Strube's premonition).

*   *   *

"It's a good thing we can translate," said Laileb, warming his hands in front of the huge grey stone fireplace in the library of Reficul's castle-appearing mansion on Mount Greylock. "The snow's so deep, only psionic transport can get us in or out."

"Why were you outside?" asked Genoveve. "I would think you have enough to be getting on with than playing in the snow." She was sitting in a rocking chair, rocking back and forth in short angry movements.

"I needed a bit of fresh air." He grimaced as he heard the rocker's wood creaking, wondering if it would collapse any second under her corpulent mass. "And besides, I'm not the one who's been sulking for two days. Shouldn't you be out there getting the formula from the Everetts, or at least making sure that kid doesn't become Ringmaster before I can rescue the Master?"

"It doesn't make any sense," she whined. "Last year, those kids beat back a whole crew of adult Black Knights and prevented our prince from obtaining the Wizard's Cavern formula. This year, that family has made Mendacci slip through our fingers, and those kids have taken out one of the most talented, experienced and powerful covert operatives of our time and busted an agent-spy we've had embedded in the Council's Executive Security forces for years—on the first day he was assigned to Everett."

"You make it sound like they did it single-handedly. They had a lot of help: rattlesnakes, griffin, dragon, adults, security agents, mountain lions..."

"But that's the point, isn't it? Somehow Brian Everett is able to summon whatever he needs, regardless of the challenge. And he finds the most incredible allies, from the most unusual sources."

"That's true. I can't think of anyone, except Merlin himself, who can (or could) call up a blue dragon, griffin, mountain lions and hundreds of rattlesnakes and get them to do his bidding. I certainly can't do any of those things and never want to go one-on-one with him again."

"What's this?" she sneered. "Are you afraid of a twelve-year-old?"

"I wouldn't say 'afraid'," he said with a growl, "but I have a healthy respect for something I don't understand. If you're so confident, why have you just kept sending others? I don't see you doing anything but yell orders from the sidelines."

"HOW DARE YOU!" she screeched, jumping out of the chair, leaving it rocking back and forth. "You know it was Master's orders that I remain covertly in the school!" She was huffing in and out and turning purple.

"Yes, I do know that," he said calmly; really pleased he'd hit a nerve. "But you're not at CKS now, and you've said you probably won't go back. Anyway, regardless of the reason, you've not faced the awesome menagerie that boy commands, so you have no room to criticize those of us who have." He stood and smoothly turned and walked away—toward the steps down to the lab.

"But—but—you can't—" she spluttered, trying to get the last word.

Yeah, I can, he thought to himself, grinning a satisfied smile she could not see, as he descended the stone staircase.

Still in front of the fire, she eased back into the rocker, barely squeezing between the well-worn wooden arm rests. Her color was no longer purple but glowed bright red—lit by the flames in the hearth. As much as she hated it, she had to admit he was right. She had never put herself (physically) on the line; always spying and planning from afar. But what was worse was what Laileb had not said, which hung in the room like a fog. Since Reficul's disappearance, she had accomplished nothing. If Laileb's team brought the Master back tomorrow, she would only be able to report a series of miserable failures, for which she was ultimately responsible. She shuddered to think of His eyes boring through her as she tried to explain.

It was time, she decided, to take immediate, personal action. And she knew just when to do it, but she had to move quickly. The schedule of events was in *Power Press* just this morning.

Chapter Twenty-Seven
The President

If packing up and leaving the manor house was hectic, the scene at the Council Executive House was absolute chaos. People were running everywhere, setting up for the three days of the investiture, receptions, banquets, balls and congratulatory meetings with Sodality/Wizard leaders from dozens of countries—not to mention, each of the permanent Council members waiting for a private moment with the new Chairman. But through it all, Brian watched in awe: chaos turned to competent organization and confusion became quiet efficiency. Somehow, the immutable bachelor and chronic prankster, Uncle Paul (still Chief of Staff) had morphed into something akin to an orchestra conductor. Events were planned, meetings scheduled, decisions made and housing was arranged for visiting dignitaries.

On the home front, Myrna immediately organized the household. Personal touches adorned every room so it felt like an Everett house, even though it belonged to the Council. Clothes were laundered and pressed, shopping done, meals and banquets organized. Brian could only hope he was half as competent when he was an adult and Ringmaster.

In the midst of it all, there were an extraordinary few minutes when everything stopped. Everyone was ordered out of the house except for family and security. Even the domestics were all given errands to run. There was an excitement in the air as Brian walked into the study his father had been using as a temporary office. He was the last one to arrive (he'd had trouble with the knot of his tie). All the men (and boys) were wearing custom-tailored suits with vests and ties; his sister, mother and grandmothers were in beautiful calf-length dresses and their hair was beauty-salon perfect. Everyone was standing, waiting for the arrival of a visitor.

There was a rustle of clothes and movement outside the door. Then a dark-suited man with sunglasses entered and took up a protective position. He looked around, then waved his hand through the doorway. Brian felt his mouth drop open and he quickly closed it (trying not to look stupid). A man confidently strode onto the room, crossing to George with an outstretched hand.

"Mr. Chairman," he said with a slight Texas accent. "Congratulations!"

"Mr. President, thank you." George firmly shook the offered hand, beaming. "You honor me. It's customary that I call on you, after things settle down a bit."

"Not at all. When Jones told me about Chairman Anderson's rapid health decline and retirement, and your confirmation, I couldn't resist the opportunity to travel through that mirror thing—"

"The FON."

"Yeah, that. Jones explained it, but I had to try it out. Couldn't let him have all the fun. I gotta tell ya, the Secret Service was dubious about it. Wouldn't let me do it until Jones went back and forth—twice."

"Well, despite all the Sci-fi movies," George chuckled, "Branglers still aren't ready for energy travel."

"Um, Branglers? I'm not familiar—"

"That's what we call those who cannot channel psionic energy."

"I remember somebody tellin' me that."

"I know you're busy, Mr. President, and the stars know we're going crazy. Please let me introduce you to my family before you go."

"I'd like that. Then, in a couple of weeks, we must meet to discuss mutual concerns."

"I will look forward to it."

Brian watched his father make the introductions as the President shook hands with each.

Then Dad said, "Thank you again for coming. And may I say, I admire your strength through the 9-11 crisis."

"Not at all, and thank you for your hospitality and kind words." He turned to Brian. "I've heard some amazing things about you, young man. We're all in a war against evil." He addressed the family: "I enjoyed meetin' y'all. Congratulations!" With Secret Service leading the way, he turned and left.

The room was quiet for a long couple of moments until Uncle Paul spoke: "The reception starts at four o'clock. There'll be a meet and greet line."

Brian, his brothers and sister all groaned—and he thought he heard muffled noises of complaint from some of the grandparents.

It was seven o'clock and he was starving. The line of well-wishers seemed endless. Brian was fascinated; the living room of the Council house was huge by normal standards, but today it was even bigger—and kept getting bigger as the crowd grew. In the end, he was sure it was about the size of a flipolo field (well, maybe not that big). For security, multiple layers of shielding and travel barriers covered the entire house and grounds, except for a small building away from the main house which acted as a reception lounge. Several FON mirrors were inside and the coordinates were made available for those who translated. It was the only way on or off the property. Brian was certain that even Brangler bombs or missiles would either bounce off or be absorbed by the massive shield dome. And it wasn't all for George Everett's sake; the Sodality/Wizard leadership from practically every country in the world was present (or sent high-ranking representatives), including the Minister from Great Britain

(George's counterpart for Europe, Russia, Asia, the Middle East and Australia).

As the throngs passed through the reception line Brian tried to remain alert to any possible problems, but it was hard. In such a crowd there were political rivals, those opposed to various policies and some who simply weren't very nice. Several times he would sense something and glance at Agent Bowyer, who would whisper, *"opposed to your dad's unification programs,"* or *"angry because your dad would not nominate him for the new SVC,* or *convinced the entire Council is corrupt and should be disbanded."* Brian wondered how he kept it all in his head. They were just about to the end. Word came down that the last group of arrivals had just finished having their names checked and were cleared by the team of empaths. As Brian scanned the newcomers, he exercised his right hand, hoping the circulation would come back and the bruising wouldn't be too bad. Suddenly his breath caught, seeing a familiar face, but not one he expected. The hair on the back of his neck bristled and he got a cold feeling in the pit of his stomach. He nudged J.J., who whispered,

"How'd *she* get in here? Surely she wasn't on the invited list."

"She's a CKS professor," answered Nicki, who overheard her brothers. "All CKS staff were invited."

"But she's on leave of absence," protested Brian, shifting uneasily on his feet and pulling at his necktied collar.

"Being on leave, she is still listed as a staff member. Now get a grip. I know she's your least-favorite teacher but smile and don't make a scene," instructed Nicki.

"That's easy for you to say," mumbled Brian with a scowl. "You never had to endure her classes." He watched her step up to his grandparents, who were the first in the reception line (Myrna and George were last). She quickly greeted the five grandparents, Willard, J.J. and all too soon she was in front of Brian with her pudgy hand extended.

"Ah, Mr. Brian Everett," she said, her high-pitched voice with controlled sweetness. "Your father has certainly risen further than

I would have expected... Anyway, I look forward to returning to beloved CKS next term and seeing your smiling face." It was clear she wanted to say something else.

"Gee, I'm sorry to disappoint you, Professor." (Brian was going to enjoy this; obviously she had not heard.) "We're not attending CKS; we're being home-schooled."

The look of shock on her face was worth having to endure her in the reception line, but she quickly recovered.

"Yes, I can understand that, as your family has so many enemies." She could no longer hide her contempt for the whole Everett family. "Pity, though; I was looking forward to teaching you a thing or two. Well, moving on. Ah, Miss Everett."

Brian thought he saw a Monēo warning, but he dismissed it because he hated letting her have the last word. He was sure his intense dislike for the woman was giving him false indications. Still, he would mention it to his father and Agent Bowyer when the line broke up.

"Hey, slow down," Brian hard J.J. complain as he and Willard tried to keep pace with Brian, who was heading toward the buffet tables. "You know Mom won't let anything run out."

"I'm hungry—"

"You're always hungry!" quipped J.J. and Willard in unison.

"Yeah, but this is different," he countered. "It's been over seven hours since dinner, and Mom said we'd have to make do with the buffet food; they're not fixin' us a separate supper." He almost skidded to a halt in front of the spot where clean plates were neatly stacked.

"What'd Mom and Dad say about Antetima?" J.J. picked up a plate, fork and napkin.

"'Bout what I 'spected." Brian was stuffing shrimp in his mouth. "I'm prob'ly reacting to the hard feelings tha's been goin' on fer years." He piled some chicken legs, potato salad and thin slices of roast beef on his plate. "But they said to stay alert. No one has been able to account for where she's been during her leave, except she's been seen around Massachusetts. They were surprised to see her here, except she's still on the CKS list." He added turkey slices and stuffing to his plate. Still, he had an uneasy feeling it was something more...

After three trips to the buffet tables, ending in almost a whole apple pie (with mounds of ice cream), Brian and his brothers sought out their mother. "Mom, we did the whole reception line and everything," stated Brian. "Can we go upstairs to our rooms? This thing is going to last all night." He tugged at his stiff shirt collar.

Myrna looked around. It was almost ten o'clock and there were no signs of anyone starting to leave. "I expect you're right," she sighed. "Be sure and let Bowyer know where you're going so they won't think you're missing. It's a busy day tomorrow with the investiture, so get some sleep."

"Thanks, Mom; we will," he said over his shoulder, having turned and begun a hasty exit before she changed her mind. A quick word with the agent and the trio was off to the second floor private quarters of the mansion. His vest and top shirt button were open and his tie off before they reached the bedroom door. (They were sharing a room, with three beds, because so many were staying overnight.)

"I need to shower. I feel sticky from being fussed over by all those people and trying to push through the crowds." He was pulling off his suit coat.

"Yeah, you're sticky, all right," teased J.J., "but it's from the ice cream you dribbled down your front." He and Willard laughed.

"No way!" Brian panicked and looked down at his shirt, inspected the suit coat and patted his chin. "I was careful!" He hoped he hadn't embarrassed himself (or his parents).

"Got ya!" laughed J.J., who was already stripped down to his T-shirt and boxers and running toward the bathroom door. "I'm gettin' the shower first!" he cackled, but suddenly went "Ummph!" He ran right into a closed door that was wide open seconds before, and fell on his backside.

Brian and Willard were bent over, holding their sides, they were laughing so hard.

"Very funny, Ringboy." J.J. scrambled to his feet, trying to retain a bit of dignity. "Hey, that was good, though; you did it non-verbally and without even waving your hand." He reached to open the door but pulled his hand back. "You did that elementally, didn't you." It was not a question.

"Wha—whaddya mean?" Brian was gasping for breath, but still sniggering.

"You didn't channel, did you?"

"I—" He took a deep breath. "I just focused on the air in the bathroom and asked it to blow the door shut. Why?"

"Well, it did what you asked and it's still doing it. I doubt all three of us could push it open. You might wanna release it. Kinda sounds like a tornado in there."

"Oooo," he grimaced. He could hear it, so he focused again and thanked the element for its efforts and asked for calm. "I didn't think of that."

"I think you can be first in the shower." J.J. backed away from the door even further. "You better clean up the mess before Mom comes to check on us and say goodnight."

"Thanks." He disrobed and slipped into his dressing robe, then approached cautiously just as Benson knocked, entered, and saw Brian's tentative steps.

"M'Lord, something seems amiss?"

"Everything is just fine," announced J.J. gleefully, "'cept for the hurricane we just had in the bathroom." Now *he* was laughing, holding his side.

"Hurricane, you say?"

"Well, more like an Arizona twister. I don't think there was any water." He really enjoyed watching Brian squirm.

"And, pray tell, why be a twister in your loo?" There was a long silence, waiting for Brian to answer.

"I kinda used wind to close the door," he finally answered, meekly.

"But?"

"Well, I made the wrong request. The wind not only closed the door but it held it fast for several minutes."

"Well, let's have a peek, shall we?"

Benson crossed the room and opened the bathroom door. Brian, J.J. and Willard were close behind. "Hmmm, seems to be a bit untidy."

"Wow!" quipped J.J. "It could have been worse—if you'd conjured up a nuclear bomb."

"Ooooh," groaned Brian, looking at shredded towels, toilet paper bits strewn everywhere, shower curtain in tatters, toothpaste squeezed out of its tube and splattered on the walls, toilet seat cover split in half, and white porcelain sink shattered and strewn on the floor. "Mom's gonna make me do extra chores for a year!"

"Not to worry." Benson reached in his coat and pulled out his wand. "I'm much better with this." He pointed, flicked and swished his wand at various items which gathered themselves whole and went to their proper places.

Brian watched in awe. Within moments the room looked perfectly normal. He felt J.J. push past him, heading for the shower stall.

"Well, if you'll excuse me, I'm going to shower." He stepped in, closed the curtain and chuckled. "Gotta be faster than that, Ringboy." Shorts and T-shirt appeared over the curtain rod and the water started spraying.

Brian just shook his head as he turned back into the bedroom to wait his turn while Benson had their suits flying onto hangers in the closet, and gathered their shirts for laundry and pressing. Willard giggled as his suit, tie, shirt, shoes and socks all tugged themselves off him and flew either to Benson or the closet. (It was an ongoing ritual between Benson and the boy.)

"M'Lord, yer mum wants a family only breakfast at seven-thirty, then scrubbed, polished and suited by nine-thirty. The investiture begins promptly at eleven o'clock at the Redoubt."

"Well, we're gettin' our showers tonight—"

"Nay. Yer mum says you bathe again after breakfast."

"But—"

"M'Lord, I may just be your butler, but I'll scrub you myself, if I have to."

"You wouldn't dare..."

"Try me," he challenged. "Wizard English butlers have some special abilities to handle unruly children in their charge. Just like yer mum and da will always have a power over you—even when you're Ringmaster."

"Oooh, as J.J. says, *I love a challenge.*"

"I will look forward to it, M'Lord. Just not tomorrow; we don't want to be bollixing up yer da's big day now, do we."

Investiture Day went by so fast it all seemed to run together in a continuous blur for the Everett family. At the end of the day, sitting on his bed, donned in his favorite nightshirt, Brian rubbed his feet, complaining:

"I don't know how men wear dress shoes all day long, every day," he said to no one in particular. His brothers were also on their beds but they were watching a late movie on TV. He thought about the day's events and only two things really stood out in his mind: First, the actual ceremony of his father's investiture. While it was mostly symbolic as transfer of power actually took place the moment the words *I accept* were uttered in Everett Manor, Carmarthen, England. Nevertheless, the ritual was steeped in tradition and solemn majesty. Second, throughout the day Professor Antetima kept showing up in the crowds nearest the family. And each time he felt prickly warnings, but not strong enough to raise an alarm.

Brian (and his brothers) were glad the day was over. After the investiture, there were endless photos with various groups; (very) formal luncheon (where is was inappropriate to ask for seconds, much less thirds or fourths); congratulatory political speeches that dragged on and on; a gift-offering ceremony (a tradition that dated back to the coronations of kings where the giver tries to curry favor with the new monarch with an extravagant gift); a quick, private family supper; then change into stiff tuxedos and attend a huge formal ball.

The brothers endured the events without complaint and performed like perfect gentlemen (well, mostly). Brian was amazed by some of the gifts, but, of course, most of them would be donated to charities, museums or for use by the Council (also a long-held tradition). The new Chairman retained only a few personal mementos of relatively small value. They had even allowed themselves to be dragged onto the dance floor by some old women and a few teen girls (who wanted the son of the Chairman for a boyfriend). Brian was not sure which was worse: the old biddies stepping on his toes and pinching his cheeks, or the girls pawing over him and trying to get him to commit to going out with them. He was sure some of them were sent by their parents. He felt sorry for J.J.; he and Willard were only twelve and eleven, but at sixteen J.J. was considered to be quite a catch.

As if having similar thoughts, J.J. interrupted his musings.

"Did you make any girlfriends today?" He and Willard giggled.

"Ewww, no. I can't believe some of those girls—wanting to go out with a twelve-year-old. Gave me the creeps."

"Me, too," said Willard.

"Ha," exclaimed J.J. "I wonder what some of 'em would say if they knew you turned into a big gold dragon."

"But I'm not a big dragon—yet." They all laughed.

"I noticed you brought back a pocketful of phone numbers." Brian lifted the sheet and bedcovers and slid his legs underneath to get warm. He could smell the sweet fragrance of fabric softener, and feel the crisp cool sheets against his toes and bare legs. "You gonna call 'em?"

"Well, they weren't all trolls, were they?" He had his mischievous, smiling look. "What'd you do with yours?"

"I put them in my pocket to not be rude, but binned them straight away. Did you see? Antetima kept popping up all day—watching us. I was also getting warnings about her, but they're all mixed up with the bad feelings between her and our family that's gone on for years. I don't know if she's a threat or not."

"She may be an awful teacher and she might hate our family, but still she's a CKS professor."

"Yeah, and that Sutton guy was a long-time agent, too."

Chapter Twenty-Eight
Antetima's Lament

The final day of investiture activities looked to be an easy one. No formal ceremonies, dances or attire. The new Chairman was hosting a totally informal barbecue, picnic and pot luck at the Council Executive Estate. The weather was perfect (as it could be in a New England February, undoubtedly assisted by some psionics).

All attendees, whether foreign or from various regions of the U. S., were encouraged to wear traditional garb and bring dishes customary in their homelands. As Brian looked on, long rows of tables were quickly laden with a huge variety of foods, and it became a marvelously colorful affair. Even the squatty witch [from the Ministry in Great Britain] was not out of place, wearing her lurid cardigan over her bright pink robes.

Brian, Nicki, J.J. and Willard circulated among the guests, allowing themselves to be tousled, pinched, patted and fawned over. But it wasn't too bad; they met some really interesting people and had lots of practice using interpreting spells. And of course, they made many trips to the buffet and pot luck tables, even trying out some of the exotic foreign nosh.

The day progressed toward evening when candles and lights lit up the grounds and garden. It was beautiful: flickering lights made the trees absolutely glow, as lanterns and candles lined the garden paths and tiki torches surrounded the patio. Brian had to catch his breath as he took it all in—and all planned in three days. It was amazing. The only bad part of the day was when he felt like he was being followed, not by the security squad which he knew was there, but he was convinced Professor Antetima was dogging his movements. He wouldn't have minded as she kept her distance, but he kept getting prickly warnings, keeping him a bit unnerved.

"She's up to something," complained Brian for the hundredth time to his unsympathetic siblings. "I know Mom and Dad think it's just the old animosity comin' out—and you lot agree, don't you?" He was clenching his teeth in anger.

"It's not that we agree," said J.J., "it's just that there's no evidence of anything else, is there." He was trying to soothe his brother's emotions.

"No, but there's something goin' on. With all this," he waved at the outdoor lighting and then pointed at the food tables, "why would she be following us around? If she's not up to no good, then she's got something seriously wrong with her."

"Well, we certainly agree with that last part," added Nicki, glancing around to see if she was still there. "It's like she's obsessed. It's creepy."

"It's getting late and cooling off." (The mages maintaining the weather bubble could hold off the February chill just so long.) Brian spotted a luscious chocolate éclair and it was in his mouth in an instant. But suddenly he was being elongated and sucked through what seemed like a long straw and being squirted out the end in a heap.

"What the—?" Brian angrily looked around and saw he was in a copse of trees. It was not totally dark; there were twinkling strings of lights high up in the boughs. Then he recognized it: at the far west end of the property was a thick stand of evergreen trees. He and his brothers had explored the area just three days before.

"How'd I?" He shook his head. His vision was somewhat fuzzy and his brain felt like it was going in slow motion. He saw some movement and squinted his eyes to see. He felt energy binder ropes pin his arms to his sides.

"Well, your gluttony finally did you in," sneered the familiar voice of Professor Antetima. "I knew your favorite dessert is éclairs—and you're nothing if not famous for your appetite."

"The shields and barriers—can't travel—" His mind was starting to clear but he could not channel his energy.

"Oh, your father's security is quite good but missed a particular method, as long as you're still under the barrier dome. Ah, I see the fogginess leaving. Now we can chat. But it will do you no good to channel. That confection not only transported you but also put a block on your channeling." She laughed evilly. "A rather clever creation of my own."

"Why?"

"Rumors abound you're the Appointed One. I don't know if you are or not, but we can't take that chance. I'm going to strip you of your psionic abilities. George and Myrna are going to get their precious little boy back but you'll be a Nomag." She cackled again.

"Why—my parents—"

"They never told you? How noble of them. Well, I'll let them do it. But of course you won't remember any of this." She sighed. "Pity! I would have preferred them knowing it was me, but we can't have the Chairman's forces looking for me. No, no! I'll just go back to CKS and be the dreaded Professor Antetima until the Master calls. But I'll be his most trusted, for it will be me who made sure the biggest obstacle was removed from his path to become Ringmaster."

Brian knew it was useless to struggle against the energy ropes and he couldn't channel, but ... maybe he could gather elemental energy. She knew nothing of that ability. Maybe whatever she did only targeted his channeling. Also, maybe he could project: mind-speak to Willard. He closed his eyes and pictured his little brother—no—a gold dragon.

Hey, Wil, can you hear me? He pushed with all his might.

Ouch! You don't have to yell. Where are you?

In that thicket of trees, west end of the estate.

How'd you—?

No time to explain. Just get here—I need help of a not-so-big gold dragon. But don't let the guests see you—

We're on our way.

That done, Brian focused on the earth—he was still crumpled up, lying on a pile of leaves. Slowly he felt it. His request was granted; almost as if Mother Earth had been waiting and was saying, *What took you so long?* He gathered her gift, a little at a time; he didn't want to alarm Antetima with an earthquake where she might do something rash. The crazy woman was relishing the idea of torturing the son of her enemies.

Don't come blundering into the trees—I'm all tied up and she might do something stupid.

Right!

Brian focused on the fire he knew was deep in the core of the earth, which also gave to his request. It was suddenly cold, except he was warm all over.

"Oh, your father's guests must be leaving. They're dropping the weather controls."

"No, that's just the icy slime running in your veins. You sure don't have any human blood."

"Oooh, trying to provoke me. Tired of the game already? Want me to end it quickly? No, no, that won't do. I've waited too long for this. Revenge is best savored slowly."

"You weren't very sneaky, were you. We saw you all day." He stopped gathering fire just before he began to glow.

"I wasn't trying to be. I wanted you so distracted you'd not notice the sudden appearance of the éclair. And it worked!"

We're just outside the clearing. We can see you.

Wait! You'll know when it's time. Have you transmuted?

Yes.

It's time for some fun.

He focused on water; it was everywhere. The ground was damp, there was moisture on the trees and plenty of humidity in the New England air. She didn't see the cloud form over her head until it was too late. Suddenly a sheet of icy water soaked her from head to foot.

"What? How?" she sputtered, trying to shake off the deluge.

Brian took advantage of her distraction and directed the stored power to blast the energy ropes—hoping he wouldn't get burned in the process. The effect was bigger than anticipated; the clash of the two energy sources—the elemental being the stronger—created a burst of yellow sparks and a loud crack as the bands burst.

"Hey! How'd?" she screeched. "That's impossible! You can't channel!"

"Hmm, you're right," he taunted. "Must be other forces at play, aren't there." He scrambled to his feet and asked Earth to shield him, and just in time. She fired off something he had never seen. He assumed it was just that nasty work she was describing. He staggered a bit when it hit his shield. He instinctively ducked.

"You waited too long. And you're right about revenge. I'm going to enjoy watching 'em haul you off, like those two fools in England."

"I don't think so. We'll meet again!" Brian knew she recognized he couldn't do offensive channeling. She started to turn and run toward the estate's perimeter where she could translate, but ran head on into a gold dragon.

"Can't be!" she shrieked. "There's—no—gold—dragons—in—U.S.—" Her face was deep purple.

"Calm yourself, Professor. We don't want you having a heart attack."

"I was warned about you and creatures." She was backing into the clearing.

"You should have listened. One day you'll understand there's a lot more than your little band of Black Bunglers." Brian laughed.

"Creature indeed," rumbled the dragon, snorting a bit of fire. "Dragons are sentient beings, much older than humans on the earth."

Antetima held up her hands in submission. "I didn't mean to offend." She was still wet and shaking all over. Just then Nicki and J.J. entered the clearing.

"She had a couple of—what'd you call 'em?—Oh, yeah, Black Bunglers hiding in the woods. Sis and I got one each." J.J. mischievously rubbed his hands together and grinned. "They'll have terrible headaches in the morning."

Brian watched the short woman tremble and back up against a tree to prop herself up; her pudgy legs looked like they would collapse at any second.

"Why?" he asked. "You've taught for years at CKS. Why would you join the Black Kni—Bunglers and try to hurt a student?"

"You have no idea. Prince Reficul is the most powerful mage of our time. He wants to become Ringmaster so he can bring order into the world. It's his destiny—his inheritance."

"Funny; I thought everyone says I'm the Appointed One."

"Then your family has—"

"I didn't say that. It's just what everybody seems to think. What do you mean by he'll 'bring order into the world?'"

"Look at all the chaos. He will bring everyone under one rule, one set of laws, strictly but evenly enforced. Everyone will work and share in the rewards evenly."

"Yeah, except for himself and his Knights who are above the law," quipped J.J.

"There have to be those who enforce his law."

"Every megalomaniac's dream," said Nicki. "Stars, woman, listen to yourself. You teach history. Hasn't history taught you anything? Hitler? Stalin?"

"They weren't pure in heart like Prince Reficul, nor were they mages."

"You know the phrase, 'Absolute power corrupts absolutely.' And besides, the masses will tolerate a dictator only so long. Then the cry for freedom would crush your prince, just like all the others."

Brian listened to his sister and suddenly had a new appreciation for her depth of thinking—her maturity, and hoped he'd be as wise when he became Ringmaster.

Her heavy frame finally took its toll; Antetima collapsed onto the roots of the tree and began weeping. "You're right, you know," she said between sobs of anguish. "I've been stupid. I let the green monster of jealousy corrupt my thinking long ago and it was easy for Master to bring me in. He can be sooo persuasive. You have no idea," she repeated and continued crying.

"Jealousy?" asked Brian. "Who were you jealous of?" He had a pretty good idea who she was referring to.

"Your mother!" she spat, regaining a bit of her strength. "I dated your father a couple of times, but then Myrna Deering batted her pretty blue eyes and she took him away from me." She started sobbing again.

"All this because my Dad was fickle when he was a kid?" Brian couldn't believe his ears. "How old was he, seventeen? Eighteen?"

"Fourteen," she barely squeaked.

"He barely knew what girls were about, at fourteen," countered J.J. "You've carried this vendetta since then?"

She nodded her head and wept some more.

I don't want to bind her, projected Brian to the dragon—his little brother. *Use your weakness mist, then go find your clothes and transmute back before security shows up.*

Willard didn't hesitate. What was left of the distraught woman seemed to be reduced to a blob, still crying. The dragon proudly padded off and a few moments later the small boy entered the clearing, zipping up his jacket—and not a moment too soon. In seconds the clearing was filled with agents in dark suits led by Agent Bowyer, who commented:

"It seems every time you lot disappear, we find you with some bad guy crumpled at your feet. I can't wait to hear the story about this lump."

Brian looked at him with pleading eyes, trying to get him to hold off on the story-telling until they were alone—with Mom and Dad.

"Right, but all that will have to wait. Your parents are anxious for you. I'll walk you back while the team cleans up this mess." He obviously got the message and turned to lead Brian, J.J., Willard and Nicki back to the Council House.

"Uh, you might want to search the area—there's two more knocked out with stunners." J.J. grinned sadistically, rubbing his hands together.

"Spread out!" Bowyer ordered. "There're at least two others—and may be more."

Chapter Twenty-Nine
"It's Moving Day!"

———◦═○═◦———

"How did she transport me with an éclair?" Brian looked around at his assembled family, Agent Bowyer, Grandma James, Benson and Professor Heady. It was 10:00 p.m. The last guests were gone and they were relaxed in comfortable armchairs in the study. The leather of Brian's chair creaked as he nervously shifted, thinking about the day's events.

"She got the idea when she was in England, directing the attacks there. It was crudely set up to work like those portal keys," answered Agent Bowyer.

"Why couldn't I channel?"

"There are actually several non-lethal poisons that will interfere with channeling. She chose one that was easily disguised by the éclair's crème filling."

"How long does it take to wear off? I feel almost naked without it."

"You will feel like you have clothes on in the morning," answered Grandma, chuckling. "If you forced it, you could probably channel now, but I do not recommend it. Control would be a problem."

"I think I'll pass. I can wait 'til morning, and I can still gather elements if I need to."

"And you won't need to use air to close any doors, *will you?*" Myrna stared at her son, chuckling. "And don't look at your brothers or Benson. You should know I have other ways to find out."

"You heard about that, did you?" Brian tried to put on his most sheepish, innocent and repentant look. "Sorry! I promise I won't. But how'd you—?"

"Now, you'll learn that when you're a parent." Everyone laughed.

"I can't believe that woman carried a grudge like that all these years," said Nicki. "She was only fourteen."

"Did you really date her?" asked J.J.

"No, not really. It was kind of an arranged thing between our parents, for a couple of school activities. And then I kept trying to keep as much distance between us as possible. She was obsessed; sending me notes, flowers, chocolates and even giving me her homework notes. It scared me. That's why it took me such a long time to get the nerve to ask out your mother. She was really popular."

"You cheated off her homework?" J.J. grinned mischievously.

"Are you kidding? I mostly earned better grades than she did. I wouldn't touch anything she sent. I was afraid of some love potion. I binned everything."

"We were all careful around her. She was top of her class in psiochemistry," added Myrna. "I received a box of chocolates that had a concoction to distort my likes in men. It was a brilliant bit of psiochemistry. We could never prove it was from her. Tonight was eerily similar."

"Were you able to get anything out of her?" asked Brian. "She sure backed down when Nicki challenged her."

"Except for what she told you, she's under an unbreakable code of secrecy for anything Reficul told her of the operation of the Black Knights," said Bowyer. "However, he seems to be missing in action, and she told us all about her, apparently unauthorized, attacks on the family."

"Did I hear right? Reficul didn't authorize the attacks in England or on Brian tonight?" asked Nicki.

"Yes. That is why she could talk about it," answered Grandma. "The oath does not bind her from disclosing things she has done on her own volition."

"Can't you penetrate the oath's binding?" inquired J.J. "You've made me give up stuff I was trying to hide."

"You were easy," she teased, then got serious. "Yes, I could do it, but it would be tantamount to torture. She might not even survive the attempt. At the very least, she would need long term care in-hospital. We do not do such things. It goes against everything we believe—tempting though it may be."

"I'm glad," said Brian softly. "I don't want her hurt."

"That is the mark of the true Ringmaster. Even though she tried to do you serious harm, you still do not wish her ill. That is the difference between you and Reficul. You reaffirm our faith in you."

"Thanks, Grandma." There was a long moment of thoughtful silence.

"Hey, Ringboy," jibed J.J., "don't be gettin' a swelled head. You're not Ringmaster yet. You still have lots to learn."

"Thanks! I can always rely on you for a reality check."

"Glad I could help."

"What's gonna happen to Professor Antetima now?" asked Willard.

"*Miss* Antetima—as she is no longer a CKS professor—will have to go into protective custody. Reficul is not going to be pleased with her. At some point she will have to account for her actions before a Sodality Tribunal."

"I want to speak at her hearing," said Brian solemnly.

"You have that right, Son," said George. "What do you want to say?"

"I don't know. I want to give her time to show her change-of-heart is real."

* * *

291

Brian lay in his bed, snuggled under the sheet and blanket. He should have been asleep, but the images of a trusted Seminary professor trying to hurt him kept him wide awake. His brothers were not seemingly afflicted; he could hear their slow, rhythmic breathing of deep sleep. The room was dark except for the faint glow of a bathroom nightlight spilling dimly into the comfortable room. He tried closing his eyes but that made things worse: the image became acutely clear. With his eyes open he could seek diversion by staring at shadowed paintings on the walls or the ornate carvings on the tall bedposts. He felt horribly betrayed, and began to wonder (over and over):

If I'm not safe at school and someone could attack me here, where am I safe?

If I can't trust my teachers, who can I trust?

Who else is going to betray me as I become Ringmaster?

What could I have done differently?

"Wha—whazzup?" muttered Brian sleepily. "Tired—need sleep." He was faintly aware he was being prodded. "G-way!" He tried to pull the blankets over his head, but they were stubbornly trying to slide toward his feet.

"M'Lord, yer mum—" he heard Benson call respectfully.

"Will haft' wai—" He flopped over and buried his face in the soft, downy pillow.

"GET UP, RINGBOY!" yelled J.J. cheerfully. "IT'S MOVIN' DAY! WE'RE GOIN' HOME!"

Brian's eyes flew open, he rolled over and quickly sat up. The room was brightly lit and he saw his brothers already pulling on their pants. He was amazed he could see anything as he rubbed the sleep out of his eyes. There were clean underclothes and jeans already laid out, which he quickly pulled on under his nightshirt, donned a freshly-laundered T-shirt and headed off to the bathroom. He almost tripped over the big steamer trunks already brought into the room. Passing by, he chuckled as shirts, socks, pants, shorts, books, mementoes, photos, shoes, study notes and other stuff they'd collected were all jammed up, hovering; literally fighting each other to be the next item to settle into the trunks (neatly folded and perfectly placed). Benson was at his best. J.J. and Willard laughed and pointed at the show (obviously done for their benefit). Benson smiled and aimed his wand at other items in the wardrobe to join the fray.

Moments later Brian emerged from the bathroom with toothpaste still on his lips when he found himself being pelted by a buttoned-up warm flannel shirt with long sleeves. The bottom kept trying to slip over his head as he flailed his arms trying to fend off the neatly-pressed menace. He was laughing so hard he could hardly breathe (along with his brothers) until finally he dropped his arms for a second to catch his breath. The shirt wasted no time; it slid right over his shoulders and arms—pinning them to his sides. He looked like a demented, multi-colored mummy.

"Very funny," he said, yet still giggling, stiffly walking toward Benson, who was grinning from ear to ear. "You prob'ly should undo these buttons. If I do it with energy, I don't know where they might go."

"An' yer mum would be tiffed if you ruined a new shirt, wouldn't she." He waved his wand and they came loose from top to bottom like a zipper. Brian's arms were freed so suddenly he almost lost his balance.

"You're really good at that stuff," observed J.J. with admiration, while Brian pushed his arms down the shirt sleeves, rebuttoned (manually), tucked the tails into the waist of his pants and buckled his belt. "I'm supposed to be the prodigy kid and I can't manipulate so many elements at one time."

"Sure you can," said Benson, "after you train and practice up a bit. Stuff like tha', they don't teach in school. We wanted to be right proper wizard English Butler and Housekeeper for a family with kids—see, Madge 'n' me can't have children—so we both studied hard to learn all the householdin' stuff."

"Wait a minute!" challenged J.J. "You wanted to be servants to rich folks or (in our case) elected officials?"

"Oh, no! We're not just servants—though some may think so. We're a proper English Butler and Housekeeper. We not only attend to the personal needs of our employers, and their children but we are more. We protect, with our lives if necessary, nurse, be confidantes, emissaries, offer counsel, maintain appointment schedules and household image and teach good moral values. We are free to choose the families we serve and leave the moment we feel our services are not properly appreciated. Yes, we are paid well, but we serve more out of loyalty and pride than for money. It is an honor to serve yer family. Believe me, there are many who queued up for this appointment. Oh, one other task we have—" He waved his wand at three boys, who were suddenly being pulled by their belts toward the open bedroom door. "We manage dawdling children who should be downstairs breakfasting with their Mum and Da. There's lots to do as Lord Jeremy so eloquently put it: it's movin' day!"

This time there was no pretense of using Brangler conveyance. There were no cargo planes or private jets. UTS had delivered large translocation receptacles to both houses and crews at both ends were either sending or receiving trunks, boxes, furniture, household goods, mementoes, gifts, hanging clothes cases, flowers, crates of books and leftover food (the Council Executive House was going to be vacant for a while). Another crew was at the rental storage facility sending all their goods packed away before Christmas.

Myrna was at her organizing finest. She translated to 128 Main Street and instructed the crews as each load appeared in the receptacle. She directed movement better than a New York traffic cop.

By the time Brian and the rest of the family arrived—either by FON or translating—almost everything was in place. Frequently though, one had to duck or squeeze against a wall as an errant item was discovered and sent whizzing to its proper location. Brian jumped sideways as a crate he was carrying suddenly burst open and books started flying onto shelves.

"Mom!" he protested.

"If you're not going to help, get out of the way!" She wiped her hands on her apron and turned her attention to another box.

"I am helping, but every time I start, you come and take over."

"I know, honey. It's just faster for me to do it than explain what I want done. I'm sorry I snapped at you."

"It's okay. Why don't J.J., Nicki, Wil and I just leave you to it and we'll go sort out our rooms?"

"That's an excellent idea! We'll all get together for dinner—maybe down to Louigi's at the Mall."

"Oooh, that'd be great! Of course, you'll give Bowyer a heart attack!"

"Hmm, such short notice... You're probably right, but it'll do him good. It's time the family got back to a bit of normalcy." She grinned a little mischievously. "Why don't you go tell him?"

"Love to!" Brian spun and headed toward the now-much-longer hallway. "HEY, AGENT BOWYER," he cried gleefully. "YOU'RE GONNA LOVE THIS!"

At the Mall, Brian was chuckling. They were strolling down the middle of the main concourse just like any other large family (Uncle Paul and five grandparents were with them.). They ogled various items in store windows, sometimes stopping to inspect something that caught an eye and waving and smiling at passersby. All the while, the ever-vigilant security team leader was muttering under his breath about short notices and wondering how he was going to keep his charges safe in such an exposed setting. But earlier, Myrna gave strict orders: the squad was to remain in the background unless a threat was perceived.

"This is totally unscheduled," she had argued. "There's no time for anyone to organize an attack. The Chairman must be visible and not appear to be hiding, protected in an ivory tower. You can put up an energy barrier if you want, but not physical. People will be allowed to approach and talk to us—except during dinner. Only Louigi and his employees come around then. That's our time." Everyone knew there was no argument, except Agent Bowyer asked:

"What about the media or press, Ma'am? Is the Chairman or any family member commenting or answering questions?"

"NO! Tomorrow's press conference is soon enough for that!"

Until they walked onto the concourse, Mall patrons had no idea. There had been no one waiting for the family in the arrival/ departure lounge. But it didn't take long as for the past several days the Everett family had been splashed across the TV screens of every Sodality household (receiving the specially-encoded cable/ satellite channels) throughout North, Central and South America, Africa, China and Japan and through wizarding households in other areas who had embraced some Brangler technology. Further, their pictures were on the front pages of every Sodality and Wizard newspaper and magazine in the world. Word of the Everetts' arrival spread pretty fast; however, while there was some pointing and staring, most were content to leave them alone, or make do with a quiet wave. A few bold ones timidly approached for a quick handshake, but the glares from the agents had them bowing a hasty retreat.

They arrived at Louigi's mostly unscathed. Only one foreign witch tried to assert her views in opposition to the Chairman's position of helping Branglers fight terrorism. Surprisingly, it was Nicki who defused the confrontation by promising she'd get a personal response if she would write her concerns in care of the Redoubt address. Actually, the most excitement came when the young waiter (the same one who gave Nicki all the attention last year) became so nervous he spilled a whole plate of lasagna in her lap (which Mom cleaned up with a casual wave of her hand— before their grandparents and other patrons knew anything had happened). Brian giggled. He wasn't sure if his sister or the waiter turned a deeper shade of red—and Nicki didn't blush easily. He was sure he saw her slip him her phone number.

At the end of the meal, Louigi approached, wearing his usual custom-tailored silk suit. "Mr. Chairman, again you honor me." He began to tear the check but George gently stayed his hand.

"Mr. Campana," he said kindly, "if you keep comping our meals, you'll go broke. As Chairman I cannot allow the best Sodality Italian restaurant in the world to go out of business—"

"But you always bring so much free advertising," interrupted Louigi.

"And besides, you've been a good friend and you watched out for my boys. This one's on us. We'll see about next time." He winked at the restaurateur.

"As you wish, Mr. Chairman." He laid the paper on the table, upside down. "Do come again soon." He made a formal bow. "And may I congratulate you on your appointment. We all look forward to your administration of our region."

"Thank you. I pray I earn your confidence."

*   *   *

Things were settling down at 128 Main Street. It was almost supper time; the moving crews were gone and only a very few boxes remained unpacked. Myrna, aided by the Bensons, was putting the final touches on a brand new house to make it look and feel like a lived-in Everett home. As promised, Nicki, J.J., Brian and Willard were allowed to customize their own rooms (and bathrooms—each had their own), though it was clear Mom was regretting the decision every time she passed J.J.'s rooms and peered inside.

"He's going to have nightmares," she mumbled, turning away and shaking her head. "And if *he* doesn't, *I* will, just thinking about him in that jungle."

297

Several times Brian wanted to look in, but decided to wait until invited for an unveiling. But just seeing his mother's reaction, it had to be something spectacular. He also wondered about Nicki and Willard—well, not so much Nicki; she was seventeen and quite a young woman. Her rooms would be all girl, with maybe a poster of her favorite recording artist or movie actor. But Willard: what would an orphan boy—raised by mountain lions, coyotes, snakes and other such creatures—think was a cool bedroom—especially one who just recently discovered he is actually a (rather small) gold dragon?

As their supper was being served, Myrna announced that, afterward, there would be a grand tour of the whole house, including the domestics' and Security agents' quarters (which Agent Bowyer code-named DLQ and SLQ). J.J. was almost jumping out of his chair, he was so excited about showing his rooms to the family.

Supper was a noisy affair as everyone was recounting the day's events and accomplishments. There was universal praise for Myrna's masterful organization. For Brian, it felt like home. The meal was the family's favorites of salad, clam chowder, pot roast, oven brown potatoes, carrots, broccoli, hot bread, deep dish apple pie and ice cream.

Then it was time for the tour. It began in the huge industrial kitchen. There were walk-in pantries, refrigerators and freezers, six ovens, two six-burner stoves, four microwaves, hanging pot/ utensil racks, butcher blocks, and long preparation counters with four sinks. Such a kitchen was not really necessary as psionics could easily make a small kitchen feed an army, but Myrna felt psionically-prepared food just didn't taste the same. So in the Everett home, energy was only used to speed things a bit; meals were mostly prepared traditionally. And like the White House, there were times they would host meals for large numbers of guests.

The formal sitting room (for receiving VIPs) was similar to the one at Everett Manor. There were clusters of seats, a huge fireplace and lots of room for milling about and talking. There was a gigantic formal dining room and a smaller one for family (and small gatherings).

The family library included desks for home schooling and was separate from the Chairman's home office. Each was comfortable with lots of wood paneling on the walls. There was now a private family room that had a fireplace, comfortable sofas, arm chairs, tables, TV and stereo.

Next (Brian was glad to see remained) was the entertainment room (now called the E.R.). It was similar to the old converted play room with computer, TV, stereo, bean-bag chairs, study/hobby desks and a sofa bed.

Finally they headed for the bedrooms. They went by age. Willard's was first (along the long hallway). The youngster's decorating was simple, and fitting. It resembled a cave den. He had artfully made the walls and ceiling look like large stone boulders. Even his desk and chair looked like something from Merlin's caves. He made his bedspread have prints that looked like fresh hay or straw. The lamps looked so much like burning torches, everyone had to touch one to see if it was a real flame. Willard was bursting with pride; Mom couldn't find anything to complain about and the rest of the family was truly impressed.

Brian's rooms were next. He went with the traditional Sodality (flipolo-loving) boy look. Bradshaw Mountaineers posters were everywhere. Various team tunics, helmets, pads and Dad's old sledge adorned the walls and ceiling. His only bit of ingenuity was making the pictures on the posters move (something he'd learned in England).

Entering J.J.'s rooms was like entering another world. Brian's first impression was they had walked into the film set of Jurassic Park. There were trees, vines, shrubs, and most impressive, were the various holographic dinosaurs that would suddenly appear, let out a roar, then retreat—only to reappear later in another location. He had suspended his bed frame between two trees and disguised it to look like a hammock. Brian and Willard burst out laughing, along with Dad, Paul and the grandfathers.

"This is not quite what I expected when you asked to decorate your rooms. What happened to your flipolo posters idea?" she said, just as a raptor flew over her head and she instinctively ducked.

"C'mon, Mom," defended J.J. "Nothin' in here is real. It's like a movie set. The trees won't drop leaves and the creatures are just holographic images. It's a great intruder alert!"

"I must admit, it's really creative. You are taking psionics into realms I've never heard of. Were Willard's rooms part of your handiwork?"

"Nope! He asked me for a couple of channeling ideas, but he did the whole thing himself. Pretty cool, huh!" Myrna just shook her head, and the small boy beamed.

"Jeremy, you make sure those creatures do not growl at me when I come to visit my overly-creative grandson." Grandma James glared at him intensely. "Or I will turn this Jurassic jungle into a pink and white lace nightmare that even your extraordinary talents cannot remove."

"You wouldn't!" He looked a bit worried.

"Try me," she challenged, smiling wickedly.

"That goes for me as well," said Myrna.

"Okay! Okay! I'll put in a threshold recognition sensor."

"It better work. I still jump every time Uncle Paul translates," Grandma muttered as she walked deeper into the faux prehistoric jungle, admiring the creation. "Extraordinary—absolutely extraordinary. I have never seen the like."

Nicki's rooms were the epitome of feminine. A queen-sized four-poster bed with a beautiful draped canopy was the focal point. The walls and ceiling were pastel colors that changed with her mood, or could be beautiful scenic panoramas or skies (she borrowed the idea from the Mall and books she'd read about that school in England). All the furniture was Victorian antiques (mostly brought from the manor house, though some were imitation copies). There were no posters; instead, a large, full-length wall mirror could become like a TV screen and display large photos of her favorite music, sports or movie idols. There were no complaints from Mom or dire warnings from Grandma—just universal praise and a suggestion: she should patent the process for the mirror. It would be very popular among Sodality and Wizarding teens. J.J. had already figured out a whole marketing scheme and ways to make it a must-have item in every Sodality household.

"It's getting late and we've all had a busy (and creative) day," announced Myrna. "During the next few days we'll have plenty of time to tour the rest of the compound. Professor Heady expects you in class at Manor House, 8:00a.m. (our time)."

"Aw, Mom," complained Brian. "Can't we wait and start next Monday?"

"You're already behind to be prepared for exams. You start tomorrow!"

The adults filed out of Nicki's rooms while J.J., Brian and Willard hung back, inspecting the poster mirror (as J.J. dubbed it). Much like FON mirrors, a simple touch on a spot on the frame and the picture changed. After a few moments J.J. challenged:

"Why'd you complain about goin' back to our studies?" He tried looking behind the mirror to see if there was any additional workings in the wall, but there weren't any. "You've been grumbling ever since we got back from England that we only made one trip to study the crystal seer stuff."

"I wish we could go back tonight," said Brian, "but I have a reputation to uphold, don't I? You're the school prodigy."

"You're unbelievable." J.J. shook his head and started off to go to his rooms, followed by Willard.

"Hey, Sis, d'you hear from that waiter yet?" asked Brian before he left.

"Not yet—no, why—I mean, why would I? What are you talking about?" she stammered, turning red.

"I saw you give him your number." He grinned conspiratorially. "Maybe he'll take you to some of your Meyor High Senior stuff—like the prom. You could do worse."

"He is kinda cute." She blushed deeper.

"I wouldn't know about *cute*; he's okay. Think maybe he'll be brave enough to call the Chairman's daughter?"

"If not, then I'm not interested. I don't want to go out with someone who's intimidated by Dad's job."

"That sounds a bit shallow."

"No, it's not. We could never get to know each other if he falls apart whenever he's around the family—and Dad's position is part of who we are—who I am. We're a close family."

"I hope he calls." Brian left to go to his rooms. He was tired.

Chapter Thirty

Guiding Principle &
Seven Laws Of Power

"Welcome back to Everett Manor." Brian heard the familiar British accent of Hodgins as he was shaking off the FON queasiness and making sure he had all his parts. "Professor waits in library. Dinner will be at six-o'clock. And may I say, it's good the house will continue to be used."

"Thanks, Hodgins," answered Brian, turning toward the open sliding doors leading to the library. There was something comforting about being in the house his family had lived in for centuries. *Lunch at eleven, our time—just three hours,* he thought.

"Professor," called Brian, breaking the silence of their studying Merlin's notes about the crystal seer cave. "I keep having dreams about our great-grandparents and Reficul keeps showing up, too." He noticed he had the undivided attention of his siblings. "I've read where there can be a connection between two people—a terrible bond—that sometimes one can see through the other's eyes. Is that what's going on with me and Reficul?"

"I don't think so, M'Lord. That kind of connection is extremely rare and in recent history we only know of it happening once. You have inherited seer abilities which show you events: past, present and (rarely) future. Much the same as the crystals in the cave."

"But sometimes I think I sense his emotions," he interrupted.

"Emotions are powerful things, full of energy. A sensitive seer is also empathic and can perceive those feelings, just as you did on September 11th."

"That's right! I sensed some of their fear, anger and frustration."

"And remember, you are only picking up what spills out into the universe. Just think how much more those brave souls were actually experiencing!"

"I don't want to go there. What little I felt was almost more than I could handle."

"That's wise, M'Lord. And by that you honor their memory by acknowledging how terrible was their plight."

"Why do I only see certain things?"

"For some reason, they are important to you, either for your educational benefit or something you need to act upon. But as you mature and refine your gift, you'll be able to direct it to specific settings—again, like the crystals in the cave."

"Isn't that really dangerous?" asked J.J. "If a seer looked into the future and saw what numbers were going to be drawn for the lottery, he could win every time. Or worse, if he saw he was going to die in an accident, he could know how to change the events to prevent it."

"Alas, you have hit on one of the reasons the gift is so rare, and it only works properly when intentions are pure—most particularly for the future."

"What about the crystals?" asked Nicki. "Do they also sense intent?"

"That I do not know, M'Lady. Hopefully an answer will be revealed in our studies. I would think your revered ancestor included such a condition upon its use."

"I've been having that dream about our great-grandparents for weeks—maybe longer. How do I know when to act?" Brian sighed.

"When the time is right, you will know," said an extremely familiar voice coming from the library's entrance.

"Grandma!" yelled J.J., running over to embrace the wise sage—his (birth) father's mother. "How'd you—why are you—?"

"I am pleased you are glad to see me, Jeremy, but do learn to finish your sentences." She chuckled as she embraced all four youngsters. "I was getting ready to make my dinner when I felt it would be nice to sup with my grandchildren—and you, of course, Professor." She nodded respectfully to him. "With all the time zones, I hope I am not too late."

"No, we haven't eaten yet." J.J. was beaming.

"I will ask the missus to set another place," said Hodgins, suddenly appearing in the room. "Welcome back to Everett Manor, Mum. Your presence is ever gracious and welcome." He turned and walked toward the door but seemed to dissolve into the air as if he were a long way off and going out of sight.

"How does he do that?" said J.J. "All the wards and shields are up. He can't be translating—they call it disabbering or something."

"Some of the old-family domestics developed special abilities they've jealously kept within their ranks," answered the professor. "They will only pass it down to the next generation bonded to the family and house."

"Grandma, earlier you were saying..." Brian eased into one of the soft leather chairs as the others followed his lead and were seated.

"Yes, before I was interrupted by my overenthusiastic grandson." Brian saw J.J. blush and his ears turn bright red (which she seemed to relish doing to him). "Each of us was given gifts that enable us to serve each other, ourselves and fulfill our roles in the greater universe. With these gifts we were also provided all the necessary tools to utilize them. Our job is to learn how to use those tools and when and where we are to apply the gifts."

Brian's mind was spinning with a veritable avalanche of questions which she sensed empathically. She held up a finger and he settled back into the leather.

"When you saw the forces assembled against Mr. Mendacci, you knew to act. When you sensed the hired operative and the Black Knight spy, you knew to act. When you experienced a bit of the emotion and scenes of September 11th, you knew *not* to act—"

"But I wanted to," he mumbled, staring at his lap.

"Yes, but you did not, because you knew it was not to be—as hard as that was."

He shifted uncomfortably in his chair, making the leather to creak, and barely nodded his head. It was a very painful memory.

"Remember the Fifth Element," she continued. "All too often we fail to realize it is just as important as Fire, Water, Earth and Air, because they are more obvious. Spirit is the essence of love and love is the essence of spirit. Neither can exist without the other. Both have energy and power. Your very thoughts and emotions send forth energy into the universe and at some time it comes back, multiplied. If you stay pure in heart, you will know when to act."

"But how do I do that—stay pure in heart? I'm just a kid and I'm not perfect. I get angry, misbehave. You know."

"Yeah, Mom will verify that!" quipped J.J., but a quick stare from Grandma had him wishing he hadn't. "Sorry."

"No one expects you to be perfect—none of us are. Each day is a new day to try again and hopefully learn from yesterday's mistakes. If you do that and share your gifts according to our Guiding Principle and Seven Laws of Power, the Spirit Element will give you direction and the answers you seek. Can you recite the Seven Laws and Guiding Principle?"

Brian's mind was in a fog. Embarrassed, he tried to sink deeper in the chair, but J.J. rescued him.

"I can! As one blessed by the Powers, I—"

"Not the Oath!" she commanded, exasperated. "You are not to say those words until you are an adult. Where did you—?"

"Books, Grandma—books." He shrugged his shoulders innocently. "Okay; the Seven Laws of Power: I will seek:

"1. Symmetry; order, balance and love

"2. Harmony; be responsible, mature, respectful and loving

"3. Empathy; show compassion, kindness, charity and love

"4. Reasoning; act with prudence, judgment, discretion and love

"5. Mastery; maintain self-control, focus, integrity and love

"6. Determination; go forth with persistence, endurance, courage, patience and love

"7. Dedication; be honorable, trustworthy, loyal, courteous, friendly and loving."

"How did you—" Brian started to ask but J.J. pushed on.

"Our Guiding Principle: Treat all creation as you would have it treat you. Thus do no harm!" He grinned mischievously, feeling very proud of himself.

"I get it, Grandma," announced Brian like he suddenly understood something that had eluded him. "Every one of the laws ends with 'love.' I've read those words many times. We even have them framed in our living room. And I can't count the times we've been reminded, *Love is the ruling power of the universe*, but I never connected it to the Laws. Wow! Am I thick? Why didn't I catch on before?" He glanced at J.J. who, with such an opening, was unusually quiet. "That's really deep!"

"No, you are not *thick* (as you say it). Each of us comes to that bit of enlightenment in our own way—though some Sodality go to their graves never having understood." She quickly wiped a tear from her eyes. "I suspect your memorizing, prodigy brother is just now working it out."

Brian again looked at J.J. and saw he was blushing; his ears were bright red, and freckles were dark blotches. He also saw Nicki and Willard were having their own epiphanies. He was pleased they each worked it out but couldn't deny it felt good to be ahead of Genius Boy for once. There was a long moment of silence while the old sage let the lesson sink in, until Hodgins silently appeared—like a ghost somehow changing into material form.

"Dinner is served," his voice almost reverberated. "There is just time to have a wash."

The spell was broken. On the Manor's ground floor there was a ladies' powder room and a men's washroom. Brian, J.J., Willard and Nicki wasted no time bolting for the door. Cook prepared brilliant meals but could get quite impatient when anyone let her dishes get cold.

"How do you memorize stuff like that?" asked Brian as they took seats at the smaller (less formal) family dining table.

"SHERMDD," answered J.J. as he placed a napkin in his lap and waited for everyone—then the food would appear.

"What'd you say? Sher—what's that?"

"S-H-E-R-M-D-D, SHERMDD! That's the first letters of the Seven Laws."

Grandma was the last to be seated. Then platters, bowls and tureens appeared in the table's center, laden with sausages, mashed potatoes ("bangers and mash"), chicken, soup, broccoli, corn, bread, butter and jam.

"Wow!" exclaimed Brian. "This sure beats the CKS cafeteria." He had his plate piled high, a chicken leg in his left hand and a sausage wrapped in bread in the right. He looked around as disapproving looks formed on the other faces around the table. "What? I'm hungry!"

"YOU'RE ALWAYS HUNGRY!" everyone retorted the family joke—even Cook, the Hodginses and their assigned agent (who were standing against the wall).

"Can't the agent eat with us?" asked Willard. "He's gotta eat."

"Not to worry," said Mrs. Hodgins. "Cook made him a scrumptious meal for after. He's on duty now. Wouldn't want him to get in trouble with your da, would we."

"Thank you, sir," said the dark-suited agent, who allowed just a bit of a smile to crack his normally unreadable look of intense professional alertness.

*　*　*

"It's not working!" Brian paced aggressively around the confines of the crystal seer cave. "We're doing everything right, according to Merlin's instructions—at least I think we are—and there's nothing." His feet lightly crunched on the fine gravel on the hardened floor, and refracted rainbows wee lit up across his face and shirt.

"Ease up!" said J.J. "It took Merlin many years to perfect the use of these crystals and construct this cave. You can't expect to master it in just a few days."

"But I need to—*we* need to see what Reficul is up to." Brian continued pacing. "All I see in my dreams is his face."

"You may not see much more than that," suggested Nicki. "Merlin himself wrote how he struggled with the meanings of the symbols in his visions."

"Ugh! I don't wanna hear that. I just don't understand it. I could see every detail about those guys trying to kidnap Mendacci."

"Maybe that's 'cuz it was actually happening at the time," suggested J.J. "The thing you're dreaming about—"

"Hasn't happened yet!" Brian's pace picked up. "Or it hasn't happened in an altered past."

"So when you dream about it," added Willard, "it's probably when he's thinking—"

"Or making his plans." Brian stopped in the middle of the room where rainbow bands streaked across his front. "That's why I haven't been prompted to act—he's not ready to do whatever he's planning."

"That's sure not going to give us much time to prepare, is it?" J.J. rose from the crude bench against a wall and glanced at the watch on his wrist. "It's almost three o'clock (back home). We'd better get going; it's late here for Professor."

Brian didn't hesitate; he slung his backpack over his left shoulder and led the four through the thick stone doorway and into the long access tunnel.

*   *   *

"She did what?!" seethed Laileb, barely controlling his temper. "Please tell me you're joking—or that the report was wrong." He angrily paced in front of the long lab bench in the basement of Reficul's mountain retreat. He glared at the woman who was cowering before his wrath.

"I'm certainly not joking! The report was written by Everett's Chief of Security and signed off by the Chairman himself," she defended, her voice meek and shaken. "Please, it's not my fault."

"You're right; I'm sorry." He stopped pacing and let his intensity soften. "Wilma, you've done exactly the right thing. I'm just having a hard time believing she could be so stupid. Would you please go through it again, and try to remember every detail."

"I wish I could have made a copy, but it was retrieved from my desk and sent to the Investigations Branch before I could do it." She went on to recite Antetima's activities in London, hiring the covert operative and recruiting Sutton to get assigned to Everett's security detail. Then she recounted how Genoveve took two Knights to the barbecue at the Council Executive House, kidnapped Brian Everett and was about to cancel his psionic abilities but was overwhelmed by Everett family members and their security forces. All three were captured, arrested and jailed. Apparently, Antetima willingly admitted her role in the plots and was seeking protective custody—though she had not revealed anything bound by her oath to Reficul.

"I knew about the operations in England; she showed me her plan. But an overt attack on the Everett boy goes directly against Master's orders. I can't believe she actually thought that would work. I still don't believe it!"

"Believe it!" said a third voice coming from the doorway leading to the stone staircase to the ground floor. "She recruited three, not two. I was there but got away."

"Oh, this just keeps getting better and better," said Laileb with a deep sarcastic scowl. "And pray tell, Myron, why would you go along with such a scheme?"

"I follow orders! Antetima outranks me, so I did what I was told."

"You're right; it's not your fault. You've always been faithful. How'd you get away?"

"I heard most of Wilma's report and it's fairly accurate, but they left out a few interesting details. Genoveve sent me to the far side of the wooded area to watch for any roving patrols. I couldn't see into the clearing very well, but I had a good view of the Everett boy and Antetima.

"The boy was drugged to keep him from channeling, yet he arranged for a little cloud to deluge Genoveve with water—as if a big tub was turned over her head. Then psionic flames blew apart the energy binder she was holding him with. I've never seen anything like it. But what came next was even more unbelievable. He conjured up the most realistic looking hologram ever made of a gold dragon. You could almost hear the thud of its feet on the ground. The thing even talked! Genoveve was so frightened, she passed out."

"Are you sure it was a projected image—not a real dragon? Remember what happened last year! A blue dragon rescued the Everett boy before Master could finish him off."

"True, but we know Blues are known to be in the U. S. This was a small gold one, and really shiny. Nah! It was a hologram. I'm sure of it."

"Then what happened?"

"The other Everett kids showed up as Brian bound Antetima. They had already stunned James and Marshall. I made a quick retreat; there was nothing I could do, especially since a security squad was also converging on the scene."

"You could have stunned Brian and tried to rescue Genoveve before everyone else got there!"

"No, he was shielded. Antetima fired some blast—I assume to cancel his powers—but it was absorbed by the shield. And we were ordered to not interfere."

"But he was drugged!"

"Maybe she made the stuff wrong."

"She doesn't make mistakes like that."

"You're right, but I also know what I saw. He was shielded. There was nothing I could do, except stick around and get captured, too."

"You, too, did the right thing. There was no point in you being arrested. It continues to boggle my mind how a twelve-year-old can summon resources of the most bizarre kind." He was almost breaking into a sweat remembering his own encounter with rattlesnakes. "Let's assume the dragon wasn't real; could you, while drugged, blast off energy binders, create a rain deluge and do a hologram of a talking gold dragon, and all the while, maintain an absorption shield?"

"I couldn't do that stuff under any circumstances."

Chapter Thirty-One
The Situation Room

"A MONTH!" exclaimed Brian. As usual, he was pacing about the seer cave, frustrated and becoming increasingly angry. "We've read almost every book and note Merlin left, and NOTHING! We're doing everything right—at least we're doing what he said..." He sat down on the hard rock floor, feeling the grit on his palms as he eased himself down. He glanced up at the various crystals hanging from the ceiling. "Maybe something is out of alignment."

"We've checked that a dozen times," said Nicki. "If his notes are right, then the alignment's right. Somehow we missed something." She was speaking softly to try and defuse her brother's unpredictable temper. They both noted J.J. being unusually quiet; obviously deep in thought. After a long moment of silence, he broke the reverie:

"We gotta start simpler," he said, just leaving the statement hanging like he'd just had an epiphany. "We gotta start simpler!" he repeated with more force, punching his right fist into his open left hand, making a slap sound.

"Whaddya mean?" asked Brian, puzzled. He knew better than to dismiss J.J.'s ideas—he wasn't called a prodigy and genius for nothing. "If we take out steps to make it simpler—"

"No! Not simplify the process; a simpler goal!" He went over, sat down cross-legged on the floor right in front of Brian and stared into his eyes. "When we first learned to do stuff, when our parents and Merlin taught us, we started with easy, simple things. When we mastered those, it was easy to move up to harder tasks. We've been trying to see back ninety-eight years into an event we've only heard about in family stories. That's too much to start off with."

"Maybe he's right," said Nicki. "I remember you guys teaching me to move just a cup of water, and I was trying really hard. Now I can use elementals and move a whole lake if needed. We're assuming we can do anything—no matter how abstract or difficult—just because Merlin taught us to use elementals. It doesn't work that way."

"It feels right, M'Lord," added Willard. "And you know what Dad taught us about the word *assume*."

"Yeah, it makes an a-- of you and me," said Brian, letting his head drop to his chest. "I've been so focused on our great-grandparents and the General Slocum, I've not been willing to consider trying something else—like practice the basics."

"Hey, don't give yourself a wedgie; we've all done the same thing." J.J. jumped up and extended his hand to help Brian up. "I'm supposed to be the genius kid and it took me a month to figure it out." Brian grabbed the proffered hand, went to his feet and said,

"Okay, anybody with an idea of something simple?" He dusted off the seat of his pants.

"It should be something current," said Nicki.

"Like when we saw Hodgins' son," added Willard.

"And I think we should all step out and let Ring Boy get it started. Even though we're all concentrating on the same thing, we each have our individual views. Maybe we're causing interference." J.J. turned toward the thick door leading to the long tunnel. "Why don't you focus on Antetima? We haven't heard from her lately."

"Hey, good idea," agreed Brian. He watched his brothers and sister file into the tunnel, just out of sight. Then he stood to the side of the huge center crystal, closed his eyes and formed a mental image of the (ex) CKS professor. He began chanting: *ilustro conspectum—ilustro conspectum—ilustro conspectum*. Suddenly one of the walls lit up with a picture which looked like a TV with no antenna attached. Brian knew he was close. He focused again on Antetima and repeated: *ilustro conspectum*. The snowy picture suddenly resolved into a full color scene—like a projection TV— showing the short, squat woman sitting in a small room, lit by bright sunlight coming in through a window on one wall. There was a bed, table and some other cheap furniture. She was sitting on a chair next to the table where she was writing on a sheet of paper.

"I've got it," called Brian. The others rushed into the cave and began examining the scene.

"That's a motel room," said Nicki, "probably one of the safe locations they're hiding her in until something permanent is found." Just then the picture changed. Now the room was dark. Someone was in the bed, under the cheap covers (probably Antetima), apparently asleep. Again, the scene changed. Outside the motel room, four dark figures were stealthily making their way through a parking lot that had no lights. Each wore a black cloak with a hood covering their heads, leaving faces obscured in shadows. Their movements were fluid and careful not to arouse any alarm.

"They've found her!" screamed Brian in a panic. He started to bolt for the door and tunnel, but J.J. intercepted, holding his shoulders.

"Hold it!" Brian heard as he struggled to break free. "It's not happening now—look!"

"You look," commanded Brian. "They're getting closer by the minute." He was breaking out in a sweat. "If we don't warn Dad or Bowyer—"

"BRIAN!" yelled J.J., Nicki and Willard together—they all saw it. J.J. walked over to the wall with the projection. "What time is it in the U. S.—right now?"

Brian looked at his watch (set to Arizona time). "It's two o'clock in the afternoon."

"What time is it in this scene?" He pointed to the dark parking lot.

"I don't know—but it's later—maybe after midnight."

"So, either this already happened or it's not going to happen until tonight, at the earliest. Also, you're not thinking. There's a satellite cell phone in your backpack. Dad's rules, remember?"

"Will it work down here?"

"Only one way to find out—but it's a special one that's used by military and stuff. It should; there's a cell tower on the hill just off the manor property." J.J. strode over to the door and backpack on the floor. He reached in and pulled out the grey unit with a thick six-inch antenna rising from the top. He pushed a button and the dial pad and screen lit up. "What was the coded number to Bowyer?"

"Star-33. Star-101 is Dad, Star-102 is Mom," answered Nicki.

"Let's call Bowyer. This is a security thing." He pushed the numbers. "Hey, it works—it's ringing."

Brian listened to J.J. describe exactly what they saw on the wall of the cave.

*   *   *

"Wha—whazzup?" Brian was groggily wondering why he was being roused from a deep sleep. "Go 'way." He pulled his covers over his head only for them to slide themselves down toward his feet. "Whatimizzit?"

"Time, Milord, for you to go to yer da's study," said Benson. "The operation is about to begin. Here's yer dressing gown."

The fog in Brian's mind cleared. He jumped out of bed, donned the robe over his long night shirt, and sped off to his father's office, meeting his brothers and sister in the hallway.

Upon entering the spacious office, the youngsters were surprised to find it was empty except for an agent standing beside a door they'd never seen before.

"Way cool!" exclaimed J.J. "One of the secret passageways Dad told us about." His red hair almost glowed as he grinned mischievously and rubbed his hands together. "We've got to do more exploring. Maybe there's a hidden torture chamber."

Brian shook his head and chuckled as he followed J.J. through the door, which led to a stairway leading deep under the house. At the bottom they passed through a massive doorway and entered a large windowless room made of thick concrete walls covered with wood paneling. A huge round table (with many chairs) was in the center and on the walls were various sizes of flat-screen TVs showing an assortment of (Brangler and Sodality) news broadcasts and some live video coming from places he didn't recognize. One of the larger screens caught Brian's attention as it displayed something very familiar: the parking lot of the motel where Antetima was staying. It looked exactly like the scene the crystals projected on the wall of the seer cave.

"All right, Dad!" J.J. was so excited he was bouncing up on his feet. "Got your own war room. This is great!" He took on a somewhat sinister look.

"We don't conduct wars." George smiled at his very imaginative son. "Branglers do enough of that—but we carry out operations in response to situations throughout the world. So, we call this our Situation Room." He was obviously proud of the facility.

Brian walked along the walls, glancing at the myriad of video displays and the other people in the room, including Mr. Jones, who was in a dark suit and standing in a shadowed corner—not speaking to anyone—just watching the activity. Suddenly Brian felt very underdressed, being barefoot and wearing only a dressing gown (robe) over his nightshirt.

As if sensing his discomfort George explained, "I'm sorry we roused you from your beds without time to dress properly, but things are moving along quickly and we promised you could watch. This is the first operation we've managed from this location." He motioned at the round table. "Please, everyone, take a seat." Discussions in the room fell silent as all were seated. "We received information from a *very* reliable source that the safe location of a person in protective custody has been compromised. Black Knights are moving into the area now."

As they sat down, the lights dimmed and everyone gasped. Above the center of the round table, a cylinder of white light appeared as if coming down from the ceiling or up from the table. But neither had a visible source. Inside the brilliant radiance, a swirling mist or smoke seemed to be boiling for a few seconds, then became an exact hologram of the parking lot (which was then on every screen on the walls).

"Ooooh!" exclaimed J.J. "Now *that's* impressive. Way to go, Dad!"

"Thank you, Son! That's quite a compliment, especially since I got the idea from you."

"But mine are always stationary images from memory. You have this doing motion in real time."

"We just incorporated scrying, satellite images and electronic video into what you did—"

Suddenly everyone's attention was drawn by some movement within the scene. Brian carefully watched as four black-hooded attackers crept into the parking lot, moving like cats, easing their way between the parked cars—always staying in the darkest shadows. These were not amateurs; their movements were fluid, agile and careful. It reminded Brian of martial arts movies he had seen on TV. But he grimaced. These were not actors playing a role. They were a skilled assault team who were powerful mages.

The atmosphere in the Situation Room was electric. Brian felt like he could actually feel the tension from all those watching the scene develop. The hologram was so realistic, everyone was afraid to speak as they might be heard at the other end. Brian had to remind himself to breathe; he was holding his breath, staring at the scene unfolding. He knew an Enforcement Squad was positioned around the area, but they were so well hidden, they were nowhere to be seen.

Closer and closer the black hoods moved toward the door where they believed their (former) associate was staying. But, of course, she had been moved earlier in the day and agents were waiting inside.

"Why don't they go ahead and arrest 'em?" whispered Willard.

"They haven't done anything illegal yet," explained Agent Bowyer. "Sneaking around a parking lot is not against the law—Sodality or Brangler." Brian saw Mr. Jones nod his head in approval. "As soon as they use psionics to enter that room, we have a large Field Enforcement Squad ready to take care of them."

During the discourse no one took their eyes off the Black Knight operatives as they steadily worked their way along the concrete walkway leading to the room—still staying in the shadows, until they stood in front of the door. Suddenly there was a blinding flash and the door burst into splinters. The four rushed through the smoking doorway. Behind them, it seemed the parking lot came alive. Agents were either running or translating to just outside the room, so they would block any retreat or assist in the takedown. There was a translation barrier bubble being held over the room.

Out of the corner of his eye Brian saw his father wave his hand. The hologram clouded momentarily in swirling smoke, then cleared; now showing the inside of the motel room (as did half the TV screens—the other half remained showing the parking lot).

Everything happened fast. The first Black Knight through the doorway was allowed to get deep inside and close to the bed so his companions would have plenty of space to enter. Once all four were inside, bright lights blared in their faces (which momentarily blinded them). Blue stun beams then blasted from several directions as the bright lights dimmed to normal room illumination. Agents poured into the room as the surprised Knights crumpled to the floor and were bound by bright orange energy ropes.

It was over. Brian felt almost disappointed; he had expected a drawn-out battle with casualties on both sides. But of course this was better; the bad guys were only stunned and taken into custody while the Enforcement Squad was untouched (except for one who was hit by a flying piece of the door).

As if by command, everyone in the Situation Room stood and congratulations were being offered—especially to Agent Bowyer who had planned the operation. Brian heard Mr. Jones inquire:

"I'm still new to all this. Do those blue bolts cause injuries?"

"Oh, no," answered Bowyer. "The stunners they used only temporarily stop the brain's conscious control. It's almost like when Brangler doctors put patients to sleep before surgery. They'll wake up in about ten or fifteen minutes with nothing more than a slight headache."

Jones could only shake his head and mutter, "Incredible—absolutely incredible," as Brian (and his brothers and sister) were dismissed to go back to their beds.

Chapter Thirty-Two
Mistaken Desire

"This isn't much different from scrying and the viewing pools Aerion taught us last year." Brian was wistfully studying a crystal projection of Coach Fleogan putting his current flipolo team through its paces; wishing he could be there.

"That's because it's current," said J.J. with a distant voice of longing as he watched the scene he participated in so many times before. "Let's try going back in time," came out almost as an afterthought.

"Boys!" exclaimed Nicki, clearly exasperated. "If you guys will quit drooling on your shirts, maybe we can get some work done." The image blinked off and they all were staring at a blank wall of the Seer Cave.

"You made me lose it," complained Brian.

"You're a girl—you just don't understand boys and flipolo," said J.J.

"Gee, you noticed," she chuckled. "You're really quick for a genius."

"Good one!" complimented Brian as he watched J.J. blush and his ears turn red. "What should we look at?"

"I wanna see what happened to my parents." They all became very quiet and Brian vividly recalled the day they learned J.J.'s (birth) parents died while investigating a cult in the Amazon rain forest of South America.

"Wait, Jeremy!" They all jumped as Grandma's familiar voice surprised them. She had never before been through the tunnel to the Crystal Cave.

"Grandma!" J.J. blurted out and stammered, "Where'd—how'd—what are you d-do—why not?"

"Have you forgotten? Complete sentences work much better." She smiled and opened her arms, expecting the rush of grandchildren for hugs.

"But—" was all J.J. could get out before he ran to her embrace, followed by Nicki, Willard and Brian for a quick flood of greetings and an excited tour of the cave—each competing to have their own say and explain their favorite parts.

"Now back to your questions—however inartfully posed." J.J.'s ears turned red as he blushed deeply. "I sensed you were about to make a huge mistake, so I came to—"

"Stop me!" J.J. stood defiant yet looked deeply hurt.

"Of course not!" She was firm yet retained her loving countenance. "I would never presume to interfere in your right to choose—even if that choice were to result in a terrible outcome. But I am your grandmother and love you without condition. I would be remiss if I did not share my fears about that which you contemplate. So, with your permission, may I share some concerns for you to consider?"

J.J. looked at the old sage in a whole new light. She had never before asked his permission to have her say about anything. She was always a commanding presence whose opinions were always considered to be second only to Spiritual Higher Power, and obeyed without question—even by adults. He looked deeply into her eyes as she kindly stared back and patently awaited his response.

"Yes, please," softly came from his lips and he smiled—feeling just a bit more mature.

"When Merlin shared the secrets and powers of the *Sigillum de Aemeth*, there were certain rules that applied. What was the most important?"

"Do not alter the past."

"Yes, and if you saw the events just prior to your parents' disappearance, you would probably see some way to stop it. Would you be able to keep yourself from going to their rescue? I could not!"

"You, Grandma?" whispered Brian.

"Of course me. Do you think for a moment that if I knew the facts this room can reveal; I would not risk anything to save my son and daughter-in-law? No—I would be just as sorely tempted to try—and it would be just as big a mistake for me as for you. It would alter history. That is one reason I have not asked you to share the secrets of *Sigillum de Aemeth*. And, even if you resisted the urge to change things, do you want to have your last memory of them being in some awful setting, or worse?"

There was a long silence.

"I have given you much to think about and have not had dinner yet. I am hoping that was Cook's famous steak and kidney pie I smelled as I arrived upstairs." She turned, squared her shoulders in a dignified way, and started for the door.

"Grandma," said J.J., his voice sounding a little deeper. She stopped and looked back with a kind look and eyes glistening from tears. "It's almost time for our break and Cook hates it when we're late." He went to her side and crooked his elbow. "May I take you to dinner?"

"Why I would be delighted, sir." She hooked her arm through his, and they eased on through the door and into the long tunnel.

"Well, I guess I get the troll and dragon." Nicki slid her arms through her brothers' elbows and they followed as the door closed itself and lights extinguished behind.

"Thank you, Grandma," echoed through the long tunnel.

*   *   *

"There they are!" exclaimed Nicki. "They're standing behind that group of kids along the railing." Brian watched her bouncing

323

up and down on her toes and pointing to the projected scene illuminated on the cave wall. "We have pictures of them in our family albums—I'm sure it's them."

"I think you're right," agreed Brian. "I count five kids in front of 'em and that's the right number for that family they were helping out."

"And that's probably their parents." J.J. pointed to the two adults just right of the children.

"I bet that's Mrs. Stube or whatever her name was, standing next to the man." Willard stooped low, walked to the wall and put his finger under the image of an older woman in an ankle-length dress who seemed to be frantically explaining something to the man and pointing to the gangway that spanned from the dock to the hull of the boat.

"Look at those huge paddlewheels on the sides," said J.J. "They're gigantic. And there's kids dancing. I wish we could hear the band playing." His face took on a very pained look. "I understand what Grandma was saying. Look at the beautiful ship, flags and banners flying, band playing, people dancing, and we know it's going to burn up. Over a thousand will be killed and we have the power to stop it. We could save them all, yet we can't. Our interference would change history in ways we could never imagine."

"But people are going to burn up and drown." Brian had tears running down his cheeks and anguish across his face. "This is awful! And we're just watching the crystal projection. It's going to be terrible when we're actually there... Over five hundred of 'em are just kids." He backed up against the wall farthest from the projection, let his knees go slack and slid down to sit on the floor—still staring at the joyful scene that would soon be tragic.

"Nicki, have you seen enough to make our period costumes?" he asked. "There's no way I want to watch that ship go up the East River and start blazing."

"I've seen all I need to. It'll be fairly easy. I'll just alter some of our clothes. The hardest thing for me is to get used to moving about in a long dress with petticoats. I'm going to practice that over the next few days. We may have to move fast, and I don't want to be slowed by my outfit."

"Why does your dress have to be so long?" asked Brian, relieved to be talking and thinking about something else. "Couldn't you make it mid-calf?"

"She'd probably be arrested or something," answered J.J. "Don't you remember your history? In 1904 it would have been scandalous for a young woman to show her ankles—especially in polite society. Remember, the June 15th trip [on the General Slocum] was chartered by the Saint Mark's Evangelical Lutheran Church—real proper folks."

"How do you remember stuff like that?" complained Brian. "I read all my history books and got good grades—even in Antetima's class—but I can't recall anything about *ladies' fashions.*"

"It wasn't about fashions. It was a discussion on early twentieth century social mores. I know you had it in Antetima's First Form—"

"I wish you wouldn't do that." Brian had a blank look on his face.

"What?"

"*Mores*—what's that?"

"Morals; morality of the time."

"Why don't you just say that?" He wriggled back up the wall to standing, brushed off his hands and seat. "Then maybe I'll understand you."

"Yeah, well, I may be able to memorize stuff and invent new psionic applications, but I can't get these crystals to produce even a flicker. Yet you can sit and argue with me and still hold a ninety-eight-year-old scene—in which the Slocum is pulling away from the pier. How do you do *that?*"

They all turned back to the projected images.

"Is that my adopted great-grandparents, there on the dock waving?" asked Willard, staring at the elderly couple standing with their arms waving above their heads.

"Yes, Wil, that's them." Nicki walked over and put a hand on his shoulder. "Your adoption, like J.J.'s, is complete and official now. You are as much a part of this family as Brian and I. You don't have to clarify family stuff with 'adopted'. That's *your* great-grandparents, not your *adopted* great-grandparents."

Brian saw a tear start to streak down the undersized boy's cheek but he stood tough and refused to draw attention to his emotional moment by wiping it dry.

"Release it, Brian," said J.J. "It's getting under way and we don't want to watch the fire."

* * *

"Why did you take so long to report back?" growled Laileb, looking up from the book he was studying. "You're a mage and can translate here in seconds. I thought you were taken into custody as well. I've been sitting here, trying to fit bits of information together and figure out what happened. You could have told me minutes afterward."

"I was afraid to come back," the dark-cloaked man snapped back. "It's obvious we have a traitor! They knew exactly what was going to happen and when. I heard one of their agents call out: 'We can stand down; we've got all four in custody.' They were expecting the four who went through the door... For all I knew, this place had been taken over as well. I hid out until I felt it was safe to stake out the castle—and I've been watching this place for days." He looked menacingly at Laileb.

"The only ones who knew about the operation were Jerry, Michael, Bill, David, myself and you," said Myron. "The others were captured, and I didn't tell, sooo—" He let the implication hang in the air, and stared angrily at Laileb.

"YOU DARE ACCUSE ME!?" Laileb jumped up, extending his right hand and ring. "I'm the one holding things together and working the hardest to bring back Prince Reficul. Now, if you want to throw around issues that are suspicious, you have been on two operation teams where all were arrested, except you."

All the color drained out of Myron's face as he realized just how shaky his own position was, and he said, "I explained what happened at the Chairman's barbecue!"

"Yes, and I accepted that as both reasonable and the right thing to do—"

"And if you'd seen that motel parking lot explode with agents, all knowing exactly what was going down, you'd have high-tailed it and gone into hiding, just as I did."

"True. Again, you probably did the right thing. At least, until you came in here accusing me of treachery." Laileb continued glaring, fully charged and ready to duel. "I won't tolerate anyone impugning my integrity or loyalty!"

"Hey!" Myron backed up two steps, carefully keeping his hands at his sides. Laileb's dueling skills and quick temper were well-known. "You're right! While hiding out I let my imagination run amok. But we have a problem. If it's not you or me, then who? It's no coincidence that all our operations have been compromised."

"I've thought a lot about that." He let his hand down, relaxed his posture but remained channeled with energy. "I'm not sure we have a traitor."

"But they knew! We have to—" interrupted Myron.

"Not necessarily—"

"There's no other expla—"

"It's Brian Everett," declared Laileb.

"Since when was he inducted into the Order?"

"He's a SEER! I'm sure of it."

"A what? You've got to be kidding. No one's had that kind of ability for centuries—maybe since Merlin, and he had that crystal cave or something." Myron pulled up one of the library chairs and sat down across from Laileb.

"It's the only explanation. Even if you or I were spies, neither of us knew all the details of Genoveve's activities in England, which were thwarted by *insider information* just like the operation at the motel. No one in the Order knew the details of all of our failed activities—going all the way back to Wizard's Cavern. Think about it; every time, the Everetts have seemingly known about everything we've tried to do—at least that somehow involved them." Laileb eased back into his chair, but did not release his channeled energy.

"Well, maybe. It *does* make sense. It would explain a lot. But, c'mon, Brian Everett? He's just twelve years old. I'd believe it more if you said it was Erin James, the one everyone calls 'Grandma'."

"I'd agree with you except I've heard her speak to groups and she was asked the difference between an emapth and a seer, and she denies any seer abilities."

"You must be talking about Grandma James," said a different voice. They hadn't heard Phusikos come back into the room after taking a break to eat some dinner. "She's the real thing. I have some empath abilities, but nothing to match hers. It takes everything I've got to block her." He paced slowly in front of the huge stone fireplace.

"We weren't really talking about her," said Myron, "so much as Laileb's convinced Brian Everett is a seer, and that's why all the operations have been compromised. I thought it might be the old lady instead."

"Oh, no!" exclaimed Phusikos, turning toward Laileb. "Not again! Last year you were convinced Everett's the Appointed One, and now your obsession has you believing he's a seer who has penetrated into the Order's operations. Get a grip, Laileb! Which is he: the Appointed One or the first true seer we've had in centuries? Hmmm?"

"I don't have to take that from you!" Laileb jumped up again, almost overturning his chair.

"You're right; you don't, but at the same time, don't expect us to buy into whatever hang-up you have with that boy. He's just a kid—an extraordinary one, I'll grant you—but there's no evidence to link him to the prophecy or that he's the reason our operations have gone sour. We've seen confidential reports right from the Redoubt and the Chief of Staff's office and there's never been a word suggesting their information comes from the boy," said Phusikos.

"But nothing else makes sense," defended Laileb. "No one person in the Order has been privy to all the information the Everetts or Redoubt agents have obtained, so we don't have a spy—"

"I'm not saying they don't have a seer! It's possible and it does explain things. But do you have any proof it's Brian and not some other Sodality mage we don't know about? They'd certainly keep whoever it is a well-guarded secret."

"But why not Brian? It could be him."

"He's not that good at blocking empath probes. I was around him almost daily at CKS, until they withdrew him to homeschool and he never hinted at Seer ability. So between that and his family history presentation last year, I think it highly unlikely that he's their secret weapon."

"Okay, okay … what about the Master? Are we any closer to being able to track him through the seal?" Laileb clearly had a different opinion, but a change of subject was a wise retreat.

"As a matter of fact, yes," announced Phusikos. He resumed his leisurely pacing.

"Really?" Laileb almost jumped to attention.

"As you know, we've known *how* to open the seal for some time, but we're still shaky on dialing into a specific destination. But, I think we can track where he went."

"How?"

"All movement of energy, magic, leaves a trace. Many can detect shields, barriers and other applications. It takes a lot of power to go through the seal, so it creates a path we can follow."

"Do we know how to hold the gate open, so we can get back?" asked Myron.

"That's the easy part," explained Phusikos—still pacing like a teacher giving a lesson. "We found an ancient, obscure text that explains it. As long as the mage who opened the gate does not release it, the gate will stay open."

"It can't be that simple! If it were, we'd all have seals and be jumping through them. There's got to be a reason the ability was abandoned," said Laileb.

"Oh, *that* part is easy. It's opening the seal that's difficult."

"Wait a minute. You said we knew how to open the seal."

"We do, but knowing how and having the energy to do it are not the same thing. In days of old, wizards were able to gather energy from the elements. That ability has been long lost, and I don't think our channeled energy is enough. You were there. It took a bolt of lightning to open the seal that day, and lightning is elemental."

"Then are you saying there's no hope?" asked Myron as he watched Laileb focus on the professor, waiting for the answer.

"No, I'm not saying that. But I am saying we need to change the focus of our research. Since we cannot gather from the elements, except in sometimes tiny amounts, we need to find another way to concentrate our power."

"That sounds reasonable. As soon as everyone gets back, we'll announce the change and get to work. That's good, Genus, real good," said Laileb. "Let me ask you: You're a renowned physics professor. Have you ever seriously tried to gather elemental energy?"

"Have you?"

"Yeah, we've all seen bits and pieces of Merlin's notes, so yes, I've had a go. Couldn't even stir up a blade of grass. Quit avoiding the question."

"Of course I have," said Phusikos, "and it was embarrassing. I felt like I gained a tiny bit of control, but it was sucked away. I almost got the impression it was mocking me and saying, *who do you think you are, commanding me?*"

"We'll just have to find another way, won't we." Laileb finally released his energy.

"It's not going to be easy, and maintain control." The professor stopped pacing and just stared at the ceiling in deep thought.

Chapter Thirty-Three
The Presentation

"Mornin'," Brian barely mumbled, shuffling into the kitchen, trying to get into his usual chair at the breakfast table before stumbling and falling asleep on the tiled floor.

"Good morning, Sunshine," quipped Mom, noticing her son's sleepy state as she finished cooking up link sausages, scrambled eggs and stacks of buttermilk pancakes. "How late did you stay up?"

"Three o'clock..." He plopped down in his chair, scraping the metal legs on the floor then put his head down on the starched linen placemat, hoping the silverware wouldn't poke him in his closed eyelids.

"You shouldn't have waited until the last minute to write your report." Platters full of food began sailing through the air and landing on the table, which was quickly laden with enough to feed the family for a week.

"All right, Mom!" exclaimed J.J. as he entered the kitchen and saw the mounds of food. "You finally fixed more than Ring Boy can eat. Did Wil transmute and you gotta feed the dragon?" He pulled out his chair, sat down and hungrily rubbed his hands together.

"Nope, I'm still boy-size," said Willard, following right behind J.J. "But, hey, Mom, I'll dragon up if it'll help." He too was surprised by the quantity on the table.

"Very funny," responded Myrna. "I always worry the agents aren't getting proper meals; cooking for themselves down at the old ranch house..."

"You've obviously not been down there at mealtimes," said Nicki, strolling gracefully into the expansive industrial kitchen, picking up a sausage link from the griddle and nibbling off a dainty bite. "You've seen those shows about how firemen eat at firehouses... Well, our agents recruited a couple of guys who went to culinary school, and Uncle Paul gives them a generous budget. They eat real well—gourmet meals."

"But they always look so hungry when we eat."

"That's because they don't get to break for meals until after we've eaten."

"I don't care." She sniffed. "This morning they're all getting a proper breakfast right here. I've already called down to let them know."

A huge platter with aromatic sausages landed right in front of Brian, who had slept through the previous exchange.

"Is it time to eat?" Brian's head came up as if drawn by the steam.

"I imagine so," announced Dad, entering the room adjusting his tie. He had on a long-sleeved, starched, light-blue shirt, suit pants and polished black shoes. "Sorry I'm late. Bloody tie wouldn't cooperate. I much preferred my sport shirts and pocket protectors."

"You're Chairman," said J.J. "Nobody's gonna tell *you* what to wear. You can even start a whole new trend at the Redoubt."

"I probably could but it just doesn't feel right. There's something about the Chairman's Redoubt office. When I walk in there, I sense all the history and important decisions made there. I never go in without at least a shirt and tie—and most times, even a suit coat."

"I've heard presidents say the same thing about the Oval Office," added Mom as she took her place at the table and reached out her hands. The whole family joined hands as Dad recited:

"For these bountiful gifts and all we have, may we always be grateful."

"EVER GRATEFUL," they all responded, then attacked the mounds of food. Brian was finally awake; sausages, pancakes, cantaloupe wedges and scrambled eggs were quickly piled high on his plate and the platters were noticeably lighter. He sensed glaring eyes and looked up (holding his fork with two sausage links and a wedge of pancake speared on).

"What?" he barely got out between mouthfuls. "I'm hungry!"

"You're always hungry!" responded everyone in the room— including the agents just outside the doors. Everyone giggled.

"Oh, I almost forgot," said Mom. "Superintendent Laedere called and you're to give your Crystal Cavern presentation today—"

"No way!" blurted out Brian, dropping his fork and sending bits of scrambled eggs to scatter onto the placemat and table. "I barely finished the write-up last night."

"Professor said your reports were due today, and because of some scheduling issues, your class presentation was moved up."

Brian heard the tone of finality in his mother's voice and realized any further argument was useless. But there was something else. She had a glint in her eyes and just the slightest upturn of a smile— as if she knew something but surely was not going to reveal it... Yet as quick and faint as it was there, it was gone. He shook his head, thinking it was his imagination running amok—and he was still very tired...

* * *

"Hey, J.J., Brian, Nicki, Willard!" Brian heard an excited, familiar voice call as the Everetts entered the CKS main hallway.

"Hey, Roger," cried J.J., breaking away to greet his (former) classmate, exchanging quick back pounds. "How're you doing? Man, you're as ugly as ever!" (Roger was really handsome and considered a great catch by most CKS girls.)

"Yeah, and you shrunk instead of growing—and your hair now is red as a traffic light!" They both laughed. "What's it like being pampered with body guards and home-schooling?"

"I'd rather be back here gettin' detention and playing flipolo—I really miss it!" His voice became distant and broken, and there was a long moment of uncomfortable silence. "Anyway, we're here to—"

"Give a history-science presentation to the whole school. We heard. Everybody's been wondering how many agents have come with you. Now that you guys are here, we went into full lock-down."

"We never know. Sometimes there's a couple assigned to us, but when Dad arrives, there'll be a whole team—"

"Hold on!" interrupted Brian. "You said we were presenting to the *whole school*? I thought it was only gonna be in History class or Elemental Physics."

"Nope. Word is, your report is an important subject the whole school should hear. A full assembly is scheduled. Cool, huh?"

"You wouldn't say that if it was you." Brian groaned. "Wait 'til I find Professor Heady—ugh!"

"'Tis time, M'Lords, M'Lady," whispered Professor Heady. They were standing backstage in the curtained wings of the huge CKS auditorium. He saw the concern in the faces of his students. "Not to worry. You'll be spot on. Just remember not to mention actually finding Merlin's Crystal Cave. Only discuss the research materials and how he made it work."

"But, Professor," said Brian, "I know some out there have empath abilities. They'll know if we're lying—and that'll make things worse, won't it?" He nervously smoothed down his robes—they had decided to wear the wizard robes they were given in England, to add to the effect of the presentation.

"You'll just have to tell the truth, won't you." He reached over and adjusted Willard's hat so it did not cover his face. "When you ask for questions, I'll stand near and help divert any that are uncomfortable. We don't lie, but we're not telling the whole story."

They could hear the superintendent call for order and introduce them.

As Brian, J.J., Nicki and Willard walked across the stage, the fairly enthusiastic applause died down and suddenly Brian felt the short walk to center stage seemed a mile long and their every step echoed on the hardwood flooring.

"Maybe we shouldn't have worn the robes 'n' hats," whispered Willard, nervously.

Brian's head was spinning. He was *very* glad Nicki was up first. And, as usual, she stepped up and took command: confidently going to the lectern (with a microphone), then smiled and asked:

"How would you like to wear this outfit to school every day?" She did a graceful pirouette, imitating a fashion model. The students laughed and clapped. "And before you ask, traditionally only underclothes are worn underneath, but today we just put them on over our regular stuff, as we're not wearing 'em all day— like most European kids do."

Brian watched jaws drop at such an intimate revelation, but it was brilliant. Even the usually disruptive students were focused on her in rapt attention and anxious to hear her presentation.

Nicki launched into a brief refresher of their family history from Captain C'Andro to Merlin to the present, then expressed their surprise at finding Everett Manor still intact and its library with details about the Crystal Cave. She touched on the general principles of how everything has energy which can be traced and examined if one has the proper abilities or technology—leaving the specifics for her brothers' parts of the presentation.

As she concluded and was about to step back, a hand flew in the air. Their friend Carl Fredericks stood and asked:

"Hey, Nicki, it's good to see you again. You said Everett Manor is located on the land Arthur gave Merlin, which was Caer-Myrddin, which is now near Carmarthen in Wales. But, last year, Brian told us the Everett name came from a village called Everett.

After Merlin's time, how did Caer-Myrddin land get the Everett name?" He smiled and sat down.

"Hi, Carl. We've missed you. Come visit us in the new house. Wow! You were listening. That's a good story by itself, but I'll give you a brief summary: After Arthur died, Merlin sent his second wife, son and daughter away to a village—Everett—that seems nonexistent today. We could not find it in any historical/geographical records, except those passed down in our family. It was Merlin's son who took on the Everett name. Then it was his son—Merlin's grandson—who came back to reclaim the land and Everett Manor was born. By then, Merlin had been sealed in the cave by Vivien."

Nicki backed up and J.J. took her place behind the lectern and microphone.

"I gotta be the luckiest kid in Sodality," he announced. "I was born Jeremy James, and my birth family and genealogy is a long and proud one, with roots going back to Caer-Myrddin and beyond. The Everetts and Jameses were close friends through the centuries. It was no coincidence my parents' and the Everetts' houses were close together in Meyor. The Everetts were *family* long before my parents' deaths and I was adopted by George and Myrna Everett." His voice broke and there was a long silent pause as he regained his composure. "Now I have another long and proud family tree—and our Chairman is my dad!" He smiled mischievously and rubbed his hands together. "And no one can mess with the short, red-headed kid any more—I've got bodyguards!" The students laughed and clapped.

J.J. went on to explain how the crystals in the cave were able to help Merlin focus on and concentrate the energy trails created by events, thoughts, emotions and actions... His was the technical and scientific portion of the presentation—the theory behind the great wizard's discovery.

As J.J. concluded his presentation, again a hand shot up from a boy who stood, looking very nervous. It was Kyle Peterson, a Fourth Form student.

"Since you have Merlin's notes and understand the science, couldn't you assemble a seer cave, or room, and make it work?" He remained standing for the answer.

"You're Kyle, aren't you? I've seen you around." J.J. paused to collect his thoughts. "Yes, I suppose we could. The principles are just as true today as they were in the fourth and fifth centuries. The hard part would be finding the crystals. They have to be pure and flawless. With all the miners, geologists and rock collectors who have explored almost every inch of the earth's surface, finding anything lying around is not very likely. You'd need ground-penetrating sonar to look under the surface—and a lot of luck.

"I'll tell you what, Kyle; if you find the crystals I'll help you assemble a seer room." They smiled at each other—if J.J. only knew... He backed up; Brian took his place and said:

"I read a line in a religious book that I've always wanted to use—changing it to fit me. I, Brian Everett, was born of goodly parents... and of course, *everyone* knows who they are, so I don't need to restate my family's history. I did that last year for most of this term's Second Form. So let's get right down to my part of this presentation: Merlin's actual use of the Cave."

Brian explained how Merlin would use his seer ability—enhanced by the crystals—to help Arthur plan political exploits, military campaigns and test the loyalty of those around him. It was the Cave that revealed how Merlin's first son was seduced by the dark magic and became a threat to his stepmother and half-brother and sister.

"In conclusion," said Brian with a sigh of relief, "Merlin's Crystal Cave was amazing technology for the era it was built and used. It's easy to understand why Arthur had some of the *miraculous* successes he achieved, with such a powerful means of help.

"Thank you for your attention and especially welcoming us back to CKS. We miss you all—and flipolo. We will be visiting from time to time; we're still registered here, even though we're home-schooled. We must take our required exams and APTs here... Next up is the newest addition to our family. He gets to answer all your questions." He stepped back, hearing polite applause.

Brian watched his undersized younger brother timidly approach the lectern, but without even blinking, his feet lifted off the ground and he hovered about ten or twelve inches taller. The ease of his maneuver and the rock-solid steadiness took everyone by surprise. Many students in the audience craned their necks to peer around the speaker's stand to see if he was standing on a stool or box.

"My name is Willard Hill Everett," he announced strongly, without any indication that holding the levitation hover required tremendous energy. "Some of you might remember me as the orphan boy raised in these mountains by coyotes, mountain lions, deer and other marvelous creatures. The Everetts took me in, adopted me and gave me a loving home and proud family heritage. Like Jeremy, I am one of the luckiest kids ever." His voice broke and tears streamed unabashedly down his cheeks—he did not make any move to dry them. "Not because my dad is Chairman and we have bodyguards and stuff, but because I have a family who loves me.

"My sister and brothers made the formal presentation. My job is to answer questions. Please, I'm being graded on my knowledge and ability to deal with whatever you ask, so don't be shy—"

"But please stay on subject," interrupted Superintendent Laedere, with an air of authority. He was seated in the first row.

Alan Nelson was instantly on his feet, raising a hand. Of course, the dreaded question came first. "Since your manor house is on Merlin's land, have you found his Crystal Cave?"

Brian, J.J. and Nicki held their breaths, but they had no need to worry. Willard was ready. "There's a hill behind the house—"

Just then J.J. had an idea. He waved his hands and a brilliant hologram of the Manor House and grounds lit up and was suspended to Willard's right. Wil saw it instantly and floated over so he could use the visual aid. Everyone's jaw dropped; his movements were seemingly effortless and he continued as if it had been planned all along.

"It's right here." He pointed to the raised area of the diagram. "It looks just like the description in the books. We went over every inch of the estate grounds." He looked up and swept his arm across the display of the acreage that surrounded the house. "And we didn't find any opening going down to an underground cave. Merlin either sealed off any entrance from the surface or he purposely misled readers with descriptions so no one could find it—which he's been known to do. He was a master of misdirection."

The answer was perfect. Every word was true. They *had* scoured the grounds of the estate (before finding the underground tunnel) and there was no hint of an entrance (on the surface).

"Which do you think it is?" asked Samantha Garrett, who jumped out of her seat.

"I think he sealed it off," answered Willard.

"Did you try the ground-penetrating sonar J.J. mentioned?" she shot back.

"No. If Merlin sealed the surface entrance, he must have had a good reason. That's powerful stuff. When the time is right, an entrance will be revealed. And who knows what kind of protections our wily old great-great-great (too many greats to count) great grandfather put on that Cave."

"Do you believe Merlin's bones are buried in the Cave? Didn't Vivien seal him in it?"

"Yes, his old mistress put him in it, but we know he appeared at least once after that, to Sir Gawain. Obviously he defeated her seal and could come and go as he pleased. But at that time of his life, he had retired to study and pursue other interests, so he let the legend stand. Beyond that, we don't know where he's buried, exactly. We're fairly sure it wasn't in the Cave."

For almost half an hour Willard fielded questions without hesitation. Brian began to think the CKS students were making up questions just to see how long he could maintain the levitation hover (they did not know he was trained by Merlin to use elemental energy and could float around all day long).

"How many agents are assigned to your protection?" asked Adam Hopkins.

"Sorry. Even if I knew—and they don't tell me—I couldn't tell you. Part of their security plan is to not reveal how many or where they are, exactly..." A big grin came across his face. "They like to be sneaky." He laughed, along with the audience. He knew his answer would please the ever-present and vigilant Agent Bowyer. He saw Superintendent Laedere stand and walk to the lectern.

"What a fine presentation—and that's the most amazing display of sustained hover-levitation I've ever seen." J.J.'s hologram winked out. "Let's give 'em a hand for a job well done and providing excellent information we hadn't heard about seer crystal projection and Merlin."

Brian could not believe it. The whole auditorium erupted in applause, with everyone standing. He expected polite clapping—they were the Chairman's kids—but this was genuine appreciation. It had gone well. When everyone sat back down, Laedere took on a somber look.

"As you know, the flu has hit our campus pretty hard, especially our flipolo team. Unless we can find a tosser and two pounders, we'll have to forfeit the match this Saturday against Salem's Warriors. It's too bad, too. I talked with their superintendent this morning and they have similar problems. Their team will be almost all second-string reserves. But they have enough, barely." Groans were heard throughout the auditorium.

Brian' heart was pounding; he was sure the whole audience could hear. Would his parents and Bowyer approve? Were he (and his brothers) eligible? Could security be arranged? His eyes searched out his parents. Then he put his hands flat together, like praying. *Please!!* He silently implored, mouthing the word. Out of the corner of his eye he saw J.J. and Willard were doing the same thing.

Then he saw it: just a nod—a worried one—but a nod. YES! From both of them. His head spun to the right. Agent Bowyer was patrolling behind the stage's wing curtains, and he was smiling and also nodding his head.

"YES," he whispered loudly; then blurted out:

"We'll play!" came out much too loudly. "If we're still eligible—are we? Can we?"

A cacophony of quick whispering went through the theater asking almost the same questions:

"J.J. and Brian were first string until their dad..."

"They're still enrolled—they should be eligible..."

"Let 'em play. We don't wanna forfeit..."

"J.J.'s cute. Love to watch him fly a sledge..."

"They should let 'em come back to CKS—security here is unbelievable..."

"Shhh! Super's gonna answer—shhh!—shhh!..."

"Well, it sounds like the vacancies are filled. I'll call Salem and let them know. I know it's asking a lot." He turned to Brian, J.J. and Willard, who were jumping for joy and making a huge racket on the stage floor. "Do you think you could work out some time to practice with the team?"

"Practices, too?" they said in unison, looking to their parents, who were laughing and nodding 'yes.' "WHOO HOO!" erupted simultaneously.

"Mom, you're not slick at all!" challenged Brian. "*Scheduling issues* ... yeah, right! You and Dad worked all this out this morning—when Super called." They were standing in the hallway at 128 Main Street, having just come out of the FON mirror from their visit to Crown King Seminary. "While we were in the auditorium, Coach posted the roster, and we were already on it."

"Why, would I do such a thing?" Myrna tried to put on her most convincing look of innocence. "Everything I said was true—just like Willard's brilliant dance around finding the Crystal Cave.

Professor suggested, and we agreed, it would be best if you gave the presentation before becoming distracted by flipolo practice. So, there were *scheduling issues*. Of course, if you feel it's too much of an inconvenience..." She let the terrible alternative hang in the air—unspoken.

"NO!" all three boys yelled in unison.

"Brian!" J.J. turned and faced Brian, almost toe to toe. "You need to shut up before you get us pulled, just when we got back on the team!"

"Okay, okay! I was just teasing. Sheesh." Just as he started to turn away, he saw his mother grinning and J.J. snickering. He knew he'd just been had. "All right, Mom. That's twice in one day. You're good. But it's not fair; double-teaming with J.J." Blushing furiously, he retreated down the hall, seeking the solace of his bedroom, but still elated. A whole week of flipolo practice and an interscholastic tournament game. Life was good.

"Don't forget," called Mom, "Coach wants you back at two-thirty, with helmets, pads, practice uniforms—everything."

Brian stopped in his tracks, spun around and a concerned glee was spreading across his face. "We've all grown, and Wil never got interscholastic gear. Can we go to the Mall? There's enough time. Please!"

"Your father already popped over to the Redoubt... I don't know. Sure! Let's go. We'll have lunch at Louigi's. Go hang up your robes and put away your—" She laughed; she was speaking to an empty hallway. "I'll just call your father and see if he can get away and meet us there," she said mostly to herself.

Chapter Thirty-Four
For The Love Of Flipolo

Underneath a shiny new helmet the cold Bradshaw Mountain air blew through his hair. His hands were almost numb as his right held the sledge's power leash and left waved about for minor balance adjustments as he streaked through the air, chasing the elusive spherule. Brian's blue and gold tunic was barely a blur to the packed stadium full of interscholastic flipolo fans.

Word of the Everett brothers—the Chairman's sons—being on the active team roster had quickly leaked out. Salem's (visitors') spectator stands were just as full as the home Crown King side. Every seat was filled and there was no longer any standing room. Reporters and photographers from a multitude of Sodality/ Wizard worldwide media outlets lined the field perimeter and the game was being broadcast live on the encoded Sodality satellite channels. But as intimidating as it was, Brian was hardly aware of any of it. During practice he had flown every day for the previous five days, chasing spherules and tossing them through goal rings. The first day he had been a little clumsy, but after that it was like he had never taken a break.

Everyone had been pleased Willard became a proficient player and flier in such a short time. Brian and J.J. were convinced his abilities came quite *natural* due to his *golden* origins (an adult gold dragon is a magnificent flier, and the maneuvers of a flipolo pounder are quite similar to the moves a dragon must make during aerial combat). In fact, he had demonstrated some loops and rolls that were well beyond anyone in the interscholastic league and most professionals.

"It's easy!" protested Willard. "I'll show you..."

"Yeah, maybe for you, Dragon Breath, but for us mortal mages it's a bit different." Everyone had laughed, thinking J.J. was just teasing his little brother, but for the three Everetts, they knew exactly what had been implied... But this was not a time to reflect on a week of practices. He shook his head and focused on the current task. The elusive spherule was only ten feet away, but the Massachusetts's tosser was right on his tail—so close he could use Brian's slipstream to slingshot around. A classic move, but easily defended. Brian pushed for a little more speed, and as he hoped, Salem's inexperienced flier paced every move.

Everett and Miller are closing on the sphere while J. and W. Everett are passing the glob—heading for the goal. What a game: three brothers on the same team...

Brian heard the announcer and wanted to look under and behind him to watch Wil and J.J., but he had learned (the hard way) that losing focus while chasing a spherule at high speeds can be disastrous.

Everett is going up for a shot, but Davies is in place to defend and the Salem squad is moving in. Everett is in the clear—the other one. And Everett is speeding up to capture the spherule... This is confusing! We've got Everetts everywhere! The crowd in the bleachers erupted in laughter.

"Just call their first names!" hollered someone from the stands.

Good idea! Brian is closing on the spherule but Miller is still tracking close behind. Jeremy is maneuvering for a better angle, but wait—he passed to Willard who passes to Reeves who swings and SCORES!

Brian's ears were filled with the cheering Crown King fans and he decided *Now!* He suddenly reversed all his energy to stop—hopefully without flying off his sledge. Miller was so close, he could only pull up hard to avoid a collision—sending him hopelessly away from the spherule's path. Of course, the elusive red ball sped away from Brian, too, but he instantly put full speed back to the chase. The idea was to grab the two-inch round rocket before Miller could recover.

That was close! Miller barely missed Brian's head but keeps control. He's racing to catch up. He won't make that mistake again...

"Yeah, I'll bet he doesn't," mumbled Brian to himself, "but he sure recovered quick—here he comes." He glanced over his shoulder and saw Miller closing in fast. Suddenly the red ball veered left and down.

What an abrupt direction change! Brian and Miller almost lost balance, trying to follow...

"Yahoo!" cried Brian; this was flipolo that he loved. The bite of the mountain air could not suppress his grin. He switched the control leash to his left hand and reached out—the spherule was almost a blur, but he was only inches away from touching it with the fingers of his right hand.

Everett—Brian—almost has it but Miller is closing in fast, trying to block or intercept.

Brian found a little more speed and his fingers closed on the two-inch ball.

He's got it! And there goes Miller to defend the goal. Salem has the glob, making short passes. Brian will have to face two defenders...

The announcer's voice faded away from Brian's consciousness. This was going to be the first time, in tournament play, he would be trying to make a toss with both the goal defender and opposing tosser blocking the goal. Always before, his (Spartans') team had been able to steal the glob and race for the goal (at the same time), forcing the defender down to the five-foot by eight-foot goal. This time, two players would be hovering in front of the two-foot ring. In all his practices, only once had he been able to toss the spherule past two goalies and score.

The rules allowed him to slow down—hoping his team would gain control of the glob—but he was required to maintain some forward motion: no hovering or backtracking allowed. But the Salem team had barely gained possession. Unless Crown King executed a steal soon, he would have to start his tossing run before play would reverse enough to cause Thompson to drop down (Berry graduated last year). *C'mon, J.J., steal!* he pleaded in his head.

As he considered his options, he was sure Salem's coach had taught the Warriors the various classic attack runs—and their defenses. He would have to try something different. He had an idea...

He dropped down in altitude and began the traditional run— the idea being to try and draw both defenders just low enough to allow a quick toss over their heads—missing the waving hands (not holding power leashes). But, as expected, the two defenders remained shoulder to shoulder with their chests obliterating the goal ring. He pulled up sharply, cocking his right arm back, like he was going to toss. As he hoped, they instinctively—almost unconsciously—eased up to meet his unexpected move (making sure the top of the ring was covered).

C'mon! Just a little bit more! cried out Brian in his mind as he saw them rise a couple more inches. *Yes!* With all the power he could safely summon, arm still ready to throw, he dove hard, flying at a steep angle toward the fifteen-foot zone bubble that glowed red against the dark winter sky and distant ponderosa pine treetops. The bottom half of the goal ring became visible below the defenders' waists and between their legs. His timing and accuracy would have to be perfect. His mind reached out:

Suddenly his whole perception changed. In his view, everything was moving in slow motion. He blinked away the momentary distortion and allowed his mind to adjust. There was a chance, but it was a narrow window. Already Miller and Thompson were dropping back down. But, as every flipolo flier learned, the hover energy dissipated slowly (for safety reasons). Brian didn't know which brand of sledges Salem used, but he hoped they bought the kind that bled off energy real slow. It was going to be close, even in slow motion. The gap was steadily closing.

With careful aim, throwing as hard as he could, Brian released the red spherule, sending it toward the narrowing goal.

And that's a maneuver we've never seen before—Brian makes his toss...

To the fans and announcer, the spherule's travel from Brian's hand until it reached the defenders took only a fraction of a second. But in Brian's perception, it seemed like an eternity. Out of the corner of his eye, his right arm seemed to take several seconds to breeze by his head and he could feel every tiny adjustment in muscle tensions to compensate for the fluidity of the scene. Later he would remember and marvel at his body and brain's ability to make such instantaneous decisions and responses.

He watched his arm and hand swing in front of his face and his fingers let go of the gleaming red ball at just the moment he hoped would result in a ten-point score. With painstaking slowness it flew, as if suspended by levitation, toward the goal. On an on it went, seemingly crossing a great divide (but it was only fifteen feet).

Movement in front of the goal caught his attention. The defenders were inching down—trying to block. Steadily, but ever so slowly, the goal's open space was closing. He cringed, hoping he had not miscalculated; every player wore mandatory protection, but still, he didn't want to hit anybody—*there*...

As the ball continued on, Brian could see its trajectory was a bit low. It would pass just below the goal—just an inch outside the gleaming suspended ring. His heart sank. He had been so careful to avoid hitting the defenders, he was going to miss. Accepting his error, he was just about to release the slow motion and turn to continue the match. It would not be his first miss. But, out of curiosity, he continued watching, hoping against hope for a gust of wind (the weather was perfectly calm). Then Brian realized the ball was going to hit one of the defenders, Thompson. Not where he feared, but on the knee pad. Thompson had shifted his legs in an attempt to block or deflect.

Brian saw his toss was lower than he had hoped it would go. It hit the bulky edge of Thompson's protective knee pad, just on the inside, between his legs. Then it happened: the bright red spherule glanced off the pad in a new direction.

EVERETT SCORES! screamed the announcer, almost hoarse. The spherule bounced off Thompson's pads and sailed through the ring!

Brian barely heard the announcer over the roar of the CKS fans (and groans of the Salem supporters) as he released slow-motion. "YES!" he yelled, pumping his fist in the air so hard he almost lost his balance. Then, as Miller flew by, giving him a polite thumbs-up, Brian knew there was no time to revel in his (very lucky) goal. The spherule was out there again and Salem's tosser was wasting no time, already in the hunt.

The score is tied at twelve-all and there are only two minutes left in regulation play...

Brian knew that with mostly second string fill-ins, neither had played particularly well—especially the CKS Spartans. Salem had made twelve glob scores against Crown King's weak defense. If it weren't for his incredibly lucky ten-pointer, the score would be twelve to two.

There goes Miller, Brian heard, and looked frantically beneath him to spot the Warrior tosser, but he was nowhere to be seen.

Surely he's not above, he thought, searching high. But then he saw him and the spherule, way up, near the 150-foot ceiling boundary and right next to the CKS side boundary. His right hand was extended, but still several feet from capture. Brian accelerated to try and intercept or send the ball in another direction.

Jeremy has control of the glob and passes to Willard... And Brian's speeding to intercept... The Everett brothers are at it again! Willard passes back to Jeremy as they are trying to zigzag down the whole field. Brian is closing in on Miller before he captures...

The announcer's voice faded out of Brian's awareness as he focused on Miller. Gauging his distance and that his opponent was only a few inches from a capture, Brian tried a desperate move. He put on all the speed he could, hoping to get close enough for the spherule's sensors to detect his presence, veer away and leave them both empty-handed. Maybe then the Spartans would make a score and time would run out. He pushed for even more speed. It was glorious!

As he hoped, the two-inch red ball shot off on a new track, but what he didn't expect was Miller's quick adjustment. He followed the direction change perfectly and his fingers wrapped around the elusive orb. But to his horror (and Brian's glee), his speed and momentum were going to carry him (and the red ball in his clutches) out of bounds. There was no help for it. The energy-lighted barrier was only two feet away and the sudden course change was going to take him right through it... Miller could chance a quick toss to keep the ball in-bounds, but Everett was good enough to scoop it up and possibly make another lucky score.

Miller made his decision: He let himself (and the spherule) be carried out of bounds. He would hope Crown King's pounders would not score and regulation time would run out, forcing overtime.

The referee's whistle penetrated the cheers (and groans) and all play stopped. A ball had gone out of bounds, carried (or malleted) by a player. Miller released the spherule, which immediately zoomed to its starting position, hovering in the exact center of the field, seventy-five feet above the ground. The glob went to the nearest (vertical) side boundary, also suspended at the same height—awaiting a player to knock it in.

CKS's Barnes went to the glob and Brian and Miller took their positions, twenty-five feet from the quivering spherule. The whistle blew. The two-inch red ball zoomed off at an angle almost impossible to see—much less for either tosser to get near. At the same time, Barnes smacked the glob with his mallet, passing it perfectly to J.J., who sped toward the goal with light taps to keep it in front of him. The other Spartans rushed to protect, while the Warriors attacked for a steal.

Only forty-five seconds left in regulation. Jeremy retains possession, despite the whole Warrior team closing in. No one in either team's bleachers was sitting. This was flipolo at its best.

Brian and Miller were both chasing the spherule, but they knew Brian's strategy had worked. By forcing Miller (and spherule) to veer out of bounds, possession was relinquished. There was no time to capture the red ball, travel the distance to the goal and make a successful toss—before regulation time ran out—especially as fast and elusive as the spherule had been that evening.

Twenty seconds... Jeremy breaks out of the surround...

Both Brian and Miller gave up their pursuit of the spherule. With forty-five seconds, there was a tiny chance to score. But with only twenty seconds, it was futile. They both went to hover over the action and watch.

Quickly scanning the play, Brian easily spotted J.J. He was deep in the mix of everything—barely keeping control of the floating white orb. A huge grin was spread across his face and flaming red hair was flitting about and aglow beneath his helmet edges. Willard was nowhere to be seen. Surely he didn't drop out...

J. J. was quickly approaching the fifteen-foot foul line when he cocked his mallet high over his head like a golfer readying for a mighty tee-shot swing with a driver. Players from both sides scattered to get out of the way. Then his mallet came down—almost in slow motion. At the last second he changed his aim to the far corner of the foul zone where an undersized boy hovered on his sledge—waiting...

*   *   *

The after-game party at 128 Main Street was somehow organized in an amazing flurry—much to the dismay of Agent-in-Charge Bowyer. There was pizza, sub sandwiches, vainabier, chips, potato salad, fried chicken, hot cocoa and some dishes Brian could not recognize. As he loaded his plate, Brian became convinced his mother had been quietly arranging the potluck affair since early that day—and possibly for several days.

Taking a huge bite of pizza and sipping from a frosty bottle of Vainabier, Brian walked past a group of parents who seemed to be having an animated discussion about whether J.J.'s faked goal attempt and pass to his brother or Willard's very covert exit from the team tangle and perfectly executed winning goal shot—just two seconds before the whistle—was the greater play. Both had been awarded (co-) Most Valuable Player status. Oh, yeah, life was good for the Everett brothers.

Finding his favorite squishy arm chair, Brian settled in, placing a plate of delights from the potluck table on his lap. As usual, his right hand felt crushed and his back was red from all the enthusiastic congratulations, but that was just fine—his mother would soothe it all away when she tucked him in bed. He almost felt sorry for Willard: being so small, cute and coming from such an unusual beginning (being raised in the wild until he was nine), adults loved to pinch his cheeks, pat his head and pound his back. J.J. thought it was wonderful; it eased some of that torture from him.

351

As the party went late into the evening, the women migrated into the formal sitting room, sipped herbal tea and hot cocoa while catching up on the latest gossip, fashions and life at the Chairman's house (the Western Redoubt). The men went into George's study and discussed (argued about) politics, flipolo (and other popular sports), latest conversions of Brangler technology to Sodality use and the new Chairman's policy to help combat global terrorism. The students/flipolo team members stayed near the potluck buffet table, in the living room or drifted in and out of Willard's, J.J.'s, Nicki's and Brian's bedrooms—admiring the creative decor—especially J.J.'s holographic dinosaurs. Brian proudly showed off his flying flipolo action figures. Many admired Nicki's Poster Mirror and wondered about Willard's dragon den.

Chapter Thirty-Five
Time To Go

"H ey! Ringboy!" Brian heard through the fogginess of waking up from a much-too-short night of sleep, and pushed the pillow out of his face that J.J. had just thrown at him. "Mom called you several times. You're about to miss Sunday morning breakfast—and I've never seen you do that! Heck, I've never seen you miss any meal" (*except on 9-11*, he thought). "Anyway, we're about to sit down. You better hurry."

"Mmm hmm," mumbled Brian, reaching for his blanket and pulling it over his head.

"Oh, no, you don't!" cried a strange, high-pitched, animated voice as something jumped out of the corner of his bed and started pummeling him with blows that felt like they were from the arms of something deeply padded. "It's time to get up!" said the weird voice between more smacks from the strange menace—continuing its attack.

"Gerroff me!" Brian pulled his arms out from the covers and tried weakly to swat away whatever had become his early-morning nightmare. But the thing—no, not a thing; it was his favorite teddy bear he'd had since he was five—seemed intent on bludgeoning him with wild, padded blows.

"Not until you get up!" the voice came very believably from the stuffed animal as it continued its relentless attack.

Finally becoming conscious, Brian flipped over onto his back, grabbed the bear around its middle and pushed it up in the air to arm's length while its stubby arms kept flailing as if it were going to beat him into submission. "Alexander, stop it!" he said to the thing he'd held close many times as he fell asleep (when he was younger—of course).

"Are you going to get up and get dressed?" squeaked the bear, now beating on Brian's exposed arms.

"Yeah, yeah! I'm up!" He sat up, covers falling from his legs—still holding the struggling Alexander (his teddy bear's name), then glanced over and saw J.J. laughing so hard he was bent over, gasping for air.

"Very funny!" He started giggling himself. "Now unenergize this poor thing before he comes apart."

"Okay," said J.J., now holding his stomach with his left hand and waving his right at the animated Alexander. Tears were streaming down his glowing-red cheeks.

The stuffed toy went lax in his grip—no longer pounding or pushing down to attack.

"Are you okay?" said Brian softly and lovingly to his beloved cuddle toy, examining it carefully for damage and stroking its fluffy fleece body.

"Of course I'm okay!" answered the bear in its weird voice. It had never spoken before.

"How'd you do that? I mean, I know how to animate toys—we've done that for years—but how'd you make a voice come from Alexander?"

"I'll show you after breakfast." He turned to exit through Brian's bedroom door. "C'mon—really, it's late—breakfast is on the table."

"Okay, I'm coming." He swung his legs out and reached for the clothes that Benson had laid out at the foot of his bed, which he pulled on under his nightshirt. Standing, he slipped off the long shirt and donned the pressed, white T-shirt, then pushed his feet in his sneakers.

"Morning," announced Brian, entering the kitchen, finding the whole family already seated at the brightly lit (from sunshine streaming through the huge windows behind the breakfast nook) large, round breakfast table—heavily laden with morning fare. He felt guilty as he knew they were all waiting for him so they could hold hands and give thanks.

"Good morning," they all said cheerily, almost in unison and smiling at him—almost too cheery and grinning wide.

"Sorry I'm late." He sat at the table.

"Oh, it's okay," said Dad. "J.J. was just explaining how you were delayed because you had to fight off a rogue teddy bear attack." He was trying to keep a straight face (along with everyone else) but couldn't hold it any longer. The whole family erupted in laughter.

Brian blushed but went right along. "Yeah! I was really in fear for my life. But I was valiant at the end." He reached out his hands to Nicki and Willard (on either side of him). "Let's do thanks. I'm hungry."

"You're always hungry!" the family responded. Then all joined hands around the table and bowed their heads.

"It's Wil's turn," said Dad quietly.

"May we always be thankful for the food before us, the hands that prepared it, each other, and everything we have, amen," said the small boy, just above a whisper.

"Amen!" the family repeated. Then a wave of Mom's hand and their plates were beautifully laden with an array of favorite breakfast delights.

"Dad, you should have seen it," said Brian between huge bites. "Alexander was trying to beat the snot out of me and was talking. I couldn't help but talk back to him."

"Your brother has always amazed us with his knack for doing things no one's thought of before—or at least doing it differently. This is just—"

"Brian, what's wrong?" interrupted Mom as she saw him drop his fork onto his plate, with a clatter. Then he held his hands flat on the sides of his head, squeezed his eyes shut and grimaced.

Willard jumped up, almost toppling his chair as it slid back, scraping on the tiled floor. He moved behind Brian and put his hands beside his brother's. He too closed his eyes, and scrunched up his face—starting to turn a distinctive golden hue.

"Wil can drain off some of Brian's pain that comes when visions force into his mind," explained J.J., whispering. No one moved a muscle or made a sound, not wanting to distract or break the spell of whatever Brian was seeing... After a long moment, he opened his eyes.

"Did you see it?" Brian's voice was almost croaky; he squinted in the bright morning sunlight and turned to Willard. "I tried to send it to you." He saw his brother nod his head.

"It's time. We've gotta go..." said Willard as if accepting an unpleasant fate to follow.

Brian looked around the table and saw the rest of his family staring back with looks of surprise—seemingly not knowing what to do or say.

"Reficul's making—"

"His move!" interrupted Dad, finishing Brian's sentence. "You sent that out with so much force, we all saw it—I think." He looked quickly to Myrna, J.J. and Nicki, who each nodded in agreement.

"I didn't know I could do that... Wil and I can mind-speak, and I can send to J.J. I guess I never thought about anyone else receiving."

"We certainly weren't expecting it: a very strange sensation. Like having a dream while wide awake."

"I want you all to finish breakfast," insisted Myrna. "You're going back to the day before the Slocum sailed. I want you to have a good meal—and I'm going to have some things for your backpacks. There may not be a way for you to find anything to eat, or if you do, if it'll be anything you want, or should eat."

"But, Mom—" J.J. started to protest.

"Now you listen to me, Jeremy James Everett!" She stood and planted her hands on the table. "If I had a lick of sense, I wouldn't let my children go time traveling to 1904, knowing they were going to confront one of the most powerful, evil mages of our time—or any time. It's insane... And without any adult help and having the additional burden of not affecting history! Give me a couple of minutes and I'll find an excuse to forbid you to go!

"But I'm not going to do that." She sniffed and tears ran down her cheeks. "It seems to be *your* calling, and not for any of us, else Merlin would have let us know. So, I'm going to send you off, praying you'll make wise decisions and come back safe and sound. But for that, you'll finish breakfast, take time to make sure all your preparations are in place and pack the provisions I give you." She plopped back into her chair, glaring at the four children, not even bothering to wipe the tears from her face.

"Yes, Ma'am," was all J.J. could get out as he swallowed a fork full of pancakes—almost whole.

* * *

"This feels weird!" Brian tugged at the waistband of his pants and reached behind and pulled at the seat. "These pants have no zippers or buttons, and the underwear; ugh! Couldn't we at least wear briefs or boxers?" Having changed into their period costumes, FONed to Everett Manor and gone through the long tunnel, the four youngsters were gathered, along with their parents, Uncle Paul and Grandma James, in the Crystal Cave. Last minute checks were being made on every detail, especially their clothes (costumes).

"Anything might happen," answered Nicki (who had been in charge of putting their costumes together). "We can't take any chance we'll be identified as being from another time." She saw Brian start to continue his objection. "Yes, even under garments. One of us could get hurt and need medical attention. We've only learned to use psionics for simple first aid. You think you're uncomfortable—you don't even want to know what women wore under their dresses back then."

"You're right; I'm sorry," he said, still squirming and tugging. "We probably should have practiced running and moving in our clothes, like you did with your dress. These shoes are really clunky and suspenders are just too weird."

"It's too late for that now," said Dad. "Just focus on your tasks and minor clothing discomforts will fade away."

"Has everyone double-checked your lists?" asked Paul. "Make sure you have everything. Each of you has period money—a fortune for most folks back in 1904. Try not to talk any more than necessary. Your accents will certainly not be right for Manhattan, New York, or the German folks from Saint Mark's Church."

"We're all set," said Brian. "We'd better get going." He looked into the worried faces of his family. "We'll be careful—honest!" He was trying to ease their concerns—and his own.

"You'd better!" cried Mom, rushing into his arms as he dropped his backpack—triggering farewell hugs and admonishments from all in the room.

"I know you have the *Sigillum de Aemeth*, in various forms, in your pockets and backpacks," said Uncle Paul, "but those are all on paper or parchment which can be damaged by water, fire or in a scuffle." He reached in a pocket and pulled out a handful of shiny chains with round, silver-looking objects attached. "I had the seal meticulously etched on these medallions with your names on the other side. Made by elves, the chains are a special alloy that makes them impervious to any damage. The medallions are made of the same stuff and won't melt or distort, except under higher temperatures or pressures than stainless steel will endure. Hanging around your necks, they will look like the religious medallions that were popular during that age."

"Wow! Thanks, Uncle Paul!" said J.J. as they each took one of the chains and pulled them over their heads to settle around their necks. They held out their medallions and examined them. "These are fantastic! Elven-made, cool."

"There's a spell on the chain," continued Paul. "No one can take or remove it from you. You are the only one who can pull it back over your own head. Also, if it's caught in something or someone tries to yank it, it won't hurt you."

"Oh, thank you!" Myrna went and wrapped her arms around her brother-in-law. "Thank you for looking out for my babies!" She cried on his shoulder. "Now I know they will always have a way back."

"I wish I could have done more—"

"But, now we must trust them," said Dad solemnly, "and let them go."

"I know." She stepped back, then touched her children's faces. "Keep our love and strength in your hearts and minds." She gathered her courage. "Go now..."

"Okay, Ringboy, you're the best at this—you know the plan," said J.J. "Light 'em up, open the seal, and create the portal."

"And you're going to hold the camoshield," said Nicki, pointing to J.J. "That was an era filled with superstitious paranoia. I can't imagine the panic we'd create if we suddenly materialized in a crowd."

"Yeah, okay, I'll do my part." He pointed at Brian and put a finger to his lips. "Shhh..."

Brian had his eyes closed and seemed to be in a trance. Willard moved behind to steady him—if needed. The ground trembled, air swirled and became drier and heat was rising under their feet as he gathered the elemental gifts from Earth, Air, Water and Fire. There was absolute silence in the room except George whispered, "Should we step out?"

"If it were me doing it, yes," answered J.J. with just a breath of a sound, "but Brian's progressed way beyond that..."

A few seconds passed, then there was a faint ringing sound as one of the smaller (suspended) crystals lit up and a beam from it struck the huge crystal in the room's center. Brilliant rainbows splashed around the room until a beam of pure white light bathed one of the cave's whitewashed walls. For a moment, there was no picture—just wavy snow—then it happened. A panoramic scene formed of 1904 Manhattan, New York. There were people, dock and warehouse workers, milling about or scurrying to various destinations. Off in the distance was the East River, Third Street recreation pier, and other boat docking areas.

"Amazing!" said Dad.

"Incredible!" said Mom.

"Such clarity!" said Grandma.

"I never imagined..." said Uncle Paul.

Brian opened his eyes and saw what the adults were commenting about. He blinked a couple of times to clear his vision. This was definitely his best work. He had spent some time online researching turn-of-the-century Manhattan and the General Slocum disaster. As a result, he was able to pinpoint the exact location and time setting, which allowed his seer ability to be amplified by the crystals in precise detail.

He studied the projected images from the past, trying to decide exactly where they should materialize—hopefully not on top of anyone. Then he saw it: there was a shallow alley between two buildings.

"Whoa!" he heard Uncle Paul say, expressing the motion disorientation everyone felt when Brian mentally shifted the direction of the view. It was like they were hovering in a miniature helicopter as it suddenly swung around and zoomed over for a closer look at the gap between two aging buildings. The area was littered with garbage, but was totally deserted. It was ideal and could easily accommodate the four Everett youngsters.

"That's a perfect spot," said Brian. "We'll hardly need the camoshield." He walked closer to the wall, trying to stay out of the projection line. "See that drain grate in the middle? That's what to focus on."

"Since Brian's holding the portal," asked Paul, "the others don't really need—"

"True," said J.J., "but if we all use a seal and focus, the gate remains open, even if Brian loses his portal hold."

"I'm going to keep sending through the crystals as long as I can," said Brian. "Maybe you'll be able to see us materialize before I lose the connection."

"Won't the camoshield interfere?" asked Nicki.

"I don't think so, since I'll be projecting from inside it."

"Let's do it, then," said Willard.

"Okay, everybody focus on the destination. Here goes..." Brian closed his eyes again, then held the *Sigilumn de Aemeth* (on the chain around his neck) in front of him. Nicki, J.J. and Willard also held theirs.

Suddenly, there was a gust of wind and a door-sized rectangle with a shining golden border appeared in front of Brian—who was staring deep into the inky black of the open portal.

Without saying anything to distract, as prearranged, J.J. stepped forward and into the darkness beyond the doorway, dissolving until he disappeared.

Behind him, Brian heard a sharp intake of breath from his mother as J.J. reappeared in the projection on the wall—like watching a live video feed. He waved, hoping all would see him in the scene.

Next, Willard eased into the seeming nothingness; disappearing and then materializing (just like J.J.). Nicki followed, giving the family a reassuring wave.

Then it was Brian's turn to enter the blackness, feeling the rush of energy and air pull him along, floating through the vastness of the universe. There were tiny twinkling lights that resembled stars on a dark, slightly hazy night, lighting the galaxy.

He kept trying to send the seer image back through the open pathway, but the disorientation of not knowing which way was up (or down) made it hard to stay focused.

Back in the Crystal Cave, four adults were mesmerized. The image remained, though only for a few seconds. Then the scene changed to what appeared to be a starlit night. Then they saw Brian take form followed by the projection going dark. The inky blackness disappeared, but the golden rectangle remained—a sure sign that the return gate remained open.

Chapter Thirty-Six
Memories

"**W**ow!" Brian wavered and stumbled as Willard rushed to prop him up. "Trying to send to the crystals, hold open the portal and travel—all at the same time—was a bit too much." He saw Nicki reach into her large bag, hanging from her shoulder.

"Here!" she commanded, ripping the wrapper off a honey-granola bar and handing it to Brian. "Eat this." He hesitated and started to protest. "NOW! That stunt took a lot of energy. You should gather more elemental before doing something like that."

"Thanks," he said, taking the bar and biting off a large chunk. "I just got caught up trying to ease our family's worries; I didn't think about how much energy I was expending." He chewed and swallowed more. "Mmmm, this is helping."

"We can't afford mistakes like that," she continued. "You almost didn't survive Wizard's Cavern because you were drained of energy. And the battle with O'Connor..." She left the perilous moments' memories unspoken.

"Okay, okay!" He swallowed the last of the honey-sweet bar. "C'mon, let's get going." He looked at Willard and nodded.

As planned, Willard would be first to exit the camoshield dome. He would walk further back into the alley, turn around, then step around the shield and exit through the gap between the buildings.

Brian watched him carry out the plan, then walk across Third Street, dodging various horse-drawn wagons clattering up and down the roadway.

Seeing he had not drawn any attention, Nicki went next, followed by Brian, who glanced back and saw the camoshield was working perfectly. The energy dome precisely projected its surroundings, so it seemed to blend in and disappear.

Brian hesitated at the exit from the alley, long enough to make sure no one was watching. No one was, so he knelt down to tie his shoes, which was J.J.'s signal to drop the shield and follow Brian out to meet the others waiting across the street.

"This is amazing!" said J.J. softly. "A few months ago we were in Manhattan, 2001, and here we are in 1904, ninety-seven years earlier. And, New York hasn't changed much. Nobody cares what we're doing; they're so used to all kinds of people. Blending in is easy."

"You're right, to a point," said Nicki. "But don't get comfortable. This is still 1904 and people are very superstitious and wary of strangers. That's why they banded together in close communities."

"But, as kids, we'll attract less attention," defended J.J.

"True—but just be careful."

"Okay, I hear you." He rolled his eyes and sighed.

"Let's check out the area and pier," urged Brian. "We can't get on board the Slocum until tomorrow morning, but we should see if there's spots where we can watch, without being noticed. We've also got to find a place to sleep tonight—unless we find Reficul today and convince him to leave our great-grandparents alone."

"Yeah, right," said J.J. "Dream on. He's here on a mission and he's not going to give up just cuz we say 'pretty please'." He led out, casually walking toward the distant pier.

"What if we go find our grandparents?" said Brian. "They're Sodality. They'd understand time travel. Reficul couldn't mess with them if they just don't show up tomorrow."

"Then what happens with that family?" asked Willard. "Maybe, without the Everetts' help, they might stay on board."

"There would be generations of people affected—a real paradox," answered Nicki, who shuddered. "Oooo! I hate to think what that could do. No, we've got to let everything take its natural course, except to prevent Reficul from messing things up."

"Brian, don't you have any idea what he's going to do?" Willard jumped across a puddle in the street. "It'd really help if we knew what he was up to."

"I don't think he really knows. You saw it: the General Slocum, our great-grandparents, the family and the fire. All I know is that he's here, somewhere. He came just yesterday, June thirteenth. I'm thinking he's making this up as he goes—trying to find a way to get his hands on our formula half."

"But that's all he could get—the Everett half." J.J. stopped and faced Brian, Nicki and Willard. "Mom's half isn't anywhere near here. That was a direct mother-to-daughter line that didn't emigrate from Europe until 1910."

"But that's enough to stop me—or anyone else—from putting the halves together." Brian shifted uncomfortably and pulled at his clothes. "And he could go after Mom's later."

"Think about it," said Nicki, with deep worry in her voice. "Even that would have profound consequences for our family..."

"We're really going to have to be careful!" Brian looked around to see if anyone was taking any notice. "It's scary to think how just a tiny change could create a future disaster."

"For lots of folks," added Willard. "Can you sense, is Reficul near—now?"

"I don't have that kind of connection. I have only sensed when he's about to do something big; like now, he's gonna mess with history—or the future from now—this is confusing!"

"Can you view him, without the crystals, now that we're in the same time?"

"Maybe—I think so—"

"Wait," said J.J., stepping back to the puddle Willard jumped across moments before. "I wanna try something." He closed his eyes for a moment as Brian (realizing what was about to be attempted) glanced about to make sure no one was watching.

"Go ahead. The coast is clear."

J.J. opened his eyes, casually reached down and touched the edge of the pool of water—being careful not to cause any ripples.

Brian (and the others) stared down. Slowly the shimmering surface clouded as colors began to waver in hazy lines. Then, like a ghost, an image started to appear. The background was dark but not black. Light seemed to be leaking around the edges of a rectangle, providing just enough illumination to show the face of a man—a man who was dressed in a hooded cloak and sitting in an old chair. He was still, except for slight movement from breathing—almost as if he were asleep. But, something told them he was not sleeping, but was in deep thought—seething, angry thought—planning a dastardly revenge for perceived wrongs.

"He's in a room," said Willard.

"And that's closed drapes or a covered window, in the background," said Nicki.

"Do you guys feel it?" asked Brian. "He's really mad."

"Not so much feel it," answered J.J. "It's just his whole presence—his posture and breathing. But yeah, he's really upset. It's as if his anger is coming out like heat from a radiator. Hmmm, yeah, I guess I do feel it."

"Where do you think he is?" asked Willard.

"We can't see enough detail," said Nicki. "It could be a hotel room or even an office in a warehouse or something. The background is dark."

"At least we know he's not out here where we are," said Brian. "We don't want him to identify us before we're ready."

*   *   *

The heat in the small hotel room was oppressive. Humidity from the nearby East River and more distant Long Island Sound made everything feel damp. The building was old. Paint was peeling off the walls and the bed linens reeked of lye soap and many sweaty bodies. A threadbare throw rug was on the floor. A tarnished brass four-poster bed frame and somewhat ornate gaslight wall sconces provided hints that, sometime in the past, the hotel had been slightly upper class. But, the ravages of time and careless upkeep had taken their toll.

With the (once expensive) drapes pulled tight and the gas lamps extinguished, the only light was what crept in around the edges of the heavy material from a bright mid-day sun. The dilapidated curtains glowed slightly as the brilliant rays penetrated the worn fabric, giving the room an eerie olive green aura.

A lone figure inhabited the room who was always dressed in black clothes, including a hooded cloak that hung to just above his ankles. He was seated on a rickety Windsor chair that had been repainted several times, making it several faded colors from years of wear exposing various layers. His hands gripped the armrests so tight, knuckles gleamed white. He was waiting for someone, but his patience was wearing thin. Nevertheless, he used the time to go over his plans—plans that would eliminate the threat of the Everett descendants being able to produce a Ringmaster.

His mind drifted back to the events that brought him to that moment: He had arranged for the theft of the formula Mendacci had developed and a blue dragon scale. But something had gone terribly wrong. As he stood near, the concoctions exploded. The last thing he had seen was a bolt of blue lightning above his head. He woke up in a strange land—or time. When he looked about, he didn't recognize anything. Except, something had been vaguely familiar, but he could not place it. Certainly he had never been to that place or time, but yet … He owned a huge library and he voraciously read books. That was it! He had read about it. But where? He frantically recalled his memory of history, geography, zoology and travel books; nothing came to mind. Magazines? Scientific journals? Archaeology? No, no, no... He sat down on a gnarly tree root that was sticking out of the ground, put his elbows on his knees and rested his chin in his hands. Was it possible?

He looked around. The trees, animals, vegetation ... and off in the distance he saw a strange tower high above a pit where huge creatures were moving about. *Was it possible?* he wondered. *Could this really be?* Almost as fast as he had the idea, he dismissed it as absurd. He looked again, then thought: *There is a series of books being written by a woman in England about a boy with magical powers. They were a huge success among Brangler children—and many adults—selling millions. Of course, in Brangler world, they were considered fiction, but any Sodality mage (or European witch or wizard) knew the stories were mostly true—with a bit of literary flair for drama. So, was it possible that Tolkien had a true vision of Middle Earth or traveled through time and dimensions? Maybe it was true. Surely I'm not the only one to somehow travel to other existences. Why not some of the great science fiction and fantasy writers? Some of those stories seemed so real—maybe they were. Maybe they chronicled actual events and characters from faraway planes of existence. What a glorious idea! But they knew something I don't: how to get back...* He did not even know how he came to be planted in legendary Middle Earth—if that's where he was.

As if some vast entity heard his unspoken pleas, he felt a presence behind him and turned quickly, channeling his energy, and extended his right (ringed) hand. Instead of finding some menacing foe, there stood a kindly old man, shabbily dressed and having long flowing grey hair and beard. The man held an intricately-carved staff with a crystal embedded in the top.

"Feeling a little lost? Confused, maybe?" A gentle smile twitched under the grey beard.

"How'd you know?" Reficul cautiously eased to standing, trying not to be threatening but still remain ready.

"I felt the burst of energy. You are not the first... You did not plan to come," he said. It was not a question.

Reficul recounted the tale of how he had been conducting laboratory experiments that exploded, and seeing the blue lightning (omitting any mention of trying to create a master ring).

The old man reached into a pocket inside his tattered grey robe, rummaged around and withdrew a round, flat stone about three inches across. It was smooth, as if polished but not quite to a high gloss. He reached out and offered it to the black-cloaked man.

At first Reficul hesitated. The old man was obviously a wizard and in Sodality world, one was always careful about handling unknown objects given by strangers. It seemed the ancient magician meant no harm, but looks could be deceiving.

"You are wise to be cautious," said the magician. "There are no spells—it is only engraved with the *Sigillum de Aemeth*—the means for you to return to your world."

"I've heard about that!" He could not contain his surprise. "It's mentioned in many of our history books. But, no one in our realm knows how to use it. The ability died centuries ago."

"I would guess the lack of instruction was deliberate. Not only can the seal open portals to other planes and dimensions, it will also provide a gateway to travel the expanses of time. It becomes too tempting to meddle in the affairs of the past, to correct perceived wrongs or create unearned wealth. Huge paradoxes have resulted. For those who learn the secrets of *Sigillum de Aemeth*, it is forbidden to change the past or use any object or knowledge obtained from the future to alter past or present."

Reficul gingerly plucked the stone from the age-worn hand. He was surprised to see the seal intricately engraved on one side. He turned it over and over, probing for any hidden spells, but found it to be exactly as the old man described.

"Will you—can you—instruct me in its use, so I can return to my world and time?"

"I will teach you, and if you are powerful enough, the seal will open portals for you. But I am sorry; you will not be able to return from whence you came—"

"But you said this was the means for me to return to my world—"

"Yes, to your world, but not to your generation of time. When one travels through the seal, if you plan to return to your own place and time, the gateway must be held open. Your accidental excursion allowed the portal to close. The only way for you to go back is for someone to open a portal from that end."

"You're sure?"

"Yes!"

"What happens if I try?" Reficul saw the old man smile under his long beard.

"It has been tried before, and you will probably have to prove it for yourself, but you will simply remain in place and chuck-up your last meal. The headache is also quite unpleasant, but after a time you'll be right again."

As Reficul listened to the old wizard, more and more he was sure he spoke with the accent of Central Britain, maybe early England.

"How soon can I begin my instruction?"

"It is morning and I haven't broken my fast yet. You may join me, and then I'll teach you. I am sure you are anxious to get going. A great battle is about to begin here and you must not interfere. Events must proceed as they will."

"If I leave here, and my people open the gate, what then?"

"You may leave instructions and they can follow, or from time to time you may try to return. If the portal is open, you'll travel. If not, well, you won't feel well."

Sitting in the chair, Reficul grimaced as he recalled the numerous times he had tried to return to his castle, on Earth in 2002. He was sure his faithful followers—especially Laileb—would eventually find a way to reopen the portal. He had thought he would get used to the terrible wave of nausea and splitting headache, but each time was just as bad as the first—maybe even worse. The old wizard gave him the needed lessons and he had visited many exotic places. He had even spent a few moments aboard the Titanic just before she hit the iceberg—which was where he developed his idea:

It was well-known among Merlin's descendants that the Everetts (George's grandparents) were supposed to be aboard the General Slocum, June fifteenth, 1904, when it became New York's greatest maritime disaster. But, strangely, unknown to most earth denizens in 2002, the Everetts rushed ashore just before the gangway was removed, along with a husband, wife and their five children. And, as Brian's paternal great-grandfather, he was a holder of the patriarchal half of the master-ring formula. Reficul (correctly) assumed the elder Everett would not sail on a ship— even for just a one-day excursion—and leave the valuable artifact behind... And that was one moment he might be vulnerable.

A knock on the room's door brought him out of his musings.

"Come." The door opened and a man tentatively eased in.

"I'm sorry I'm late," groveled a middle-aged man, obviously hardened by years of working New York's docks. "One of my lookouts had a last-minute delivery to make."

"I'm paying well..." Reficul's deep voice reverberated off the lath-and-plaster walls. "I expect punctuality."

"You also wanted results, and the man who was delayed was in the best place to watch." He was used to being chastised by ships' officers and belligerent passengers, but the man dressed in black was really scary—terrifying.

"Give me your report, then!" he growled.

"Right you are, Gov." He wiped sweat from his brow with a handkerchief. "We've had eyes turned on the pier and all up and down Third Street. As of a half-hour ago, nothin'. No kids, other than the us'al urchins we sees every day. No strangers in funny clothes."

"You're sure?"

"Ever'body stayed zac'ly where you said. I checked. A'course, as I said, ever'thin's a half-hour old. They coulda come since then."

"Fine!" He reached in his pocket, pulled out some coins and held them out for the visitor. "Report back to me this evening, six o'clock sharp. Make sure that riffraff of yours keep their eyes open—all night if necessary."

"Oh, they'll keep 'em peeled; spec'ly for this kind of coin." His eyes bulged wide, seeing the generous payment in his hands.

"There'll be a bonus for the man, or men, who can discretely keep them in sight and lead me to them. I'll be down in front of Slocum's pier at seven o'clock tomorrow morning. But remember, be here at six, or anytime if something comes up before then." He folded his hands in his lap; the gruff dockworker knew he had been dismissed. He wasted no time exiting the room. He was outside the hotel and in the street before he felt he could breathe again.

Chapter Thirty-Seven
Third Street Dock

"We still have to be careful," cautioned Nicki. "He could have spies out and we wouldn't know it." She glanced about furtively, trying to see if anyone was paying attention to them.

"C'mon," said J.J. "He's as much a stranger here as we are."

"Remember who we're dealing with," she argued. "Reficul is clever, cunning, smart and has tremendous resources—even in 1904. He's a powerful mage. Any one of these workers would spy for him, in a second, with the kind of money he can spread around. Each of us is carrying a fortune, by 1904 standards."

"Okay, you're right." Brian intervened to keep his brother and sister from bickering. "But how do we check out the area and make plans for tomorrow unless we do something?"

"We split up," suggested J.J. "They will be looking for the three of us—or four, if he knows about Willard. Also, let's at least change our hair colors. My red hair is like a beacon and the Everett blond is just about as bad. Dragon Breath can stay the same. Even if Reficul knows about him, his appearance isn't quite as famous—yet."

"Good idea," said Brian, watching J.J. remove his newsboy cap and instantly his shoulder-length red locks practically lit up in the bright sunlight. Nicki reached over and brushed her (ringed) hand along the crimson strands. With each stroke they turned silky black. Seconds later he looked totally different.

"We should have thought of this before," said Nicki, repeating her ministrations on Brian, changing his hair to dark brown. "J.J., you do mine. Go for a light auburn—not red like yours—a reddish brown."

"Unless we used real hair dyes…" He brushed his hand over her long, straight hair. "…the energy changes probably wouldn't have held through the portal. That's why we decided our costumes had to be real and not illusions… Oooh, Sis, that's a good look for you. Your boyfriend would like it." He grinned mischievously.

"What boyfr—"

"C'mon. Did you think we'd miss you inviting that guy from the Mall to the after-game party? You were pretty cozy in the den. Do we need to remind him to be nice to our sister?"

"No! Don't you dare! Anyway, do you think you're a bigger threat than Dad and his security team?"

"YUP!" J.J. rubbed his hands together and smiled, showing his teeth.

"Brothers!" She rolled her eyes and shook her head. "We'll talk about this later. Right now, let's split up and check out the area."

"Let's meet back by the alley entrance in an hour," said Brian, stopping the verbal sparring between J.J. and Nicki. "Remember, we're looking for places to stay out of sight, but still watch the boarding—and our great-grandparents come back off. We also need a place to stay tonight."

"Nicki and I will take the left side," suggested Willard. "You guys can go down this one." He didn't wait for comment; just started strolling across the street, imitating some local children they had observed dodging horse-drawn wagons, carts and trolleys being pushed by sweaty men, and other people seeming to be hurrying about on some business. Nicki hiked up her skirt and followed—keeping some distance away.

"I guess that's our cue." J.J. stepped out to stroll down the street with his hands in his pockets. Brian watched and allowed him to get a good lead, then leisurely plodded behind, looking in small alcoves until he heard a man's gruff voice:

"Hey, you!"

Brian kept about his business, hoping he was not the focus of the man's attention.

"HEY! BOY!"

The voice was closer and obviously being shouted his direction. Brian started to turn—channeling his energy and gathering some power from the earth.

"Who, me?" he barely spoke, pointing to his chest, acting as if he hadn't heard the first call.

"Yeah, youse!" came the angry voice—almost a growl. "Youse seen eny strange kids 'roun' here, mebbe dressed funny?"

Brian heaved a great sigh of relief; their costumes were convincing. The man thought he was a local. He shook his head.

"Thar's a dime innit, if'n you do and bring word back to me."

Brian grinned wide, hoping the man would be convinced he was excited about earning ten cents (a lot of money in 1904).

"Youse kin find me 'roun' Third Street Pier. Dock foreman, I am. Jus' ask fer Jake. I'll be here all day."

Brian nodded (he understood), turned and walked away at a fast pace—looking for J.J.

"There's all kinds of crates and stuff around the warehouses," reported J.J. "Lots of places for us to hang out and blend in." They were back at the entrance to the alley and J.J. was energizing a camoshield.

"But we won't know what's available until the last minute," added Willard. "I listened to some of the workers and they were saying most of the crates we see will be loaded onto boats that dock here—and more are coming in."

"There are some alleys and alcoves, but they are a little way away from the pier," said Brian. "It's going to be hard to know when he'll make his move."

"It would be best if we can spot him before he tries to attack our great-grandparents," said Nicki. "We'll have a better chance of interfering with his plans without throwing history upside-down. Also, there's an old rundown hotel over on Avenue C. I found a room for me and my three sisters."

"SISTERS?!" they all objected.

"How are we supposed to be your *sisters*, wearing these clothes?" asked Brian.

"Girls in 1904 didn't wear pants—EVER," added J.J.

"Well, just in case," she reached into her bag, "I brought—"

"OOOH NO!" J.J. backed up, holding his arms outstretched, with palms facing Nicki. "I'm not changing into all that girl stuff and put on a dress!"

"You don't have to put on any of the underthings. I made 'em big enough to slip over your clothes. They have high collars, long sleeves and are floor-length. I can energize your hair into a feminine style... And, J.J., you're the only one whose voice has changed; just don't say anything."

"That'll be the hardest part," quipped Brian, "gettin' him to shut up."

J.J. looked very strange: he still had black hair but his cheeks were glowing red. "Keep your voices down!" he admonished as he waved his hand. "I forgot to do the audio shield—there—now we can't be heard."

"You can do that?" asked Nicki. "You're sure it works?"

Brian watched him shoot a nasty look of disgust.

"Silly me—I shouldn't have asked. Sorry... It's just—I know I could probably do a camo *or* an audio shield, but to integrate them as effortlessly as you do—your multitasking is amazing."

"C'mom, Sis, stop it! You're about to ruin our carefully nurtured sibling rivalry we've enjoyed so many years." He sniggered.

"Yeah, you may be a multitasking genius, but you're still an incubus troll."

"Ah, now all is right with the world—'cept you still need some new material."

"And you're going to put on a dress."

"Okay!" he conceded. "But if you ever tell anyone, you'll see what I can multitask!"

"Enough!" cried Brian. "Give it a rest! We've got more important things to worry about. We're going to have to really be careful. Reficul has hired spies everywhere. One of 'em offered me a dime if I were to spot three kids—two boys and a girl—dressed funny—and take word back to him." He took a breath and described the whole scene with dock foreman Jake.

"As I see it," announced Nicki, "that's really good news. We know what he's doing: relying on a network of spies. He hasn't thought about us being in special costumes, connected Willard with us, and doesn't know we're here yet."

"And," interrupted Willard, "if he hasn't thought we'd be in 1904 clothes, he may not have thought of some for himself—"

"Yeah," interrupted J.J. "He's probably wearing that long, black cloak of his. He'll be easy to spot." Instinctively, they all glanced around for a tall man in black. "And, I doubt he knows we can scry him." He looked at the ground. There were no pools or puddles of water to use. He pointed at Brian. "Can you *see* him?"

"I'll try." He closed his eyes and concentrated. "Yeah…" he said, moments later. "He's still sitting in that chair, but the light has changed. I can see a bed and some old, peeling wallpaper. I think he's in a hotel room or rooming house. It's pretty run down… Close your eyes and I'll try and send it to you."

"Eeww!" exclaimed J.J. "Run down hardly describes it."

"Is he asleep?" asked Willard. "He's not moving."

"Maybe he's viewing us," suggested Nicki, "like we're seeing him."

"I don't think so," said Brian. "He's not looking into a pool of water. The *seer* ability never went down that side of Merlin's family."

"But he could use a pool if he wanted to," said J.J.

"Sure! Any mage can scry, using a pool—if they know how."

"So at least for now," said Nicki, "we have the advantage."

"Okay, before we go to the room Nicki got, let's find something to eat. I'm hungry."

"YOU'RE ALWAYS HUNGRY!" they said in unison, and laughed.

"With spies about, we should avoid sitting down in a restaurant," said J.J. "That'd surely attract attention."

"I saw a place around the corner on Avenue C," announced Willard. "It had breads, meats, cheeses, salads, hot dogs and sausages. I think they make sandwiches to order. Lots of kids, like us, were buyin' stuff there."

"That's perfect," said J.J. "We can get take out. And Chow Hound here can get enough—well, we may not be able to carry that much."

The sign above the door said: "Mother Stepley's Hotel and Boarding House." All four entered.

When they saw Mother Stepley, Brian and his brothers' jaws dropped. She was an older woman with gray hair, rather short, and wore an old dress covered by a drab apron. She had a pleasant voice. And she looked exactly like Frau Strube. "What can I do for you young people?" she asked.

Nicki kept her wits. "We want to rent a room for the night. I inquired earlier. We promise to stay quiet and not disturb the neighbors, and will leave it cleaner than we found it."

"Oh yes, I remember, but don't you have any adults with you?" asked the old woman.

"I'm eighteen," Nicki lied. "I'm in charge of these three." She glared briefly at J.J., hoping to quell any wisecrack or prank. J.J. tried to look innocent, which fooled neither. "We can afford to pay extra, if it's going to be a problem." She fished five silver dollars from her purse and held them out.

"No, that's all right," said Stepley. "We served supper at six p.m., so you missed it."

"I'm sure your supper was better, but we picked up some sandwiches at the deli around the corner."

The landlady took four coins. "Your room is five fourteen, fifth floor. There are two beds in it." She frowned, wondering how they would share them.

"That'll be splendid," said Nicki. "We're used to doubling up."

The Everetts trudged up the stairs, finding the room open and empty. "At least it's clean," said Nicki, sighing. They divided the beds and found chairs around a rather small table. "Don't look at me like that, Wil," she said after seeing the expression on her littlest brother's face. "People shared beds all the time in earlier years, and it meant nothing weird. It's economy. And I think if you split with Brian, there will be less mischief."

"Fine," said J.J. "I'll volunteer to sleep on the floor—again." He spoke in a high girl's voice. He glanced at Brian. "No warnings?"

"No," he barely said—his mind was spinning. "But did you notice how closely she resembled Frau Strube?"

"So you think we're safe for the night?" asked Nicki, wanting her own feelings confirmed.

Brian nodded, but had no time to voice his thoughts.

With a knock on the door, Mrs. Stepley arrived with left-over bread, cheeses and a pitcher of water with four glasses. A man helped carry the tray. Brian looked disappointed by the meager quantity. Nicki whispered, "This isn't the time and place to be a glutton."

Brian sighed and sank back.

The old woman produced a registry and had Nicki fill it out. She gave their names as Sally, Jean, Mabel and Linda Bowyer. J.J. was Jean. They got a receipt for the four dollars Mrs. Stepley had collected. Then she settled at their table and began to ask questions.

Brian (Mabel) stopped her. "Please, wait a moment while we offer thanks." Mrs. Stepley looked surprised but allowed the blessing of the food. "Now we can talk while we enjoy this sumptuous repast."

That startled the old woman, but she recovered quickly and began: "Why are you four in New York?"

"For the sailing of the General Slocum," said Nicki. Brian's mouth was full. "That's why we need only one night's lodging. We arrived a day early."

"You arrived by train?"

"From Poughkeepsie, yes, ma'am," said J.J. (Jean), still keeping his voice high. "Our aunt and uncle invited us, but we lost their address."

"I'm part of the St. Mark's congregation," said Mrs. Stepley. "If you give me their names, I can probably direct you aright."

"Deering," said Brian. "I know we look different, but we're really sisters."

"Their address I don't know. I can ask my sister; she's supposed to be on that old bucket, too."

Brian looked shocked. "What's wrong with the Slocum?"

"It has run aground six times, collided with four other vessels, and it can't pass a U. S. steamboat inspection without the owners bribing the inspectors. But, they keep bringing it back to life. A fresh coat of paint doesn't make a ship safe to sail on!" Mrs. Stepley put on a sour face, but rose and left, closing the door behind her.

J.J. was locking it at almost the same moment. The only lock was inside, a deadbolt. It had to be unlocked to get out.

"You handled that well," J.J. complimented his sister. "Even thinking of giving us fake names just in case someone tries to trace us."

"Wow. I can't get over it," said Brian quietly.

"What?" responded three voices.

"She looked like Mrs. Strube, from my dreams." Brian thought she seemed like a dear grandmotherly type he'd feel very comfortable around. "Maybe Mrs. Strube and Stepley are sisters."

"Then I think we were led by Spirit," declared Nicki. "Now we have just our sandwiches left. Let's eat them and get some sleep. We'll want to be up early."

"Ugh! How can girls stand these things?" Brian was hurriedly pulling off the dress he had worn to be one of Nicki's sisters. He saw J.J., already busy moving about the room, setting shields and wards on the door, window and perimeter walls. He hoped his comments were not overheard before the audio shield was in place.

"Sometimes even I struggle with dresses," said Nicki. "I grew up wearing pants and shirts. I only wear dresses for special occasions. That's why I practiced running and stuff, before we translated."

"Um glud ids oo, no mme." Brian was wasting no time unwrapping and devouring his deli sandwiches. "Thi pus—tromi izz ood!" He looked around and saw confused and disgusted looks on the other faces in the room. He swallowed hard. "I said, 'I'm glad it's you' and 'this pastrami is good'."

Suddenly Brian dropped his sandwich and grabbed his head, swayed in place, and squeezed his eyelids tight. Willard and J.J. rushed to steady him.

"What is it?" asked Nicki, barely whispering.

"I don't know," answered J.J. "When he gets like this I just wait for him—"

"Put up mind barriers—now!" Brian barely croaked, still concentrating hard. Each youngster focused their energy.

Brian opened his eyes then seemed to go limp, being held up by his brothers. Nicki scrambled for a chair, and she pushed it behind his legs as Brian was eased into an old wooden armchair.

"Wow! That was intense. Reficul sent out a mind probe. It was nothing like Laileb did last year. This was much more powerful, and he tried hard to get it past my shield."

"Why didn't you reflect it back?" asked J.J.

"Because it was splattered everywhere—not from a single direction. He was just sending a general broadcast, hoping to find—me."

"Why didn't we feel it?" asked Nicki.

"He was targeting me, somehow."

"Does he now know you're here? Did he get in before you shielded?"

"He knows there's Sodality here, because I blocked him. A Brangler wouldn't know how. But, I don't think he knows it was me. I could sense his questions: 'What is your name?' 'Who are you?' 'What do you know?' 'Where are you?' He got really mad when he couldn't get past my barrier."

"If he was targeting you," asked Willard, "why did you want us to put up barriers?"

"I figured since he couldn't get anything from me, he'd widen the search."

"Hold it!" said J.J. "That doesn't compute. If he was targeting you and was suddenly blocked, wouldn't he automatically know it was you—and we're here?"

"I don't know how to explain it. I got the impression he's not convinced his targeting worked. He's doubting a twelve-year-old has the strength or ability to block him. He thinks I'm an adult, with considerable skills, that somehow got caught up in his sweep."

"That's scary," said J.J. "Can you read his mind?"

"No! But while he tried to get past my barrier, we were connected. I could sense what he was thinking right then. Kinda like what Grandma does with her empath abilities. His thoughts were exposed, but mine were closed to him. Really irked him!" He chuckled.

"Could you tell where he is?" asked Nicki.

"No, but he's close."

"He'd have to be," added J.J. "Remember last year? Dad told us mind probes weaken quickly with distance and you said this was really powerful."

"I wonder..." Willard drummed his fingers on the side of his head. "Hmmm." He looked about the shabby room.

"What?!" demanded J.J., impatiently staring at his undersized sibling. "Don't just stand there like a dragon who just ate a farmer."

"Gold dragons don't eat farmers!" he insisted, but laughed. "Just smart-alec brothers!" They all laughed. "Does anything about this room look familiar?" He waved his hand at the dilapidated room and furnishings.

The others quickly scanned the once-luxurious walls, furniture, window drapes and tarnished lighting fixtures.

"Familiar, no—I mean, I saw a room like it for a second, when I stopped by earlier," said Nicki, staring harder at their surroundings. Then a look of discovery swept across her face. "Oooh! I think I see it! Yes!"

"Yeah!" exclaimed J.J. "This room looks awfully similar to what we saw in the viewing pool with Reficul. Dragon Breath thinks the creep is in this hotel. And I think he's probably right." He was bouncing on his toes in excitement. Then he went over to a wash stand that had a large porcelain ewer and basin. "Let's see what he's up to." He poured water into the wide, shallow basin. As the others gathered around, he touched his finger to the edge of the water. The glassy surface went cloudy. Then rainbow colors streamed across as a dark picture began to emerge.

Chapter Thirty-Eight
J.J.'S Change Of Plan

Inside the gloomy room the small light, leaking through the shabby drapes, faded as the mid-June sun disappeared below the horizon. The cloaked man was again sitting in the spindly Windsor chair. But instead of being rigid, with his back straight and shoulders squared, he was bent over with his head in his hands and elbows propped on his knees. Slowly he swiveled his head left-then-right and grumbled.

"I can't believe it! No one, in this time, should have been able to block my probe—unless it was Old Man Everett—and he shouldn't be anywhere close until tomorrow. He's certainly not living in this dump. There's no way the kid could do it; why would they be here anyway? I'm just being paranoid."

Slowly he stood up, feeling exhausted. Sweat beaded on his forehead and trickled down his chest. His movements were slow and unsteady as he began to pace about the room; contemplating what had just occurred and how it could impact his carefully-crafted plans for the following day. He could not remember the last time he had put so much energy into his psionic channeling.

"If only I could tap into elemental power like Merlin did. I could sustain probes like that forev—"

His musings were interrupted by a knock on the room's door. He straightened his back, squared his shoulders and wiped his brow with a cold hand.

"Enter," he said, with all the firmness he could muster. He screwed his face to the intense scowl that was so effectively intimidating, and he watched the door slowly open as Jake, the dock foreman, cautiously eased inside, staring at the floor and fumbling nervously with the worn flat cap in his hands.

"You're late again," scowled Reficul—just to set the mood.

"S-s-sorry, S-s-sir. A late d-delivery of glassware for the German church group a-g-goin' on the Slocum held us up."

"I don't need your excuses!" He was enjoying watching the man squirm. It was making him feel better—stronger—as if he were feeding off the Brangler's fear. "Just tell me what you found out!"

"Me scouts have had eyes and ears ever-whar. There aren't been eny strangers about, 'specially chil'en dressed funny. Course thar's been a bunch 'em Luthern folks, bringin' stuff, but they's all 'counted fer. I even put word out with the newsies—an' nuttin' gets pas' 'ems."

"I assume your spy network will continue watching until tomorrow?"

"Aye, Sir. 'Tis suppertime so's easy to spot eny strangers."

"I will see you at seven-o'clock—"

"In front of the pier entrance. The Gen'l should be dockin' jus' then. Right you are, Sir." He hesitated, nervously waiting for his next payment.

"Yes, at the pier entrance!" Reficul waited a long dramatic moment, then reached into his cloak and produced a pouch, tied with a string. "This is payment in full. I expect you and your friends will be keeping watch and not celebrating in local pubs."

"Why, thank 'ee, Guv'nor. We'll keep watch—I'm not payin' eny of 'em 'til after the Gen'l puts out tomorrow." He was surprised, not expecting the final payment until they met the following morning. They would be celebrating tomorrow evening. Many of his spies were earning more on this job than they usually received for a month (or two) of hard dock work (including what they could steal). Jake bowed to the mysterious man and exited without further ado. He was glad to get away. Despite the generous money, there was something about the man that gave him the willies. He shivered and shook just thinking about him.

* * *

"Hey, that's Jake, the dock foreman I talked to," cried Brian as they peered into the picture on the surface of the water. "He's the one who tried to hire me to watch out for us." He chuckled. "If he only knew…"

They had watched Reficul talking to himself, then Jake moved into the scene.

"I wish we could hear what they're saying," said J.J. "I'm going to learn how to lip-read when we get back."

"I could listen in," said Brian, "but I'm afraid he might sense it."

"Wait a minute," announced J.J. "I've got an idea! Nicki, reach down and touch the water to hold the vid-pool. If Wil's right, I should be able to amplify the sound from the room…"

Brian watched as Nicki eased the tip of her finger into the water, concentrated on Reficul and the scene. The picture wavered as J.J. lifted his finger, but she quickly stabilized it.

J.J. picked up a dingy, spotted drinking glass from the bureau, held it in front of him, circling the bottom with his thumbs and first fingers. He cupped his other fingers so they formed a bowl (with the base of the glass in the bottom). It faced away from the direction he was looking. Then he raised his hands (and glass) to chin level, closed his eyes, channeled energy and suddenly loud, tinny sounds blasted into the room.

This room is terrible! … It's all we have. … Okay, I'll take it. … Where have you been? … I went to the privy. … Let's go get something to eat. …

J.J. almost dropped the glass.

"It's too loud!" complained Brian, putting his hands over his ears.

"Sorry." The sounds stopped. "I wasn't sure it would work so I put too much energy into it." He held up the glass again and the voices returned, but much softer. He turned some other directions; it sounded like radio stations fading in and out as a radio's dial is tuned. He pointed the bowl of his hands towards the ceiling and floor. Each time, different voices and noises would momentarily be heard. He quickly passed anything that didn't sound like Reficul's distinctive deep voice—trying not to intrude on people's privacy.

I assume your spy network will continue watching until tomorrow?

"Stop!" commanded Brian. "That's him! I'd know that voice anywhere."

J.J. hesitated. His hands were facing up and toward the right.

Aye, Sir, said another voice. *'Tis suppertime so's easy to spot eny strangers.*

"That's Jake…" whispered Brian. They listened to the rest of the exchange between the two men while Nicki kept the scene pictured in the viewing pool.

"Okay, we know when he's going down to the pier," summarized Nicki. "He doesn't know we're here yet. Our costumes are working."

"And lots of people are looking for us," interrupted J.J.

"And, for sure, he's in this building," concluded Willard.

"I tunk ee sud ma u pla," spluttered Brian; he was back to his sack of sandwiches and using a small, flat wooden spoon to shovel potato salad from a cone-shaped paper container.

"Hey, Ringboy," chided J.J. "How many times do we have to tell you? We don't speak glutton!"

Brian swallowed hard and blushed. "I said, 'I think we need to change the plan.' Since we know he's in this boarding house, maybe we should try to deal with him here—tonight."

"We can't do anything yet," objected Willard. "He hasn't done anything."

"What? You gotta be kidding!"

"No! Remember when Dad let us watch that operation in the Situation Room? Agent Bowyer told us they couldn't arrest anyone until they did something illegal. Reficul's got every right to be here—even send spies looking for us. Until he makes a move against us or Grandpa, we can't do anything—but plan."

"Oooh, that's deep for a baby dragon," quipped J.J.

"But we're not cops, constables or Redoubt agents—" argued Brian.

"No, we're more." J.J. sighed and became uncharacteristically serious. "We're Sodality mages who are citizens of a wonderful community and country. If we attack without good reason, we're just as bad as he is." He spoke just above a whisper, then smiled. "What do you think he'd do if he knew we were here?" J.J.'s grin and excitement was so mischievously strong, the spell keeping his hair black was broken and he seemed to glow red...

*　　*　　*

Inside the darkened hotel room a single candle burned, providing an eerie flicker of light that bounced off the peeling paint of the walls and ceiling. The lone occupant had just retired to the lumpy bed, fully dressed as he was loath to lay his pale skin on the dingy sheets. And besides, he was restless and expected to sleep very little. But at long last his eyelids fluttered, then closed.

*　　*　　*

"Are you nuts?" cried Brian, walking beside J.J. as he turned onto Third Street, working his way right out into the middle. "His spies are going to spot us for sure." He hurried his pace as his brother lengthened his stride.

"That's the whole idea!" J.J. reached up and removed his newsboy cap and let his bright red hair fly in the breeze like a beacon. "I'll explain when we get into the pier. Trust me." He glanced over his shoulder toward Willard. "Wil, let's keep you a surprise. You walk along the buildings, keeping us in sight. After we've gone inside the pier, you ease in. Try not to be noticed... Better yet, you go find one of the spies and tell 'im you've spotted us and are going to follow to see where we go."

Brian watched Willard peel off and start ducking in and out of shadows, pretending to follow and avoid being seen.

As they approached the expanse between the last of the buildings and the pier and docks, Willard found Jake perched on a shipping crate, just outside a warehouse.

"Hey, Mister!" He tried his best to imitate the accent of the people he'd heard earlier in the day. "Wasn' youse the one payin' a dime for info about three kids, two boys an' a girl? Strangers to the area?"

"What of it?"

"Gimme a dime!"

"Yeah?" He jumped off the crate, becoming excited. "Ya seen 'em? Where?" He reached into his pocket and pulled out a thin silver coin, then held it tight between his thumb and first finger—showing it to the small boy.

"They're right there." He pointed to Brian, Nicki and J.J., who were halfway to the pier entrance. "An older girl and two boys—one of 'em has bright red hair." He grabbed the dime. "I'm gonna follow 'em—see what theys doin'." Willard stuffed the coin in his pocket and moved away quickly, still staying in the shadows to keep up the ruse.

*   *   *

As the frantic knocking at his door continued, Reficul cleared his sleepiness, straightened his clothes, donned his black, hooded cloak and barked, "Who is it?"

"Jake," came an excited, whispered voice.

"Come in!" He watched the door ease open and the shabbily dressed, dirty dock foreman squeezed through and closed it. He stood, backed up against the peeling paint, with cap and hands behind his back.

"Well?"

"They're here—we spotten 'em. Beggin' yer pardon. Theys walked righ' down Third Street, toward the pier. But they wuz hard to spot 'cuz theys weren't wearin' eny funny clothes. But the rest fit. A slightly taller girl—good looker—an' two boys—one of 'em short with bright red hair." He nervously shifted his weight back and forth between his feet, and clutched the flat cap he held at his back while the strange, scary man contemplated the news.

Hmmm, he thought. *I don't know how, but that Everett brat always shows up. Just like 'em to put on period costumes to avoid disturbing history. They must be heading down to scope out the pier. That's perfect. I'll deal with them tonight so they can't interfere tomorrow. They won't be so lucky—I don't know how they conjured up that dragon last year, but there's no dragons in 1904 Manhattan.*

"Come, Mr. Dock Foreman. Show me where you saw them and tell me everything. Don't leave out any detail."

* * *

Brian had watched Willard point them out to Jake, who immediately left in the direction of Avenue D and the dilapidated rooming-house. He, Nicki and J.J. approached the huge covered pier. To call it a pier did not do it justice. It was a long, two-story, triangular (hip) roofed building that jutted out from the dock over deep waters of the East River, suspended on giant pylons. The front was flat, with a great, wide entrance door in the middle and two smaller doors to each side.

As they passed through the center doorway, the depths felt much bigger than earlier in the day. It was dark, except for a few flickering lamps providing a ghostly illumination. Big square, wooden columns rose up to support the second-story balcony. They seemed to be apparitions of sentinels guarding against all who dared enter the inner sanctum.

Brian felt like an intruder. The hardwood floors, walls and vaulted ceiling amplified every step as their leather-soled shoes seemed to hammer and echo throughout with every step. He wished he could have worn his sneakers. Then he noticed: they weren't alone; there was scurrying along the walls and across the great, spanning beams.

"This place is creepy at night," exclaimed Nicki. "And there's rats!"

"Aw, is our big sister afraid of the dark and a few rodents?" teased J.J.

"Only because it's as empty as your head—including the rats."

"Oooo, Sis, that doesn't sound like your diplomatic best. I've heard better comebacks from my dirty socks."

"Only an incubus troll, like you, would have moldy, stinky animated socks!"

"All right! Now you've graduated to first form jokes—"

"Will you two give it a break?" hissed Brian. "There's no time! We probably only have a couple of minutes…" He turned to J.J. "Okay, Prodigy Brain, you wanna explain why we've completely thrown out our whole plan of staying concealed and surprising him when he goes after our grandparents?"

"Look, maybe the Black Bungler doesn't care about changing history and creating paradox—that's what Merlin warned us about—even he might not survive the mess, but we do. Tomorrow there's going to be a couple thousand people all crowded around the General Slocum, this dock and the pier area. If we confront him in the middle of all that, there's no way bystanders won't be drawn in, hurt and maybe worse. In here, tonight, we have a chance to keep that from happening."

"Hmmm…" Brian pulled at his chin. "You're probably right."

*   *   *

"They be walkin' right down Third Street, here, big as you please," Jake barely whispered, panting, trying to keep up with the tall, black-cloaked stranger.

"Where did they go?" rumbled Reficul's deep, bass voice. "I don't see them now." He was moving along the south side of Third Street, staying close to the buildings, using shipping crates and shadows to avoid being seen.

"Mebbe theys went inside the pier. That be the way they be goin'." Jake broke into a few-step jog to catch up. He could not remember ever walking so fast.

"Where did the boy go who reported them to you?" He suddenly stopped before crossing an open area.

"Dunno..." Jake almost ran into his mysterious employer's back. "He said he was gonna tail 'em." He stood, still holding and fumbling with his flat cap—wringing it between his hands.

"Hmmm... I wonder..."

Chapter Thirty-Nine
The Tale Of Long Tail

"**W**here do you think he is?" asked Willard. All four were crouched behind two large wooden shipping crates.

"I don't know," answered Nicki. "He should have been here by now. Surely, after hiring spies to spot us, he's not going to pretend we're not here."

"Think about it," said J.J. "If you knew your enemies were in here, all channeled up for a battle, would you simply stroll through the front door?"

"But he isn't sure we know he's here—"

"Of course he does!" interrupted J.J. "Why else would we be here—just to watch our grandparents get on, then off the Slocum?"

"I've got an idea." Brian put a finger to his lips. "Shhh! Don't move or you'll scare 'em."

"Scare what?" whispered J.J. "The fishes under the pier?"

"Shhh!" came from three directions as Nicki, Willard and J.J. turned to stare at Brian through the darkness—barely illuminated by distant, flickering oil lamps. He closed his eyes, mumbled *rodontia intelligo* (interpretation command) and reached out with his mind (and softly speaking aloud so his siblings could hear): "Can you hear me?"

"*Ch-ch-who are you?*" Came a chittering, squeaky, high voice in his head.

"I am Brian, one of the humans in the pier. Do you have a name?"

Ch-ch-We do not have names like you, but Long Tail will do. We were told you might come.

"Really? Who told you?"

Nicki and Willard could barely restrain J.J., who was squirming, mouthing questions, wondering who (or what) Brian was talking to. Of course, they were all curious.

Ch-ch-the ch-wizard from ch-long ago.

"Merlin?"

Ch-ch-did not say his name. Ch-ch-said ch-you going to ch-keep bad man from ch-hurting future ch-time.

"Will you help us?"

Ch-ch-yes. Ch-what can we do?

"Maybe watch for that bad man. Create some confusion."

Ch-we are good at ch-that. ... Ch-ch-my nestmates ch-say a local boss and a man in black clothes ch-are ch-coming and ch-hiding in dark ch-areas along the road.

Brian closed his mind-speak projection and explained about talking with Long Tail, asking the rats for help and that Reficul and another man were creeping up and staying in the shadows. He saw Nicki and Wil were excited, but J.J. became serious and deep in thought.

"What's wrong with you? The rats won't get hurt, if they're careful."

"I'm not worried about our furry helpers. We're in the wrong place."

"Wrong place?" Brian peered into the gloomy, dim light from the few lights. "But maybe you're right; there's bigger crates over in that corner." He pointed.

"No—I mean—we shouldn't be in here." J.J. waved his arms at the pier's interior.

"Wait a minute," interrupted Nicki. "You're the one who dragged us out here, throwing away our plan of staying hidden. You insisted we should confront him tonight. Now you're—"

"I didn't say we shouldn't take him on tonight." J.J. stood and started for the door. "Just not in here. We're hiding behind a crate like it would protect us, when we know it can be brushed aside like it was nothing. We need to get away from here and pull Reficul away to make sure nothing happens to mess with history—and give us more room to maneuver."

*   *   *

"Where are your other spies?" growled Reficul.

"Begging yer pardon, when I saw 'em kids wit' me own eyes, they was still at their posts, an' still should be … 'ere, now!" He kicked at a rat that ran across the toe of his shoe, missing the rodent by a wide margin. "Rats are always roun' the docks, but ne'er had one be that bold. I hate rats!"

"Never mind a stupid little rodent! What the—?" He jumped sideways to clear a path for two rats that were scampering directly toward his right foot. But, as soon as he landed, he began dancing and hopping in circles as his arms flailed at another pair that leaped off a nearby crate and onto the back of his long black cloak. Just then, two others scrambled up his heels and over the cuffs of his trousers, clawing their way up the back of his leg.

"Hey, now!" yelled Jake, backing away from the incredible scene. "Youse got pockets full of cheese or strong-smellin' food? I ain't ne'er seen rats go after a man like—sweet Moth—" Jake barely ducked in time as a pure white, pink-tailed rat tried to sprint onto his shoulder from a tall shipping container he had backed up against.

"IT'S THAT CURSED EVERETT BRAT!" roared Reficul, swatting at a small brown-and-white rat that, somehow, had gotten onto his left sleeve. "I don't know how he does it! Aaarrgh!" He screamed as yet another landed on the cowl (hood) of his thick cloak. "I'm going to kill him!" Off in the distance he heard the screams of Jake's hirelings.

"Rats! There's hunnerds of 'em!"

"Help! They's crawling all over me!"

"Where'd they all come from?"

"Let's go, boys. We didn' hire on to battle vermin."

There was a rustle of tromping and running feet as the spy network disintegrated and the men ran up Third Street, away from the East River docks, piers and hopefully, the marauding army of rats.

Through the gas-lamp lit darkness Reficul watched the unbelievable scene unfold. Men were retreating from an ever-growing horde of rodents that were intent on exterminating all human presence in the area.

"Sorry, Guv, I'm wit' them." Before his employer could stop him, Jake broke into a run. Reficul was almost mesmerized by what was unfolding. It would have been comical, especially when a tiny white mouse joined the pursuit, little bulging, pink eyes glowing, smiling, chittering and doing his best to run down one of the dockworkers, except at that moment Reficul was being surrounded by dozens of rats in a coordinated attack...

* * *

"Oh, wow!" exclaimed J.J. as he snuck around the edge of the pier's huge doorway. "Listen to those guys buggin' out. Your little friends are doing a lot more than keepin' watch and creating a distraction."

"I wonder if they attacked Reficul," asked Nicki. "We haven't heard—"

"IT'S THAT CURSED EVERETT BRAT!" came from down the street with the rumble of Reficul's deep bass voice.

"I guess that answers that," whispered Brian, following J.J., Nicki and Wil as they worked their way along the dark river bank.

"I'm going to kill him!" floated above the din of the retreating spy network.

"Ooo! He sounds mad," said Willard.

"Yup! I'm getting' a bunch of Monēo warnings from all the anger he's putting out." Brian shook off the spectral vision and ran to catch up with the others, who were passing in front of a dock for another excursion steamer.

"I think this is far enough," said J.J., slowing to a stop. "We're away from the Slocum's recreation pier and there's some places we can fall back into if we get in trouble. And over there," he pointed to some dock area buildings, "is a place for Wil to hide."

"Oh, no! I didn't come all this way to be left out, and safe—just because I'm little." Willard stood defiantly, glaring at J.J.

"Cool your jets, Dragon Breath. No one's being left out—especially you! Look, he doesn't know about you yet—particularly your gold nature. If you stay out of sight and watch, you'll know when you're needed, or Brian can call you with mind-speak. But remember, he's smart and knows dragon lore. The second he sees you, he'll shield against your fire and cone of weakness—and they may be reflected at us."

"As far as we know," said Nicki, "he can't draw on elements. So, our tactic's to keep pounding on his defenses and absorbing whatever he throws at us. Eventually he'll exhaust his channeling power and then we'll have the advantage. Maybe then Wil's weakness weapon will work."

"HEY, EVERETT!" boomed Reficul's deep voice. "SHOW YOURSELF!"

Chapter Forty
Willard's Plight

"**G**o, Wil! That little alley will be perfect," whispered J.J., pointing to a gap between two buildings. He and Nicki turned to Brian, who took a deep breath.

"Hey, Black Bungler!" taunted Brian. "Yeah, we're here, a little up the river bank. Been expecting you."

Suddenly there was a burst of twinkling, multi-colored lights and a metallic ringing sound. Reficul materialized about twenty yards away. Seeing the (translation) lights, Brian, J.J. and Nicki readied themselves. They had already gathered elemental energy, and Nicki was holding a protective energy-shield over them. Brian and J.J. were prepared to take over or assist where necessary. But unfortunately, the energy dome she had woven would not allow them to propel anything offensively ... and not a moment too soon. Out of the midst of the translation lights burst a huge stunner, hitting the dome with such force Nicki almost went down. The others were rocked, as if there had been an earthquake.

"Hmmm, that was good," goaded Brian. "You learned a few new tricks. But, as you can see, not good enough."

"I can see that." Reficul grinned menacingly, but inwardly thought that should have leveled them. He slowly paced in front of the three youngsters, but at a respectful distance. "You've expanded your mind-speak powers to include genus rodentia. They certainly chased off the branglers I hired."

"They were marvelous. I must thank them when we're done with you."

"Well, now, I'm thinking that might be a bit more difficult than you imagine."

"Maybe. Maybe not," interrupted J.J., who could not stay quiet any longer. "We have a few new tricks ourselves." He smiled mockingly, but Reficul simply ignored him and continued speaking directly to Brian.

"I was just about to ask you why you're here—or, better yet—how you knew to come, but I think I just figured it out. Merlin was an extraordinary seer who, obviously, could time-travel. He taught you and he's been feeding you information. It all makes sense now. We've wondered how it is that you keep showing up to interfere with our plans."

Brian heaved a sigh of relief. Reficul did not know or had not guessed about his abilities.

"Or you inherited *seer* abilities, when you joined with Merlin's personal power ring, last year."

Brian tried hard to control his emotions and what could be read in his face. He could barely be seen from the dim gas street-lamps.

"Which is it?" he roared, frustrated because he was not accustomed to anyone not quaking under his intimidating gaze and mannerisms.

"You just can't stand it," jeered J.J. "You're one of the most powerful channeling mages ever, yet here we are, just kids, standing here ready to take you on... And you're supposed to be so smart, yet you just learned about time travel. We've been doing it for a long time ..."

"You are so self-absorbed." Nicki picked up where J.J. left off. "You think you know everything. You can't even imagine there might be some new technology, or a very old one that went into disuse and was lost—that we discovered and you don't know about."

"Either way," said Brian, "you can huff and puff all you want, but we're not telling you anything, except: I almost wish I could see the expression on your face—if you ever get back to your own time—and you find out Antetima is in protective custody. Your European operative, O'Connor, was captured along with several of your Black Bunglers—including the spy you had on the vice-chairman's security team. Oh, yeah, my dad is now Sodality Council Chairman."

It was glorious. Very little rattled Reficul, but that news clearly unsettled him. He felt like he had just been hit in the gut and could barely breathe. But, he used his considerable skills to prevent the Everett youngsters from seeing most of his surprise and agony. Ten of his personally chosen Black Knights had been captured. Two had been carefully placed as undercover operatives, and one had been one of the best spooks in Europe. He took a deep breath.

"You have been busy."

"We can't take all the credit," said J.J. "Can you believe it, a bunch of 'em were stupid enough to attack a highly-protected Sodality safe house? An enforcement squad easily dealt with them."

"They got what they deserved," sneered Reficul with his deep, growly voice, still pacing some distance from the youngsters. He was trying to say something that would distract them and give him an opening. But so far he was the only one getting rattled.

"How fast can you reset your shield?" whispered Brian to Nicki.

"It takes a few seconds to weave the layers," answered Nicki, barely moving her lips and speaking low.

"I'll send a *drenching fireball*," suggested J.J., "right behind your stunner. That should keep him busy while she resets the shield."

"What's that?" asked Brian. "I've never heard of a *drenching fireball* before."

"Of course you haven't. I just made it up. It should work."

"Should work? It better." Brian looked over at the black, almost spectral, image pacing some distance away. "He'll be shielded, but we've gotta start wearing him down. Let's use regular-looking attacks for now; save the elementals for later—when he thinks we're out of energy. ... Okay, Nicki, on three: One! Two! Three!"

Their timing was perfect. Nicki dropped her shield, but was already starting to weave the energy layers to reset it. At the same time Brian let loose with a massive stunner, sending a brilliant blue bolt at Reficul that was almost three feet wide and was as long as the distance between them. (Usual stun energy is only two or three inches across and less than two feet long.) The blast lit up the whole area for about a city block—especially as it was a new (moonless) night. It was even bigger than Brian expected.

Reficul was totally taken by surprise. He did not expect them to drop their shield for an offensive attack. And, he surely did not expect anything like that! His shield barely held as he was thrown backward a considerable distance, causing him to run and stumble to keep his feet under him. But it did not end there. Just as he was regaining his balance and preparing to launch his own attack (while their shield was down), he heard the unmistakable whoosh of a fireball coming his way. Instinctively he ducked down.

There was no need to crouch down; his shield could easily deflect fireballs. But this one was different. Instead of bouncing away harmlessly, it stuck to the dome of his shield and spread like lava engulfing a rock in its relentless path, until it completely covered him with a hot, glowing bubble. As with the giant blue stunner, he had never seen nor heard of such energy manipulation. *Maybe*, he thought, *this isn't going to be so easy.*

As J.J.'s *drenching fireball* dissipated, Reficul channeled up an attack of his own. He was a master at instantaneously dropping and resetting shields and firing offensive energy between—especially after the disaster at Wizard's Cavern the year before.

The moonless dark night lit up again with a blast of *knockdown* white energy (normally only mages, witches or wizards could see channeled energy, but the huge power being exerted that June 14th night was so intense, anyone could see it.).

Nicki had rewoven and reset the shield; the Black Knights leader's energy deflected off and hit a nearby packing crate, sending wooden pieces and splinters flying, sounding like it had been hit by a large, swinging wrecking ball. Nicki, Brian and J.J. were not injured. The concussion sent them scrambling back to stay standing. Nicki almost lost concentration and let their protection collapse.

Reficul could not believe it. Even shielded, no one had ever been able to stand against one of his strikes. Yet the three youngsters—seminary students—were unscathed after two. He channeled practically everything he had into the attacks and was fast depleting his store of energy. As much as he hated to admit it, he would not be able to handle many more of the blasts those kids were coming up with—and they did not look exhausted at all. So, he decided, it was time to show some (dirty) tricks he was sure the Everett youngsters had never seen nor thought of. He just needed to stall them for a few minutes so he could take some deep breaths, clear his head, steady his emotions and covertly down a few energy pills (he had personally developed).

"Impressive," said Reficul, his voice almost rumbling. "I see you have added to your arsenal as well. But, like you, I am still standing." He began pacing again and when he turned away from his foes, he secretly swallowed six of his power pills. He needed only two or three minutes for them to start working. "You know, no one needs to get hurt—including your great-grandparents. History can go on unaltered. Just surrender your ringmaster formula-halves and we'll all go back to the twenty-first century and get on with our lives."

"Yeah, right," said J.J. "And what would you do as Ringmaster?"

"Bring order and uniformity to the world."

"If you truly believe that drivel, you're more deluded than we thought," said Nicki. "I'm not empathic, but I don't think you buy that junk any more than we do. It's really pathetic; you have tremendous abilities, and yet you use your talents to persuade and browbeat poor lost souls into becoming a rabble of non-thinking followers."

"Wow, Sis," whispered J.J. "Why don't you say what you really feel?"

The distance between them lit up with brilliant blue stunner light. Again, the pounding on the shield drove them backward.

"I think you've made him mad," said Brian, as the blue turned white from another *knockdown* strike, then blue again before they could regain their balance. Nicki stepped on the hem of her dress and fell, hitting her head and left arm on a dislodged paving stone. Their shield collapsed as she struggled to remain conscious, and a sharp pain wracked up from her wrist.

J.J. saw the translucent glow of the shield begin to dissolve and did not hesitate. He launched an elemental-assisted *knockdown* blast. It lit up the entire (Third Street) dock area with white light—as bright as noonday sun. But in his haste, it went wide and high; harmlessly dissipating into the inky-black sky. Yet it did have an effect: everyone was momentarily blinded from the huge flash. Which was fortunate; Reficul's next energy punch (barely) missed its mark. It still grazed Brian's shoulder, blasting open the seam of his shirt and bruising the muscle as he knelt to check on Nicki.

"Ow!" cried Brian, but ignored the pain as he felt under Nicki's head. There was a small amount of blood. "She's still breathing but she's really dazed." He took a deep breath and called out to earth, air, fire and water, pleading for an extra amount of their bountiful gifts.

"See what you can do. I'll keep him distracted." J.J. stepped between the black-robed man and Brian (tending to Nicki), then twirled his right hand in the air.

"What the—?" grumbled Reficul as a whirlwind started around his feet and quickly grew until he was totally engulfed with swirling winds. It was not strong enough to knock him down, penetrate his shield or spin him around, but it picked up debris and dirt, obscuring his vision. He waved his arm over his head and uttered: *energia dissipatus*, which should have countered the annoyance. But to his surprise, the wind seemed to feed off his channeled energy, growing in intensity.

"Wh-what ha-happened?" stammered Nicki, sitting up and rubbing the back of her head (with her right hand).

"You tripped and banged your head." Brian helped her to her feet. "I did some first aid, but you'll want Mom or maybe a clinic to fix it better, when we get home. You okay?"

"Yeah, thanks. Just a bit sore and I've got a headache. I think I maybe sprained or broke my wrist." She gingerly held up her injured left extremity, already starting to swell.

"Yuk! You better get behind Wil in the al—"

"No way!" She stood defiantly. "I'll be fine! Help J.J. keep Reficul distracted for another minute or two." She started to apply healing energy to ease the pain.

"Oooh," said J.J., still twirling his finger to maintain the twister. "I almost feel sorry for him. She's MAD now." He giggled.

Just then a white *knockdown* blast lit up the area—punching through the whirlwind. It did not even come close to the Everett trio, bolting down the East River dock area, exploding as it hit something beyond their sight.

"C'mon, Brian," said J.J. "This thing isn't over by a long shot. My twister's done about all it can do. He's gonna bust out any second." But before Brian could respond, his sister spoke.

"Let's give him another elemental experience." Nicki smiled sadistically, closed her eyes and focused on the river's energy.

Finally, thought Reficul. *I knew he would run out of energy.* His imprisonment by Wind was starting to collapse, but he sensed motion over his head and looked up. "Uh-oh!" he mumbled, seeing a long tendril of water snaking out of the river and coming down on him.

Reficul was dumbfounded. Hundreds, maybe thousands, of gallons of cold river water were being pumped on his head and back—then skittering away and returning to the East River. He could not understand how they had such elemental control.

"Good one!" said Brian, rubbing his shoulder. He had been hit harder than he earlier thought.

"ENOUGH!" Reficul slowly stood, as if unfolding himself. The water stopped hitting him, being shed around by an invisible umbrella. Then, from under the sheeting waterfall a blue stunner blasted through the deluge and night air, hammering the ground at Brian's feet.

Brian jumped backward, but not before a small amount of reflected energy hit his left ankle, causing it to go numb. He tripped and fell into Nicki and J.J. They all ended up in a tangled heap. Nicki lost her concentration, shutting off the tendril of water.

Reficul pressed his advantage, launching a white knockdown right into the middle of the intertwined, flailing arms, legs and bodies.

"Ooof!" Brian's eyes went wide as the air went out of his lungs. The strike hit his middle, just below the ribs. "Nicki! Shield!" he gasped, trying to get his breathing going again. He felt like he had just been punched by a prize-fighter.

Nicki did not wait to get untangled or stand up. She waved her right hand, wove energy layers and set a dissipation barrier—just in time, as a fireball whooshed toward them with bright orange, red and blue flames. They could barely feel or hear the loud crackling heat as it splattered across their protective bubble, then grounded itself to the earth below.

Brian pushed, tugged and scrambled to his feet—shying away from his left ankle, still weak and numb. With a determined look of concentration on his face, the ground began to shake under their feet; the air swirled and became drier and the temperature turned noticeably cooler as he gathered from all four elements. *Wil, have you—?* He projected.

A long time ago. Are you okay?

I'm a bit shaky, but yeah, I'm doing okay. You got enough room to spread your wings and take off?

Barely, why?

Just for effect. Fly up and take a dive at Reficul.

Now?

Now! projected Brian, just as the concussion of a blue stunner hit their shield, knocking them around again, but their opponent was running out of channeling energy. Suddenly there was a flap of wings in the air, drawing everyone's attention skyward. Barely visible from the glow of a gas street lamp a magnificent, not so big, gold dragon was soaring overhead with a menacing look on his face, making a steeply banked turn.

Reficul's jaw dropped open. A dragon—a rare gold dragon—had suddenly appeared, dipped a wing and was gliding directly at him. He barely overcame his surprise in time to put up a shield against dragon fire and weakness mist.

As Nicki and J.J. were getting untangled and to their feet, Brian struggled to maintain his balance and ready himself for another attack. But, instead of another stunner, fireball or knockdown barrage, he saw something quite strange—and scary.

Reficul was facing them, easily seen but only in silhouette. A fist-sized orb was hovering behind him, shining so bright that he cast a distinct shadow on the ground at his feet. That, alone, was nothing to fear; Brian and J.J. had pestered Nicki with light orbs since they were little. But the shadow: it was coming to life. Reficul remained absolutely still, while his shadow was moving, stretching and becoming a three-dimensional form. It then stood up, becoming taller than its conjuror. It took a long stride toward the Everetts, then stopped.

As soon as the ground (in front of Reficul) became clear of the shadow, the glowing orb behind Reficul's back created another outline and new shadow that extended (again) from his feet, took form, stood and took a long step away from the black-robed man. The two apparitions stood still, as if waiting for something.

Again, another shadow formed, but this time it did not follow the previous shapes. The edges swirled around, finally coming together in two outlines that wriggled and shifted until they were silhouette profiles of large dogs or wolves.

Brian, Nicki and J.J. looked on in fascinated horror. "What are—?" whispered Brian.

"Shadow wraiths and wolves," said J.J. "I read about them in an obscure book in Dad's library."

"You mean, one of the volumes he said not to read—?" said Nicki.

"Of course. Tellin' me not to read a book is like gift-wrapping it and putting on a tag sayin': 'Read me first!'"

"Okay, Prodigy Brain, what do they do and how do we defeat them?"

"Depends on who conjures them. They mostly do their creator's bidding, but shadow wraiths usually take away the will to fight."

"And those great big wolves?" asked Nicki.

"They can't do actual physical damage, but their bite sends spasms of pain that feel like they're tearing off a big chunk."

"This just gets better and better," said Brian.

"It's worse. They're Spirit conjurations, so energy shields and barriers won't stop—or even slow 'em down."

"Here they come," said Brian, seeing the shadow wraiths take long strides toward them, with their wolf companions dutifully padding along at their sides.

Instinctively, J.J. sent a huge fireball, but it passed right through one of the shadow apparitions, only causing them to momentarily hesitate.

Brian sent out a stunner at Reficul, hoping that if he lost concentration the shadows would disintegrate. But his shields were firmly in place, so that theory could not be tested. Before any of them could try anything else, the shadow creatures were on them.

J.J. screamed as his lower leg was attacked by one of the canines and the other chomped onto his right arm. The wraiths descended on Brian and Nicki, enveloping them in their wispy arms.

"Nicki, just give up," said Brian. "It's just too much—"

"I know," she answered. "No! That's not right! Fight it!"

"Why? We can't win. I'm just a kid. He'd make a better Ringmaster."

"Maybe you're right—no, no, no! C'mon, Brian. You know better ... but ... "

"I'm tired..."

"AND I'M HURT!" screamed J.J. "WILL YOU TWO GET IT TOGETHER?"

"That's right," coaxed Reficul. "You can't win." His deep voice cajoled.

Brian slid out of the wraith's embrace, sat on the ground, scrunched his eyes together and covered his ears. His will to fight was just about gone, but he had a fleeting idea: *Willard*, he projected, *I don't know if you can help, but try.*

I'm on my way! When I attack Reficul, those things should come after me. When they do, put up dragon fire shields.

Reficul was so focused on his shadow creatures he momentarily forgot about the (not so big) gold dragon that was making another circle overhead.

Willard swept around and again dove at Reficul. When in range, he let loose with a huge stream of dragon-fire.

As expected, Reficul was shielded, but the blast was so intense a few bits of flame leaked in. It had the desired effect. "What the—?" he roared, wondering aloud: "There're no gold dragons in 1904 New York! Where did you come from?"

Willard gracefully landed between the Black Knight and Brian, Nicki and J.J. "I guess there are now," he taunted.

"Ha, ha! Look at you! You're just a wyrmling—a baby. I've got bigger gargoyles on my home castle."

"Maybe so, but I was able to penetrate your shield; your cloak is on fire."

"What?!" He twisted, now smelling the smoldering fabric. He summoned some water and doused the blaze.

The plan worked. Reficul had created the shadow conjurations with the sole mission to attack whatever was perceived to be a threat. The apparitions turned their attention to the gold dragon.

"No! You fools!" he growled, but it was of no use. He knew, once created, whatever intention they were instilled with would dictate their actions. He could no longer command them. And he did not have enough energy stored to create more.

As they rushed on, Willard turned to face the shadow creatures and started circling to put himself between his family and Reficul and his dark defenders.

You better do something fast, Brian heard in his mind. *I don't know how long I can hold these things off. I don't think I'm immune from their touch or bite.*

Maybe just give u— Brian started to answer. *No—I mean—er—I'll try.* He was no longer being touched by the wraith, but he could still feel its effects. In his mind, he was still struggling with feeling helpless.

"Only something from good Spirit can defeat a dark, or bad, spirit creation," whispered J.J. He too was agonizing from the bites on his arm and leg—even though the teeth did not penetrate or inflict real, physical damage.

"Look at Willard," said Nicki. "He's holding them off with dragon fire but it's not destroying them."

"It's not the fire," said J.J. "It's the light from the fire. And see, his scales are glowing. That's repelling them, too. They're from dark; only light will destroy them. Spirit light."

"Where do we get Spirit light?" asked Brian. "I've never heard of it."

"I don't know," said J.J., still barely able to speak from the pain of the shadow bites. "But we've got to hurry. Look!" He pointed a finger at the standoff between Willard and the shadow beings.

Brian was immediately worried. At first Wil had been able to breathe fire (light) every few moments and keep his scales glowing bright, but that required expending huge amounts of energy.

And, while in dragon form, he could gather and store elemental energy but could not act like a conduit and let it flow through him endlessly—like humans can (or he could, in human form). There was no time to break off and fully replenish his energy; soon he would be unable to hold off the dark creations.

"Why don't we help him with fireballs?" asked Nicki. "Or that enveloping fire thing?"

"It won't help," answered J.J. "Remember, I tried that. Our fireballs aren't as bright as dragon fire. And the gold glow from his scales must be a special color."

"Arrrgh!" roared Willard. One of the (shadow) wolves attacked between fire streams and bit him on his left (rear) ankle, causing him to almost fall over on his side. He reached deep and blasted some more fire and drove the shadow back. But the damage was done; his left (hind) foot felt like it was "asleep"—tingling and limp.

Brian closed his eyes, trying to call forth the knowledge (long ago) infused in his ring. But it was hard, distracted by Willard's plight. The shadows were mounting a coordinated attack. Willard's respites to draw deep-stored energy had become long enough to allow them to rush in.

"We've got to help him!" cried Nicki. "He's exhausted!"

"I know," said Brian, tears streaming down his face. Again he closed his eyes, tried to block out the feelings of defeat and summon a mental picture of Merlin's face…

Chapter Forty-One
The Fifth Element

*S*ummon the Fifth Element, Brian heard in his mind.

"What?" he asked aloud.

"We didn't say anything," said J.J.

"I know … I mean—"

Summon the Fifth Element.

"C'mon! We need more than that!"

"Who're you talking to?" asked Nicki.

"I don't know. Merlin, I think—or his ghost—or his knowledge in my head or ring—I don't know."

Summon the Fifth Element.

"Yeah, I got that!" snapped Brian. "But how?"

"Got what? How, what?" said J.J.

"Aarrrgh!" roared Willard as one of the shadow wolves leaped and bit down on his left front foot (hand), which instantly went numb, asleep and useless, and giving him more tingly pain. He could not bring forth any more fire (at least for a few minutes). He used his last reserves to brighten his golden glow; driving back his attackers one more time.

Summon the elements.

"Yeah, I said I got—uh—no…"

"Brian," said Nicky softly, "what does the voice say?" She was trying to calm him down.

"First it was 'Summon the Fifth Element.' But this last time is was different. He said, 'Summon the Elements.'"

"That's the answer!" said Nicki and J.J. together.

"What?"

"We need to summon Fire, Water, Earth and Air to call up Spirit," said J.J.

"But, if each of us invokes an element," observed Brian, "there'll be one missing. Wil can't do that, too."

Summon the elemental, he heard in his head.

"Huh? That makes no sense." Brian saw inquisitive looks on J.J.'s and Nicki's faces. "Now it said, 'Summon the elemental.' What the heck is that?"

"Oh, I know," said J.J. "Each element can send forth a structured form of itself to carry out a needed task. It takes a real personal connection to summon an elemental."

"I can do it," said Nicki, surprising Brian and J.J.

"Oh, really?" said J.J. with a smirk.

"We don't have time to argue," said Brian. "If you think you can, do it!"

Nicki closed her eyes and began chanting: *Aqua Elementis, I seek you to help our brother. Aqua Elementis, I seek you to help our brother. Aqua Elementis, I seek you to help our brother...*

"Look!" said Brian, pointing to their left and the swift East River. The glow from Reficul's orb and Willard's scales reflected of a human-like form lifting itself out of the dark depths. It then strode across the watery expanse, becoming more solid, yet it was still fluid and rippling on its surface—as if its flesh were constantly flowing like a swift brook. In the dark they could not see through it, but it was easy to imagine it would be a beautiful translucent aquamarine color in bright sunlight.

Somehow, Brian and J.J. instinctively knew what to do next. Each needed to summon and join with one of the other elements. Brian started: *Mother Earth, please join with me to help our little brother*. J.J. chanted: *Brother Fire, please join with me to help our brother.* Then Nicki: *Sister Air, please join with me...*

As each felt the elements freely give their gifts, Water Elemental reached the Everett trio and extended its arms to J.J. and Nicki. They joined hands, including Brian, forming a circle. They all bowed their heads and Brian called out:

By the powers of Water, Air, Fire and Earth and the bond of love we share (being the greatest of all), we call on Spirit—Spirit that the Creator put in all things in the heaven and the earth—to take away the dark shadow conjurations and save our brother who has protected us.

While the actions of Reficul's dark creatures were dictated by the initial intention of their maker, their energy came from his channeled power, making it necessary [for him] to focus on them. He was so engaged with Willard's weakening struggle, he almost missed the Water Elemental and the curious ritual happening on the far side of the (not so big) gold dragon. And when he did, he scoffed and dismissed the whole scene. "You can't pray your way out of this one, Everett!" he taunted. But, then...

There was a huge bolt of lightning and a deafening clap of thunder. Through the air, high above, a brilliant light streaked through the inky-black, moonless sky. It circled the whole area once, then came rushing down at a blinding speed, leaving a long contrail of residual whiteness.

"NOOO!" cried Reficul as he realized what was coming. "It's impossible! There's no way you could..." But even as he said the words, he knew. Somehow, again, Brian had marshaled forces from the most improbable—even incredible—sources. This time it was a Luminous Dragon—an elemental of the Fifth Element. Pure light. Spirit Light—that could defeat even the strongest dark conjurations. His shadow wraiths and wolves were pretty pathetic by comparison. There was nothing he could do but accept the inevitable.

The sight was glorious. The Luminous Dragon slowed and swooped over Willard, then floated over Reficul. Sensing a different, greater threat to their creator, the shadow wraiths and wolves broke off their attack on Willard and leaped at the oncoming radiance.

It was all over in an instant. Like a spectacular sunrise consumes a dark night, the shadow specters were obliterated by the splendor of the essence of all creation—never to return.

Are you okay? Brian sent to Willard.

No; I can't move my—

Do not worry yourself, Little One, all the Everetts heard in their minds. *You fought well and protected your family. The bond of love you share and willingness to sacrifice has summoned me.*

With a flutter of huge wings, the magnificent, great dragon landed next to Willard, who tried to bow in respect, but collapsed onto his left side from his still numb and non-working limbs.

"He looks so small, next to the great wyrm," whispered Nicki.

Maybe so, retorted the Luminous One, *but ofttimes size does not matter. This little one was willing to sacrifice himself for you and the future Ringmaster. There is no greater love, and such has great power.* With a tiny whisp of breath, Willard was completely healed. He stood tall—as tall as he could—and the two dragons turned to Reficul.

"Human Reficul," called the wondrous Spirit Elemental in a voice aloud that was both terrible and embracing, "you were entrusted with a great gift: to travel via the *Sigillum de Aemath.* You have violated that trust by attempting that which is forbidden. You have not only sought to change past events, but have done so for personal gain. Fortunately the damage, thus far, is repairable."

Surrounding Reficul there was a burst of multicolored lights as he tried to translate and escape. But, instead of the usual metallic ringing, there was a reverberating, metallic thump—like a rubber hammer hitting a metal barrel half full of water. He shook his head in disbelief.

"Foolish mortal! Did you think you would be permitted to continue on in this time to create havoc? That will not happen. You will *travel* once more: to a non-earth time, dimension or plane of your choosing, being stripped of all psionic or magic abilities."

Reficul thought he was going to be sick.

"Or you may retain your abilities, except for *traveling*, and your memory of these events will be erased. Then you will be returned to your present-moment earth."

"Not much of a choice," he growled, feeling like an errant schoolboy being lectured and punished by the principal. "I'll return to my present."

"If that is your choice; I believe your followers are trying to open a portal, even now."

*   *   *

"Look!" yelled Laileb, pointing: a black rectangle had suddenly appeared, extending up from the floor of [Reficul's] underground laboratory. It had a brilliant border that looked like a brightly-lit silver picture frame.

"It's a portal!" said Phusikos, his voice high with excitement. "I'm sure of it. It looks exactly like the ancient writings and drawings described. Careful now. Keep your focus so it doesn't close." He circled the doorway, examining it from all directions. "It's blank on the back, like it's not even there. How'd you do it?"

"I'm not really sure," Laileb barely whispered. "I'm not completely convinced I did it. I mean, I did—but I'd swear I had a lot of help. That's just it. I have no idea. I felt a huge burst of energy, much greater than I can channel."

"That's scary!" Phusikos backed away, fearing being sucked in.

"Tell me about it." They stared at it, in wonder. "Hey!" The portals' inky black inner surface began to ripple and distort with blue-grey smoke swirling in its depths. "Something's happening ... and I'm not controlling anything."

"Better channel up," cautioned Phusikos. "Who knows what might come flying through." They both extended their right (ringed) arms and hands, focusing their psionic energies.

Suddenly out of the swirling smoke and darkness, a figure appeared. It tumbled out and onto the flat-stone floor and was hit by two powerful stunners.

* * *

"Wow," said Brian, awestruck and amazed. "That was quick. A portal opened right around him and he was gone."

"He made his choice," said the dragon. "He has done enough here that will require much repair to maintain historical correctness. All must be made as it was." The luminous being turned and blew a soft breath at Brian, Nicki and J.J., who (like Willard) were instantly healed of all their injuries from Reficul and his shadow creatures. "I can relieve that which is physical—even perceived physical. It is up to you to conquer your personal, inner emotional traumas. That is never easy."

"I think we understand," said Nicki, "and thank you." She turned to the water elemental and bowed (curtsied). "Thank you, Great Being, for answering when our brother was in peril."

The water elemental did not speak, but respectfully returned Nicki's bow, turned and with long strides walked back to the mighty East River and dissolved into its dark depths.

"Now I must take my leave. You have done well. Remember—"

"Love is the governing power of the universe," said Brian, finishing the line the dragon was going to say.

"Well said, Ringmaster." It seemed the luminescence of the Spirit elemental brightened with approval.

"Wait. You said it wrong," said J.J. "Our parents taught: 'Love is the *greatest* power in the universe.'"

"What do you say, Ringmaster?"

"I'm not Ringmaster yet. But he's right; that's how we were taught. But, somehow, for me, 'love is the *governing* power of the universe' feels more right."

The great wyrm, the Spirit elemental, Luminous Dragon, bowed low in reverential respect and said, "Then you ARE Ringmaster."

Chapter Forty-Two
Going Home—Again

"Wow!" Brian heard Nicki exclaim. "Look at the crowds." They were mingling among the throng of people gathered at the Third Street dock area and the recreational pier where the [side-paddle steamer] General Slocum was tied up—waiting to make its 17th annual excursion to Long Island Sound and Locust Grove Picnic Ground on Eaton's Neck.

"As I remember, one of the internet articles said there are 35 [mostly inexperienced] crew members and 1,331 passengers. More than 500 are kids under twenty," said J.J.

"Yeah, and one thousand twenty-one are going to die," whispered Brian, his voice breaking. He wiped away tears with the sleeve of his shirt. "I can't stand it! We have all these psionic abilities and could stop the disaster before it starts. But, noooo! To keep history intact and avoid a huge paradox, we've gotta stand here as Captain Van Schaick steams the Genral Slocum up the East River and it burns down to the waterline. Kids are gonna die!" He could barely maintain his composure and hide his anguish from the crowd of passersby.

"Do you just wanna go home?" asked Nicki. "We don't have to stay and watch the sailing."

"I know, but we haven't seen our great-grandparents yet. I really want to do that, and make sure they get back off—along with Mrs.

Straub and that family. For history to be right, that's got to happen. Just us being here, yesterday and today, could have affected something."

*   *   *

"Oh, what have we done?" whined Laileb. "What have we done?" He stared frightfully at the still-comatose body of his leader, Reficul. Over twelve hours had passed since he and Phusikos had (each) blasted stunners at the flailing human form that had been ejected from the portal in Reficul's basement laboratory.

They had gently moved the infamous Black Knight from being a twisted heap on the stone floor to Reficul's own sleep chamber and four-poster bed, given him a sponge bath, and dressed him in comfortable, black satin pajamas. Phusikos and Laileb applied healing energy, but neither were trained psionic healers or Sodality physicians.

"Master has never trusted sodality-trained doctors—only European wizards and witches for medical issues. We cannot summon anyone local—and bringing someone from London creates too much exposure." Laileb went to the bedside and (again) fluffed and straightened the down comforter covering Reficul to the middle of his chest.

"If he doesn't come around soon, we'll have to take him to that hospital in London…"

"If you do," growled a deep, bass voice, "I'll boil you in oil!"

"You're awake!" Laileb tripped over his own feet as he spun to greet the source of the voice. "Master! Thank the stars! We were so worried."

"Which one of you hit ME with a stunner?" His eyes cast about like a laser detector. He almost grinned when he saw both of his followers stop in mid-stride and slowly raise their hands as their chins dropped to their chests and they stared at the floor. Then he cringed at the thought of being hit with two.

"How long have I been out?" He stared at the bed, covers, pajamas and his freshly-washed hands.

"Almost thirteen hours," said Phusikos sheepishly.

"What else did you use—a bat?" Reficul rubbed the temples on the side of his head to ease his pounding headache.

"No, just stunners," said Laileb, regaining his composure— after the tangled feet mishap.

"Hmmm. I wonder ..."

* * *

"There they are!" cried Willard, pointing down at an elderly couple entering the (covered) pier from the dockside doorway that led from the starboard side of the General Slocum. Since he was adopted by the Everetts, he had spent hours memorizing all the faces from family photo albums, slides and old home movies—the faces of his family.

"I think you're right," said Nicki. The youngsters were on the upper, second-story recreation deck of the pier—often used for parties, dances and concerts.

"And there's Mrs. Straub," exclaimed J.J.

"And the family!" Brian let out a sigh of relief. "Now we can go home."

* * *

"I did what?" questioned Reficul, listening to the story of his being stretched out and sucked into the page of an old book. "That's impossible!" He shook his head in disbelief.

"When you're up to it, we can show you," said Laileb. "Remember, we installed a video monitoring and recording system with cameras in the lab? It captured everything."

"This I've got to see." He threw off the bed covers, grabbed his sleek, black dressing robe and strode off toward the staircase and his library below. He ignored his throbbing headache—he'd had worse.

"I don't understand it!" said Laileb. "I swear! It was there!"

"I concur, Master," said Phusikos. "For weeks we studied that recording, looking for clues to reopen the portal." They all stared at a blank video monitor screen. The images of that fateful day had somehow been erased.

"Weeks?!" yelled Reficul. "How long have I been gone?"

"Several months," said Laileb—under his breath.

"Months?! My brain feels like it was yesterday. Have I been unconscious or in a coma for all this time? I don't remember anything."

"We don't know, Master," said Phusikos. "The only clues we have are the things we found in your pants before sending them out for laundering. There was a stone with some engraving, but it was sanded off to where nothing was recognizable. And there was some old U.S. currency from the late 1800s. Does any of that ring a bell?"

"No, nothing."

* * *

"What does it say?" asked Willard. He was standing on tiptoes, trying to look between Brian's and Nicki's shoulders to read the note they were both holding. It was found taped to the door of the Crystal Cavern when they arrived through the portal.

"Dearest Children,

We check back every few hours to see if you've returned. There's been much political unrest and other national and worldwide events that require the Sodality Chairman's attention. Go to the Manor House and call the house in Meyor or the Chairman's Office. Then wait for us to bring you home.

Love always,
Mom and Dad"

CPSIA information can be obtained
at www.ICGtesting.com
Printed in the USA
BVHW081252020919
557346BV00001B/30/P

9 781733 4028